BETTER WHEN THE SUN GOES DOWN

HUNTER HYDE

Synopsis

Ezra Gray is a recidivist...

... but an innocent one. He is not a convicted criminal who repeatedly offends, contrary to what the government would have their citizens believe. But that doesn't matter in the eyes of a prejudiced population because people like Ezra—people with special abilities—instill fear in the powerless.

Conin Bresshet is normal. He's co-captain of the football team, a hard-working student, and Ezra's only friend. When Ezra lands on the radar of a recidivist trafficking network, run by the infamous Angela Barclay, Ezra discovers how coveted his powers truly are and the lengths Barclay's mercenaries will go to obtain them. He's instructed to find a boy named Atlas who promises safe passage to an elusive haven for AWOL recidivists—to get there, Ezra must leave the world he knew behind before he's taken captive.

What holds him back is that Conin now knows what he is. But if Ezra goes, he will lose the only boy he's loved. If he stays, he will endanger them both. Conin cannot bear the thought of Ezra's uncertain future. He's torn between following Ezra wherever his path will lead him or staying behind and being without the one boy who makes everything bearable. Will Conin continue to live his normal privileged life, or will he give up his hopes and dreams to protect Ezra in a life on the run?

TRIGGER WARNINGS

<u>Disclaimer:</u> Contrary to the extensive list of trigger warnings below, "Better When the Sun Goes Down" has prevalent queer joy. (Wait, really?!) Yes, really. It also has many fun, light-hearted domestic scenes between our three beloved MCs. So, don't fret! While the rest of it may be a dark and dreary thriller, I'm positive you'll find something good within the book's contents :)

(Alphabetized)

1. Ableism

2. Alcohol/Alcoholism (excessive)

3. Anxiety (excessive)

4. Assault (familial)

5. Attempted Suicide

6. Blood (excessive)

7. Death

8. Depression (excessive)

9. Eating disorder

10. Emotional abuse (excessive–familial)

11. Fire

12. Gore (excessive–severed body)

13. Gun violence

14. Hallucinations

15. Homophobia (use of the word f*ggot)

16. Murder

17. Physical Abuse (cutting)

18. Profanity (excessive–I like the word f*ck, okay?!)

19. PTSD (prevalent)

20. Religion (The LDS Church is a background for many of the characters–based in Utah)

21. School Shooting (but with superpowers rather than guns.)

22. Self-harm (cutting)

23. Violence (excessive)

24. Excessive Vomiting

To my biggest cheerleader,
Riley, I wrote this for you

Prologue

Atlas

I know the moment he passes on. His aura, our tether—that strong, once unwavering bond dissolves into the universe. There one moment, and then gone within the blink of an eye. I choke out a sob and fall to my knees. My shins scrape against the asphalt. I momentarily wonder if my parents know or how long it will take them to find out about his passing. I wonder if I will be the one to tell them, thinking I'm not sure I can fathom their reactions.

With bloodied kneecaps, I bolt to my feet. I need to do this, I need to see him. And then I'll have to tell the Angelics of his passing. Maybe they'll assign me to continue with his work. The thought evokes a bittersweet pang and lingering throb in my heart. Is this what grief feels like? How long do I have to feel this way?

A sudden, audible pop follows my vanishment. I don't care if anyone saw it. He's far more important than the discovery of my powers. My world is crumbling around me—a physical, sturdy object now parting like sand through the cracks of my fingers. What the hell am I going to do without him? How the hell will I navigate this world without him guiding me or . . . imparting his wisdom?

The living room is silent. The door to his room at the very end of the hallway is ajar. Lights are on inside. My parents must be at his bedside. A cry from Máma and her pleas in Spanish indicate they know he's gone. I don't want to have to deal with them—I just want to mourn in peace, alone . . . I want to be alone.

PART 1

FAUX

Chapter 1

Ezra

The sun drips its light onto the blank page. It's been empty for a while and will most likely remain so. I tap my pen on my makeshift desk—a small fold-out table found curbside for free. It's not much, but it's something—just like everything I own—the bed frame and the sheets over the mattress from the D.I., to the splintering nightstand.

Orange hues paint the tone of my room. The space is scarce. The twin-size bed adorned with the worn bed set, a three-cubed organizer brimming with Conin's recommended books, and several posters tacked to the wall: *Star Wars* and my favorite CHVRCHES album cover. I glaze my eyes over the sheet of paper. Miraculously, words haven't written themselves onto the page. The lyrics are lost—they won't come to me, no matter how hard I try to coax them out.

This song has been in my head forever. I know what message I'm trying to convey, but I can't commit those words to written form. I had finally mustered enough courage to write the song, but another unwavering, cemented wall blocks me. I don't know how to push through the worst of it. I don't know what it is. My frustration builds, and in a flurry of defeat, I toss the pen and watch it scatter to the floor in two pieces. My gaze lingers where the ink spills. I don't care enough to clean it. Instead, I wonder if Conin's ever been this frustrated with his writing.

I'd probably be a shit songwriter anyways. Better to acknowledge it now rather than later. I prefer not to give myself false hope. But then again . . . some of the best songs take years to finish. So, perhaps today isn't my day. Maybe tomorrow will be.

A muted numbness creeps into my chest. I know this numbing sensation. I'm acquainted with it, used to its debilitating effects. I can't ignore the feeling, so I let the permeations wash over me like roiling waves at sea, numbing me, numbing me, numbing me. Of course, I'm left with no choice. There are always ways to dull the pain.

My parents' bedroom door is cracked open. I sneak inside, though no one is currently home. My dad stashes his alcohol in the corner of their closet, hidden behind the drapes of hung clothes. He's not discreet about it. He thinks Thax and I aren't stupid enough to steal from him. Luckily for us, whenever alcohol goes missing, Dad assumes he consumed it because he never remembers. Thax and I caught on pretty early that all we needed to do was return the empty bottle to its home. Lukeman Gray was none the wiser.

A fresh, gleaming bottle of amber liquid bestows itself when I swipe the clothes away. Tequila, an alcohol I can stomach. I grip it hard, return the clothes to their original positions, and rush back to my room. I choke down the scalding liquid. It tears at my throat, but I relish the burn. It's comforting. Familiar. Before I know it, the world is tilting and my vision sways as a burst of euphoria replaces the numbness. The alcohol sloshes in my belly, distending tight against my abdomen. After a while, the need to puke washes over me. The pounding of my heart is loud, but all I can think about is the incessant worry that I don't want to vomit. *I don't.*

I carry myself to the bathroom and release the regurgitated liquid into the toilet bowl. It makes me feel disgusting. I'm disgusting. The thought of what I just did replays, triggering another gag reflex. I sit over the basin for what feels like hours. The wave of nausea doesn't pass, not for a while, but it eventually does.

I've all but forgotten the split pen and the barren sheet of paper in favor of wasting away on my bed. The world tilts. My eyes shut. Eventually, Thax lets himself in with some weed and an unfamiliar bong in hand. It's new, crystalline. But its presence is alluring, and I'm tempted when he offers to take a few hits with me. I cave in like I always do. Guilt rises in my throat, though I'd rather not piss him off. Weed is what keeps the peace between us. So, he and I take turns passing the bong.

The sun sets. Moonlight filters through the blinds. And it's silent, too silent between Thax and I. We don't talk. We never do. There's this mutual understanding between us. I'm not sure you would call this brotherly bonding, but I'll take this momentary truce. Smoking weed is about the only thing we hold in common, besides our abilities. Even then, our powers are nothing alike.

Today, I chose my battle. This is how I avoid the inevitable.

Then, miraculously, he speaks. Even as I buzz from head to toe, I'm floored.

"I met up with an old friend from high school the other day. It was crazy," Thax says.

I can't get my lips to move. Instead, I opt into listening, not caring enough to wonder why he's telling me any of this.

"He asked about you, actually. I told him there wasn't much to know. He's like us."

I'm already forgetting, losing consciousness, watching Thax's face muddle into hues of peachy skin and brown hair. If he told me what the name of his friend was, I can't remember. Frankly, I don't care.

I don't know when Thax leaves. He's no longer with me when I slump onto the bed. I pass out immediately after laying my head on the pillow. A null world of black envelops me, beckoning me into its depths.

— ◆ —

It takes me a couple of minutes when I wake to realize that I'm late for school. I'd rather not go, but Ms. Bernard would be pissed if I missed today's rehearsal. I finally managed first chair and I don't want to fuck this up. But the second I stand, I know today's going to suck. My head pounds in a ruthless rhythm. I feel sick to my stomach.

In the same fashion as yesterday, I flee to the bathroom and discard the remainder of my belly's contents. It only induces my already rising anxiety. It lingers and sticks to the muscles of my chest. But I need to get to school, no matter how shit I feel.

I hurry to get ready and find a clean long-sleeved shirt to cover the scars along my arms. I toast some bread, something bland, and drink about a pitcher of water before I bolt to school. It's about a five-minute walk, but I'm already an hour and a half late. Above all my worries is the thought of if I'll see Conin today. I haven't seen him in a while because of how busy he's been. And come to mention it, I forgot to reply to his text from yesterday. I fire a quick response and shut off my phone when I arrive at English. Conin's taking AP this year. I miss the days when we'd share the same classes.

Thank GOD I missed chemistry, though suffering through Math is now the bane of my existence. By fourth period, the tension in my shoulders eased as I entered the orchestra room. The anxiety is still there, still persistent as I unpack my violin, tighten and thoroughly resin the bow hair, then tune the strings. Ms. Bernard greets me with a curt nod but smiles, nonetheless. Students pile in. Gleaming ebony shines under the rough fluorescents. My head is a dull ache now. The more I sit here, the more I start to believe that I won't be able to do this today. I'm not sure why today out of all days is the exception, as every day before has been just as shit as the last, but I know without a shadow of a doubt that today is worse and that my performance is going to be severely lacking because of it. And I'm not at all wrong. In fact, I am downright terrible. Fuck this hangover.

My head is not in the game, and it shows. Ms. Bernard's glance flicks to me, her lips pursing tightly. The movements of her baton become less languid and more rigid. My classmates' gazes hold on to my every movement. The ensemble starts to unravel, the tempo and notes missing after every interval. Clara, sitting right next to me, casts cautionary looks my way. Ms. Bernard pauses us so often that I start to lose track of how many times we need to replay a specific section. I never heard my name uttered with so much disdain before. Well, apart from the way Dad said it, I suppose.

Ms. Bernard is ruthless, but I can also tell she has no idea how to properly reprimand me for such a heinous performance because it's never been an issue before. Her nose twitches, and the wrinkles on her forehead solidify into deeper indents. Eventually, she tells me to practice alone. My classmates are just as shocked as I feel at that moment. I don't complain. I say nothing as I bury myself in one of the practice rooms.

I worked so fucking hard to get here. I wanted this with every fiber of my being, practiced countless hours at school to audition for Chamber Orchestra, and even managed to get first chair. Pathetic. But instead of practicing, I reprimand myself over and over again. When the bell finally dismisses us, I break out of my self-deprecating inertia. I slip the instrument gently into its case, loosen the bowstrings, and tighten the clasps. Everyone else stuffs away their stringed instruments, lazily and without the careful, deliberate movements I take to ensure the longevity of mine—the one possession I hold dear. I suppose my classmates don't have the same type of father I do. I suppose they don't fear for their lives and possessions like I do daily. It's exhausting.

Lukeman Gray—my dad, if you will—gets off by holding the looming threat of my violin's destruction over my head whenever I do something to upset him, but that never matters. I usually upset him regardless. Nevertheless, I try not to do anything on the off chance he decides to stay true to his word one day and execute his usual empty bluffs. I'm positive he hasn't yet because he spent too much money on the damned thing, even when it was the cheapest, decent model one could get. My mom, for all her worthlessness in my life, talked him into it. It was the one time I was ever grateful for her—grateful I have a mom.

I'm cautious while using the strap to carry the case on my bony shoulders. I hug the case to my chest. Only once everyone's gone do I attempt to leave. Ms. Bernard, however, intercepts.

"Ezra . . . what was that today?" she asks. It's not cold nor callous, but I can't help but recoil and feel an immense amount of guilt. Concern laces her eyes as she considers me. My instinct is not to respond, but Ms. Bernard isn't Thax or my dad. I shouldn't be rude to her just because I fucked up big time.

"I don't know," I say, honestly. Her nose scrunches and the indents along her forehead crease tighter.

Ms. Bernard sighs.

"Is something going on at home?"

My heart thuds against my chest. There's no way she could know. My chest is tight and every part of me buzzes. Her conclusion was so abrupt that it caught me off guard. I genuinely have no idea how to answer. Though, if I don't say anything, she'll assume her suspicions are correct.

"No," I say, "everything's fine at home."

"Are *you* alright?" Ms. Bernard questions with narrowed eyes. "If you're not, you can tell me. I won't judge. We can get you the help you need."

"My mind just wasn't here today. That's all. I'll do better on Tuesday."

There's a momentary pause. I can see her working on a reply.

"Ezra. Do you trust me?" she says.

"Of course," I answer quickly.

To an extent. I can say the same thing about everyone. I like Ms. Bernard over so many others—I can admit that. But there's still this barrier, this wall I put up. There's only so much trust I can allow and there's only so much people can know about me. I refuse to let her in on any of it. She may have an inkling, but an inkling is all she'll ever have.

"A word of advice?" Ms. Bernard sighs.

No. I really just want to leave. I keep silent and study her intently as if I'm interested in her advice.

"You may be one of the best violinists in your class, but I've noticed how you isolate yourself. Try to open yourself to your classmates. Make some friends."

"I have friends," I interject.

"I know you do. All I'm saying is that to learn and grow, you need to put trust in others. Not everyone is out to get you, Ezra," she says and purses her lips.

I have genuinely no clue where this came from. My performance today had nothing to do with my trust in others, but perhaps Ms. Bernard can see right through my bullshit. I nod, slip in a thank-you, and get the hell out of the orchestra room. I find myself mindlessly walking to where Conin and I usually meet after school gets out. When he isn't there, I peer down both ends of the hallway. He's at football practice. Of course, he wouldn't show. And why should I expect him to when I've ignored him for the past several weeks?

Deflated, I make the trek back home. The house is silent when I return. Mom's most likely hiding in my parents' room and Thax is either at work or hanging out with his stoner friends. Dad, on the other hand, is probably out at some frequented bar. I open the door to my room and let out a long, heavy sigh.

And there, half an empty bottle of tequila in hand, is Lukeman Gray wearing a livid expression.

Chapter 2

Conin

A weakening ache travels from each shoulder, each bicep, pec, quad, hand, and toe. My ass is on fire, and I will definitely be feeling this sore throb tomorrow, but for now, I'll let sleep wash it into a cool numbness.

After Dan gave me the okay to go, I left our concluded football practice where I was tasked to put away equipment and push the blocking sleds back into place. I trek home in the waning light of the sun. Days like these remind me why I should have never accepted the co-captain position. Too much wasted time.

Ogden High's team is far from perfect. We're a 3A team and haven't won a state championship in well over a decade, if we've even made it that far. News flash: we haven't. We've won our fair share of playoffs, qualifying for regionals only once since I've taken the title, but each failure is another regret.

There's always regret.

The sun sets behind the peak of Mount Ogden, shading the sky in blends of inky orange and yellow. I'm so sick of these long hours, how the evening is upon us every time I set foot back home—another reason in the long list of reasons why I hate this as passionately as I do.

My thoughts were preoccupied throughout most of the training session. For one, I was hyper-fixated on the staggering amount of homework that currently sits in a haphazard pile across my desk when I stumbled into my room, which is cast in a paradisiacal orange glow. The sore sight of it elicits a deep, guttural yawn from me. These stupid, unrelenting AP classes. They're going to be the death of me.

I can't glance at them another moment—instead, I fall loose-limbed onto the full-sized mattress placed alluringly before me. Its warm, soft reassurance ebbs the tension suppressed in my shoulders. God. This feels amazing. I turn onto my ass, head propped up on a pillow. Absentmindedly, I gaze at the wall ahead and watch as the shadows from the blinds slowly dissipate.

A buzz vibrates in the pocket of my shorts. A sliver of hope wells until I grip the phone and pull it out, realizing it's only Mom letting me know she'll be home late tonight from her shift at the library. I sigh and thumb to my text thread with Ezra—see that the last message I sent sometime this morning has been left unread. *Again.* The longer I stare at the text, manifesting Ezra to reply, the more I succumb to disappointment and the sleep that threatens to pull me under.

Sleep should wait, but it tugs on my eyelids. I haven't seen or heard from him in a while. As a final admonishment, I remind myself that I could have visited Ezra, called him more often, and searched for him at school in my free time between classes. But I didn't. I wonder if he's okay and if shit at home has worsened or if I need to intervene with Mom. Maybe Mom could speak with Rochelle, Ezra's mother—though, their tight-knit friendship is nonexistent now, ever since Lukeman began his drinking tirade.

Loyalties were put to the test back then.

I can't do the same thing to Ezra. I've been such a terrible friend.

Shooting another message, I let the fatigue wrap me in its embrace. I wake up an hour later drenched in sweat, panting from some nightmare I can no longer recall when the brain fog overcomes me. Every limb and every muscle shakes violently. I heave myself out of bed and move to the bathroom where I run hot, scalding water down my spine. The water drenches the curls atop my head and cascades down the stomach I've let go, inflaming my feet until they're beet red, almost purple, from poor circulation. When the shivers cease, I pat dry my damp body and moisturize. I glare at the inflamed acne that dots my chest and back until I can stand it no longer.

Homework and sprawled-open notebooks taunt me from my desk. Simultaneously, colorful spines aligning a vast bookshelf tempt me from the far end of the room. The books beg to be read, but I can't give in. This coursework will only collect and build if I leave it alone. I can't help but think I made a mistake trying to pursue a writing career instead of my predestined path into a life of football. I should never have accepted the full ride to the U of U knowing well in my heart that it wasn't what I desired for myself. It had felt obligatory—as if I was doing only what was expected of me. And I know I was, I know what I must do, and working my damn hardest to get into a university near wherever Ezra goes needs to be a top priority. And well . . . I suppose I don't have a fail-safe if everything goes awry.

Because Ezra will get admittance to whichever school he wants based solely on how talented he is with the violin. And because he's expressed interest, I've scoped the universities nearby with decent creative writing programs, most of which are in New York, where I could have a decent enough chance of acceptance. If I'm honest, I want to follow my dream of becoming an author and I want to do so with Ezra at my side as he takes on the unfamiliarity of a new life—far away from this one in Utah, one made abhorrent by his terrible excuse of a family. Not only do I need to make this a reality for myself, but for Ezra too. He deserves that much.

So, I must remain diligent as an exemplary student.

It's so exhausting. Most days I want to tear my hair out, sleep forever in the comfort of my bed. Why am I doing this to myself? Why don't I just quit football?

"Why don't you?" Ezra asked after I told him I'd be signing up for AP courses in our senior year.

"It's expected of me. I'm not sure I can handle my mom's disappointment."

"Your mom will accept whatever you decide to do, Co" he said.

"I know." It was the truth. "But accepting the full ride meant that she wouldn't feel the need to help me with tuition costs. If she knows I don't want that for myself anymore, she'll want to help me pay for whichever university I decide to go to. She's done so much for me already."

I hate football. It no longer brings me joy.

And I hate even more that I suffer through it—a tiny, screwed-up part of me grasping at straws for some of my dad's approval. Maybe if I made it big, he'd come back to us.

"You'll have to tell her eventually," Ezra muttered. His nonchalant, yet sarcastic retort set me on edge. He sounded almost resigned, but maybe even a little kind. I couldn't stay mad at Ezra for long.

Our conversation then proceeded into a heated debate which resulted in Ezra's convincing me to tell my mom and work harder to get where I wanted to be. That had been weeks ago. I haven't said a word since—haven't taken the necessary steps except for piling an excruciating amount of stress on top of the sport I no longer enjoy. So much is on my plate, I find little time to fulfill other hobbies or wants or needs. I'm falling apart at the seams. I could burst or implode at any moment, frozen within a vicious cycle.

So, I begin where I ended off, analyzing "The Yellow Wallpaper" for AP English. I don't enjoy it. It's boring. Sitting here, lost in mind-numbing texts makes me crave something more exciting—something queer, fun, adventurous, dark, or thrilling—everything I enjoy writing about.

Gilman's words are a bore. Sorry, I said it.

How is this a classic again?

I would much rather write than lose the ability to retain anything I've read. I've had this novel brewing for years, but never had the willpower to execute it onto the page. Maybe one day, if I can get my shit together.

I breathe out an exasperated sigh. Casting a dirty glance at my phone, I type a message to Melissa.

Conin: Want to come study?

My thumb shifts to Ezra's message thread in one subconscious movement. Nothing. No reply. I hover over the call icon, find myself pressing it before I sissy out, and listen to the ring perpetuate. After an entire minute, nothing. No dice.

A text chimes.

Melissa: *Hell no! It's a Friday, Conin. I'm coming over and we're going to watch a movie.*

I chuckle and emit an exhale of relief. An excuse not to work on homework is one I'll welcome with open arms. But in the meantime, I set the phone down and return to the endless sea of cracked-open books.

Chapter 3

Ezra

The bottle tilts in Lukeman Gray's hand. For a moment, I think he threatens to throw it at me, cut me open with the shards of glass. But it stays gripped in his calloused fingers. He stares daggers that pierce into my soul. His brow is furrowed with suspicion.

"You've been stealing my alcohol, you little shit?" Lukeman accuses as if it's a question. He knows the answer.

Dazed, I don't respond at first. I hug my violin to my chest.

"Answer me!" he bellows.

"What?" I finally say. "No! Thax must've—"

"Don't you fucking lie to my face! Thomas sure as hell didn't do this, the fucking pothead."

I'm quiet. I let the insults hit me. The obscenities keep coming. After the shit day I had, I can't take it. Not this time. I crack.

"No wonder he's a pothead! You're insufferable!" I exclaim.

"Excuse me, boy?" Lukeman hisses.

"I've had enough of your bullshit," I say.

In a drunken rush, Lukeman Gray is on top of me. I grip my violin case closer to my torso and know the moment I transform into my mother in self-defense—the only person my father refuses to abuse. I let the familiarity of my ability overwhelm my body, let it shift into a body that is not my own. It's not a power I use often, but it comes as naturally as breathing.

"That won't work on me again!" he says.

He keeps the bottle in his right hand while he lunges for the violin case. I fight for it, glue it to my body, and wrap my wrist and fingers around the handle. My grip is slipping. Lukeman twists the case at an awkward angle—I can feel my wrist start to tear. I let go. He wins. In horror, I watch my father unclasp the case and fling the flap open. With one last, final attempt to stop what he's about to do, I close the distance between us and attempt to pry the violin from his grasp. I'm decked in the chest, sent sprawling backward. My vision blurs for a moment. He then releases the stringed instrument.

It splinters onto the floor with bone-crushing force. The reverberation chills my body, and the fading echo of the violin trill diminishes entirely. My world shatters. My heart plummets into the earth. I stare at this person who's supposed to be my father. I see nothing but a violent man—someone unrecognizable, someone I couldn't possibly be an offspring of. I need to get out of here. I need to get out of here now.

"I should have registered you and your moronic brother!" Lukeman screams in finality.

He wouldn't dare do that. Not only would the government find my parents complicit, but registering me and my brother would mean signing our death sentence. Momentary regret flashes in Lukeman's irises, but it's gone a split second later. I'm frozen, wondering if it was a trick. I don't dare stick around to find out.

I could kill him, but what would that do? I've thought of it plenty of times. There are cops, laws to worry about, my abilities in danger of discovery. It would cause me more harm than my father ever could.

I flee into the drizzle that's started to weep from the clouds. I think of the violin remnants—the pieces of ebony scattered along the floor. I think of class tomorrow and if I should even go. And I realize then that I have nowhere to go now. Nowhere to call home, because the house I left behind sure as hell was never a home for me.

I think of Mom and how I shifted to take on her appearance the moment Lukeman attacked me. Like countless times before, I wonder why she never bothered to leave him. *"Your father is misunderstood,"* I recall her saying once. *Misunderstood.* No, he's just a fucking terrible excuse of a human being. And the rare attention I'd get from Mom would always leave me craving more. It would be those brief, solitary moments when either Thax or Lukeman hurt me, when I needed to be patched up, that she'd be the attentive mother I craved—a mother who acknowledged my existence. She was invariably silent. She never spoke up about the injustices—about the constant abuse. I know that it did more harm than good in the long run. I know that now. More importantly, I know that they never loved me.

Chapter 4

Conin

Melissa lets herself in, as usual. I only knew she was here because I overheard her and my mom talking from the kitchen. Mom arrived about a half hour ago. We interlocked in an entirely familiar conversation about Ezra, which resulted in an indistinguishable tired look in her eyes—the look she often gave my father after a heated argument or a belligerent rage, the reason he no longer lives here with us. She said she'd talk to Rochelle about Ezra's silence, but I'm not counting on it.

"Hi," Melissa says and situates herself on my bed.

I'm at my desk, slaving away at this excessive amount of homework.

"Hi," I reply.

Mom isn't concerned about Melissa being a girl and hanging out with me in my room. We're strictly platonic bros. It's never been a problem, especially not while she's dating Dan. Dan, however . . .

"Do you ever stop? You're worse than I am," Melissa whines. She chucks something at my head with surprisingly accurate precision. Well, I suppose her boyfriend *is* the star quarterback and captain of the football team.

"You made me this way," I rebut.

She scoffs. I tab a page, then close the book. We're off to the living room where we start cycling through the movie options. A cheesy, but comfortable Marvel movie is selected. Melissa rolls her eyes, but she concedes because all the men are hot. They are, but I won't verbally agree. Mom passes the living room where Melissa and I sit in anything but silence. Five minutes in and Melissa's already complaining.

"Want to join us, Mom?" I ask.

She lingers behind the couch and studies the movie for a second. I don't see her commit to the act, but I can practically feel her eyes roll.

"Thank you, sweetheart, but I think I'm going to get ready for bed," she says and saunters off with a "good night."

The movie ensues in its disorderly fashion. Melissa's silent when she's invested, but these moments are familiar and comfortable. When we arrive at a particular lull in the plot, I crane my head in her direction and notice her bored expression.

"Does Dan know you're here?" I question.

"Nah," she says, "he thinks I'm out with Emery. He'd *flip* if he knew you and I were hanging out. He's still convinced you like me."

"I do like you," I joke, which elicits a playful slap to my deltoid. "It's ridiculous though."

"Such is the way of a heterosexual man, my not-so-straight friend. How's Ezra, by the way?"

My shoulders tense as a hot, pricking heat flushes my cheeks. I don't think Ezra is interested in anyone, which at one point or another made me believe he could be aroace. It'd be weird to try to hit on my best friend of fourteen years, though.

"Fine."

"Just fine? When was the last time you talked with him?"

I ponder for a moment, reluctant to confide in her about this—the severity of Ezra's situation. I could probably omit that part, though.

"A little while. He hasn't responded to me."

"Have you bothered checking on him at school or going around to his place?"

"I haven't had the time," I say with an immense amount of guilt pressuring my lungs.

"Sure," she says, unfazed. "If only you would confess your feelings for him, then maybe—"

"Shut up!" I exclaim.

"Conin!" Mom calls from her bedroom.

I quiet down.

"I hate these movies. They feel so prevalent today," Melissa says under her breath.

They do. The accords are like our registration policies and the Recidivism Act, or the mutants confined to a school due to the world treating them like freaks because of a trait that sets them apart from everyone else. Our world is downright cruel. And this movie? I find no enjoyment in it anymore.

I'm about to suggest we turn on something else when a knock comes from the door.

Chapter 5

Ezra

I pound hard on Conin's front door. The world shakes, blurred at the edges of my peripheries. My damp clothes cling to my skin. It continues to pour warm, relentless rain. I can barely stand upright. I can barely think straight. God knows I've never been able to do that. Like the masochist that I am, I met with Thax and his stupid friends to get high. And now I'm at Conin's doorstep because it's the only damn place I thought I could go to. Is he mad at me for being quiet these past several weeks? Will he turn me away when he realizes that I'm high as a kite? Conin answers the door, though I hardly register that he's there in the flesh.

"Ezra?"

Conin Bresshet. The man I love with every fiber of my being. He's eighteen now. I can call him a man. That's sorta cool. I notice the way his belly fills out the T-shirt he wears, his strong chest, and his muscled arms. The mop of blonde curls that falls onto a faded undercut. His azure blue eyes. I ogle at him, not caring if he notices. He repeats my name.

Melissa Abernathy materializes at his side. My mood instantly sours. I may or may not have whispered that I didn't want her here. I don't know. I'm mad that she is. Why the hell is she here? Were she and Conin—

Conin and Melissa whisper to one another. This sours my mood even more. I can make out bits and pieces of their hushed conversation, but nothing concrete. The next second, I'm somehow inside. Melissa is still fucking talking with Conin! She offers to help, but he says that he has it under control. Smug, I nod. *He's got it.* The two say goodbye to each other. Melissa sounds concerned. I hate that she does.

And before I know it, I'm in Conin's bedroom, sitting on the toilet in the attached bathroom. It's cold. Everything is so cold. The damp clothes continue to soak my body.

"Angle yourself this way, please," Conin says while nudging me. His voice sounds admonishing. I can't help but feel guilty at his tone. Expertly, Conin ties my hair into a bun. His tongue pokes out slightly as he wraps and cords the long locks of hair. I see the subtle quirk on his lips—the smile tilting slowly upwards. This makes me happy. It makes me so undeniably happy.

I remember when I first showed Conin how to tie it, a year or two ago when my hair had finally become long enough to achieve a bun. This memory is muddled now, but I remember how eager Conin was to learn. My heart could not be tamed through the entire process.

As my traitorous mind does, another thought arises. Melissa.

"What was she doing over here?" these traitorous lips ask.

"We were hanging out, Ez," he responds.

"You like her, don't you?" I say. I can't fucking shut up.

"We're just friends," he says back.

I scoff. He clucks his tongue—similar to Ms. Bresshet. Conin asks me something, and I might've said yes, and then I'm being stripped of my clothes. I'm too much in a daze to do anything about it. There may be vomit on my hoodie. I feel a tad better when I'm bare of the wet apparel, but I'm suddenly aware of my body, its scars, and Conin . . . how he can see me. Conin's seen my scars, but never like this. Not all of them. Not all at once. The ones on my arms, sure, just not the scars etched into my chest, stomach, back, legs. Exposed, I start to cry, grateful for Conin's careful attentiveness through the state I'm in.

"Don't look at me," I sob.

"It's okay," he says. His voice is soothing. "Let's get you into new clothes."

In the blink of an eye, I'm lying atop Conin's bed. I'm clothed and under the sheets. They're warm and inviting. They smell of him, of Conin, of the man that I love. In heavy droves, the numbness of sleep washes over me. I succumb to its bliss.

Chapter 6

Conin

Ezra's in my bed asleep while I sit curled up in my closet, a hysterical mess. The tears fall copiously in large, uncontrollable drops. And no matter how hard I try to keep them at bay, they slip from my eyes in a torrential downpour.

I rub my palms on the carpet. They grow angry and red. But compared to Ezra and the absolute bullshit his family put him through, this pain is nothing. I'm angry. I'm so, so angry. I'm furious that the family which was supposed to show Ezra unconditional love failed him so miserably. I'm enraged they'd abuse him this way—enraged at myself for never doing anything about it even when I knew his home life was grisly.

The excruciating images of his scars stain my mind. My shoulders are still tense from the sore sight—a lingering pain that sprouted and worsened from football practice earlier in the day.

I've seen the lacerations on his arms before but was clueless about the ones on his torso and legs, the unmapped portion of his body in the early stages of exploration. My culpability increases. I've wanted to see him, to have him, but not this way . . . not with this tainted image and with him at his most vulnerable.

What kind of shitty friend am I? When I've had time to breathe and let my sobs run their course, relief washes in. Above all else, I'm relieved Ezra is okay. Starting today, I'll become that better friend Ezra needs me to be.

I'll sleep on the floor tonight, so I rummage through my closet for the sleeping bag Ezra would use on the nights he stayed over. It's rolled up, clasped together with a single strap. I let it unravel near the base of the bed—Ezra's soft snores carry from on top, instilling ease I haven't felt since he arrived. If I leave Ezra unattended and if I'm not by his side like those nights in junior high when we'd share the same sheets, I fear what could happen.

Because I wish I could join him in bed. Share it like we used to. The comfortable flush of our bodies, his mirth over whatever show I turned on for the both of us, the way he'd fall asleep with his head on my chest and his fingers clutched to the fabric of my shirt. But I won't join him. I won't be someone Ezra can't trust or confide in. I need to be the one to hold him up and the pillar to help him back on his feet. I can't be the one who uses him, have him realize he made the mistake of ever being my friend in the first place.

As the night carries on, these cycling thoughts lull into whispers. Ezra's reassuring breaths are a merciful reprieve. And after an hour or so, I'm enveloped in a faux calm—enough for me to sleep.

Hours later, a flash of panic finds me. I scramble to a standing position and almost totter to the bed, but Ezra is safe and sound, snuggled under the weight of the blankets. He's asleep, unstirring, hair in disarray. Ezra is adorable with his mouth parted slightly. He looks tranquil, like the innocence of a child. I move to gently brush the locks of hair that scatter over him. His hair is ridiculously long now, but it's easily his best feature.

In this state, it's almost easy to forget his scars, a reminder that he isn't the undefiled boy of our past. The upset and worry from last night returns. I know I won't be able to sleep any longer, so I turn to my desk and continue the onslaught on the never-ending pile of homework. Another two hours pass in complete silence. Nothing I've studied is retained. And I've managed little more than staring into the void for the last half hour.

I need to fix this. Ezra needs to leave his home, come live here, and be safe under my protection. I'm familiar with what it's like to be hurt by a father. What happened with my dad isn't the same as what's happening here. It's worse, it's so much worse, and I can't subject Ezra to the abuse any longer.

"It's the fucking weekend, Co. Cut that shit out," Ezra says.

I place the pen on the sprawled notebook and turn to take him in. He's pressed against the headboard, hair disheveled, but tied into that signature bun. A stony mask blinks back. Does he remember what happened last night? Does he know why he's here?

"What are you looking at?" he retorts.

"Nothing," I say and laugh in relief. "Want some breakfast?"

Chapter 7

Ezra

The scent of pancakes and sausage wafts into the dining room. Conin's at the stove, dutifully preparing a meal that I'm not sure I can stomach. I haven't been able to keep most food down lately. And even more so, the humiliation from last night won't stop. It rattles me. I'm so fucking embarrassed. What did I say to Conin and Melissa? Did I say anything at all?

There are brief glimpses of Conin undressing me . . . he saw everything, though I'm grateful he kept me in the same pair of underwear. My cheeks are heated, and my heart beats a million miles a second. Conin doesn't say anything, nor acknowledge what happened the night before. His eyes, however, look blotchy. Did he . . . cry?

The news channel is on, for whatever reason. Ms. Bresshet, most likely. Their house is liberal and modest, decorated with Ikea furniture and adorned with photos. I'm in a good chunk of these pictures—like I'm a part of the family. The time I got to experience Disneyland because Conin's mom was kind enough to bring me along; she insisted on buying the two of us Mickey Mouse ears, to my chagrin. The time, on the same trip, at a pier of a beach I can no longer recall—Conin and me, arms draped around each other's shoulders. The time I attended Conin's first football game; he, Ms. Bresshet, and I were amongst the field of burly football players. Our first sleepover at five years old and the blanket fort we built in that very living room. Mom and Miss Bresshet were close back then. Lukeman Gray widened the rift between them, but Ms. Bresshet kept me in their lives.

This only makes my guilt over the silence much worse. I shouldn't have ignored Conin as I did. The tension at home, Conin and Melissa and their more frequent hangouts . . . Maybe that's why. Maybe I saw it as more than what it was. When the two would ask if I wanted to hang with them, I'd say no. Being the third wheel in a relationship with someone I wanted to be with would suck. And I didn't want to confirm my worst fears. That's when the texts went ignored. Conin was persistent at first, until he gave up, and the messages tapered down to once a day.

Vaguely, the memory of last night resurfaces. I asked if they were an item. I think, and god, please let me be correct, Conin said it wasn't like that. But the damage was done. Lucky for me, he hasn't said anything about it.

"A recent recidivist attack at an elementary school in Chicago has revived a debate on recidivist reform within Congress. According to the Recidivism Act of 1994, every individual to possess transcendental abilities, or the more popularly dubbed term, superpowers, must register and be closely monitored by the U.S. government. However, the House of Representatives at first debated whether this act would directly violate the constitutional right to privacy and anonymity. The verdict declared mandatory testing for traces of transcendental abilities unconstitutional. Thus, a great many unregistered recidivists have existed under the government's nose. U.S. citizens have flocked to their congresspeople in droves to express their outrage on the attack on Buford Elementary and demand a permanent solution to this age-old conflict. We will keep you updated when more information as the ongoing situation unfurls."

Conin abruptly changes the channel. My heart won't slow. A trembling sensation erupts from the tips of my fingers and swiftly spreads. I try my hardest to suppress the shakes so Conin won't notice.

"We don't need to watch that," he says and switches the news to a *Star Wars* movie. *Attack of the Clones.* My favorite of the nine. He judged me at first, until I recited an extensive list of why it was my favorite and why others should overlook its shittier qualities. I don't need any judgment, thank you.

"Shit's just depressing," Conin whispers and hurries back to the stove before he burns the entire meal. It wouldn't matter to me—I can't eat after what I heard.

Another recidivist attack . . . and it's no wonder the world views us as criminals. I first learned of the law and people's animosity toward someone like me back in sixth grade. In school, we were taught about the Recidivism Act of 1994—proposed legislation set into fruition that would criminalize people with superpowers under the Second Amendment. Some argued that powers were a right, considered a concealed weapon. Although it is an American's right to possess a concealed weapon, the discourse over dangerous abilities was a heavy topic of discussion because those who possess offensive, potentially dangerous powers are in direct violation of the law. They always harbor these abilities. Naturally, these supposed "weapons" are not typically possessed by law-abiding citizens nor those of the police and military. Recidivists are unpredictable; these abilities could be used to benefit for personal gain or perpetrate unlawful acts. Or in many cases, are simply too powerful for the beholder to control.

And what if these powers were to fall into the wrong hands? What could they do in sensitive places like schools or government buildings? What damage could they wreak? Buford Elementary will now serve as a reminder of the harmful consequences superpowers can cause. Every single one of these factors is why these people, people like me, are named a recidivist—someone who repeatedly commits a crime.

It was clear the American people were scared. Soon, our neighbors turned against us. Superpowers were no longer deemed concealed weapons or a means of self-defense. When our superpowers were considered an infringement upon the Second Amendment, recidivists were only ever viewed as the result of their sinful behavior. It became our prominent feature. The government created the Scarlet Letters. In our case, if you're a registered recidivist, you had to go out in public with an "R" badge pinned to your clothing. It's humiliating, but not common.

Meanwhile, concealed firearms were encouraged by the government. Guns could protect American citizens from recidivists. They were willing to overlook the prevalence of gun violence over what they couldn't understand. States offer concealed carry permits, which in return will require background checks. If these individuals are lawful, they will be protected by the Second Amendment. This idea was quickly twisted from a place of prejudice. Citizens used this opportunity as an excuse to carry guns around with them. And if this resulted in someone getting shot? The perpetrator could claim self-defense.

However, the government would *protect* powered individuals if they were registered. The downside would be living a constant, monitored life. Certain rights would be revoked and the way you'd be treated by others . . . it's no wonder so many committed suicides. So many runaways . . . to seek refuge even with the possibility there is none. And, in certain cases, if the government believes your power to be dangerous, they have the right, under the law, to deactivate or strip you of it. This always results in the recidivist's death. This, or you're detained for the rest of your life. If Congress finds a reason to break our right of anonymity, we're all screwed. As much as I hate to admit it, I hope the anti-vaxxers speak up again. Not everyone sides with mandatory testing.

I was eleven when my abilities first manifested. Before then, there was this instinctive knowledge to keep silent about my powers, if my parents' reactions to my development were any indication. Our technology isn't advanced enough to detect powers at birth and it doesn't remain a concern, as so many recidivists' powers don't develop until later in life. So, I've lived a life under the radar. Thax and I both have. But it'll be harder if we're required to test within the near future. It's difficult to believe the government will be forgiving when we've kept our identities a secret for most of our lives.

My parents have remained silent because they'd be complicit if we were found out. Lukeman's threats over the years were only ever that: threats. My parents made it clear as they raised us that we were freaks for the powers we possessed. Thax needed to vent, didn't know how to control his pent-up frustration and hurt, which is why all his scorn and spite were taken out on me.

And yesterday . . . I have no doubt there was truth to Lukeman's words. Something changed. I could hear it in his voice, the indication he'd finally cracked. Moving forward, I need to tread carefully. I fear now more than ever of my discovery. If Conin finds out, would he turn me in? We haven't talked in weeks, but we're still close, akin to brothers. I want to believe we'll always remain close. His comment about the news, however, didn't sound promising. It sounded downright belligerent.

"It's scary, huh?" I say, ignoring the movie. Conin's opinion is something I need to know. We don't talk about this often enough.

Conin shifts and bends over. The softness of his belly bulges over the waistline of his joggers. I nearly faint—melt into goo. One thing's for sure that will distract me: it's fucking Conin Bresshet. His ears are adorned with fresh studs that weren't there several weeks ago. I don't remember him telling me about them. Maybe he mentioned it in one of the many unread texts, but the sight of them catches me off guard. I like how they look on him. I really, really like how they complement his already handsome complexion. And I realize, in that excruciating moment, the hard-on pressed against the sweats Conin dressed me in. My dick pitches a tent against the fabric. My face grows hot. Thank god for the cover of the table.

Conin finishes the food, but he takes that moment to glare in my direction, hands on hips, stern disposition in full display. He looks like Ms. Bresshet. Ms. Bresshet is scary at the worst of times.

"Are you not going to tell me what happened last night?" Conin asks instead.

"I was hoping not to," I reply. More often than not, Conin tends to evoke the truth out of me. He's one of the rare souls I can open my heart to, though there are secrets I keep to myself—things that are better if no one knows.

Conin's pause is loud. Shattering. I deflate. There's no deflecting this.

"We haven't talked in weeks," he says. "Not properly. And then you showed up high on my doorstep last night. I had to change your clothes and put you to bed. I was afraid you were going to choke on your fucking vomit."

He's angry. Seething. He trembles and I can see the tiny reverberations of his body even as the darkness of the kitchen masks his silhouette. Shit. I totally fucked up. Conin hasn't been this mad at me in so long. He rarely gets mad. Under that stoic facade is someone brimmed with emotion, I know that much. Conin's sudden change in mood has me disoriented.

"Jeez, Co. I've never seen you this angry before—"

That was the wrong thing to say.

"We're not going to joke about this, Ezra! You didn't tell me your scars were . . . all over you! Some of them are even fresh."

"Conin—"

"Is that why you've been quiet? Because things at home have gotten worse?" he mutters. The plates of food have been abandoned and forgotten. I can't conjure a sarcastic retort—there's nothing in me. And as usual, I keep my mouth shut. Better that way.

"And what about all my texts? You haven't responded to a single one! I even called you, for fuck's sake!"

Oh, he's swearing now. This is serious. I look at my phone and groan when I see that the text was never sent. I tell him as much, but Conin isn't having it.

"That's it. You're not going back there. I'm texting my mom and you're staying here until we figure something out," says Conin.

I don't speak. There's half the urge to run, but where would I go? Conin's texting his mom and when he finishes, his eyes find mine.

"Where are you?"

Without fail, he knows. When we were kids, he'd point out when I stared off into space—those moments I was lost in thought. I wandered far away. Somewhere dark. He reels me in, a fisherman at sea.

"I'm here," I lie. The fallacy escapes as a stutter. The tears well, though I demand them not to come. I don't want to cry in front of Conin. Not again. "Thank you," I whisper.

Conin sits down. He's adjacent to me, his whole body sitting in attention to mine.

"You don't have to tell me, but what happened?"

The question can remain unanswered, but I feel compelled to tell him. He deserves this much.

My voice cracks. It's pathetic and embarrassing. "He shattered my violin."

Conin lets out an audible gasp. A sob parts my lips. Even as my body numbs, I can sense the anger that emanates from him. Conin reaches out, just as he used to when we were kids, and embraces my bony figure. The embarrassment is there at first—tiny, insignificant, until it dissipates. I take the intimacy of this moment to break down and cry.

Chapter 8

Conin

To say I'm fuming is an understatement. I'm seething the longer we watch *Star Wars* in silence. I hope that it takes Ezra's mind off the horrid events of last night, but it does nothing to alleviate the bottled anger that threatens to pop inside me. The movie is more so for him rather than my entertainment. I've only watched *Star Wars* for Ezra's sake. And it seems to be doing the trick.

I could care less about him ignoring my texts. Taking away Ezra's violin is like amputating an extra limb. He cherishes it more than any possession he's ever had. I possess half the mind to storm the Grays' home and give Lukeman a solid beating, but realistically I know nothing will come of it. Mom's spoken with Rochelle before, but she said it was all gaslighting and false assurances that Lukeman was going to get better, that she as Ezra's mother would do something about it. All lies.

Ezra is alarmingly thin, with gaunt cheekbones, bags under his eyelids, and bony shoulders hidden under the oversized hoodie I fit him in. Regardless of these faults, Ezra is undeniably attractive. He may not see it, but I do. I love his heterochromia even when he complains there's nothing cool about his one green eye and its blue counterpart. As a kid, I was convinced they gave him magical powers—my friend was a superhero—invincible, powerful, and special.

Ezra's slender frame is attractive as hell. I suppose I have a thing for skinny boys, though really all body types are perfect. Will he like me even though I've gotten fat? Would he and I look good together even when we're completely different people? His hair is long and dark brown. It's soft to the touch, perfect for raking fingers through it, which I'd do if he didn't find it weird. But his hair is downright swoon-worthy when it's tied into a bun. He taught me long ago, and when he wasn't around, I would practice on Melissa, who was more than happy to offer her services to get me to "first base" with Ezra. I had flicked her forehead.

It's those intimate moments between us I appreciate—Ezra trusting me to handle him, the inside jokes, the memories only he and I share. Casual glances, secretive smirks, the way we open up when we're around each other. Before I realize it, calm has settled in my chest, and a grin works itself onto my face. That sensation comes crumbling down when I cast a glance at Ezra.

There's a deep rigidness in the posture of his frame. He looks exactly how he did when the news played the segment on Buford Elementary. It was devastating what happened, but what about it put him so on edge? I don't know. It worries me because his whole body seemed prepared for fight or flight. Does Ezra believe recidivists are inherently evil? Was he hurt by one?

I hold no animosity against people with special abilities. In my eyes, they aren't any different from other marginalized groups ostracized for simply being different. I'm queer, for hell's sake. No, I may never face the cruelty others have, and being a straight-presenting white dude is a privilege in and of itself, but I understand. And it's with that I wonder if Ezra thinks the same. Or could he have reacted that way because he's a recidivist, too? I'd know if he was, right? He would tell me. He'd have to.

Or maybe he's trapped, afraid of what I'd think, of what everyone in his life would think if they knew. He's ghosted me over the past several weeks. The trust I thought we had maybe shattered somewhere along the way. The idea is too much to bear.

My phone vibrates.

Melissa: *Party at Emery's tonight. Want to come? Ezra should come, too.*

Ezra abhors social events, situations, and interactions of any kind. He's a champ enough to attend my football games and participates in everything related to orchestra, but parties? Out of the question. Despite knowing this about him, this could be a good idea. For both of us. I know I want to go, drink a beer or two, lose myself in the moment. Maybe that's what Ezra needs. It's worth a shot.

"Melissa invited us to Emery's party tonight. Do you want to go?"

"Invited . . . *us*?" he questions. His genuine surprise kind of hurts. If only everyone knew Ezra as I do, he wouldn't be shocked when someone actually cares enough to invite him to a party.

"Yeah, how about it? Could be fun," I say.

He scrunches his face in consternation. I knew better than to be hopelessly optimistic.

"Sure," he says.

And . . . I was not expecting that. I suspect it's the alcohol because there's no Ogden party without it, but if it helps in getting Ezra's mind off his current predicament, I'll take it. I note to watch over him. He tends to get carried away with drinking. I can't say I fault him for it.

"Are you sure?" I ask.

I want to be one hundred percent certain before I drag him into a throng of drunk high school students.

"Why not?" he rebuts.

Ezra's eyelids are scrunched as if this conversation is bothering him. I want to push him for the truth but think better of it. His attention returns to the movie. For some odd reason, I feel like I've failed, that I lost him. There are just some things we don't talk about—a mutual understanding. So, I toughen up and don't pry.

"I love this scene," he says more to himself than me.

I glance at the TV but move to my room and grab my homework since Ezra is so enthralled with a scene he's watched thousands of times. Upon my return, he eyes me in exasperation. With dramatic gestures of his hands, he says, "It's the fucking weekend."

"AP test Monday!" I argue.

"Ah, right. I forgot you're abandoning your full-ride scholarship for no life," Ezra says, exuding sarcasm.

"Don't be a dick. You know why," I say and hit him with one of Mom's designer pillows. "And besides, if we're talking about people with no life, you take the cake."

Ezra hits me back. The grin from this morning makes a triumphant return.

"I do know why. Have you told your mom yet?"

I sigh. "I haven't figured out how."

"You'll figure it out. You're a great writer," he says.

My stomach flips, elated by the praise. But wait . . .

He *didn't*.

"When the hell have you read my stuff?"

I'm sure he hears the mortified tone in my voice because he suppresses a snigger and smiles a shit-eating grin.

"That one time."

I guffaw, reach for the pillow, but Ezra is a blur, stealing the homework from my lap. I move to intercept. Ezra bounds to his feet and holds the papers high in the air. He's using his goddamn height against me!

"You tall little shit, give it back!" I exclaim.

Crouching low and lunging forward, I tackle Ezra to the carpet. He strains against my muscles, but he puts up a decent fight. We wrestle, rolling along the floor. My leg hits the coffee table and I stifle a groan. Ezra takes advantage of my momentary blunder to get on top of me, gripping my wrists and holding them to the carpet. He pins my legs together and I suddenly feel myself go hard. I could push back and easily overpower him, but I keep lying here, crossing my legs together to hide the erection. Whatever just happened has become too intimate. Too intimate for even us. Maybe not when we were in junior high, but we're different now.

We pant, collecting our breath. He stares at me uncomfortably for longer than anyone would have otherwise. To play it off, I decide to redirect with lighthearted humor.

"We haven't done that in a while. When did you get so strong?"

"Pfft," he blows. "Your wrestling phase did nothing to prepare you for me."

In his distraction, I snatch my homework and kick him off when I'm in the clear. I sit on the couch and pretend nothing happened—there was no disruption, and I *did not* get an erection. I cross my legs again to mask the obvious effect Ezra has on me.

He joins me seconds later, but he's farther away this time. Distant. He returns to the movie as if he wasn't bothered by our farce. It sure as hell bothered me. This may not have been a big deal to him, but it certainly evoked a multitude of hormones, emotions, and desires out of me. Does he really not see the effect he so evidently has? It's not his fault, I suppose. He has no idea. Yet, it hurts. I'm seemingly invisible to him—nothing more than a childhood best friend and a brother.

I can't focus on homework anymore.

Chapter 9

Ezra

As soon as the worn-down Chrysler pulls into Emery's packed street, I regret saying yes to Conin. Her home is decked to the nines with students. Half of them probably don't even go to Ogden High, in need of something mundane to occupy their weekend with cheap thrills and stale beer. A claustrophobic agitation itches my skin. Conin glances at me with a furrowed brow, trying to detect the bullshit—I don't want to be here. I slip on my signature resting bitch face. I pull on the hem of my sleeves to make sure they're covering the brunt end of my scars even when most of the people here have probably seen them at one point or another. Together, we shuffle inside.

We can hardly move. The throng of people won't budge, relentless at the threshold of Emery's home. Conin pushes our way through. There are a few grunts and stifled protests, but he manages.

"Is this okay?" he questions once we've skirted around the worst of it.

"Why wouldn't it be?" I lie. "I'm fine."

He's skeptical, but I won't admit anything. Instead, I chart my course straight to the alcohol. I'll take cheap, stale beer over sobriety any day. With each step, that numbness settles in, and with it, the craving for liquid death. Conin's eyes sear holes into my flesh. They burn into me until I arrive at the kitchen where an honest-to-god keg sits on top of the island. Tommy Donahue pours a gold liquid into his red solo cup. I have the sudden urge to turn away. Right as I'm about to, Tommy looks up, and takes this unfortunate opportunity to call my name. I redirect myself to the keg and act unbothered by the encounter.

"I haven't seen you in a while," Tommy says, reminding me too much of Conin. I ghosted him, too. "Are you all right?"

"Yeah, I'm fine. I've just been . . . busy, with orchestra," I lie.

The third or maybe the fourth time tonight.

Beer sloshes into my cup. I half-ass a smile at Tommy and then move in search of Conin. Tommy sighs and hurries to stop me. He grabs my wrist. The act itself isn't violent, but the swift suddenness of the action makes me flinch. I whirl at Tommy and he backs away with arms raised in surrender. Understanding dawns on his face.

"Sorry," he says.

"What do you want?" I hiss. The music's loud. There are so many people. I feel backed against the wall, the air is tight, my throat closes.

"You've been avoiding me."

"No," I say, "I haven't."

"Yes, you have," Tommy persists. I glare daggers at him, willing him to push me to the edge.

"I've been texting you, calling you even. We need to talk—"

"About what?" I contend.

The speakers blast. Everyone's voices drown under the blaring music. I quell the urge to be sick.

"I'm assuming you saw the news, about the recidivist reforms . . . the mandatory testing. How are you holding up?" he asks. On instinct, I check to see if anyone overheard. I don't think they could even if they tried. Tommy is barely audible. I have to seriously strain to hear him.

"I'm *fine*," I insist.

Recidivist or not, I don't want to be having this conversation with Tommy Donahue. Not here, not now. The beer suddenly vanishes in my cup. I down it in one gulp and push past him to refill it to the brim. Tommy, like the indelible stain that he is, follows. Even after I've filled my cup, he idles close behind me. He watches as if he's my guard, there for protection, but allowing enough leniency for me to do as I please. I get sick of it really fucking fast. I ignore Tommy in search of Conin. My search is for naught as the throng of students has multiplied. They're everywhere and it's hard to breathe. I can't breathe.

"Ezra?" comes Tommy's voice.

"Leave me alone," I shout. He cringes.

I push through the sea of people, but Tommy is nothing if not persistent. He was persistent back then, too. When we first met, it was in the music hall. He looked nervous, wringing his hands together as if he were about to confess unrequited feelings. I ignored him at first until it became clear he was there to see me. I'd seen him around, but he and I never interacted. I was confused and thought it was some prank, or perhaps a friend of Conin's I wasn't aware of, but I decided to concede.

"Hey, sorry, um . . . my name's Tommy. You're Ezra Gray, right?" he said.

"Yeah?"

"Can we talk?"

Turned out Tommy's a recidivist. He told me he could feel my presence, sense it unmistakably. When I was hurt and confused, attempting to understand how he knew and what was in it for him, he conceded by presenting to me his abilities. Tommy said not everyone had the capability of sensing other recidivists' presences, that others were just more attuned to the sensation. If I felt broken then, I certainly felt irreparable afterward. We soon were acquainted and resembled friends in some regard. Admittedly, Tommy's helped me through a lot. I may be angry with him now, but I am grateful he reached out to me all those months ago.

I just didn't need a constant reminder of what I am when I've been trying so hard to forget.

And in the waves of never-ending bodies, I see Thax. He sports a bruised eye and a bloodied lip that's dried over. Lukeman Gray did this to him. As much as I hate my brother, it breaks me to see him this way. Knowing that, even through all the pain Thax has caused me, he and I still have the same father. He and I had to go through this shit together. If I had stayed in the Gray household, what more would our father have done to me? The violin would not have been the means to an end. It would only have been the start of something more.

I want to kill Lukeman Gray.

Next to my brother is a stranger. The two are unmistakably at the party together, but this . . . friend, he's different. Thax shouldn't be here in the first place, as he dropped out of high school a couple of years ago, but that never stopped him. He's here, maybe, because of this friend—this stranger who locks on to my eyes and keeps them trained on me. A prominent scar dashes across the man's cheek. That sickness from earlier pits in my stomach. I search for a bathroom, in disregard of Tommy. When I find an unoccupied one, I dive for the toilet. The stranger's sick, hostile gaze sets me over the edge.

The ripple of students outside undulates. After I've closed the door, their voices swell and threaten to burst in. Someone knocks, but I can't be bothered. I recheck the lock and feel the trill of my heart quicken, closing my throat, creating a barrier that cuts oxygen from my head. I spit into the toilet, fearing what comes next. The sickness is based at my throat, and I refuse to let it rise, so I swallow and wait and eventually, the urge to vomit relinquishes after time. I stand and turn to the sink.

The mirror on the wall taunts me and beckons me to peer into its depths. I avoid it like the plague. I don't want to see my face. The water scalds my skin at first until it cools. Deliberately scrubbing my hands, I rub them raw. I breathe in and out. In and out. In and out. And then hear a low, malevolent chuckle.

"It was such a big mistake to isolate yourself," says the man in the mirror.

Chapter 10

Conin

Dan and the football gang drag me far away from Ezra. I was trying to intercept him to the keg when Dan pulled me outside. He led me to the beer pong table where the other guys from the team were already mid-game.

"I know he's your friend, Conin, but why the hell would you bring him here?" he says sloppily. His voice slurs with inebriation.

"Ezra?" I ask, though it's clear who he speaks of.

"He follows you around like a stray puppy just to get inside your pants. He's a fag, Conin."

"What did you say?"

"He's a faggot. Why the fuck do you keep him around?"

The irresistible urge to sock Dan in the face is impossible to overcome. No one insults Ezra in front of me and gets away with it. Melissa will understand if I knock her boyfriend out.

"You know what, Dan?" I say and he turns to me, but he's no longer there. I've lost him to the recesses of his mind. "I quit the team."

"You . . . w-what?"

"I quit the team," I hiss, enunciating each syllable. "If you're captain, I want no part of it."

Well, that's not the only reason.

The boys boo. They've started listening and I ignore them.

"And we're breaking up," says Melissa defiantly. "Asshole."

I have no idea where she materialized from, but I'll use the excuse to escape Dan any time. She takes hold of my wrist and starts to tug me away from my former football team and her now ex-boyfriend. God, I love this woman.

"Babe . . . what? Where are you going? Where did this come from—"

"Swallow it, Papenbrook. We're over."

We don't stick around to hear the rest of his drunken tirade, knowing none of it will be good. Melissa leads me inside the house. We're swallowed by flashing lights, deafening music, and a multiplying crowd. I twist myself to take in her reaction. From what I can gauge, she's apathetic, but I know her better. Relief loosens the tension in her eyebrows and cheeks. Her lip curves into a subtle smile.

"Jesus. That felt good," Melissa says for only me to hear.

"You were badass," I say.

"Damn right, I was."

The crowd thickens and suddenly there's no leeway to move. The room throbs and pulses, students jump and sway, push and pull. I feel an overwhelming sense of claustrophobia and a ceaseless worry for Ezra. I haven't seen him since he disappeared to the keg. I shouldn't have followed Dan. That was mistake number two. My first mistake was coming here in the first place and dragging Ezra along with me. I wanted to deny it, but I knew—*I knew* shit would happen. And I'm responsible for it.

Melissa bumps into someone I can't see. I hear her attempt to apologize, but whoever it is is not having it. They're belligerent. Their words slur.

"Hey—" I protest, ready to make them back off.

I recognize his voice.

Thax rudely gestures at Melissa, shoving an indignant finger at the base of her sternum. I slap his hand away the second my own is free from the sea of people. The look he casts me is callous and hostile, but he grins when he realizes who I am. It's unsettling. All I want to do is pummel his face into the ground. Thax takes that same index finger and thrusts it into my bubble. I notice the prominent black eye.

"You can't protect him anymore," he slurs, maintaining that dreadful curve of his mouth.

He's upset and I can only imagine why. But fuck will I tolerate him threatening Ezra. I will not let him carve one more single line into Ezra's skin. I don't know whether Thax is high or extremely intoxicated. Either way, I have a strong sense this interaction won't end well.

"Ezra's actions have consequences," Thax continues, his gaze held on me. "Whatever the fuck he did to my dad, he needs to fix it." Thax got in trouble. Lukeman didn't have an outlet, so he chose his older son instead. How utterly useless does Rochelle need to be to let this continue to happen? I shouldn't sympathize with Thax, of all people, and I understand that their mother must be scared, but this treatment is blatantly unfair and cruel.

"I made a deal," he spits.

Melissa backs into me. She says nothing, waiting for me to react first before she intervenes. She's letting me handle this on my own terms.

"I'm sick of his bullshit. I'm so sick that he has the power to leave, to get far away from here, but he never does. He always fucking stays! He's useless! Imagine what I could do with that kind of power." Thax pauses, thinks. "Nah. Ezra's going to be dealt with."

What the hell is he talking about? *Power?* What power?

"All right, this is enough," Melissa says sternly. "Let's go, Conin."

She tries to pull me away, but I stand still, firm and unwavering. I wring my wrist from her grip and get close to Thax. We're face to face, nose to nose. He's unstable on his feet as he leans with the sway of the partying students. He trains his look on me regardless.

"What do you mean? What did you do?" I ask.

"Where is he, Thomas?" I spit.

He hates that name. Thax's eyes narrow into slits. And in one swift, blundering movement, he shoves me with a freakishly strong force. It is taking every fiber of my being not to explode on him. I try to suppress the urge to rip his throat out while students take an interest in the unfolding fight. Not knowing where Ezra is has spiked the worry that's been churning in my stomach since I was driven away from him. I need to know where he is. I need to know now. I need to know before I break and someone ends up hurt, or worse.

A hand finds my shoulder. At first, I think it's Melissa abating the situation, but a much deeper voice emanates from the stranger. Tommy Donahue. He pulls me aside and I let him. Melissa waits on the sidelines. Thax is now nowhere to be seen. The crowd of people return to their partying as if nothing threatened to ruin their fun tonight. Tommy leans in close. His breath is warm.

"Have you seen Ezra?" he whispers.

Chapter 11

Ezra

S ilence.

I will myself not to speak. It's easy. When Lukeman Gray verbally abused me in the past, I quickly learned to keep my mouth glued shut. Maybe I should scream, but I can't. This trait has coded itself into my very existence. Even when Thax carved lines into my skin, I kept silent. Now, I wish that I wouldn't. I wish I could scream and scream and scream.

The defining scar across the man's cheek haunts me. I dare a glimpse over my shoulder and see that the stranger isn't there. I whip my gaze back to the mirror and notice that he remains within, still watching and carefully calculating. He's a recidivist. There's no doubt. He laughs again, a mirthless, pathetic thing.

"Admittedly, we have our methods of snuffing out people like you, but your brother was very willing to offer you up," the stranger says. "Don't worry. Thax and I go way back. He'll be safe with us. You, on the other hand . . . not so much. Though I'll admit, he's kind of a dick for turning you in."

And with those words, my compassion for Thomas Gray diminishes. I take an involuntary step back. The stranger, wherever he is inside that mirror, looms closer.

"Someone's willing to pay a pretty sum for your powers, Ezra Gray." Then he pauses and the world stands still. "Faux."

He knows what I am.

I shouldn't be surprised. He and Thax are apparently well acquainted with each other. It's been so long since I've heard that term—the appellation given to those with shape-shifting abilities. I can mold myself into anyone I want. Yesterday, when Lukeman destroyed my violin, I shifted into my mom. Her body was unfamiliar, untouched. The sensation was new. But I'd done it as if it had been the easiest thing in the world—instantaneous as the snap of my fingers.

Faux.

The coined name for those with shapeshifting powers. Me. And this man, the man in the mirror, who speaks, but whose words don't make sense, says that my abilities are desired by someone. That they're willing to do whatever it takes to have them. It's true, though, what they say. A faux's ability is rare. Faux possess the power to undergo separate aliases, which makes them a rarity for trafficking networks. They could become anyone—leave the life they were born in for a new one.

But not me. I never had the guts to leave and start a new life. There were always tethers reeling me back. My love for orchestra, my unhealthy attachment to Mom, lack of funds . . . Conin. I could never leave him. Even now, when it's clear my life is in danger and staying will only guarantee my death or capture, Conin holds me back. I can't leave him. I *won't* leave him. And then the cold, cruel image of his pale, lifeless body flashes in my eyes. If I stay, I risk his life too. Because whatever this means . . . it's not good. It won't end well.

I edge toward the door. And to my horror, the stranger phases through the firm mirror—a solidified, corporeal body. He lunges and pins me against the wall. I struggle against his considerable strength, waiting for the inevitable to happen. But it doesn't. Just when I am convinced I'll die in this bathroom, Tommy Donahue barges in. The handle splinters, the knob clattering to the tile.

Everything that transpires afterward is a blur. A large amount of water splashes against the man's head and bubbles around it, drowning him while the rest of his body remains untouched. Tommy grabs hold of my hand. We dart out of the bathroom. Conin pushes against my shoulder, teaming up with Tommy to usher me out of the house as he trails close behind. We burst out into the night.

Chapter 12

Conin

Cars line the curb of the street as far as the eye can see. I promptly forget where I've parked mine, which jolts me into a panic. High school students dot Emery's yard and send amused looks our way for our sudden outburst. I twist my head back and forth excessively, but I can't seem to recall where I've parked, nor do I see the Chrysler in the endless lineup.

"Conin, over here!" Ezra says.

Tommy takes his wrist and pulls him forward. He gesticulates his hand in rapid movements to follow. Neither Thax nor the stranger he arrived with have come to pursue us. I'm going to hope they're trapped in the unceasing pool of partygoers. If I hadn't pushed everyone aside, we might have been goners. Who knows what the hell that recidivist was capable of? Granted, I watched Tommy bend water to his will and drown that man in an airborne sphere. Which means Tommy is also a recidivist.

Do Ezra and Thax possess special abilities, too? Is that what Thax was on about?

I fumble for my keys and unlock the car through the driver's door. The other two pile in—Ezra in the passenger seat and Tommy centered in the back row. He leans forward and curves his fingers over the backrest as the vehicle roars to life. I swerve the car out and press on the accelerator. Minutes later, we're cruising out of Emery's neighborhood.

Streetlights swim past us the longer I drive aimlessly ahead. Everyone's quiet, but I can't take it anymore.

"Tell me what's going on," I say with fake composure.

Tommy shoots Ezra an incredulous glance.

"Does he not know?" Tommy asks.

"No," says Ezra.

He's paper-white—jaw locked, fingers clenched tightly. He just continuously shakes his head like he can't believe his answer, either. Ezra's ruminating, lost somewhere deep in his mind.

"Good god," Tommy sighs. He sits back and raises shuddering hands to the nape of his neck. "Ezra, tell him. He needs to know."

Ezra huffs, consuming air through the thin gap in his mouth. He's transfixed on the road ahead. Shadows watch connivingly from the sidelines. I half expect Thax and the stranger to manifest from one of the pitch-black pools. The steering wheel slickens under my touch. Somewhere in the distance, a siren wails.

"I'm a recidivist," Ezra mumbles. It's faint, barely audible over the roar of rolling tires.

I heard what he said, but I'm having a difficult time processing this world-shattering confession. A part of Ezra I never knew—a secret he kept from me our entire lives. And I know I shouldn't, I know it's not my right, but I feel incredibly betrayed. How could I not see through his deception? How was he able to hide his powers all these years?

No. This isn't about me. Ezra's life is in potential danger and I'm being selfish. If he didn't say anything, there must be a reason.

"Okay."

Ezra's dubious expression swivels to me. He's right in believing it wasn't that easy. I need to know more.

"So," I say, "you have powers?"

He nods. Although I'm driving, he's aware my attention is focused on him. His adam's apple bobs. In a hoarse voice, I hear my best friend of fourteen years admit what he is.

"I'm a faux . . . which means I can shapeshift and take on the form of anyone."

"Right."

Ezra's crestfallen. What the hell do I say?

I refuse to believe Ezra embodies what recidivism means. Our government has fed us lies so we can turn on our most loved ones, to snuff out the people they're so afraid of. It infuriates me.

"I don't know who the man was that came to the party with Thax. But he . . . I found him in the mirror. No one was in the bathroom when I walked in. I turned around and he was gone. When I looked back, he was still standing in the mirror," he says. "He said Thax turned me in. I don't know to whom, but whoever it is is willing to pay a large amount for my powers. I'm not sure who he means. Or why."

"The man at Emery's is Callum Finch. It was quick, but I knew by the scar on his cheek. If you said he can transport through mirrors, it can only be him," says Tommy. I honest-to-god forgot he was in the car with us.

Putting a name to the perpetrator unsettles me further, somehow solidifying our predicament into something more real. I shiver in the cold of the air conditioning.

"Callum belongs to the Barclay Network; they're a trafficking network that discreetly hunts recidivists for deadbeat politicians and rich assholes who want the powers for themselves. The death and capture rate are proportionally higher than that of any legal penalty or hate crime targeted at a recidivist."

We learned about this in school. Recidivists slated for prison often face a cruel, brutal death at the hands of other prison mates—even that of other recidivists. A plethora of hate crimes broke out—so much so that most aren't even worth any news station's consideration anymore. I flick Ezra a look, feeling guilty for using the term even if it was only in my head. That's not what Ezra is. A criminal isn't what most super-powered individuals are. But if our world profits from recidivist labor or widespread fear, then it doesn't matter what becomes of the innocent. I feel like I'm going to be sick.

"Callum's a mercenary for the network. How he knows your brother is a mystery to me. But if he's after Ezra . . . let's just say Ezra's in big fucking danger. I will need to get in contact with the Angelics—tell Atlas to arrange a meeting with them," Tommy says. He has a flip phone in hand. I hear the clacks of his typing.

And I have so many questions.

First things first.

"Why would a trafficking network hire individuals with powers? And why the hell would one work for them?" I ask. I'm not sure where in town we are now. I've wandered so far, but I don't stop driving. I cast the occasional peek through the rearview mirror.

Tommy looks up from the phone.

"The Angelics call them jingoists. Essentially, our own people turned against us. I can't testify for other trafficking networks, but the Barclays hire jingoists for more high-profile cases. It makes them more imposing. And the powered individual will work for the Barclays because it grants immunity. Protection. They pay handsomely, too . . . or so I heard."

Ezra's a high-profile case? He says nothing, nor does he question Tommy's words. Ezra is a blank slate, stone-faced and dead to the world.

"Who are the Angelics?"

"Shit. Hold on, Conin. Sorry. I got a reply," Tommy says, and the vehicle falls silent.

I have no idea what to do. I don't have the slightest clue what position this puts me in. Ezra is in danger. He can't return home; Thax also lives with the Grays, and this Barclay Network will know where to find Ezra if he returns. The only viable option I can come up with is to get Ezra far, far away from here. Somewhere out of the state, potentially even out of the country, though I'm not positive how doable that will be without illegally crossing the border.

He can't leave by himself. Who will take care of him? I don't know Tommy well enough to trust Ezra with him—I'm not aware of their history or how far back it dates. What I do know is that I can't abandon Ezra. I don't want to abandon him. When I thought about my life and future, Ezra was always a key factor in it. He was always a part of it, no matter where I was or what I was doing. He's a staple—an irrevocable, static part of every imagined scenario. I can't live my life without him in it. Not to be dramatic, but I'd rather fucking die.

My future flashes before my eyes. Every created scenario. Every goal I made for myself. I will be tearing down what I worked hard to accomplish. All those hours clocked for coursework, the constant state of studying. Leaving football, a scholarship, to work tirelessly to create a new life from the ground up. All of it will be gone if I decide to stick with Ezra.

I was working to become a writer for my sake, but it was he who stayed in the forefront of my mind. Could I really go on without him? Could I live with myself if I stayed behind?

The truth of the matter simply boils down to this: Ezra can't stay. He's dead otherwise. I'm not foolish enough to trick myself into believing they'll let him live after he's been siphoned of his abilities. Besides, the process might just kill him. If I leave the world I knew behind, I can take on a new one with the boy I love. If I stay, any shot at normalcy is tainted by the image of Ezra dead and forgotten. I won't let that happen.

Oh my god. Mom.

Leaving her will tear me to shreds.

Leaving will kill her.

But I don't see any other option. And Mom can't join us for whatever perilous obstacles stand in our way. The existential guilt holds me at gunpoint. Fear says hello and tells me it's going to stay for a little while. It's choosing family over a boy, but Ezra is family. He needs my help. I can't in good conscience let him go.

"No, Conin. You won't," says Ezra.

He took my silence and determined it for what it was. My decision.

"It's my choice, Ezra," I whisper.

I feel utterly defeated.

"Find a motel at a good distance from here. We'll ditch the car a couple blocks away," Tommy says.

"Isn't that dangerous?" I question.

"We don't have much of a choice. I'm going to need to make a call and solidify our plan."

I don't like this.

Tommy pockets the burner. For now.

CHAPTER 13

Ezra

Conin is not coming. I refuse.

At least, that's what I say to him—those are the words that escape my mouth. I don't believe them because I know how stubborn Conin can be. And if you dug far for the truth, you would find my selfish, petulant in my desire for him to stay. A life without him is not a life I could live. I would be alone, and life would be pointless. An unhealthy mindset or not, that's the truth.

Tommy, who's also eighteen, checks us into a motel room with two beds. We don't bother with the logistics of who will sleep where, because Tommy instantly makes a phone call.

Conin paces. I sit, back pressed against a wall. Why do I feel as if a pierced blade will crush through the plaster and stab me at any given moment? As if hands could plow through the drywall and pull me into its depths. Still, I remain pressed against it. My eyes track Conin's movements. He's only ever this nervous before his football games. But I know, this time, his worries are much, much worse.

Despite the morbidity of the situation, I feel relieved. At ease now that I am free of the burden that's my family. The sensation is odd but liberating. With these emotions comes a sadness that creeps over the other feelings. It reminds me of what I will lose, the music I may never get to create, the possibility I might lose Conin, though he remains persistent that he's going to come with me. Wherever that is. I have hope for the safe haven Tommy mentioned on our way here. It could be a fruitless hope, but I cling to it, even as my world crumbles before my very eyes.

Conin continues his pacing. The hammering of my heart is relentless.

"You have a life ahead of ou, Co'," I say. He ignores me. "Think about your mom—"

"Shut the fuck up!" he tears at me. Tommy glances over while he remains on the phone.

My back molds further into the wall. Carpet grazes skin, fingers, forearms. He's not my dad. He's not my dad. The air is difficult to inhale, but I manage, and repeat those words like a mantra. *He's not my dad.* In a flash, Lukeman's figure looms over mine. Then he's gone. Conin stands above me. His expression is contorted with horror. Lips move, but I don't hear him at first.

"Ezra, I'm sorry. I'm so, so sorry. Are you okay? I'm so fucking sorry," Conin blurts.

God, he's swearing a lot.

"Sorry," I mumble.

"Don't say that. I shouldn't have blown up on you."

"But this isn't fair for you."

"This isn't fair for you either and it's my decision to make," he says, then ensues the pacing. Tommy is still on the phone with Atlas when Conin kneels and whispers so only I can hear.

"So, this superpower of yours . . . it's rare, right?" he asks.

I hate how I find his use of the word "superpower" cute. *Not now, Ezra.*

"As far as I'm aware. It's not like faux are easily found," I whisper.

"But you were found—"

"I also have a dick of a brother," I rebut. He flinches.

"Sorry, that was the wrong thing to say. Again," Conin says, then stands. "I made my decision, Ez. I'm coming with you."

"You are not," I say. But I want him to. My heart aches for him, the proximity of his body.

"I am. Don't try to stop me."

I won't. I couldn't even if I tried. It just doesn't make any sense. Why would he upheave his entire life to aid me in a future on the run? Conin has a full-ride scholarship if all else fails in his literary journey, other friends who care for him, and a mom he would be abandoning. I've known him like a brother since we were so little. That brotherly love may have manifested into something more, but it's not like we'll be anything more. Maybe that's all we need—maybe all the love required to upend everything he's known is that sibling love, to ensure my safety. But who will protect him? I'm not capable of that if push comes to shove. I'm not strong enough. After all, it was Tommy who came to my rescue at Emery's.

Though, if the roles were reversed, I would do everything in my power to protect Conin. It would be because of that love that transformed into more. This unwavering, romantic attraction has far exceeded my ability to control. Conin inhales—a deep, guttural breath, then releases it. He pulls out his phone and makes a phone call—his very last.

Chapter 14

Conin

Revealing who Ezra is isn't my right to share, so I must be discreet with what I say to Mom. I want to believe this won't be my last time talking with her, that one day I'll be able to explain everything. But it's official. I've made up my mind to aid Ezra in whatever lies ahead. The phone rings and rings as I pace the length of the hallway. She answers on the fourth ring. I freeze.

"Conin, sweetheart. Where are you? It's getting late."

"Hi, Mom," I say and try to remain casual.

She knows something's wrong immediately.

"Baby, what's wrong?" she says. Her panic jumps from zero to a hundred in seconds.

"Nothing, Mom. Seriously. I'm fine."

"Then what is it? Do I need to come pick you up? Is Ezra alright?"

My heart skips a beat. No, Ezra is not alright. And I can't tell her why. If my heart were an alarm, I'd be blaring for the world to hear. *Stow it, Conin.* I need to get through this.

"He—"

Lie. I need to lie. My tongue dries and I lose the ability to speak. An itch crawls up, pausing at the base of my throat, choking me. The words cling to the cornice of my tongue. I'm stuck. The longer I stay silent, the more Mom will freak.

"Conin?"

I opt for a partial truth.

"He's not okay, Mom. I need to handle a few things," I say—a massive understatement. "It's going to take a while, but we'll be okay. I love you so much. I want to tell you how much I appreciate you, everything you've done for me . . . for supporting me when Dad wouldn't."

"Conin, you're freaking me out. What's happened?" she sputters.

"Something happened between Ezra and Lukeman. It . . . put things into perspective for me. I wanted to call you to say how much you mean to me—"

"Come home! Bring Ezra with you. We'll handle this together!"

"I . . . can't." The earth stops rotating. I hold my breath. If it wasn't for the noise of passing cars, I would've thought the world had ceased to exist around me.

"I love you," I mutter and hang up.

She calls back without hesitation.

My thumb hovers over the block icon, shaking uncontrollably. I hit it before I can chicken out, then delete the contact altogether. With a quivering breath, I shuffle to our motel room. Ezra's still on the bed, but Tommy now sits across from him on a rolling desk chair. Neither acknowledge the phone trembling in my hand, nor do they inquire about the conversation I had with Mom.

"Are we safe?" I find myself asking Tommy.

"We'll be fine. There's a plan now," he says, but I can see the skepticism in the whites of his irises. The sight of it sets me on edge.

"I'm a cohort with the Angelics."

"What does that even mean? You mentioned a safe haven. Are these Angelics like you guys? Do they have somewhere safe where we can take Ezra?"

Ezra keeps quiet, eyes trained on the bedding.

"The Angelics are an organized group of AWOL recidivists. They were founded long ago by their leader, Esther Brown. And they do have a safe haven; it's located somewhere in Northern California. I can take you there with the help of another Angelic. His name is Atlas. He resides somewhere in Eureka, which is about a two-, three-hour drive from here. He told us to meet him at first light and can explain the rest then."

"And how do you know we can trust him?" I ask.

"Co'—" Ezra warns.

"I'm simply looking out for us. Atlas is a stranger, and we don't know anything else about these Angelics," I say, exasperated.

"Do we have another choice?" he says.

I clamp my mouth shut. I'm worried about what I say around him, but he's right. I don't know what else we can do. A safe haven sounds too good to be true, but if bringing Ezra there is an option, we have to take that risk. I'm not completely on board—I'll just need to put a little faith in Tommy and hope for the best. Ezra appears to trust him, for the most part. And I'd trust Ezra with my life.

"Atlas is good people. I've met him a few times. He's who convinced me to join the Angelics, to aid recidivists in need," Tommy tells us.

"Fine," I say. "Let's get some sleep and leave first thing."

Ezra rejects the bed and opts for the floor. I give him the comforter and a couple of pillows. He arranges them on the carpet, then lies down and faces the wall opposite of me. Tommy shifts in the sheets of his bed and I stare up at the ceiling. I won't get much sleep tonight. Uncertainty hangs like a hook over our heads, biding its time to snatch us up. I close my eyes and search for Ezra's soft breathing. It's there, but subtle at the foot of the bed. I listen, I lie here, and I wonder . . .

How the hell did this happen?

Chapter 15

Ezra

The carpet has a musty scent to it. The motif is some ugly green atrocity probably coated with bodily fluids of every kind. Conin and Tommy offered to take my place or share the queen-sized beds, but I declined in favor of the stiff floor and its familiarity. It reminds me of Conin and the sleepless nights at his home where I'd take the floor, comforted knowing he was nearby.

And it's not the stiffness that keeps me awake, but the incessant pounding of my heart, and my mind which won't shut up. Are any of us actually asleep? I doubt it. How could we when the Barclay Network is potentially after my ass? Every car, every burst from a pair of headlights, makes me freeze like a deer afraid of its impending doom. Subtle noise from the city's nightlife travels into the room. In a way, it's the most comforting reassurance tonight will bring.

"You awake?" Conin's voice is small, but it penetrates the night.

"I don't know how anyone could sleep," I say in place of an answer, hoping Tommy's passed out.

"Will we ever be able to sleep again?" he asks. The joke doesn't land, but I don't think it was meant to be one. My mouth is zipped shut. I don't have a response, not one we'd like.

"Why didn't you tell me that you were a—"

"Recidivist?"

"I don't like that word . . . I never did," says Conin.

"We never talked about it," I answer.

"I wish we had. I don't have a good enough answer to why it never came up. It just felt taboo, I suppose. Maybe if we had . . . you would have felt comfortable telling me."

"To answer your question," I whisper, exhaling a perpetuated breath, "I thought you wouldn't look at me the same."

An unmistakable, choked-back sob emanates from Conin's bed. I sit up, feeling the urge to join him there, embrace him, pull him close—share that comforting heat that exists only between two pressed bodies.

"I should have said something," he says. It's unmistakable, the way he suppresses that sudden outburst of emotion. I wish he'd let himself cry.

"Conin. You had no way of knowing."

"It doesn't matter. It's like the time Dan and the other guys made these homophobic slurs and I did nothing about it. I had the power to, but I kept my mouth shut. Maybe then, like now, I could have changed something. I could have made an impact—made someone feel comfortable in their own skin."

My mouth goes slack-jawed. My hands tremble, and an abrupt cold runs down my spine. We've never approached queer topics, as I've always been afraid of outing myself to Conin. And now, at this moment, I have a strong desire to tell him I'm demi and admit the truth I've kept to myself.

He wasn't aware of it, but Conin accomplished the impossible. I thought I was broken. Boys in the locker room would brag about body counts, scrupulously detailing a woman's body in the most derogatory manner. I didn't understand why I couldn't feel the same. Girls were fine enough, and so were boys, but the idea of kissing them or . . . having sex with anyone was nothing short of horrifying. When Conin and I would lie next to each other watching movies, I'd feel a slight shift, a subtle crack inside me. During a particularly passionate kissing scene, the damn broke loose. The thought of kissing Conin, having sex with him, hit like a sucker punch—an irremovable want that only he could satiate.

Every day after was full of sleepless nights researching what the hell this feeling was. Conin and I carried a deep bond only years of friendship could cultivate and so that could be the only reason I was brimming with embarrassing, sexy thoughts of him. I figured that's what it was, that could be the only logical explanation, so I typed that feeling into the search bar. Lo and behold: demisexuality.

It felt right.

If I keep this part of myself hidden, would I be smashing or setting barriers? On the off chance Conin doesn't reciprocate those feelings, how would my confession affect over a decade of friendship? And given our situation, now's not the time to admit I'd move the moon and stars for him, not when our lives are at stake.

"I don't believe you're capable of what the government would accuse you of. It's not fair to criminalize an entire people for their mere existence," Conin says after many beats of silence.

"No," I say, "but that's the world we live in."

Another beat. Two, three.

"I never noticed, growing up."

"My powers?"

He mumbles a yes.

"I slipped several times and shifted without meaning to. My abilities didn't manifest until I was eleven. Thax was maybe . . . nine or ten. It can be the easiest thing ever, but it requires a lot of energy, so I can't always do it," I say.

"What are his abilities?"

"Thax can manipulate sound and mimic it, too. He hates it—said that I had the far more practical ability."

"Is that why he—"

Someone barges through our door. A crackle of electricity thrums in the silence of the night—a searing, blue light that echoes in the dark room. Tommy is immediately on his feet, and I quickly follow. A blast of lightning erupts into the space and misses Tommy by mere inches. The figure clad in all black enters the motel room. Small bolts of electricity fly from their fingers, dispersing like a thunderstorm. The attacker sports a skull mask, realistically bone-like, with gaunt cheeks and faux teeth. Tommy lunges at the unwelcome stranger and attempts to drown them the same way he did the other mercenary back at the party. I don't stay long enough to learn if the tactic is successful.

"Get out of here!" Tommy screams.

I can't leave him like this. I won't, after all he's done for us. But Conin adheres to Tommy's panicked request and drags me to the room's only window. The issue is that we're positioned on the second floor. There's not much time to think about the repercussions as Tommy starts to show signs of struggle, his strength loosening, giving out.

"I'll catch up with you!" he cries.

Conin swings a leg over the ledge. In a split-second decision, he jumps. I watch his feet crash into the mulch below. His leg twists at an unnatural angle.

Chapter 16

Conin

Pain jolts icy hot sparks in my ankle. A numb, pricking sensation coerces me to instinctively clutch on to the appendage even as chaos unfolds above. Lightning crackles and zigzags out the window I jumped from, narrowly missing Ezra by an excruciatingly small margin. I crane my neck to look at him. If he jumps the same way I carelessly did, the two of us, injured, won't be able to get far.

I crawl forward and raise unsure arms in the sky. Ezra stares at my outstretched limbs, perched on the windowsill, turning to watch Tommy fight off the mercenary before screaming a very audible "fuck" and falling right onto my torso. The air is knocked out of me, scorching my lungs and chest.

"I'm so sorry," he whispers. "I'm so sorry."

The ability to speak has been knocked out of me and all I can manage to is a raspy exhale. Ezra hauls himself to his feet and helps me stand.

"I'll have to drive us out of here. Do you think you can walk?"

"Uh—"

I set the hesitant, injured foot down and regret it immediately. It burns hot and bright. Ezra flinches and wastes no time in draping an arm around me, taking my own, and pushing forward while I hop on my good foot. Three blocks of this. I don't know if we'll make it. His struggle in carrying half my weight is obvious. His mouth is pursed in concentration, face scrunched as we skirt around the motel.

"I don't think my ankle's broken," I say.

Ezra doesn't reply. We keep on going, almost passing the second block. We parked in a vacant lot near a bus station, which takes shape in the dark. I'm panting now and my uninjured leg is screaming for reprieve. But we're almost there and giving up now will mean death.

Ezra's strength wavers when he starts to tilt at my side. Boldly, I press my foot harder against the concrete. The pain is outrageous, but I push and push. I've dealt with worse; at least football was good for one thing. Ezra and I scramble to the bus station, where my car awaits us under a post's harsh, fluorescent light. I rummage through my pocket for the key I kept on me, when a shadowed figure emerges through the glass of the station. He stalks in front of the vehicle and glares with malevolent disdain. The scar on his cheek is more prominent in the vivid white of the lamppost.

"Going somewhere?" Callum mocks.

He flaunts his pistol at us.

This part of town is dead. When a car passes by, Callum lowers his weapon but keeps it at the ready if either Ezra or I feel brave enough to make a move. We're completely alone otherwise. But maybe that's also a good thing.

"Hands up," instructs the mercenary.

Ezra steals a glance my way, but I nod enough for him to let go. He raises his hands in the air, and I mimic the same, putting all my weight onto my good leg.

Is this really how it ends? Mere moments after our escape? After I said goodbye to Mom with the foolish optimism that one day I'll be able to see her again? What was this all for if Ezra and I perished here? Callum certainly won't let me live after taking Ezra from me. And then Ezra and I will never just . . . *be*.

Guilt emerges from somewhere deep—from leaving Tommy behind just so we could be stopped as soon as we made it to the car.

"I'll go with you. Quietly. Just leave him alone," Ezra says, voice piercing the night.

"No, Ez!"

He shoots me a furious glance. One wrong move and we're dead. Ezra keeps his hands suspended in the air and walks unsurely to Callum. Callum then trains the gun on Ezra, half parts watching his every move and keeping an attentive eye on me. My arms grow heavy, gravity pulling them relentlessly to the earth. The farther Ezra is from me, the more I deflate, my adrenaline depleting fast.

Ezra does what he's never done before.

He fights back—

—and rams into Callum like how I've tackled players on the football field. I'm thoroughly impressed, embarrassingly aroused, but we have a chance now. And I take it.

Callum almost loses his pistol in the scuffle. It comes tumbling down with him and fires aimlessly into the night. The shot cracks and leaves a lingering echo—a ringing that reverberates in my ears long after the bullet's been fired. Callum nearly loses purchase on the ground, resetting to aim. I have ample time to intercept, so I waste none of it. Despite the shrill pain in my ankle, I push forward and slam Callum into the car with brutal force. I topple over with him from the sheer torture of my foot, but I'm successful in disarming the mercenary—the pistol clatters to the pavement.

I roll to grab it. The sound of Callum's attempt to stand is swiftly squandered by the noise of a thorough pounding and the squelching crack of bone. I slip the gun into my possession and flick my attention to the chilling noise. Ezra mercilessly kicks the already unconscious man with the sole of his shoe. Crimson bursts from Callum's nose, misshapen by Ezra's nonstop blows.

"Ezra!"

He doesn't hear me.

"Ezra, enough! We need to get out of here," I say.

He halts and looks at me with an expression I've never seen on his face. It chills me to my core.

"O-okay," he croaks.

Ezra helps me to my feet again. He lowers me into the passenger seat and takes off for the driver's side. I hand him the key, he twists the ignition, and we idle there for several moments. Several moments too many. Ezra watches the way we came, as if willing Tommy into existence. I grow antsy, nervous that Callum will wake from his unconscious stupor any second.

"Ezra, we need to go," I urge.

"We can't leave him—"

"He told us to go."

He considers this another minute before shifting into drive. We zoom away to the distant wails of police sirens. Ezra navigates to the highway. After a while of driving, I notice our trajectory shift to the interstate leading to Salt Lake City.

Neither of us speaks. We don't need to.

We just carry on and hope for the best.

Chapter 17

Ezra

"Where did Tommy say we needed to go?" I ask Conin while I navigate the highway interchange, directing our course toward Tooele, and trying desperately not to think about the way I hurt Callum.

It made me feel things . . .

"He dropped the burner phone in his struggle with the mercenary. Let me check it."

Conin produces the flip phone and scours through it. He decides to call the last dialed number. The beating of my heart picks up pace, muscles shocked he took the risk of calling. It rings several times before a voice sounds from the other end. My shoulders tense. I try to listen over the sound of roaring tires and the staple Utah wind.

"Hi," Conin says, awkwardly. "I'm the friend of the recidivist Tommy was talking about. Yeah. We ran into trouble. He said to escape, that he'd catch up. Where do we go? Eureka? Okay. Okay, I will." Conin hangs up, snaps the burner phone into two severed pieces, and chucks them out onto the highway. In another brief decision, he holds his phone in a white-knuckled grip before tossing it into oblivion. The act, the brevity of it, what it means, throws me into a loop. It makes sense—our situation is dire. I don't have anyone who would care enough to contact me, or I anyone else. The only person I love is in this car with me, taking on the unknown dangers ahead. So, I dig my phone out of my pocket and hold it in my sweating palm. Miss Bresshet takes this moment, the perfect opportunity, to call it.

Conin pales. My thumb hovers over the answer icon. He wants to talk to her, I know he does, and a part of myself wants him to, but we shouldn't—not when there's the risk of someone, Barclay Network or otherwise, that could glean any pertinent information on our whereabouts. Finally, breath hitched, Conin says, "Don't answer it."

With a trembling hand, I discard my phone. It's engulfed by the black of night, its fate to be determined by the road. I grip the steering wheel tighter on ten and two with sleek, sweaty hands. Conin's breaths are heavy, labored with suppressed panic. As we near the turn of the mountain, I can't find the proper words to comfort him. I wish I was a writer like Conin with the knack for always knowing what to say, but I'm not. I need to say something, though. None of what's happened has been fair to him.

"Are you okay?" I ask. It's a stupid question. He's obviously not.

"Yeah, I'm fine."

Seconds pass, though they fill the space with silence, as if hours have gone by.

"You can talk to me about it—it might be better to let it out-"

"I said I'm fine, Ezra!" Conin seethes.

"Okay," I say and zip my mouth shut.

The only lights we can see are the Chrysler's, limiting our view ahead. The rest of the world around us is draped with the light of the moon enshrouded by stubborn clouds. A maintenance icon flashes on the car's dashboard. I ignore it and maintain a steady 80 miles per hour. The interstate remains relatively isolated and scarce. My heart leaps every time a vehicle passes, or a pair of headlights warns us of their presence.

"Sorry," Conin says.

"Don't be sorry," I whisper. "This situation is fucked. I'm so sorry you had to leave your mom behind."

He didn't need to apologize. Better not to rehash our argument from earlier, so I keep to myself.

"She'll be okay," he says, more to himself than to me. He wants to believe this. I do as well.

"We should try to make as much distance as we can. Who knows if anyone else is following," Conin mentions.

I nod and check the rearview mirror. Headlights from a vehicle, probably miles away, blink back. I press on the acceleration, barreling us into the unknown.

Chapter 18

Callum

Callum's consciousness pieced itself together little by little. His back and shoulder blades ached tremendously, and the skin of his hands was inflamed, cuts and scrapes oozing coagulated blood. He blinked death from his eyelids and opened them to a searing pain that made him want to close them right back up. Callum forced his eyes wide open. When he did, he was met by two pairs of boots on the dimly lit asphalt.

"The disappointment awakens," came the voice of a woman he vaguely recognized.

The second set of boots rushed forward while Callum recoiled from the blow that was likely to follow. Instead, he was hoisted up and slammed against the glass window of the bus stop. The air was knocked right out of Callum, who had already been struggling to breathe since he awakened from the hellish nightmare he was forced into by those damned kids. He blinked and found the face of his younger brother glaring back.

"I'm always picking up after you," Levi said vehemently. Callum didn't like his brother. He didn't like his brother at all. He loathed him with a fiery passion that could rival Levi's fire abilities.

"Where'd the boys go?" Mara asked Callum, but Callum didn't want to listen to her either.

"They got away," he rebutted sarcastically.

"No shit, Sherlock. Levi, kick some sense into your older brother."

Levi must've rearranged some organs with the aftershock his kick left roiling in Callum's stomach. He bunched over and spit phlegm into the grass. On second thought, he hated them both.

"Remember now?"

"Of course, I don't, bitch!"

Another swift kick to Callum's midsection knocked every last dreg of air from his system.

"Do not . . . talk to her that way. Do you hear me, Cal?"

He nodded if only to get Levi off his back long enough for him to collect himself. Levi stood, ignoring Callum in favor of a silent discussion with Mara. Callum desperately wanted the night to end, so he glared disdainfully at the asphalt and didn't utter another word.

"My guess is they're heading for the Nevada border now that they think they've outsmarted us. I'll start moving that way. You take this pathetic bastard home," Mara said. Her boots stomped away.

Callum was lifted once again and shoved into the backseat of the car. Levi slammed the door shut and rounded his vehicle to the driver's side. Callum didn't want to face Angela's wrath, but he was too tired and too defeated to make himself care what punishment was sure to follow his failure tonight. The car's ignition roared to life, and they pulled out of the desolate parking lot. When the vehicle hit a particularly large bump in the road, something big and cold was tossed Callum's way.

He craned his neck to find what had shifted on him and saw Tommy's unconscious body sag next to his. He shoved the boy away in disgust. Tommy's head smacked the glass and slumped down, folding over his chest. Levi laughed from the front seat, delighted in Callum's displeasure.

"Don't damage the merchandise," he chuckled.

Chapter 19

Conin

Tooele appears in the horizon as a half-lit green sign and a cluster of small lights. Ezra takes the off-ramp after gesturing at the fuel warning icon. He's resorted to silence—a mute press of his lips. A heavy trepidation takes hold in my chest cavity, lingering as we pull up next to a fuel pump at a vacant gas station. I think of Mom—of her phone call I ignored. An immense feeling of loss washes over, making it hard to breathe.

I'm killing her.

"Conin?" Ezra's voice calls from the abyss.

He reels me in from the deep, forcing me to look him in the eye. His irises are as full of concern as they are of fear. Something shatters inside me.

"I'm not sure how much I have left on my card, but it should be enough to keep us going for a little while," he says.

It takes me a moment to register what he said.

"Are you okay?" he asks.

We both know I'm not.

"Yeah," I lie. "And don't worry about it. I'll pay and then withdraw some money from an ATM to keep us going for a while. I'm using our joint credit card, so she'll know where I am. If I use it this one time, we should be fine."

"Are you sure?" he asks.

"Positive," I say and glare at the road behind us. "Keep an eye out, will you?"

He nods and I limp over to the convenience store. The lady behind the counter shoots a questionable glance my way before returning to her phone. I amble over to the only ATM, then withdraw a thousand dollars. This should immediately alert Mom. I then scurry over to grab a map of Utah, some snacks to tide us over, and several water bottles.

It takes a second for the lady to realize I'm standing in front of her while I pile the groceries onto the counter. She eyes me wearily and mumbles a pathetic excuse of a greeting before telling me how much I owe.

A pair of headlights flood the store, but they flee faster than they came. I will my beating heart to slow. The lady repeats the total cost.

"Oh, sorry. Can I add sixty bucks to pump four, please?"

She bags the water and snacks, then leaves me to my devices. When I return to the Chrysler, Ezra's gaze is transfixed on the highway off-ramp. No sign of mercenaries, or *jingoists*, yet. A subtle wind blows through the strands of his hair, rustling the plastic of the grocery bags I carry.

"Nothing yet," he whispers.

I hand him the snacks, then punch in the authorization code, and begin to fill the car. With each guzzling noise, my chest constricts and grows tighter—a fear the worst has yet to come sprouts like poison entering my bloodstream. The pump clicks and the echo of a gunshot crackles all around. It's in my hands and it's not a gun. Of course, it's not. We're fine.

"What's wrong?"

"Nothing," I lie again. "Let's get moving."

"Where to?" Ezra questions as I unfold the map.

"I don't feel comfortable heading directly to Eureka," I admit and thumb through the paper.

Charting out a course, there just so happens to be a more direct way to get to Atlas, but I know better than to potentially lead a mercenary to our only saving grace.

"UT-36 would lead us to the turn-off for Eureka, but I'd feel safer if we continued on I-80 to Wendover so we don't hint to the Barclay Network of our true destination. That's if we're still being followed. It's better to play it safe than sorry."

"Sure," Ezra says. He's off. He's *been* off since mercilessly kicking Callum to within an inch of his life. I stash away the urge to probe for later.

He pulls onto the highway and proceeds as if we never had this detour to begin with. As time trickles forward, Ezra's indiscreet glances in the rearview mirror become more obvious. The emotion in his eyes is indiscernible, as if he's caged it behind a practiced veneer. His mouth is pursed just as tight as before, his knobbly shoulders rigid and locked into place. Ezra's hair is a disheveled chaos, though the bun from the other night withstands the test of our predicament.

Looking at him, at the boy that I love, I promise myself I will do everything in my power to keep him safe. Ezra and I might never be, but I cannot live in a world without him. The promise has been made, though my lips remain glued together.

"Co," I hear his faint voice.

"What?"

"I might be paranoid," he says, "this car's been following us for a while now. Same distance, too, it seems."

I twist to get a good look behind the passenger seat and stare at an endless sea of black. But in the considerable expanse between is a pair of daunting lights—a vehicle that gains with each mile we drive. It could be any random car on its way to a far destination, but I trust Ezra's judgment. We're certainly not alone.

"I'll keep an eye on it," I say. "You focus on driving."

Ezra nods again, a frantic bob of his head.

"How's your foot?" he asks.

I settle on the truth.

"It hurts like a bitch. I'm worried about it getting swollen . . ."

We won't be able to go to a hospital, though neither of us says it.

"You've had worse from football, right?" he says.

"Yeah," I say, though I've had little time to assess how bad the injury is. I try desperately not to think about it. "I'll work at getting a brace on it as soon as we can. Maybe Atlas or the Angelics will be able to treat it."

"Maybe," Ezra echoes and casts another peek through the mirror.

I take that as my cue to return to my post.

The pair of headlights is dangerously close for comfort. It's uncertain whether this is the same vehicle or just some random driver, but the tension solidifies in my body. The throb in my ankle makes me clamp my teeth together and grind them mercilessly. The car looms closer, its ray of light growing, blinding our view from the back, not that we could see much in the first place.

Lightning strikes from the pursuing vehicle. The bolt targets the asphalt ahead of us. Sparks rain down and scatter as we cruise by. I wince, craning my neck back at the mercenary from the motel.

Is Tommy . . . *dead*?

"Oh shit, oh shit," Ezra panics under his breath.

The vehicle lurches.

"We're going to make it," I say and try to believe it.

Another burst of lightning vibrates the car, although we can't see where it struck, and the vehicle lurches and groans with protest. Ezra veers the steering wheel to the right in one swift, panicked move. He loses balance momentarily—an excruciatingly painful moment—before correcting himself and pressing hard on the accelerator. The mercenary's vehicle, pitch black in the dead of night, cruises forward and stays glued to our side.

A final bolt of electricity stuns the road ahead. Ezra slams on the Chrysler's brakes. A deep, audible pop rattles us in our seats—a blown tire followed by a shrill screeching. When we've come to a complete stop, the mercenary's vehicle pulls ahead and parks in front of our headlights. We waste little time. The handgun I stole from Callum is in the glove compartment, so I snatch it and unclick the safety. Ezra's out the driver's door, taking refuge behind the Chrysler's trunk. I have another plan in mind—a reckless one, but fuck it, I'm terrified.

The mercenary emerges from their vehicle, their skull mask a black hole. I cock the chamber of the gun and fire in their direction. Several wayward bullets are absorbed by the land, their destination unknown. The flare of each shot flashes in my eyes, blinding the world around me. In a last desperate attempt, the skull mask directs a lightning bolt my way. I lunge, feeling the disturbing pain of my ankle and the scorching burn of flames erupting from behind me.

"Conin!" Ezra shrieks.

The hood of my car is on fire, a vivid contrast to the obsidian night. I crawl away as I feel flames eat at my clothing. I remove my hoodie and chuck it into the dark. The pounding of footsteps near, and my attention darts to Ezra's frantic approach.

"Holy shit," he breathes. "Are you okay?"

"I'm fine," I say. "Where's Skull Mask?"

Ezra's blue and green eyes search the dark.

"I don't—"

A crackle of blue webs disperses out of nowhere. I release two more shots from where I saw the electricity form. There's a gasp, followed by a large thud, and then silence. I don't have time to react. I don't have time to understand what I just did, what it means. Ezra is pulling me up and telling me we need to leave . . . people are coming . . . cars are far off but approaching. I have to accept I won't know if our pursuer is dead. Time is of the essence.

Fire consumes the Chrysler's hood, quickly scorching the interior. Ezra is leading me away, right to the mercenary's vehicle. I search for the body, see them lying there on the asphalt, but I'm then being shoved into the passenger's side and Ezra's fumbling for the keys still inserted in the ignition, bringing it to life.

Every noise descends into static. I can't breathe. Endless darkness stretches ahead, perpetual and unrelenting. We move forward and cruise into the unknown.

Chapter 20

Ezra

Wendover reveals itself on Nevada's border, at the foot of a jagged, rocky mountain. A sore, stinging tiredness tugs at my eyelids. When they droop downwards, I'm jolted awake by the rumble strips on the edge of the highway. Conin startles and now we're both painfully awake. Minutes later, we pull into the bright luminescence of Wendover's nightlife; the view of the Rainbow Hotel Casino is a reminder that life moves on, even when it feels as though ours has ended.

"Let's grab a motel," Conin mutters. His voice is tired but steeled off. I want to ask how he is, but he'll only avoid the question. Shooting someone . . . that's not easy. Neither is kicking someone ruthlessly in hopes it'll end their pathetic life, but I shove that thought far, far away.

"Are you sure?" I ask, matching his tone of exhaustion. "What if the Barclay Network comes this way?"

"Ezra . . . you're tired. I'm tired. If we continue like this, we'll get in some accident, and then what would have been the point of everything we just went through?"

That's fair.

"Besides, I can't see them exerting their resources on just one recidivist, no matter how coveted your power is. If the mercenary on the interstate isn't dead, it will take a while for them to get back to the Network. We should be long gone by then," he says.

"I'm not sure about this, Co," I say.

"Can you just trust my judgment for once?"

When have I not? But, like usual, I shut my trap. He's staring at me expectantly, so I concede he navigates with the map, and we drive off in search of a place to stay for the night. Or what remains of it. The mercenary's vehicle feels evil and vile. Using it is necessary, but I feel just as estranged driving it as I did Conin's Chrysler.

We end up at a decent-looking establishment, where Conin pays for our stay with the wad of cash he pocketed at the ATM. Conin tells me not to fret when the clerk walks away to grab our key, probably noticing the panic in my eyes. I'm fretting, okay? I've been doing nothing but fretting since my dad shattered what remained of my good life in the Gray household. Now, I'm fretting some more, though this time under the roof of a piss-covered motel.

A single queen bed greets us upon entering our room. We turn to each other with equally coy expressions, though this should really be the least of our worries. Sharing a bed, after everything that's happened, should mean nothing, right? Besides, he and I had sleepovers all the time while growing up—shared an intimate space that could only come from years and years of friendship. He eyes me warily and says he wouldn't mind taking the floor. I refuse. And part of my refusal, I admit, is my selfish desire to have his body next to mine, the safety of his strong frame against my back, the reassurance of his closeness.

When the awkwardness mellows, we situate ourselves on the bed. I told him I didn't mind if he slept in nothing but his sweats. I'm thinking about things I know I shouldn't. It's crappy timing: leaving our lives behind, the shit we've seen, his injured foot, the mercenary's uncertain status. But I want him. Despite all that, I want him, if only he'd have me. A gag reflex surfaces, and I forcefully swallow the sensation down. While I wait the horrid feeling out, sleep swallows me whole. And when I wake, Conin is gone.

Time passes slowly and it's excruciating. It's sometime in the afternoon when I wake up. I stand, a tremor in my movements and an uncomfortable buzz centering at my fingertips, creeping up my nervous system. The curtains are closed horizontally, blocking light from entering the tiny room. I part them slightly, that tremor persisting, enough to ascertain that I slept for an ungodly number of hours, evident on the digital clock that reads 2:43 p.m.

I have no idea where Conin is.

He isn't in bed, nor is he sitting on the only chair. The bathroom's vacant. Conin is *gone.*

There are no telltale signs of struggle, nothing that indicates something bad went down. Do I wait him out or do I go in search of him? There's the option to shapeshift—a tool I haven't utilized since the night at the party due to all my efforts to just fucking forget. Now that the one person in my life I actually care for is missing, I should probably get over myself and put my powers to some use.

A mirror that's seen better days is plastered to the bathroom wall. Looking at my reflection in one makes it easier to transform. The shift is simple—getting the looks right, however, can be difficult. Two distinct eyes gaze back at me: one green, one blue. *My eyes.* The ones I was born with. They are the first to change. I decided on complete blue since it's the color that comes to mind after imagining Conin's azure in my head. It's oddly intimate and awkward, so a vibrant hazel it is. I contour my face next, mold it to my will. My jaw and cheeks fill out more, my long brown hair shortening until it's cropped around my head with some length at the top. My stomach, chest, arms, and thighs grow until I'm roughly the same size as Conin. I'm . . . attractive. No acne, no scars, the perfect hair, the perfect angular face . . . the perfect body. My clothes have shrunk—I should have considered that. It looks nice, in a way. You can see the most prominent features through the tight clothing. They're not mine, and a part of that makes me feel defeated. None of this is who I am.

An unsettling pain lingers, starting at my clavicles and spiraling down through my ribcage. The buzz returns with a vengeance—a panic attack-level of reprisal. The creak of the motel room door opening, then abruptly closing, sends vibrations to the bathroom. In a flurry of panic, I rush to see who it is, if Conin's arrived. Underneath the entrance stands Conin Bresshet in the flesh—alive and well. He carries bags loaded with items. And when he sees me in a body that isn't mine, he freezes and stares at me with equal parts childlike horror and curiosity.

"Ezra?" he says, uncertain. I've forgotten I've only shown him my ability once.

I shift to my normal self and feel the clothes loosen around my frame. Conin visibly relaxes.

"I was going to look for you," I say.

"Sorry. I didn't want to wake you."

I'm mad at him, but I keep the sentiment to myself. Frankly, I'm not sure I have the right to be angry when he's done so much for me already just by being here.

"What's all that?" I ask.

"Stuff for the road," Conin answers, heaving the bags onto the bed. Right—what we had was destroyed in the fire.

I spy clothes for him and me: shirts, sweats, joggers, underwear, and socks are in plastic bags while the rest are filled with mostly non-perishable foods and other miscellaneous items. He even bought a cooler to stuff the frozen goods inside of. He produces a box of store-bought hair dye, sunglasses, and a baseball cap from one of the bags. I glare at the box of bright red hair dye. My eyes flick from it to Conin and back.

"You can't be serious," I protest. "Out of all the colors you could have gone with—"

"This one will make me the most unrecognizable. I mean, as far as cheap hair dye goes. I need to disguise myself and you have powers that can transform you into anyone, so you're set."

Conin's about to ruin his perfect hair, but there's no stopping him. I hate to admit there's apt logic to his idea. Dreadfully, I watch as he tears open the box and gets to work in the bathroom. I pace, making occasional glances at the map we bought. Fifteen or so minutes pass and Conin's hair is already shifting into a vibrant, unnatural red.

"I made sure to get an ankle brace, too," he says, lifting the hem of his joggers. He sways on his feet, the momentum driving him forward, a limp in his gait. My hands levitate in the space between us, ready to catch him if he falls over. Conin smiles, recognition dawning on his face.

"I'm okay."

I'm not.

Hopefully, the brace will help him get back to normalcy. There's no way we could go to a hospital without outing ourselves. Perhaps the Angelics, or this Atlas, will have resources we can use.

The dye settles for a little while longer. Eventually, Conin escapes to the bathroom to wash off the excess color. The door shuts and the sound of cascading water spills into the room. I am *not* thinking about him undressed. It wouldn't be the first time, but these thoughts are entirely inappropriate, given everything.

Guilt for harboring these thoughts in such a difficult situation racks me. They're normal, sure, but I shouldn't feel this way, shouldn't submit to these feelings after Conin's left his life behind, injured himself in the process, and had to abandon his mom to aid me in a life that may inevitably end regardless of how hard we try to escape.

That's what I don't tell him. I'm not confident we'll get out of this alive. I possess half the mind to abandon Conin at the earliest convenience, but what that would do to him . .

. what that would do to me, is beyond what I want to allow myself to think about. It is, in a sense, a betrayal. Leaving him would essentially act as the biggest "fuck you," and I can't do that to him. I can't do that to him. I can't. Conin's complicit now, whether I like it or not. Abandoning him would be like offering him to the Barclay Network, exactly what Thax did to me. I will not sink that low, no matter how terrified I am.

And if I'm being honest, I can't survive on my own. I hate this.

"Let's map out our way to Eureka," Conin says while he exits the bathroom.

His bright burgundy curls are tousled. The room's low lighting reveals a glistening, damp sheen. I gape, not sure what to think. It makes me sad, almost, as if I'm mourning something that belonged to me. Conin's shirtless. His skin shines and I follow the thin trail of hair on his stomach that dives below his waistband. His soft belly erupts me into flames. I dart my eyes away. And Conin, to my relief, obliviously reaches for the ball cap and sunglasses. He puts them on and looks like he could pass as someone else. This could work.

"See? A whole new person," he says, satisfied.

"Sure," I mutter.

"I was thinking of growing out a beard, too."

"Oh god, but it's so patchy when you do!" I exclaim. He's tried it before. It was a rough time.

Conin is unimpressed. "Ezra—"

"Fine, it'll look good."

"And I don't need your sarcasm, thanks," he says and slips on a new shirt. No longer able to ogle at his perfect body, I deflate on the bed.

He joins me, pulling up our gas station-bought map. He unfolds it, smoothing its creases. Conin draws his index finger across it, circling it uncertainly, before settling on a spot. Eureka isn't that far. He estimates it should take us three to four hours from Wendover to arrive there. In the meantime, he says that we should spend another night here—get some more rest, and be masked by the shade of night, before we attempt our journey again.

I agree with him.

The night is subjectively scary. Too much can happen in the dark—too much dangerous potential. But for me, night has always felt safe and comforting. In the dark, no one can see you. In the dark, expectations are subverted. We're less exposed. I don't have to be self-conscious of myself, as if I'm a grave disappointment. And at night, Thax and

Lukeman Gray sleep. At night, I can be myself. It's a reset. A reminder tomorrow might be different.

When morning comes and the sun shines on our corner of the world, I must remake myself as a different person with a different alias. Conin sits against the headboard, turns on the TV. My legs drape off the bed, my body facing the masked windows. I breathe again. The curtains are musty. The carpet is laden with stains.

"What should my name be?" I ask. Conin's frame rustles against the sheets. "In case it comes up . . . I should go by a different name. You should, too."

"Our IDs say otherwise," he deadpans.

"Yeah, but like . . . in passing. What do you think I look like?" I say and transform into the outline from before.

"Oh fuck. You look like a Brad," Conin says.

I feel like socking him in the gut.

"Hell, no!"

"Wait . . . what about your middle name?"

Tatum. It's not a bad idea.

"I was hoping for a superhero's name, but that'll work," I say, sarcasm dripping off the edge of my tongue.

Conin erupts into a fit of laughter.

Chapter 21

Conin

Ezra's passed out next to me on the bed. I lie on my side, arm denting the pillow, hand propped up to support my head and watch him. The faint movement of his body rises, then lowers—an endless flow of hair masks his face from view. He's so peaceful-looking that I'm envious of his ability not to be bothered by sharing the same mattress as me. Meanwhile, I'm losing my mind. It was the same deal as the night before and it's much worse now.

Does he really feel nothing for me? Does this truly not bother him?

I want to rip my fucking hair out.

Carefully, without rustling the sheets, I remove my hand from under the duvet. It stays suspended in the space that separates me from Ezra. Raising a hesitant index finger, I wait with a trembling wrist. I want this more than ever; the comfort and solace from Ezra's touch is a pang of hunger in need of satiation. Ezra, and only Ezra, can satisfy it. My skin grazes the fabric and lingers on the small of his back. I breathe deeply, a scream lodged in my throat, a desperate plea to stop—stop before I do something I'll regret.

Ezra shuffles, then positions himself on his back. His eyelids are shut, his mouth is parted slightly, and I hear his small inhale. Relief washes over the storm brewing in my chest. He's still asleep. I turned over, away from him, and let the tears well—the shuddering sob suppressed long enough for me to abscond to the bathroom. Once inside, I quiet my cries, but they burst out anyway. Tears stain the linoleum floor.

Loneliness is a double-edged sword. And I'm bone-deep pierced to the heart because even as I'm here with Ezra, I feel so alone. These ruthless feelings for him have nowhere to go, and no place to call home. What happens at the end of this road? What happens once we've found safety and there's nothing left but to exist? I'm not like Ezra. I don't possess any special abilities of my own. It's selfish of me to think that despite having Ezra's friendship, I may never have more. There may always be this rift between us, and knowing this makes every inch of me ache. I'm so lonely and that reality only digs deeper, made worse by the realization that I may never get to see the second-most important person in my life.

And she has no idea what's become of me.

I left for a boy who may never want me . . .

. . .leaving a mother who can't live without me.

But Ezra must be protected, no matter how much it tears me apart.

Crying silently in the bathroom reminds me of all those long nights of countless, unrelenting arguments. My father's booming voice. Mom's silent pleas.

I peer in the mirror, my grip tight on the counter. There's a crack at the top corner, alongside some spots and smudges with a story to tell. With one good look at myself, a spike of rage ignites. The slap to my cheek was brutal. And the mark it left is a hot, stinging red.

"Conin?"

Ezra's voice is soft. At first, I thought I imagined it, if not for him repeating my name. It sounds like salvation. It drives me insane.

I open the bathroom door, hoping he won't see my tear-streaked face.

"Yeah?"

"Is everything alright?"

No.

"Yeah, I'm fine. Just stubbed my toe . . ."

He's quiet—assessing.

"Okay. You should try to get some sleep," he whispers.

I can't read his face.

I want to ask . . .

Where are you? What are you thinking?

I know I'm your friend . . .

But I love you. I love you so much.

If you knew how I felt, could our friendship remain the same?

Do you reciprocate these feelings?

Do you feel the same?

I join him under the sheets. His smile is sad, worried, fake.

"We're safe," he says. It's a lie, though it's somewhat comforting. Maybe that's why he told me.

"Good night."

"Good night," I whisper back.

An hour later, I'm asleep.

———◆◇◆———

We're up very early the next morning. When Ezra shakes me awake, I jolt upright, head pulsing with a ridiculous migraine, and reach for the handgun on the side table.

I see skull mask thud onto the road, bullets tearing into skin. Whether or not this last detail is a figment of my imagination, the panic it instills clutches me.

"Jesus, Co'! It's me! Ezra!"

"Sorry," I gasp and see that it is indeed him.

"It's alright," Ezra says, gauging my sorry state. "We should get going."

"Let's map out a course first."

I'm drenched in sweat again from the nightmare. Before Ezra can say anything else, I shower and dress. After I'm finished, we unfold the map on the bed to chart a route from Wendover. Ezra is attentive as I run a dragging finger along the highway.

"It might be a safe bet to avoid the area where we had the encounter with the mercenary," I say.

"Right. How about Skull Valley Road past Lakeside? It's a much longer route, but it avoids Tooele entirely. We'll need to make sure we're filled up on gas and check again once we hit Dugway," Ezra tells me.

His face is scrunched in concentration and the determination in his eyes evokes a genuine grin out of me. He looks up, notices my smile, and grins too.

"What?"

"Nothing," I say.

I fold up the map and we're out in a matter of minutes. Once back on the highway, we fall into silence—Ezra at the wheel and me trying to navigate the map. Time slows into an endless hour. The mercenary's vehicle feels taboo to drive in. It's about a half tank full, so Ezra and I decide to refill and head directly to Eureka afterward.

A skull mask falls to the ground in front of my eyes.

They were going to kill Ezra.

I did the right thing.

This is something I must remind myself of, over and over. I suppress the urge to panic because I don't want to worry Ezra. Besides, there's a chance the mercenary is still alive. There's a chance I'm not a killer. And no matter how evil the person, that hope is there, and bright.

"Are you okay?" Ezra asks.

I break from my stupor and focus on the road ahead.

"Yeah," I lie.

Chapter 22

Ezra

The road winds ahead. It wraps around the base of a mountain and dips into the crevices of a canyon. Blackbrush and purple sage dot the terrain. Spindly junipers and Joshua trees scope the road's edge, resembling a fence guarding the land beyond. The sun is bright enough to cast the sky in a brilliant baby blue. I'm slow around the tight bends to let Conin doze off in the passenger seat. A dollop of drool hangs from his lips. It's cute, but distracting, so I return my attention to the road. We hit a rough patch, shaking the car, which jostles Conin out of his stupor. My eyes glaze over his waking body.

"I'm sorry, I didn't mean to—"

"Stop that. It's fine," I say. "We're almost there."

"How's your foot feeling?" I inquire moments later.

"I've had much worse, but you knew that. The brace should help it," Conin says, grimacing.

Got ya.

The fall was a nasty one. As far as second-story jumps go, the height could've been worse, though it was lengthy enough to do some fair damage. His vague answer prompts me not to pry further. I'm not willing to try getting the truth out of Conin when he wishes to keep it to himself.

"Where are you?" I ask, using his words against him.

"I'm here," he answers. He shuffles and faces the passenger window.

Cheap move.

I push on the accelerator, watching the outskirts of a small mining town grow from a speck into a sign labeled *Eureka: Population 651.*

Then, it hits.

An innominate force pressures my shoulders, pushing down like it wishes to bury me deep in the Earth. It's a sensation I've never experienced before; I grasp for ways to describe it, a feeling so surreal. It binds and tethers me to something unknown, tugging at my heart, pulling, and crushing. I nearly careen to the side of the road.

Conin asks what's wrong, but my ears are ringing.

In an overwhelming rush, I pull over. The sensation intrudes and permeates my every synapse, but then it feels as if it's always been there—always a part of me. The force doesn't exactly hurt, nor is it uncomfortable the longer we idle against the side of the road. What I thought was pain soothes into a steady hum.

What is this?

What's happening to me?

"Ezra? Are you okay? What's wrong?" Conin berates, but I can't be bothered.

I wait and hope that the sensation relents. The feeling dwindles more, not so much a hum, than a buzz after several alcoholic drinks, sourced at the back of my head. It's present, it's there, but bearable. I'm not sure if I should be terrified or relieved. Maybe both.

"Ez?" Conin says.

I can't look at him.

"What happened?"

"I don't know," I say in earnest. "I think I'm okay now."

Conin quiets and lets me proceed when I'm ready. On our right is a relatively small brick building with the ugliest blue-stained roof. In bold letters at the front are the words *Tintic High School.* The familiar name rings a bell. Several paltry mining cities must be nearby with the name, in the days when Utah mined for silver. I kinda went through a mini ghost-town phase.

Farther down the road, past sheds and warehouses, are the residents' homes. We pass an elementary school across the street from an LDS church, because of course there's one out here in the butt crack of nowhere.

"Where should I go?" I ask.

"Well, this should be the place. Maybe that motel over there? We can stay until we figure out what's going on," Conin says.

I acquiesce and pull into its vacant lot. It's a tiny establishment, perhaps five, maybe six rooms in total with a check-in office on the far left. Conin turns to face me when the car shifts into park.

"Are we sure about this?" he second-guesses.

"Do you think Tommy was lying?"

"No, it's just . . . what if this Atlas person isn't who they say they are? What if we put ourselves in more trouble?"

"Co," I whisper, "what else are we going to do?"

"Right," he murmurs. "You should shift," he says.

And I do as fast as possible, walking out with a confidence I do not possess.

We're across from a Methodist church—a quaint white wood-paneled building with a small tower and spire on top. Conin limps toward the motel's office while I trail behind. His gait is clunky, his movements deliberate, masking the fact that he's obviously in pain.

That tether, the sensation from earlier, instantaneously blooms at an unprecedented speed. I'm suddenly deprived of air when we enter the office space. An invisible grip tightens my lungs, then relaxes, but that feeling reverberates in my chest and echoes long past the moment I can breathe again. There's a boy behind the counter: tan, golden skin, brown eyes, and brown hair with blonde highlights that streak its tousled nature. Freckles constellate his cheeks, complemented by sleek black, square glasses. He has a nasal piercing, a black loop that glints in the morning sun. Impressionably, he's objectively cute, which makes me feel guilty since I am undeniably infatuated with Conin. He and I aren't an item, and I don't even know if Conin is queer, so wherever this guilt stems from, I'd appreciate it if it would fuck right off.

Plus, I'm demi, so . . . if I can equate this feeling to attraction, which I'm not even sure that's what it is, then this is unexpected as hell.

It's undeniable this tether binds me to him. Our eyes meet and he sharpens into focus, almost like the universe is feeding me a sign. Those overwhelming sensations roil off him in relentless waves. My eyes gravitate toward his chest where a nametag reads *Atlas*.

This is Atlas. This boy, who must be around mine and Conin's age, is the person Tommy told us to find. A boy. A boy I already feel a staggering connection to. And why? I'm being lured toward him as if I'm a fish hooked at the end of a line. My mouth glues shut. I'm rendered totally and utterly useless, though that isn't anything new.

Atlas's velvety-chocolate eyes find mine again. We hold each other's gaze for one, two, three seconds before the boy returns his attention to Conin, who inquires about a room and its rate. I cannot pry my eyes away from him, a supposed Angelic, someone who can lead us to Proctus. This is the guy. This is the guy who will lead us to our salvation.

Atlas shifts uncomfortably under my intense gaze. I look away, anywhere but at him, though it's too little, too late. The damage is done. Conin's thanking Atlas for his time, then scurries to usher me out the door. Did he notice Atlas's nametag? The question's tipped on my tongue when Conin leads me to our room. It takes him several minutes to pry open the door with the key, but we manage. A single queen-sized bed awaits our arrival. Together, we groan.

Chapter 23

Conin

"What the hell was that back there?" I ask.

Ezra situates himself on the bed. His jaw contorts as his brow wrinkles.

"Don't think I didn't notice, Ezra."

"Notice what?" he says as if I'm unaware. He's deliberately avoiding the question. An unnecessary, totally unwarranted rage ignites within me, and if I'm being honest, I'm not sure where this anger is coming from. More importantly, I'm unsure why I'm directing it at him.

"The way you two looked at each other . . . it was more than just recognition. It was so much more than that. I want to know why it looks like you and Atlas have known each other forever," I say.

"We haven't." He focuses on the floor. "I felt this strange . . . sensation the closer we got to town. Atlas was exuding that same energy. And the way he looked at me . . . I wonder if he could feel it, too."

The loneliness from last night pierces me like a blade. What do I make of what Ezra said? An energy that connects him to Atlas? One I can't see or feel or hear? I felt estranged from Ezra before, but that feeling has only amplified a hundredfold now. If there's a connection that intertwines recidivists, one that ties itself between Ezra and Atlas, well, that distances me further from Ezra, doesn't it? How is it that they have a connection when the two have never met? Ezra has no incentive to lie, and I have no reason not to believe him. Fatigue claws at my eyelids while my irritation cools. I exhale an exhausted breath.

"Conin?"

"Sorry," I sigh.

"Don't be," Ezra mutters.

"I suppose nothing is keeping us from talking with Atlas now."

"Should we?"

"Let's wait. See if he comes to us."

Time slows. The sun shifts, casting its orange glow onto the blinds. We keep the television on for background noise, neither of us paying attention, too lost in our thoughts to be comforted. Ezra turns on the news. He and I watch in silence, trepidation present after each passing second. There are no reports on the past several nights—zero coverage about two missing boys and mercenaries with a vendetta.

I tell him to search for another channel. He listens without refusing. He rises from the bed but pauses to stare down the beaten threshold. His features scrunch up in consternation. Seconds later, a knock comes from the door.

Chapter 24

Ezra

Atlas is haloed in the overhead light. The way his eyes flick away from me makes me wonder if he feels this tether, too. The closer he is, the more I pay attention to it, the more it pulses. My breath hitches and I'm suddenly hyperaware of Conin. He tries not to act it, but he's been closed off since I mentioned the sensation earlier. Now, it's as if I'm dancing over pins and needles, carefully skirting around the issue. Knowing Conin, he'll suppress it. And knowing me, I'll continue to believe it's my fault.

"Did Tommy send you?" Atlas whispers. Conin peers back at me. Visible relief floods his face. We've been stewing over it the entire day, waiting and wondering if we should be the ones to initiate the conversation—if this boy in front of us is the true Atlas. I mean, how many "Atlases" could there be in such a small, remote town?

"You're Ezra and . . . Conin, right?"

"That's right," Conin says reluctantly.

Atlas hesitates a moment and lets himself in when Conin shifts to make space. A blanket of tension weighs heavy on my shoulders.

"I'm Atlas MacPherson, an Angelic stationed here in Eureka," he says. "What happened to Tommy?" Straight to the point.

"We don't know. We were hoping to meet him here but were delayed in our arrival after an excursion on the highway," Conin answers. He shifts on his feet, leaning away from his injured ankle.

"Is he not here?" I interrupt.

Atlas trains that distinct, calculating stare on me, almost as if he's sizing me up. An itch crawls over my cheeks, searing my forehead. I'm not sure if I like it.

"No."

"He lost then . . . in that fight against the mercenary," Conin murmurs.

"What are you talking about?" Atlas questions.

"There was another mercenary," I say. "They beat Callum to us on our way to Wendover. Whoever it was possessed lightning abilities and wore a skull mask."

"You're kidding me," Atlas whispers.

"Who is it?" says Conin.

"Mara Barclay. Angela's adopted daughter, the leader of the Barclay Network." I could feel the power those names carried—their insidious weight.

"And Callum. I recognize that name. What did they look like?"

"He had a prominent scar across his cheek, green eyes, ashy hair," I say. The image of the man in the mirror is ingrained in my mind. It haunts me. *He* haunts me because my old life ended the moment he came into it.

Just how I know Conin is haunted by Mara's fall—whether or not they're dead, it must be a frightening thought.

"Jingoist scum," Atlas says. "I've only heard of him. He's infamous in our world. When Tommy mentioned the Barclay Network, I hoped it wouldn't be him. Or Mara, for that matter."

"That klutz?" Conin guffaws. "He could hardly stand upright on his own two feet."

"Don't underestimate him. The stories I've heard . . . Callum's done some pretty fucked-up shit. And Mara's worse."

I don't know if the mercenaries had just been having a bad night or if we'd bested them with sheer dumb luck, but we're both thinking it. We *must* be. There's absolutely no reason we should be alive.

"Anyways," Atlas says and directs his attention to me, "what can you do?"

"What?" The subject change leaves me with whiplash.

"Your abilities."

The clothes are still tight over my frame and my hair isn't veiling my face. Nothing prominent or distinguishing about me is up for display and it's been hours since we left the check-in office. This disguise was Atlas's first impression of me. Great.

It's easier to shapeshift into someone after I've done it once or twice. I kill the disguise and transform back. Atlas's eyes widen with excitement.

"You're a faux! No wonder they're hellbent on capturing you."

Oh, that makes me feel better.

"Angela must be desperate for your power, Ezra. Faux are rare, very rare, and you're one of the few who didn't drop off the face of the earth. Her daughter isn't expendable. If Angela sent Mara after you, we're in trouble."

This news makes me sick to my stomach.

"What do we do? Is Ezra safe here?" asks Conin.

Conin's safety is just as important. If he held his life in higher regard than he did mine, then maybe he wouldn't be here. Words cannot even begin to express how happy I am that he is. I wouldn't have made it this far without him. I'll need to do everything in my power to ensure nothing happens to him.

"Tommy said you might have a lot of questions. And I can answer them, just not here. Ezra will be safe if I take you to the bunker. It's a safe house here for passing recid—I mean, Angelics. I can explain everything there."

I want to believe him, I really do, but that instinctive urge to close myself off settles in the cavity of my chest. Turning to Conin, I find he's caged off and unreadable. His smile is wry, perked at the edges, though it doesn't reach his eyes. Nothing displaying on his face is incriminating enough to distinguish how he feels about this. Does he see my body shaking? Does he see how this feeling . . . this tether that somehow binds my existence to Atlas is tearing me apart at the seams?

Is this what Tommy meant when he said he could feel the presence of other recidivists? Is it always this overstimulating? Whatever it is, this isn't normal. I thought I was inept at sensing recidivists' presence, but maybe I wasn't. Maybe Atlas is the exception. It's the *why* that jostles me from the inside.

Conin reveals the Glock he stole from Callum. Atlas gapes at it—there's a momentary flash of surprise in his eyes, but he tries to mask his shock with indifference.

"I want to trust you, Atlas," he says, "but I need to be on the safe side here. In case . . . in case you're lying about the bunker." He's determined, his face plastered with the same expression he's worn in football games. I remember it well—have it ingrained in my memory.

"I understand," mutters Atlas. "I'll let you two get situated and then we can go."

Conin nods and moves to collect what we've brought. Minutes later, we're stashing what we can in the mercenary's vehicle. Atlas hops in the back to give us directions. The night is upon us and there's very limited lighting throughout the town. It's quiet and eerie. The solace the dark would often bring me is enshrouded by preying eyes watching our every movement, the ghosts of mercenaries haunting our hope for safety.

I ignite the car's engine, let it roar, and Atlas tells me where to go.

PART 2

THE ANGELICS

Chapter 25

Atlas

I'm scared shitless.

I have no idea what the hell I'm doing.

Why hadn't I listened to abuelo more when he was alive? And as much as I hate to admit that I kinda forgot all about Tommy Donahue since he joined the Angelics (because I DID forget all about him), seeing his name flash on my phone startled me so badly that I had to hide in the back of the motel office until my heart slowed to a healthy rate. Because he would only call for one reason, and one reason only (which was the agreement we had): call if you're in trouble or if you've found a recidivist—correction—a *powered individual* in need.

Tommy was sending two high schoolers my way. A powered individual discovered by a trafficking network, and his lifelong friend, who possessed no abilities of his own, was along for the ride. That was some dedication. I mean, how else would you react to this kind of situation? Maybe they're even in love. How sweet.

No matter what it may seem like or even that abu tasked me to carry on his work (not by my own free will, I can assure you), I'm woefully unprepared, with no clue what the hell I'm doing without him here to help me. Mamá and papá are convinced I listened to every lecture he ever gave me—that I was present for every Angelic visit, but that's not the case. That's not the case at all.

Because it's not what I wanted for myself.

I am so incredibly fucked. I was so focused on school and tutoring and seeking out cute people that I lost complete control over the operation abu had run for decades. He would be gravely disappointed in me (no pun intended; I promise).

That was so fucking morbid. God, I'm a sick person.

I need to act as if I have my shit together, that I know what I'm doing, and that I'll safely get these friends to Proctus. They'll be none the wiser when my part is over and done with. Meanwhile, I calm the creases scrunching up my forehead, the tension in my cheeks, and the lock in my jaw. The job *will* get done.

Conin parks on the opposite side of the street, per my request, a bit of a distance away from home. He listens, albeit reluctantly. Telling him what to do almost made me shit myself when I remembered the gun he kept in the pocket of his hoodie. I should warn Mama and Papa of that.

The walk to my house from the car isn't a long one, so I feel comfortable enough to lead them through the dark, lightless streets of Eureka at night. I swear to god, if they think I'll jump them or lead them into an alleyway so I can murder them in cold blood, I'll . . . well, I won't do anything, but I *will* panic. I don't want them to believe I'm up to anything nefarious. If I mention that, I doubt it will do me any favors. They most likely won't believe me. And I'll most likely be shot.

Instead, I say, "I'm sure ma and pa are still awake. They don't normally go to sleep until I get home from a shift."

"Okay. Thank you," Conin says. Ezra is cold and silent beside him, his unique eyes gazing speculatively at me, calculating, as if he's trying to decide whether I can be trusted. Fair enough, I suppose.

The presence of another powered individual breezed through me like an intense wind just minutes before they arrived at the motel. It had been so strong, so overwhelming, I had keeled over for several minutes to compose myself. It was unlike anything I had felt before—certainly not anything like the bond I shared with abu, and most definitely not like the feelings I'd get when the Angelics came around for a visit.

This sensation is utterly new to me. It's intoxicating and my every waking thought is glued to the way it makes me feel. What's different about Ezra? Why do I feel innately tethered to him, as if I've known him my entire life? Ambrosia said once after she broke the news she and Matt had gotten together, that their bond had always felt like something more, but she hadn't had the words to explain it until they'd started dating. That can't be possible with Ezra. I only just met him. There's no way something's already happening between us. To even entertain the idea is asinine.

Can he feel it?

I'm not sure how I'd react if he did.

I burn the thought from memory. Because at the end of the day, Conin and Ezra are going to leave and live their lives out far away from here. This is only a temporary fleeting moment in time. I can't entertain the idea there's more to this tether than just being near another powered individual. That means something more than what I'm willing to handle right now. It's only been a month since abu's passing. I shouldn't move on from my grief that fast.

The front door light is on as we approach home. I double-check to make sure the friends are still following close behind before taking my key to unlock the door. I enter first and hold it open like the gracious host I am. Ma and pa are, as usual, lounging on the couch in the living room when we enter. They peer up—ma from her phone, pa from some ex-Mormon book he's been reading, and their eyes widen in surprise.

Shit. I forgot to update them that two teenagers are on the run from an infamous trafficking network and need asylum downstairs in our basement. And now, the more I think about it, having the Barclay Network after their asses is absolutely pissing-pants scary. God, they better not track them here. Ezra and Conin would tell me if the mercenaries were still on their trail. I hope.

Maybe I should ask.

"Mamá . . . Papá, this is Ezra and his friend Conin. They're seeking asylum after a run-in with someone dangerous. Tommy contacted me about them. Remember him?"

I'm handling this so well.

"Of course, mi corazón. We just . . . weren't expecting this so soon," says ma.

What she means is I forgot to tell them, and I'll be hearing about it later in her overbearing, loving Latina fashion. Pa remains stern next to her, his mouth stretched thin as he takes in the newcomers. They should understand. Not everything is going to be planned. Abu certainly reminded my parents of this.

Ma stands, a whole foot shorter than me and the others. I got pa's tall, Scottish genes, which is evident by the way ma looks up at me with concerned eyes. They see all. They tell all.

"*Were they followed?*" she speaks in rough, rapid Spanish. Pa listens in, his two years of missionary experience and two decades of marriage kicking in.

"*No,*" I say. "*They lost the network's trail a while ago.*"

She goes slack-jawed.

"*The Barclay Network?*" she questions incredulously, emphasizing *Barclay* in heavily-accented English.

I nod but break the conversation so Conin and Ezra don't think we're plotting against them. Conin wouldn't kill all of us, would he? Pa stands, ambling over to shake hands with them both, forever stuck in his missionary ways. Conin smiles, his studded earrings distracting me as the overhead light reflects off them while Ezra attempts an awkward grin. For a brief second, the tether pulls with every bit of energy it has. Ezra winces. He looks at me but quickly glances away when he notices I'm watching him.

Way to be discreet, Atlas.

"Let me show you around," ma says. "Then Atlas can take you to the bunker."

She casts a backward glance at pa before beaming a brilliant smile and leading the two boys out of the living room. I make to follow her, but a large, firm hand grips my forearm before I get a chance to leave.

"How was work?" he questions.

It was abu's idea to have me work for our family's motel down the street in case any wandering recid——powered individuals passed through. He claimed I was more attuned to sensing their presence than most people like us, so I acquiesced. Ma and pa were skeptical at first, but they knew one day I'd take over once abu passed. It was always in my cards and my parents were aware of the dangers of having both a father and a child with special abilities. The argument hadn't lasted long.

"Work was fine," I say.

"Do you think these kids will be trouble?"

I don't blame my parents for being extra cautious since abu's passing, but I'm almost an adult. This was always a risk. I was told all my life that I'd be continuing his work, so they can't suddenly change their minds now. It is arguable that this is their home, after all, and that I am their son. I sigh.

"I don't think so. Tommy said he knew them from school. But if I start to think there is a potential risk, I'll notify Ambrosia."

Besides, this is what the bunker was designed for.

Pa releases his grip and ushers me along. "Just be careful," he says. I go in search of ma and our guests. In the morning, I'll make sure to contact Ambrosia. I haven't spoken with the Angelics in over a month because they remind me of him and my failures.

They probably think he's still alive.

I'll tell Ambrosia the truth of his passing and notify her of Conin and Ezra's arrival. What I won't say is that I have no idea what the hell I'm doing. I wasn't prepared for a life without abu—without my rock, the man who taught me everything I needed to know about my powers. I only watched and helped where I could, letting the desire for a life I couldn't have overcome me.

I'm such an idiot. It's time I finally get over whatever fears are holding me back and contact the Angelics. There's no choice now when I'm aiding a runaway-powered individual in the flesh.

Ma and the others are in my room. Conin is acting as polite as can be, but Ezra could care less about any of it. Ma smiles and whispers she'll make us some food before disappearing around the bend.

"Sorry about that," I say.

"It's alright."

"Let me take you to the bunker now."

The two cast each other a look. I turn my foot and lead the way.

Chapter 26

Ezra

The ties that bind us increase in strength. The longer I remain near Atlas, the more I feel a part of myself entwine with his being, merging until our essence becomes one. He certainly acts unperturbed, but my composure is leaning, crumbling before my very eyes.

I don't want it to be like this forever.

Atlas introduced me and Conin to his parents; his father has bright, fervent red hair due to his Scottish lineage, and his mother is Latina-Caribbean—the two had met when his father served his LDS Mission somewhere on the Caribbean islands. Atlas's mother moved to start a family in Utah, and they settled in Eureka almost a decade ago.

I can't imagine their family as devout members. The LDS Church took a neutral stance on the matter, though many of their more conservative members chose to side against recidivists. My family and I have never been religious, but I do have a small vendetta against the church, as I grew up surrounded by its influence.

It doesn't help that the church neglected our family when we were in need. Conin's stories of his time as a member are also horrifying.

As Atlas leads us into their basement where he says the bunker is located, an uneasiness prickles at the nape of my neck. Not all those who are part of a denomination are prejudiced, and I shouldn't act as if they are, because that isn't fair, but I have these overwrought thoughts that this is a trap.

I snap out of my daze when Atlas pauses in front of an aluminum door reinforced with a locking mechanism, where he punches a code in to gain access. An abrupt hiss emanates from the threshold. Several locks click. Atlas pushes the door open and leads us inside an unexpected luxury. The bunker is state-of-the-art with a modern sleekness that does not resonate with the rest of the MacPherson household. I wonder as I gawk at its homely coziness, why their family doesn't live down here full-time, especially when at risk with Atlas. What I would've killed for to bask in the luxuriousness of this cellar. Most of its technology, some of which I can't put names to or recognize, is mind-boggling to see.

Conin lets his guard down. It's enough for me to witness his impressed look. Atlas leads us through the kitchen, passing what appears to be a living room mixed with an entertainment center, to a bedroom with rows of twin-size beds. I deflate. While Conin appears relieved, maybe even unburdened by our change of scenery, I can't help but feel that I have lost a part of what's comforted me throughout this trip: Conin's back pressed against mine, the warmth and heat of his body, the gentle rise and fall of his stomach and chest. *Him.* Right next to *me.* And now there are no more excuses. What could I possibly say that wouldn't out myself to him? The fear of him thinking differently of me plagues me enough with worry that I keep my mouth shut. I won't ruin this.

"This is where you two will sleep. You can leave your stuff in here and then I can give you a tour of the bunker," Atlas says with a subtle grin quirked at his lips.

We place our bags on the spare beds, claiming them as our own. Conin keeps the Glock in the hoodie's pocket. Atlas tries to act as if he hasn't noticed. When we're ready, he nods and proceeds out of the room and into a hallway aligned with a closet, bathroom with shower, and laundry room. This makes me question the extent of our stay.

"The bunker was my grandpa's idea and the Angelics helped bring it to life. The goal was to design it as impenetrable and impossible for intruders to get in. It's where we keep AWOL powered individuals until the Angelics can extract them and take them to Proctus, the Angelic safe haven," he continues as he presents a bathroom the size of my room in the Gray household.

"Tell me more about the Angelics," Conin says.

"Besides what I already told you, essentially, they were founded about twenty years ago or so. The Angelics were small back then. They grew through the wealth and influence of Esther Brown, their founder. She bought some small town sequestered in California after a wildfire and established it as the Angelic safe haven, or what we call Proctus."

"How are the Angelics able to stay off the radar? I can't imagine no one's stumbled upon an entire town of AWOL recidivists," says Conin.

"It's been years since I've visited Proctus, but back then Esther had to spend millions to hush not only the government up, but any poor soul to stumble upon it. From what

I understand, one of their own possesses an ability to mask it using a force field of sorts. He's a more recent addition," Atlas says.

"The government knows?" I ask.

"Well, you buy an entire town—granted, one that burned in a wildfire—and that's going to draw attention. As far as I'm aware, California is one of the more accepting states. In more recent years, they passed legislation to protect recidivists. After the attack on Buford Elementary—Well, there's a lot of work to be done, but Esther plans on more widespread influence. She's been brewing on bigger courses of action for years, though nothing concrete yet. There's not enough of us."

Conin nods. He nudges my shoulder, catching me fixating on Atlas. This draws the boy's attention, and I subvert my gaze when he peers over with a curious expression. He says nothing about it and for that I'm grateful. Atlas proceeds with our tour of the bunker. He takes us into the entertainment center, complete with a grand television set, and a wall lined with shelves that sport a plethora of books, movies, and vinyl records. The record player, a fancy system with a glass cover and conjoined speakers, sits on a nightstand at the end of a large, L-shaped couch. I'm excited to see it, but immensely jealous. I could never afford one of my own.

A large abstract painting takes up most of the accent wall, outlined with crown molding. The rest of the space is furnished in a very homely way, albeit sleek and modern. There are video games, a couple of arcade machines, and other shit I can't put a name to. The kitchen is across from the living space, adjacent to the door that leads to the house. All the normal amenities are there with a stocked fridge and pristine, white cabinetry. It appears as if no one's used the bunker in a hot minute. It's nice—too nice. It seems too good to be true.

As if reading my mind, Atlas says, "It's cool, isn't it? Esther was very generous when my grandpa presented the idea to her. He was a devout Angelic and wanted to do what he could here in Utah. Esther liked the idea so much that she stationed small groups of Angelics in every state, and made sure there was a safe space for AWOLs to stay at until they could be taken to Proctus. She pays them handsomely, that's for sure."

He sits on the plush couch, sinks into its cushions. Conin places himself on a rocking chair and I take the other half of the couch, leveling my knees to my chest and propping my chin on a kneecap. Atlas props his feet on the glass surface of the coffee table. He's perfectly at home. He probably spends a lot of time down here, more than he'd admit.

"So, is that how you know Tommy?" Conin questions after a momentary silence.

"Tommy is a newer recruit. It was sort of a chance meeting at a protest in the city last year. My grandpa and I went; he liked Tommy's 'spunk.' His words, not mine," Atlas says in an attempt at a joke. He coughs and plays it off when it's clear neither Conin nor I found it amusing.

"Weren't you afraid of attending the protest? What if they had you arrested or you were found out?" I say.

I always wanted to participate in one, but I never had the courage. There was an immense, persistent fear of my discovery or the possibility of arrest. Atlas looks me dead in the eye. A small frown tugs his lips downward.

"You can't live your entire life in fear," he says, his focus entirely on me.

Conin shuffles on the rocking chair. It's silent longer than feels comfortable. Ms. Bernard's words drift in like a whisper, brushing against my skin, raising the hairs on my arms. A cold shiver takes root.

"Anyways, it was a peaceful protest—nothing the police or government could act on. And there were hundreds and hundreds of just normal citizens, all there in support of recidivist rights. If the authorities had done anything, shit would've gotten ugly quickly. And many were fearful of the recidivists in the crowd, of what they could do. The unfortunate truth, but we used it to our advantage."

I possess nothing useful to contribute to the conversation, so my lips stay zipped.

"How long do you suppose we'll be here before the Angelics can extract us? Who will it be? Esther herself or a smaller group of cohorts?" says Conin.

Atlas's posture straightens.

"I'll need to contact Ambrosia in the morning. She, along with several others, is usually in charge of extractions in Utah. Depending on whether they're in California or somewhere nearby, it could take up to a week. Shouldn't be any later than that."

He stands abruptly. I mimic him, cursing my legs for betraying me, and almost sit back down, so as not to out myself that his entire presence has me on edge. Atlas studies me for a moment; our gazes locked, tension potent, palpable enough for Conin to squirm in his seat. Atlas blinks, then grins. His stubble is prominent in this lighting.

"Knowing ma, she's probably whipped something up for you two, so I hope you're hungry."

It's eleven at night, but I don't point that out. Conin's stomach grumbles. I stifle a laugh because the timing couldn't have been more perfect. Atlas, however, lets out a cordial chuckle.

"I'll take that as a confirmation. The fridge and cupboards are stocked, but ma tends to cook whenever we have visitors. It's just how she is," he says, catching my eye one last time before disappearing through the secured door.

My gaze lingers long after he's left, and a sigh presses out my lips. I hadn't noticed it was queued for Atlas's departure, but now that he's gone, I regain the ability to breathe. Conin's intense glare sears my peripheries. When it's clear I've spotted him, his focus darts intently to the abstract piece of art hung on the wall. We stay like this for a long time.

Chapter 27

Conin

I hate how calm my nerves are—like a significant burden was relieved from my shoulders as Atlas showed us around. I'm not completely at peace, because that would signify a wholehearted trust that isn't there yet. We may have achieved some semblance of safety, but my worries for Ezra are persistent and my distrust of Atlas needs work. When he leaves, I turn to Ezra and notice the sickly look on his face.

"Are you okay?" I ask.

He isn't.

He shakes his head and doesn't speak. Instead, he stalks off to the bathroom, shutting the door with a jarring slam. It's obvious he's experiencing one of his episodes and I can do nothing to help him. Our conversation will have to hold out for later. In the meantime, I re-explore the bunker and get acquainted with its amenities. I enter the bedroom, staring down at the row of twin beds. Ezra can no longer share a bed with me. His body near mine was a comfort, an essential I needed, a means to keep me sane through the horrible things we've been through. I have no excuses now without outing myself to him. His friendship means the world to me. Creating a rift is the last thing we need.

I return to the entertainment room and rummage through the extensive array of books aligning the shelves. There are some greats mixed in with the bunch and several more notably queer titles I recognize. I file that information away for later, then make myself comfortable on the couch since Ezra might be a while. Moments later, the bunker's entrance emanates a low hiss and Atlas enters with a tray in hand.

"Pa had a look at the vehicle you arrived here with. Thanks for the keys, by the way," Atlas tells me while setting down both keyset and tray on the kitchen table.

"And?" I question, leaning in and clasping my fingers together. I clench tightly and watch my knuckles grow white.

"There was a tracker placed inside, just as he suspected. The Barclay Network was smart in placing it there, probably for situations like these. He's erasing its history, then he'll destroy it," says Atlas.

I'm not at all relieved. A sharp stab pierces my chest—a hint of worry. Tommy was beaten by Mara, which means these mercenaries still have a means to find us.

"My car was destroyed on the interstate," I say. "In our scuffle with Mara, we stole her vehicle and diverted paths for a while. Then we came here."

"I figured that was the case. It's not the first time we've had to deal with a situation like it. Scanning's now become a precautionary measure."

"I don't believe the tracking device was their only method of finding us. The Barclay Network has Tommy now. They could torture the information out of him," I say.

When the panic comes, I'm on my feet in a flurry. Ezra's still in the bathroom, but I'm wired with impatience. The bunker's a facade, one I'm more eager to escape. It's only a matter of time before the Barclay Network picks up on our trail again. I'd rather not be here for their inevitable arrival. Atlas soaks in the hysteria I attempt to mask. He tests the waters by moving closer, but I'm feeling territorial and downright defensive. If he doesn't back away, something of his is going to end up broken. The gun still weighs on me.

"Conin, I know what you're thinking," Atlas says calmly. "But leaving here will only condemn you and Ezra. This bunker was designed to withstand intruders. It will hold and you two will be safe."

That brief calmness returns because I want to believe him. But what if belief is not enough?

"What about you and your family? We're putting you at risk by staying here."

"If we feel our lives are threatened, we'll resort to staying down here, too. Right now, I need to discuss the situation with Ambrosia. I'll make sure to do that in the morning."

Realistically, Atlas is right. There's not much we can do and nowhere to go without the Angelics. When had I become so distrusting?

"Is everything alright?" says Ezra, who joins us in the entertainment room.

"Yeah, everything's fine," Atlas says while casting a cautionary glance at me.

Ezra's face is curious when he turns to me.

"Food's ready. Let's eat!" our host exclaims.

A silent truce is established between Atlas and me. We keep quiet about the risk of the Barclay Network finding us. If it's pertinent information later, I'll tell Ezra, but for now, I don't want to worry him. He has enough on his plate. And I must protect him, no matter the cost.

Chapter 28

Ezra

I can't eat. Atlas was kind enough not to mention it and offered to store the food in the fridge for later, but I insisted I'd finish. Even after he left because he had school in the morning, I couldn't give the lovingly home-cooked meal the proper attention.

Comfort food is always easier to stomach.

So is tequila, but I don't have that.

Ice creeps through my body.

And now, sleep is hard to come by. The tether persists, clawing at my eyelids to stay open while Conin stains the brunt end of these intoxicating thoughts. His expression was brief, only catchable if you were already suspicious that he was upset. I was lucky enough to catch the momentary chink in his armor.

He's dissuaded by mine and Atlas's tether, but the distrust is there and it's ravaging his insides. There's more to it, there must be, either because his protective instincts are kicking in or he really wants to believe we're safe now, out of the home stretch.

I can't say my faith in Atlas is concrete, but a spark has been kindled, and the tether urges, no, *beckons* me to trust him without any substantial reasoning.

Or could Conin's strange attitude be—

No, of course he doesn't love me. Not in that way. He made it clear he saw me as no more than just a brother. I shouldn't get my hopes up. After all, his expression could have been many things. Would he tell me if he liked me in that way? I know I wouldn't. I doubt he would.

Atlas is a stranger. It makes sense that Conin's hesitant. Though he's relaxed some now that a part of the burden is on Atlas's shoulders, Conin's guard's still up. He carries that damn gun everywhere, waiting for the moment everything goes wrong. Atlas attempts to warm up to him, but he maintains his distance. Rightfully so.

When it's obvious that I won't get any sleep tonight, I toss in bed and check to see if Conin is asleep. The steady rise and fall of his stomach, and the subtle noise rising from his mouth are indications enough. I move stealthily, a skill I acquired over the years in the Gray household. The sheets rustle gently when I stand.

Exiting the room, I hadn't realized I'd been suffocating, the claustrophobia pressed tight against my lungs. There must be a distraction, something to alleviate this anxiety. The arcade machines look enticing, but that'll be loud—so, no point in listening to any of these records, either. There's a gaming console near the TV and I browse through the selection of games. Nothing piques my interest, so I end up perusing through the movies instead. And to my delight the second *Star Wars* movie is aligned with the other films. It's slotted into the DVD player immediately. But when my favorite scenes unfurl, their enjoyment is lost. The past several days have sucked the joy from me.

One Halloween a handful of years ago, Conin and I decided to dress as *Star Wars* characters. We were seven, maybe eight—he'd settled on Obi-Wan while I was Anakin. Conin was large for his age at the time and could have easily passed as a fledgling middle schooler. I reached out for him in a bout of confusion, coming to find out he wasn't the only one dressed in the costume. Somehow, we'd been separated, and being the kid that I was, I panicked in silence. I searched and searched and searched, but to no avail.

Eventually, I crumpled on the curb. Tears welled, but they wouldn't shed. The panic surged and people passed, but no one stopped—no one cared. Until, suddenly, his voice sounded in the dark. It called to me—concern, fear, and eagerness wrapped into this voice that brought me immense comfort. A pillar of light, Conin came back to me. His lightsaber was ignited, pail brimmed with candy, and his stance hero-like amongst the hundreds of passersby. My Jedi knight in shining armor.

A crash echoes just beyond the sealed door, thrusting me into the present. I jump, then peer at it skeptically, unsure whether anything should be done about it. What if Callum or the masked mercenary tracked us down? What if that's one of them behind the door? I find out when it slides aside a moment later. Atlas steps through the threshold.

Tucked in the crook of his arms is a box that clinks with every movement. He doesn't notice me here, not yet, as he makes his way to the kitchen island with a disgruntled expression. The bottom of the cardboard box thuds to the counter and Atlas starts to unload bottles of alcohol. He has yet to notice me uselessly standing here in the entertainment room.

When he finishes stuffing the cupboards full of booze, he turns for the box and sees me standing there in the exact position I was in when the door opened. Startled, he clutches his heart and shuts his eyes, glasses askew.

"Jesus fuck," he whispers.

"Hi," I say.

Hi? Are you fucking kidding me, Ezra?

"I thought you were a ghost," Atlas says.

"Nah, it's just me," I whisper, to be cordial while playing cool. Atlas ambles over to the TV where I remain. He grins with an awkward tilt of his lip, then notices what's playing.

"Good choice."

Does he like *Star Wars* too? Who wouldn't? Is he a toxic fan or is he one in a million like me with a secret love for everyone's most hated prequel movie? I study his fixation on the screen and realize too late that I need to say something.

"Which is your favorite?" I ask.

"Oh, *Revenge*, hands down. This one's a close contender," he answers.

"Everyone thinks I'm weird when I say it's my favorite."

"Really?" he inquires. "Not at all. But out of all the content, or just the saga?"

"Nah, just out of the main nine," I say.

"Preach," he says, that grin plastered on his face. Atlas is lost in the movie. This mysterious boy is mesmerizing, from his darker skin to his tousled brown hair, glimmering from the gleam of the TV screen that reflects off the lenses of his glasses. His lips are plump, his body lean, several inches shorter than me, but with an overall attractive persona. I know almost nothing about him, though it feels as if I've known him for so long. The binding force lures me toward his being, toward his heart. If I plucked it from him, could I then be at peace?

"Ezra, you alright?"

"Sorry, what?"

"You blanked out. Are you okay?" Atlas repeats.

"Yeah, fine," I say. "What's up with the alcohol?"

Atlas's countenance shifts into a sheepish look. He brushes his fingers over the nape of his neck and lingers their touch where strands of hair branch out. There's that numbness, lodged in my throat. It craves the taste of alcohol—a temporary means to end the numbing.

"Ah, I tried to be discreet about that," he says. "Can I admit something to you? You won't judge, right?"

I won't, but I'm not sure I like the sound of that.

"Of course not."

Atlas wrings his hands together and lets out an elongated sigh. He chuckles, but his eyes crease sadly. They glisten behind their mask.

"I have no idea what I'm doing," he sputters, sprawling out on the couch. He inhales sharply, gazing off into the distance. Hesitantly, I lower myself on a cushion about a foot or two from him, unexpectedly ready to listen to this boy who took us in with the kindness of his heart.

"My grandfather passed a month ago. This was his thing, his operation. I should've taken this safe house stuff more seriously because I wasn't prepared for the moment he would leave us behind. Leave *me*. Neither of my parents has abilities, so they can't teach me and I no longer have him to learn from. I wish I'd paid attention more, listened to him, and helped him out more where possible. Before, I was obsessed with an unachievable normal life—crushing on people at school, tutoring math, working on college applications."

Atlas collects himself.

"Deep down, I always knew a normal life wasn't for me. With my abuelo's legacy, our ties with the Angelics, these powers? I was working so hard for nothing when I knew that one day, I would need to continue abu's work," he says, sounding lost, his words weighed down by the grief he carried.

He's unabashed over admitting his deep insecurities to me, a total stranger, someone he only met yesterday. I feel compelled to comfort him in some way.

"I'm sorry—"

"I didn't share this with you so you'd feel bad . . . I guess, what I'm trying to say is, I understand . . . needing to leave a life behind. I'd want to dull these worries and thoughts if I were you, especially if I was in a similar situation. Abu would be pissed if he knew. He never allowed alcohol before."

I won't say how badly I want some—

—nor do I ask how he got his hands on the various bottles of booze. He hasn't shared his age with us, but he mentioned he'd been applying to colleges and attending school, so he must be around my and Conin's age.

He and I are quiet for a while. The movie continues. Atlas then inches closer, the tether subtle but there in the subconscious, a pull in my chest. My entire body freezes when he's near, waiting for what he'll do, expecting an unprecedented move. "Across the Stars" swells in the background, though neither of us is watching. Atlas's lips, round and thick, are close. His breath tickles my ear, grazes my neck. I suppress a shudder.

"Do you feel it, too?" he whispers, barely audible over his breath.

I whip my neck to stare at him, mouth agape.

"Wha-what?"

"This binding force that shackles me to you. I've never felt anything like it before. It's strong . . . I can't describe it."

I'm speechless. My hands tremble, but not because of his proximity. He doesn't have that control over me. I'm frightened at the implications, and what this means. I'm frightened that I'm staring the issue straight in the eyes, faced with it with no option to go back.

"I feel it." My voice shakes. "I-I've always been inept at feeling other recidivists' presences. I don't know why this is different," I say.

The arcade machines are shut off, their presence looming like figures in the shadows. The paintings behind us, this couch, watch over our conversation, watch the way my body tenses from head to toe. Atlas blinks, then blinks again.

"I'm not sure what it is, either," Atlas confesses. He backs away, his warmth dissipating. Cold waves wash over the room. "It's . . . intoxicating. I wish I knew why. It feels . . . it feels as if I've known you for a long time."

"I thought I was going crazy," I admit and let out a relieved chuckle.

"Me too," he says. "I've felt others in the past, but nothing like this."

That inadequacy rears its ugly head once more, but I stifle it and shove it back from where it came. Not all recidivists can feel when another is close, I need to remind myself. It would be a disservice to Tommy if I didn't heed his words.

"That reminds me. I never showed you my ability."

The awkward tension from before melts into curiosity. Atlas stands, moving farther from me. I stay rooted, unsure why. He settles in the space between the entertainment console and the billiards table. In a moment of concentration, he scrunches his face, and is gone the next. I stare at the empty air his body no longer occupies. An eerie silence rings through the bunker.

A tap on the shoulder confirms the presence of someone behind me.

I whirl on the spot and see Atlas MacPherson gazing at me with wonder in his brilliant eyes.

"Hi," he says.

"Hi," I say back.

"Everything alright?"

"Yeah." *Sure.*

He furrows his brow but doesn't persist on the matter. My spine is straight. My shoulders are tense. I look at Atlas and see everything that I'm not. I look at Atlas and see a boy who has come to terms with his powers, is unashamed of them, so freely uses them without a care. Every time I use my own, I feel like I'm caving in—hiding from my true self. I hate it. I hate it so fucking much.

"So, you can teleport?"

"Yeah. Not as impressive as your shape-shifting. You should do it again," Atlas says.

"Um," I say. "Maybe some other time. I'm tired."

"Right." He looks at his phone with eyes that pop out of their sockets when he sees the hour. "Oh, shit. School's in like . . . two hours."

I nod and bid him good night. He leaves me here alone in this dark room, this quiet bunker, reeling from his secrets. Secrets told at night.

Chapter 29

Atlas

So many secrets.

Too many for my liking.

My bond with Ezra, telling him about my feelings of inadequacy, me and Conin refraining from telling Ezra about the tracking device, the possibility the Barclay Network can still track these two down, not mentioning that fact to my parents, and now . . . well, I have to tell Ambrosia about abu. She needs to know.

How can one prepare for this?

The burden of keeping these secrets is enough for me to blow a gasket. The thoughts keep me awake (I may have tried to doomscroll through TikTok at one point or another), so by the time 6 a.m. rolls around, I'm bone-tired and refuse to go to school. Ma makes her rounds and raps quietly on my bedroom door.

"Mijo, school starts in an hour—"

"I'm not going."

She leans against the doorframe with her arms hugged tight against her chest. She absorbs my sorry sight, ambling over to tuck me further into the sheets.

"The boys' arrival must be weighing heavily on you," she says.

"You could say that," I quip.

"¿Qué más?"

"Nope, I'm fine. Just tired. I didn't get any sleep."

She's trying to get me to confess my feelings about abu, but I refuse to give her satisfaction. We haven't broached the subject since he died and I'm not about to discuss it today when I have two AWOLs in my basement fleeing from a trafficking network.

"Let me tell you what," ma says, "you get some sleep and I'll tell the boys to expect you up around noon. You can keep them company."

"Sure, Mom," I say. "Thanks."

When she leaves, it's about an hour before I get any rest. Within that hour, I'm stuck staring at the ceiling and the washes of cobalt pa painted when I was younger, leaving puffed spaces around to resemble clouds. I wish I could redo the entire interaction I had with Ezra hours ago. A big part of myself wanted to tell him he didn't need to feel ashamed of his abilities. But after teleporting in front of him and asking if he could rehash his powers so I could witness them again, I could see he was scared—frightened, even. Everything I had been going to tell him had vanished from my mind.

It was exhilarating being so close to Ezra. The tether tugged and twisted, tying a precarious knot around my heart. At that moment, when he turned to find I had teleported behind him, the strange urge to kiss him had rattled my withering composure. The idea of his mouth on mine had left me trembling. None of it made any sense.

I don't know who Ezra Gray truly is.

So why is this happening?

⊰◦⊱

"Keep our visitors company." ma pounds on the door.

I blink grogginess away from my weary eyes and sit up in bed. My room's the same as it's always been: creaky wooden boards aligned on the floor; a carpet in the center with a faded motif. The walls are a light beige spaced with posters of my favorite bands and movies. There's a wall of shelves adorned with a myriad of trinkets, photos, awards, and papers establishing accomplishments achieved throughout my life. It's the same as it's always been. Even when Esther pays us handsomely, all the money is tucked away for a rainy day or put toward the bunker to heighten its security.

These limbs are tight when I stretch out and emit a guttural sigh. My attention snaps to the high-frequency radio on my desk. It's programmed only for communication with the Angelics, though sometimes it feels as if someone who shouldn't be listening is overhearing everything either I or my abu have ever said through its microphone. There's a brewing uneasiness whenever I use it.

The time has come. Stalling is a thing of the past. Dreadfully, I take the necessary steps to the desk and flip the power on, switching for the receiver. I slip on the headphones and hear static swell through my ears. I press down on the button to speak and cry out for Ambrosia, my voice lost in the endless stream of airwaves. Static returns and cycles through phases of deep crescendoes and tiny, motionless ebbs. It extends and just when I'm about convinced I won't hear a reply, a woman's voice echoes back.

"Eureka101, this is Callahan speaking. I copied your message loud and clear. Over," Ambrosia speaks into the mic. It's so good to hear her voice again. It's been weeks since I've last heard it, months since I saw her.

"I've missed you, Callahan," I say. A longing to see my friends burns a hole through my chest.

"Eureka101, you need to say 'over' when you're finished speaking and 'copy' if you understood what I relayed to you. Over."

(She's really going to be this way, isn't she?)

"Copy. Over," I blurt sarcastically.

"Copy. You're a little shit. Over," she croons through the waves and swirls of static.

Haha.

"Eureka101, what's new with you? It's been so long since we've heard from you and abuelito."

I love that she still calls him that. He'll always be her abuelito. He was everyone's abuelito, after all. But it's time to tell her the truth, no matter how morbid it may be or how drastic it changes our radio reunion. I shudder in a breath, hovering my finger over the button. Before I can back out of this, the reluctant finger lowers.

"Um, well," I choke, scrounging for the proper words, "Abu is dead. He passed away twenty-seven days ago."

Oddly specific, but it's the truth. The truth is out there and there's no taking it back.

The radio remains silent for far too long. I'm starting to fear Ambrosia left the moment I uttered the dreadful news.

"I'm so sorry, Atlas," she says through the static. "We loved him, you know."

"I know. He loved you too," I say.

"It won't be the same without him, but I know you have what it takes to continue his work. He was integral to the Angelic operation and you will be, too."

Suddenly, I'm pissed she isn't as distraught as I've been these past twenty-seven fucking days. It's immediately back to business, but that's how she always was. That's all the Angelics can afford. Business. Stasis equals death in this game. I take another careful inhale and breathe slowly out my mouth.

"Thank you, but that isn't the only reason I called. Over."

"Copy. What is it that you need? Over."

I tap my middle and index finger repeatedly over the desk, feeling the increasing nerves slowly climb and climb.

"Copied. I have two AWOL powered individuals secured safely in the bunker. Tommy Donahue sent them. They'll need to be extracted and taken to Proctus. Over," I recite.

"Copy," Ambrosia sighs before she can cut off the mic. I wait for her voice to return. "We're stretched extremely thin as it is. It may take upwards of a week before we can reach you. Over."

A week suddenly feels too long. What if Conin's right and the Barclay Network *did* use Tommy to track us down? What if they're on their way here as we speak? Regardless, there's nothing that can be done. We'll have to bide our time and hope the bunker remains resilient like I promised it would.

"Copy. I'll let them know. Over."

"Understood. You did good, Eureka101. And again, I'm so sorry about abuelito. We'll miss him. Over and out."

Over and out.

Chapter 30

Conin

Pan-panic. I'm suffering from it—it's obliterating my senses and distracting me from Ezra, but I cannot easily let it go. Because Atlas is undeniably attractive. I look at him and my body erupts all over. There's something about the way he treats Ezra that just . . . turns me the fuck on. His constant smiles, his infectious mirth, their never-ending conversations about *Star Wars*.

And then there's the way he treats me, like he's intentionally flirting—like he can see right through me. Despite his best efforts, I'm hesitant to trust him completely. It's difficult to pinpoint whether it's the tether Ezra's spoken of or my fear of Ezra's safety, but I've yet to fully warm up to Atlas. He notices, but he's too kind to say anything.

Damn his kindness.

I hate it. I hate his charity. I hate his stupid face. And I hate myself for thinking anything of him when my feelings for Ezra remain unresolved. I love Ezra and that won't ever change, but I'm simultaneously feeling things for Atlas while silently denying my jealousy over the bond he and Ezra have. I don't know what's happening to me, but I'm not liking it. Not at all.

Atlas grew up distant from Proctus. He met Ambrosia and Matt at a relatively young age, the Angelics he keeps in contact with for emergencies like ours, to extract AWOL recidivists and bring them safely to Proctus. Matt and Ambrosia were orphaned in an attack on a recidivist safe house. From there onward, they dedicated their lives to the Angelic cause.

Atlas, Ambrosia, and Matt met in the least likely of circumstances. It was through Atlas's abuelo they ever crossed paths in the first place. His grandfather was born and raised on the Caribbean islands where he and his wife had Atlas's mother. His abuelita passed away before he was born and when Yailin decided to follow Scott back to Utah in the small, once-bustling mining town he grew up in, abuelito journeyed with.

Abuelito discovered the injustices committed toward powered individuals in the States and wanted to advocate for the rights of people like him. Atlas is skeptical of how his grandfather achieved what he had in the early days of the operation, but his abuelo's heroics and efforts attracted the attention of Esther Brown. She personally located his family's place of residence to commemorate him for his bravery. They were in talks for days, weeks, and months after their initial meeting. The operation bloomed from there.

—◆◇◆—

Staring at the words, their meanings are lost—incomprehensible. I chose one of the queer selections from the MacPhersons' book collection, one I haven't read, in hopes that it will occupy my mind. Every thought drifts to Mara's limp body thudding onto asphalt, flames licking a dark infinity, Ezra's mortified expression when our chances of escaping were so bleak. And above it all, my ankle fucking hurts. I'm positive I didn't break it, but it's definitely sprained. I forgot to mention the injury in all the commotion and getting to know Atlas. Maybe I should suck it up and say something before it worsens.

When the clock hits three in the afternoon, the familiar hiss of the bunker's entrance sounds, and Atlas comes strolling in with coursework in hand. He huffs and sits on the floor in front of the couch where Ezra and I lounge, then splays an array of papers onto the coffee table. I sneak a glance over his shoulder, noticing the different names on each assignment. Atlas slumps against the couch, sighing until he's completely deprived of air. The histrionics are almost enough to elicit a smile out of me. Almost.

There I go again.

Who the hell uses histrionics?

And why the hell am I feeling guilty when Ezra and I are nothing more than close friends? Atlas is a stupid crush—an infatuation that will go nowhere. Ezra's napping, curled up at the far end of the couch while the millionth rerun of the same movie plays on the TV. The sight of him evokes a broad smile that hurts, which Atlas notices when he cranes his neck back.

"So," he says and I'm not sure I like the tone of his voice—the playfulness of it. "Are you and Ezra . . . you know . . . a thing?"

"What?" I splutter. "What makes you think that?"

That would explain Dan's words at Emery's party. Am I bleeding through that badly? Atlas sports a shit-eating grin.

"The way you two look at each other. It's obvious to anyone with eyes," he mocks.

"We're not . . . dating—"

"But you love him, right? You have feelings for him."

I must go beet-red by the way his grin widens, and he merrily chuckles to himself, throwing his head back. The messy tousle of his hair, the glasses, his full lips, his perfect teeth. I'm doomed. The queer book in my hand comes as a reminder that I'm safe here. I'm okay to express myself, but that doesn't mean I can entertain these thoughts about Atlas. They'll lead nowhere.

"But he doesn't reciprocate those feelings," Atlas states.

"I don't know," I answer, miserable at the gloomy reminder.

"What a shame," he says. "You should tell him."

"No," I bluntly state. Atlas's leer falters.

"You'll regret it if you don't. Life's too short for secrets." He looks guilty for saying this. "I'd want to know if I was him. It's only fair to you both."

I ruminate over what he said, but I worry more about what Ezra will have to say if I tell him the truth. However, Atlas is right. It pisses me off that he is.

Atlas attempts to work on the papers displayed in front of him. I watch, masking my gaze with the cover of my book, feeling like a creep. An unknown amount of time passes before he dramatically melts onto the carpet with a loud groan. His dramatics wake Ezra up, who blinks groggily at the unfurling scene. I smile at him wearily.

"What is it?" I ask.

"These are the math assignments I need to grade as a tutor," Atlas replies.

"Come on then," says Ezra with a hint of his sarcastic nature. A part of me revels in the way he's opening up, showing his true self to Atlas, but the selfish part of me fears what that means.

"I don't wanna," Atlas bemoans.

"Whatever," Ezra whispers and wraps himself further into his hoodie.

It's fucking adorable.

"This calls for some alcohol," our host says and stands up. "Who wants some?"

Ezra perks up at this. I remember the times he'd take hits from Thax's bong and drink himself silly. For hell's sake, he showed up at my doorstep high as a kite while I had to explain to Melissa the very bare minimum, fishing for lies from nowhere.

"I do," he says. And of course, he does. With everything that's transpired, I don't blame him, but I don't want him to lose himself to the substance. I'm suddenly very, very angry at Atlas. I keep to myself, silently watching as Atlas roams over to the kitchen and grabs one of the various bottles Ezra told me he stocked the other night.

"Conin?" questions Atlas.

He's removing glasses from the kitchen cupboard, placing them pristinely next to a bottle of amber liquid. He nurses the third glass in his hand, waiting expectantly for my answer with a subtle quirk on his lips. The stubble running across his jaw and below his nose is pronounced in the kitchen lights. I feel my blood heat.

"I'm good," I say.

The truth is that I don't trust myself around alcohol. I don't trust myself to not say anything or act on any impulse desires while drunk. What would happen if I gave away that I find Atlas attractive? What would happen if I confessed my love for Ezra and not in just a bro-friend way?

Atlas returns with the bottle of tequila and two clear glasses. He places them on the coffee table. Watching him pour a hearty amount in each, there's the trepidation of the possibility of where this night could go. Ezra takes the glass Atlas proffers him with a small "thank you" before downing the entirety of it in one gulp. Ezra mentioned once his liking for tequila above other alcohols. That worry from before settles in my chest cavity, hurting the muscle and bone that surrounds it.

"Damn, Ezra. Slow down!" Atlas says, but he's smiling. That stupid shit-eating grin.

"I can handle my alcohol," Ezra rebuts with an equal grin of his own.

He moves for the tequila and pours himself another shot. Atlas chuckles. He holds out his so Ezra can give him some more. They both down their shots after a clink of their glasses, Atlas with a fervor he didn't before, making a race out of it. I don't believe Atlas will be getting any grading in tonight.

⊰•◦○◦•⊱

I'm the only sober person in the room. Atlas has practically told us his entire life's story, everything about his abuelo, his parents meeting on his father's mission, how badly he wants to be a math teacher, but how he may never get the opportunity, given his recidivist status. And Ezra shared about Lukeman destroying his violin and Thax turning him in, revealing that Ezra's a faux. That's not even what pissed me off—

—it's their conversation now while they play a video game on the PlayStation. Ezra's sharing too much. He's never had this issue before, but it seems he can't get himself to shut up now. He's sharing things he never would have and with someone we barely even know. According to Ezra, we do know Atlas—whatever the link between them is. I try not to let jealousy get the better of me when I have no right to be jealous.

And *of course*, they're discussing *Star Wars*, a topic I'm hardly knowledgeable about. I've watched the movies and shows for Ezra's sake, but the information didn't stick.

Atlas and Ezra are shooting opponents in a game I don't recognize, not because of indignance, but more because I am hardly a video game person. Ezra finishes spitting some rant about certain characters in one of the various spin-off shows.

"Factssss," Atlas agrees and headshots an enemy.

Mara falls to the ground in a perpetual reel, slowed down so I can agonizingly witness the event again and again. Ezra fires at some incoming enemies, which he surprisingly downs with ease despite his inebriation. Blood splatters on the asphalt, a skull mask, lightning erupting midair. I see fire and the way it burns and burns.

I can't take it any longer.

"Turn it off, please," I mutter.

Neither of them hear me. The gunshots continue.

"Turn it off, please!"

Atlas startles, but listens. The game is quickly shut off. Ezra's face is plastered with concern, yet he says nothing, trying to understand my sudden outburst.

"Are you okay?" Atlas asks.

"I'm fine," I say, ignoring Ezra's gaze. "I'm going to bed."

I leave the two of them without another word.

Chapter 31

Ezra

Atlas is sprawled out on the couch when I regain consciousness, head dangerously close to mine. His glasses are discarded on the table, his eyelids shut peacefully, hair as messy as ever. My accelerated heartbeat is far too much to handle, so I back away. The distance I put between us does nothing to help slow it down.

The movement stirs Atlas awake instead. He blinks life back into his eyes. Groggily, he notices me at the far end of the couch. He grins and checks his phone, mouth gaping when he realizes what time it is.

"Fuck, I actually need to be at school today," he says, then zips out of the bunker faster than I can reply.

Conin chooses that as the perfect opportunity to set foot in the entertainment room. He's shirtless: bare, chiseled chest imprinted from the sheets, his stomach hanging over the waistline of his shorts. An erection pushes against my sweats. I move one leg and drape it over the other, hoping it'll mask any evidence.

"Did you sleep well?" he asks.

There's no hint of accusation in his voice, not one I can detect. Still, I can't help but wonder if he's secretly admonishing me under all those thick, collective layers.

"I slept fine," I say without any mention of Atlas, though Conin most likely heard his departure mere minutes ago.

"Good," he says.

"What do you think our next steps should be?" He's acting like nothing happened last night.

"What do you mean? I thought the plan was to wait here until the Angelics could extract us, take us to Proctus," I answer.

"Is that what you want?"

"I want us to be safe," I say and glare at him dead in the eyes. "Is something changing your mind? It was our goal to get to a safe haven, right?" Or so I had thought.

Conin exhales and blows the air until there's nothing left in him. His inhale shudders. The second chink in his armor.

"I've just been thinking . . . about options. I want a safe haven. I want us to be safe. But what if Proctus isn't what it's cracked up to be? What if it's a fallacy?" Conin says. He can't look at me.

Again with the words!

"Conin, we have no way of knowing. I'm skeptical too, but we can't keep living with no clear end in sight. This could be our break. This could be our only fucking chance. If we keep aimlessly driving into the unknown, the Barclay Network will catch up to us. We'll be as good as dead."

Is this what he wants to hear? Is this the reassurance he needs? At this moment, Conin's unreadable. Maybe he always has been, and I've been too ignorant to realize. No matter how hard I try, the wall he keeps up to guard himself remains impenetrable.

"Where are you?" I ask.

"I'm here," he says.

⸻◆⸻

We're lounging on the L-shaped couch, a *Sleep Token* record winding down to the last songs. A movie plays in the background, though neither of us pays attention. Conin's feet are close to my lap while I'm stretched out, my legs facing the other direction.

"My dad called about a week or two ago saying he was no longer going to be paying child support because I'm eighteen now. Which, I mean, I get it. I do. But at that point, I planned to live with Mom for another year before going to college. He was so adamant about it. It seemed he was ready to be finally rid of us," Conin says as I gaze up at the ceiling.

"What an asshole," I whisper. "I'm sorry, Conin. You deserve better from him."

"Can't be as bad as your dad." It wasn't meant to be a low blow, but it hurts, nonetheless.

"Conin," I say. "That doesn't invalidate your experiences or your problems. It isn't a competition. What your dad said, what he did to you and your mom, was bullshit. You deserve more than that."

"Yeah, well. Here we are," he says.

Now that was a low blow. His defenses are up, but I won't confront him because I know the sacrifices he had to make to be here with me now. This is a delicate situation; he and I are charting unfamiliar waters. But I wish he'd dismantle those barriers, look me in the eye, and confide in me all his pains, thoughts, and emotions.

"I'm sorry, Ez."

"It's like I said. You're allowed to feel this way. What's on your mind? And don't say 'nothing' . . . I know something's troubling you." Conin ponders long and hard. His mind is far from here as he stares out into space, on the carpet below. Telling me about his dad was a step in the right direction and it's not like he hasn't laid himself bare to me in the past, but since his dad left him and his mom years ago, he's erected a wall I can't break down. I know I'm not the one to talk, but the longer he suppresses the conflicting emotions sweltering inside him, the more in danger he is of imploding. Leaving his mom behind, his promising future, his foot injury—which, now that I think about it, we still need to address—shooting the mercenary on the highway, his sudden outburst last night . . . he'll self-destruct and I won't know what to do when that moment arises.

"I don't want to talk about it, Ezra," Conin finally says, and stands.

He shuts himself in the bathroom. The shower starts seconds later.

Chapter 32

Ezra

In the following days, I deliberately avoid any war-related or shooting video game that may trigger another outburst from Conin. Yes, it sets off a PTSD tick of my own, remembering the flagrant fear in the blue of his eyes, but more than anything, I want to ensure it won't happen again.

The hours trickle by. Conin finds a book to read that keeps him occupied for a good chunk of the time. The familiar sight provokes happy, sentimental memories. I can't help but smile.

"You know what this reminds me of?" I ask, poking at him with my big toe.

He recoils even when a laugh escapes his mouth. Conin pushes back, farther from me, which cracks me the hell up.

"What? What does this remind you of?" Conin says. He clutches his stomach. I avert my gaze.

"All those times growing up when you'd have a book propped open and I was on your TV, playing some *Star Wars* game. You remember? That's how we spent most days. We'd help each other with our homework. You would listen when I practiced on the violin. I'd avoid going home, spend so many nights in a sleeping bag on your floor . . ." I choke. A sob crawls up my throat, lodging itself somewhere in the larynx.

"Fuck," he says. "Ezra—"

He wraps two big burly arms around my neck and pulls me close. There's a hint of shampoo, something citrusy in his hair, and a musky body wash. Clean, yet entirely familiar.

"This is so awkward," I mutter. "I'm okay. Promise."

"You're okay?"

"Yes, Co. I am," I emphasize.

"You sure?" He pins me down. His kneecaps find both outer sides of my legs, and his hands grip my wrists, glued to the couch cushions behind me. He straddles me, perhaps unaware he's doing so, and I plead desperately for the blood in my dick not to betray me, though a tent already pitches itself against the fabric. Conin hasn't noticed yet—he's not privy to the way his body has a direct effect on mine. It's only a matter of time before he does. There's enough space for me when he moves off that I can quickly prop a pillow over the direct giveaway. Conin's face is close—too close. I can feel his sweet, minty breath brush against my nose. What's he doing? What the fuck is this?

This feels like the other day when he tackled me to the floor of his home. I wonder if he's thinking the same.

I choose the most horrible, terrifyingly sarcastic comment that will obliterate every sense of normalcy we have left.

"Jesus, Co, just kiss me already, won't you?"

The sudden energy shift is tangible. Conin blinks, then blinks again, aghast at my comment. He's petrified. Perhaps I revealed a part of myself he'd been suspecting for a while. I confirmed his suspicions with one stupid comment meant to be a joke, even if it was what I wanted. He backs away. I've scared myself shitless, so I'm relieved that my erection is gone.

"Conin, I was joking." I laugh to play it off.

"Yeah. Right," he says and plasters on a grin that doesn't reach his eyes.

"That was weird. I'm sorry. I was trying to lighten the mood," Conin clarifies. He returns to his book, and I resume my game. An indeterminable amount of time passes before he speaks again.

"Do you trust Atlas?"

Oh god. Did my quip prompt him to ask?

"Where did that come from?"

"I'm curious. That's all," Conin says.

"Considering he hasn't done anything suspicious over the past two days we've been here, I think that's a sign enough to trust him," I answer, alluding to nothing.

He studies me for a moment.

"What were you two talking about the other night?"

The panic swelters to a boiling point. Kill me. Now. What does he think is happening here?

"Atlas brought the alcohol, saw that I had a movie on. He and I talked about it. He remembered that he hadn't shown me his ability yet, so he did. Atlas can teleport, by the way," I say with some snark. "Whatever you're worried about, there's no reason to be."

Why is he so damn persistent?

"I see," Conin says quietly. "I don't know. I'm on edge since Tommy."

Understandable. But what does any of that have to do with my joke about a kiss? Seconds later, we hear footsteps carrying closer to the secure door. Atlas crosses the threshold, backpack slung over his shoulders, a notebook in hand.

"I don't know why I do this to myself. It's not like this shit's useful anymore," he exclaims, exasperated.

Atlas has become overtly cordial around us. I'm not opposed to his openness or vulnerability—it's just . . . jarring.

"What?" I say.

"Homework. It's bullshit. If I need to continue abu's work, why the hell am I working so hard for a future I can't have?"

Conin cringes. Damn, that hit too close to home.

"Because your parents want you to?" I suggest.

"Yeah, and it makes no sense!" he says, tossing his coursework on the floor.

"How old are you?" questions Conin, eyes peering over the top of his book.

"Seventeen. I turn eighteen in several months. I hate that I rely on my parents so much. I need their help because I can't do this alone." Atlas sighs. "So, I adhere to their requests. I suppose it's the least I can do."

"You're a good son," I say. "A good grandson."

Conin murmurs in agreement. Atlas thanks us and hunches over his homework pages that are sprawled out across the coffee table.

"Shit," Atlas says under his breath when a text chimes on his phone.

Conin and I glance at each other in apprehension. Atlas inquires if he can change the channel. He clicks through a few before settling on a local news station. Pure dread blankets the room. Photos of me and Conin transition into the other and I know, we *both* know, who's responsible for this.

Joyce Bresshet. I've never met another worrier like her.

"If you see these two, please contact the local police," the news reporter says before the segment changes.

"Ah, so you're a blonde," Atlas says.

"We've received word about recent investigations on a car that mysteriously caught fire outside Tooele on I-80. It is believed the Chrysler exploded because of fluid leakage or an overheated catalytic converter. Forensics has reported that no bodies were found in or outside the immediate proximity of the car. It is also said that whoever was driving the vehicle fled the site and failed to report the accident to the proper authorities. No further information has been provided at this time. Now, back to you John."

Every drop of blood has fled my face. Conin doesn't seem any better than I am. He stares at the television, blanched paper-white, far after the segment's end. Atlas takes a seat on the rocking chair.

"I texted ma and asked if she watched the entire segment on you two. I'll let you know what she says," Atlas informs us. But we're not listening. How could we?

"There was no mention of Mara," Conin says. I noticed that too, and it doesn't sit well with me. It doesn't sit well with me at all.

"What happened to her?" Atlas questions.

Conin hesitates. There's that disconnect, the buildup in his decision, but it's clear when he caves into confiding in Atlas.

"I shot her. I saw her go down. It wasn't certain whether she had died or not, but it seems now that she got away," Conin mutters. The relief on his face is evident. I hope that this takes away part of what was burdening Conin.

"It's a good thing you disguised yourself," the boy says. "Let's see if it's effective."

Another text alerts on Atlas's phone. He reads it with a grim expression.

"Ma said she caught the middle of it. Looks like Conin's mom filed two missing person reports. Nothing on Ezra's powers yet."

I'm not surprised the Grays have kept their mouths shut. Typical. They're so keen on forgetting they ever had a second-born son because if others were to find out about my abilities, the repercussions would be too much to bear. I can imagine Thax wants no one to know, either. I shouldn't feel hurt. I shouldn't.

"We require alcohol," Atlas decides, moving to the kitchen. "I'll contact the Angelics in the morning, but in the meantime . . ."

Excitement perks at the mention of the substance that will dull all this anxiety and worry—this overwhelming stress that builds and builds, collecting like layers of earth. I'll be buried in it—my grave of all my inane fuckups. I get up to follow Atlas when a strong set of sturdy fingers wrap around my wrist.

"Ezra," Conin says deliberately.

"I need it," I say and he lets go.

His gaze sears into the back of my head as I enter the kitchen.

Chapter 33

Conin

Another day passes. The stubble running alongside my jaw has set in and it won't be long until I have a considerable beard, even if it is patchy like Ezra fears. The red in my hair is as vibrant as ever, though I can't help but worry I'll still be recognized somewhere and somehow. Apprehension gnaws at my stomach, spreading like a raging inferno. I remind myself how the Angelics plan to extract us from the bunker and take us directly to Proctus. So, realistically, there's nothing to fear, but after the missing person reports, that does little to comfort me.

Mom is stubborn. She won't rest until we're found.

The MacPhersons have a fenced backyard, a red brick-and-mortar wall casting the illusion of privacy and allowing the five of us to spend some time in the sun after Ezra and I have been cooped up underground for a while. We hang out with Atlas and his parents while we laugh and joke over lunch.

Atlas sits adjacent to me, pulling me out of a daydream I'd wandered into by nudging my shoulder. His eyes display an encrypted message while Ezra's distracted by an animated discussion between Atlas's parents, most likely telling me that I need to stop giving Ezra wistful glances and being so damned obvious over my infatuation.

God, I can't get his words out of my head!

Atlas's advice tremors in me like seismic earthquakes. Each repetition urges me to tell Ezra the truth, the whole truth, and nothing but the truth. I've thought of it plenty since then. Every instance I get close to letting my confession slip from my tongue, some incorporeal hand glues my lips back together.

"You haven't talked to him about it yet, have you?" Atlas whispers, his eyes gliding over the other three.

"Of course not," I hiss. "It would fuck up our friendship."

"You don't know that. He probably reciprocates those feelings."

"Let me figure it out, please."

But he's right. I know myself. And I'll regret it if Ezra doesn't hear the truth from me before something bad happens to us.

When our awkward conversation tapers into silence, Atlas's mother ushers us back inside with regret. There's evidence in her eyes that she doesn't enjoy this any more than we do, but it's better to play it safe than be sorry.

"Conin?" Atlas says. He holds a clear glass in hand, raising it so I can give in to his offer. He never pushes, but he continues to ask despite my constant refusal. This time, I cave in.

"Sure," I say.

Atlas blinks, his lips parted in disbelief.

Ezra turns to me as if I've sprouted a new arm and leg.

"Okay," says Atlas.

He pours three glasses, handing one to each of us.

"¡Salud!" he exclaims.

We toast, clink crystalline cups of tequila together. Ezra has his downed in seconds, with Atlas as a close contender. I'm more deliberate with my drink, but I finish not far after they do. Atlas pours another round. We toast, drink, and succumb to the mind-numbing effects. I'm a lightweight, contrary to what my belly would have you believe, so even with food in my stomach, it's not long before I feel the pleasure of being drunk. Time passes at an unknown pace before I'm being offered more tequila. I drink without hesitation and with no thoughts in my mind. It's nice.

Ezra and Atlas play video games as I attempt to read. The reading doesn't stick, so I watch them play a more lighthearted game. He hasn't mentioned it, but it's clear that Ezra understood the reason for my outburst the other night. There's a sudden surge of gratefulness and fondness when I gaze into his one blue and one green eye. He's beautiful. Ezra's stunning.

Some movie gets turned on and the three of us mind-numbingly watch it. It's hard to pay attention when Ezra's right fucking there, looking gorgeous with every follicle of his being. It's movie after movie in an endless cycle thereafter. I pretend to be attentive, yet it's the boys who captivate my eye: Ezra and Atlas, both. They're so attractive, so fucking attractive, I could burst into flame on the spot, and I'd be okay with it. I'd be content. And

I don't know what it means. I don't think I care to know what it means. I know I find them both attractive. I like Atlas because he treats the boy I love most in this world the way he deserves to be treated, nothing like Dan or the guys or the Grays would. I know I love Ezra with every fiber of my fucking being, so much so that it hurts. It hurts, it hurts, it fucking hurts.

I'm so drunk.

Atlas chooses a vinyl from the shelf and places it delicately onto the record player. Music plays from a band I don't recognize, but I let myself sway to the beat, get lost in the good vibes and how it makes me feel. I'm having genuine fun. There's guilt underneath all these layers, but for tonight I don't care. I let it go. I sway and dance and raise my hands into the air like I just don't care. Because I don't care. Tonight, I do not care at all.

"Let's do this again," I yell.

Ezra and Atlas agree.

"Let's do this every night!"

We dance and dance until we can dance no more.

⁕

I wake up to an unimaginable hangover. My mouth is dry and my throat burns. It feels like death. It feels *worse* than death. I'm sprawled out on the couch. Atlas's silhouette lies on the carpet, and my tangled limbs entwine with . . . *Ezra's.*

I spring away, clutching my knees to my chest, and watch in horror as Ezra slowly comes to. He blinks several times. He must notice the departure of my legs from his own, though he displays not a single ounce of remorse and also no signs that he was fine with the innocent entanglement.

Was it innocent?

Last night was blurry.

Instead, Ezra exudes an impassive expression. He mutters a "good morning" before settling his gaze on Atlas below. Seeing the other boy still asleep with an arm under the coffee table gives him the okay to drift off again. Ezra relaxes, the tension in his shoulders dissipates, and his face untangles from its intense knots.

A quirk in my mouth makes me realize just how happy I am. Ezra's regaining the ability to trust someone else after years of difficulty. Before, it might have felt like jealousy. Now, I can't help but feel grateful for how close he and Atlas have been getting. It proves that he's opening up, taking risks, and growing from the immense pain of his previous life. Ezra has a new friend, someone he can trust and confide in. Someone, perhaps, who can teach him the ropes—help him come to terms with his abilities.

Atlas will be there for Ezra if he needs it. The hope is that after we leave the bunker, the Angelics will show him the path to acceptance. I can feel it. But a tinge of sadness lurks behind the swell of positive emotions. When everything is said and done, what will my purpose be? What will I be to Ezra apart from a childhood friend? The sad bit is I'm not sure I'll be ready when Ezra doesn't need me anymore.

So, maybe it's time I confess. I have nothing to lose, right?

Chapter 34

Atlas

Pa shuffles the stack of papers, filing it in the cabinet for later use. He stands, groaning, while theatrically stretching his arms and legs. I roll my eyes, sheltered behind the motel's front desk and the wall space that separates me from him. He slams his briefcase shut (which, for the record, he doesn't need) and zips it closed. Loudly. As I clack my nails over the granite desktop, I feel his sudden presence loom over me.

"Alright, hijo," he says, having picked up the term of endearment from ma long ago. "I'm going home. Here are the keys to lock up shop," he says.

For real?

"No fair. Why do I have to stay? We have *guests*," I say emphatically.

He makes that small grunt of disapproval he doesn't think anyone can hear, but that we can all hear regardless.

"Because you're my son and I asked you to. Our guests have plenty enough distractions to entertain themselves while you're gone."

"What's so important you need to go home for and abandon your only son?"

"Mamá and I are going to watch *Housewives*. The new season just came out," he says in the most nonchalant way possible.

I groan, then keep groaning until all the air has traveled out of my lungs. Pa slaps me playfully on the shoulder and laughs boisterously. (I'll get you, old man. Nowhere will be safe. Perks of teleportation.) He rounds the desk, hooks his finger under my chin, and lifts it so we look at each other face-to-face. Pa has a bright, red beard he brags about because he was in the habit of excessively shaving for the longest time (looking at you, BYU), and the sparks of fiery red hair that are as vibrant as ever, though now balding, and frayed.

Please don't let me go bald like he is. I must retain my gorgeous, luscious locks for as long as I'm alive.

"How are you holding up, hijo?"

"It's only a matter of time before Ambrosia and Matt show up. So, I guess I'm alright. I'll miss Ezra and Conin, though. They're good guys."

Pa smiles. His hand lingers but finds my shoulder, where he squeezes it gently. Reassuringly.

"You always did carry your heart out on a silver platter," he whispers before saying goodbye and strolling out of the motel like he didn't just shatter my entire world with those . . . eleven words.

WHAT DOES HE MEAN!

I'm not instantaneously in love with the first pair of nice boys that come my way. There are plenty of decent people at school (some dicks, too), but he's never commented about them that way. Or maybe it doesn't mean anything. Maybe I'm too bottled up—too on edge to think straight (yes, pun absolutely intended).

It's math test after math test afterward. My tutoring has helped improve some students' scores, but the rest continue to fall short. Why do I torture myself with this? I don't need the experience, I don't need the pay, and I sure as hell don't need the credit because when high school is over, I'll be stuck in this small, shitty town for the rest of my cruel existence.

Why the hell did I have to be born this way?

Perhaps Ezra would listen to me if he knew how I truly felt.

A bell dings overhead. My attention is drawn to a couple: a white man with disheveled hair as bad as mine and a cocky, hungry grin, followed by a Black woman sporting a buzzcut. Her piercing eyes tell me she does not want to be here. I wouldn't want to be here with this man, either. There's just something about him that screams *NO*.

"A bedroom for two, please," the man says. Meanwhile, the woman leans against the table with the coffee decanters and sugar packets. She's unimpressed, watching the vacant road outside.

"Okay. I'll need a few things from you first," I say, pulling out several forms. I've been asking Pa to go digital for years.

The man presents me his ID and fills out the form until his phone rings, loud and clear. The woman breaks from her daze, casting a furious glance at the man. He shrugs, gesturing with his hands for her to finish the check-in process, and stomps out the door.

"Let me just grab your key," I say.

I fumble for it in the key box. She stares blankly into my soul when I finally present it to her. I gulp back the urge to tell her to stop looking at me like that. When our hands graze, an unpleasant jolt of electricity shimmers through me. The woman mumbles a "thank you" and leaves without another word. I gape, left wondering what just happened, when it hits.

Ambrosia better answer, otherwise, I'll be pissed.

◆◇◆

"Hi, I have to take care of something in my room. Please don't interrupt, okay bye," I blurt when I enter the house.

"Mijo!" Ma yells.

"I can't right now. I need to contact Ambrosia."

"Is everything okay?"

"I hope so," I say, slamming the door to my bedroom.

The radio thrums to life and the headphones clasp over my ears. I withhold the prevalent urge to scream into the mic. This is urgent. This is life or death. Ambrosia or Matt or whoever else better pick up on the other end.

"Callahan, this is Eureka101. Do you copy?"

Nothing. Seconds lead into minutes. My patience is wearing thin.

"Callahan, this is Eureka101. I repeat, do you copy?" A surge of static answers.

The headphones are discarded in a flash. White noise spills out.

"¿Atlas? ¿Estás bien?" Ma's voice asks from the hallway.

Para nada, Mamá.

Noise filters through the speakers. It's incomprehensible—enigmatic the higher in volume it increases. I rush for the headphones and plug them in. The sound from the opposite end enunciates more clearly as seconds pass by. A voice plunges from out of the static, flooding my ears.

"Eureka101, this is Callahan. Were you attempting to make contact? Over," says Ambrosia's sultry tenor.

"Yes, yes!" I exclaim into the microphone. "Sorry, copy. I did attempt to make contact, yes. Over."

"Copy. What do you need? Over."

"I . . . I think the Barclay mercenaries caught on to our trail. They're here, disguised as citizens. Over," I say.

She doesn't even bother to correct me on my radio etiquette.

"Copy. Keep them hidden in the bunker. Under no circumstances are they allowed to leave, understood? We're about a day out. We can be there tomorrow at noon. Do you copy?"

"Copy," I say. "Over and out."

Lowering the headphones, I take heavy gulps of air. The woman I checked in at the motel must be Mara Barclay, I have no doubt. Pa disabled the tracker, so there was only one other way the mercenaries knew where to look. They gleaned Tommy's information, the location, and possibly where to go. My feet find the wood floor.

I don't want to cause Conin and Ezra panic, so I won't tell them the Barclay Network's mercenaries are in Eureka. I will, however, tell them the Angelics are slated to extract them by tomorrow. When the door to my room cracks open, ma steps in.

"I heard," she whispers.

"Don't say anything. The Angelics will handle this. We have nothing to worry about," I say, skirting past her, and beeline to the bunker.

The truth is, I'm not sure I believe myself.

Lies upon lies upon lies.

Chapter 35

Ezra

On our fifth night in the MacPhersons' bunker, Conin, Atlas, and I surround the coffee table, each with a deck of cards. It's been a week since Callum Finch phased through the mirror at Emery's party. It's been a week and a day since Lukeman Gray destroyed my violin.

Story of my fucking life.

Conin's stubble sketches his face across his jaw and neck. It offsets the sapphire red of his faux hair: two nuanced shades of red and one considerable headache for me. Stubble looks nice on him, though. I wonder how it would feel to caress his cheek, kiss the line of his jaw, his lips . . .

We're playing a card game, Ezra. Focus.

Atlas stares at me. His lips are compressed, and his cheeks are puffed like he's on the brink of laughter. I cast a furious glance at him that should wipe the smug look off of his face, but he only bursts into a fit of giggles, back pressed against the carpet as he kicks his legs in the air. His cards get discarded somewhere on the floor in favor of clutching his stomach. It's not like I've said or done anything that would give away my love for Conin. Or have I? Am I that obvious?

This card game is no longer fun.

I chuck the deck of cards onto the floor. They scatter over the living space, one nicking Conin on the cheek as he elicits a slew of stern protests. He has this endearing habit of scrunching his face every time he's captivated by whatever's caught his interest. Conin always had a competitive spirit. It's hilariously cute.

Atlas ruptures into another onslaught of laughter when he captures Conin's scrutiny. I'm the next to break. He and I are bunched up on the floor while we howl with laughter.

That wall, that protection, has a chasm in it now—an Atlas-shaped chasm. I'm not certain when it happened, whether it has anything to do with this link, this tether that intertwines our existence. But this chasm is being chipped open more and more each day, flooding over with Atlas, Atlas, and nothing but Atlas.

Our society and the people in it are loathsome (Conin and his mother have always been the exception), but I like Atlas, and the notion fucking terrifies me. The bubbling mirth welling inside me fades. I'm left rocking with a developing headache.

When Atlas's laughter dims, he moves to the couch and shuffles into a comfortable position. A familiar ease. Conin discards his pile, then sits back.

"So," Atlas says, an icebreaker, "tell me about a mutual embarrassing moment from your childhood."

You never know where our conversation will lead with Atlas.

Conin gives me his full, undivided attention with a wry grin. He's about to embarrass the ever-loving fuck out of me. When Atlas discovers Conin's dead cadaver tonight, it wasn't me.

"I have this distinct memory from when Ezra and I were kids. God, we were probably like twelve or thirteen," Conin starts the tale, and I already know where this is going.

"Shut up!" I swat at him, and he swats back with a giggle.

Atlas sits up in earnest.

"I dragged Ezra along for all my little daring expeditions back then, so one night we decided to go skinny dipping and—"

"Shut up!" I yell.

I lunge for his mouth and press a firm palm against it so he won't speak. My body pins him to the floor, but it doesn't feel right. Larger legs fasten kneecaps, meaty hands snare wrists. The frame of someone more imposing, large, and threatening to look at: the husk from the motel. We're suspended while time involuntarily slows. I hover over Conin's figure with a faux strength in these muscles that carry none of their own. Panting breaths escape my mouth.

Conin looks taken aback. The glimmer in his azure eyes is a dead giveaway. They swim in an unspoken guilt. He crossed the line and it's evident in his eyes he realizes this—I don't want Atlas, a stranger, to know my most embarrassing moments. No matter the ties that bind us or that chasm, this is my and Conin's secret—ours alone, witnesses aside.

Not only had my underwear been snatched by some feral dog, but I had emerged from the water with an erection I couldn't placate. The mere closeness of our naked bodies had been scintillating with the boy that I loved. Conin played it off as a normal teenage occurrence, so I was never suspected. Still, I doubt Conin would share that more intimate aspect, but he'd surely tell the tale of our arduous journey home. How humorous he finds it.

"I'm sorry," Conin whispers.

The broad stature of this projected facade fades into a slim body, scarred and imperfect. It feels like the moments in my childhood when I'd slip and shift—a mistake that would have been a detriment to my entire life if I had been caught. The impression is degrading. *I hate it.* I recoil from Conin and sit against the couch, a hot flare reddening my cheeks when I remember Atlas is in the room with us.

"Sorry," says Atlas. "I shouldn't have asked."

"It's not your fault. I shouldn't have brought it up," Conin says.

He takes the rocking chair. The piece of furniture has unquestionably become his in our short time here. His foot kicks the chair into motion, followed by smooth, repetitious movements, vacillating to and fro.

"I remember this day when abu was alive, my first time meeting the Angelics," Atlas tells us, maybe to break the sudden awkward tension that permeates the air. "I was so determined to make a good, lasting impression. Something they would remember me by and be like, Oh! That's Augurys's grandson! He's going to amount to something great one day. Remember him—'" Atlas trails off, his expression grim, but then he smiles as if the memory is bittersweet.

"I wanted so badly to show them what I could do, that I wasn't just this nerdy, useless kid—a kid who was picked on, bullied for who he was," he says.

He notices the shock on my face, the curved O of my mouth. Did they—

"They didn't know about my powers, no. But I was determined to show the Angelics and prove I had prowess. So, I did. I teleported. But I was thinking about those kids at school and materialized in one of the hallways."

"Shit," Conin mutters under his breath.

"I just realized how not funny this story is," Atlas guffaws.

His display of emotions is difficult to face when all I do is hide, but if I can challenge myself for Conin, I can trudge through this too.

"Go ahead," I say.

"No one was in the hallway, not at first. A staff member came strolling through, and asked what I was doing out of class . . . I skipped because I didn't want to miss the

Angelics' visit. When she spoke, I ran. I ran the mile home and walked in on my panicked grandfather giving orders to the Angelics on where they could go to search. The relief on abu's face made me believe it would be okay, but I knew the others were silently scrutinizing me. They asked what had happened and I told them, thinking it would win me some brownie points. Even when no one witnessed me teleporting into the school, the Angelics still thought it was necessary to wipe away the memories of everyone there. It's not a large school, so it was easy. I was embarrassed and hid from the Angelics for the remainder of their visit."

Atlas chokes on his next words, and they stumble one over the other as his eyes develop a glassy sheen. "When the Angelics left, abu took me aside, lifted me, and hugged me tight against his chest. He told me what I'd done had been an honest mistake, that he was proud of me, and that he knew my heart was in the right place. I never thanked him then, but at that moment . . . it was paramount. It helped me as I grew up. Shaped me into who I am, knowing he'd be proud no matter where I ended up and what I did with my life."

"He sounds like an amazing man," Conin says. His sentiment shocks me, but that's Conin. He's kind and understanding.

"He was," Atlas choked. "I wish he was still here. I don't know what I'm doing."

"Well, if it's any reassurance," I say, "I think you've been doing a good job."

My voice trembles with this complete and utter vulnerability amidst a stranger—except, is that really who Atlas is to me anymore? It's as if I've known him for years.

"Ezra and I are indebted to you. I can't thank you enough for saving our necks," Conin says.

Atlas nods and mutters a "thank you." He blinks rapidly to suppress the tears. "I want to do the right thing and continue abu's work. But I also know I'll miss you two."

Had I heard him correctly? I'm as confused as Conin appears. Atlas turns his head, grumbling under his breath when neither of us replies. If I pause to sit and reflect, can I say I feel the same?

"I'll miss you, too," I whisper.

Atlas's eyes dart to mine. In that suspended moment, I know he will forever remain prevalent in my life, a mark fated to stay for eternity.

"I'm queer!" he blurts out.

It's not Atlas I turn to, but my unsubtle want to memorize and ascertain Conin's feelings. He gapes, his maw open. He clenches his jaw. *Oh god. Oh, motherfucking god. Kill me kill me kill me kill me kill me.*

"Oh," Conin says. "That's awesome!"

What?

"I'm pansexual," he tells us.

What? The fuck?

My jaw is on the floor, and I couldn't pick it up even if I tried. Atlas's stunned expression is like mine—I don't think he was expecting Conin's confession, but maybe he's not surprised. Maybe, it's just the sudden brevity of those words. Those two words that rattle my entire world.

Chapter 36

Atlas

Why the hell did I admit to them I was queer? What are they supposed to do with that? They leave tomorrow and I'll be stuck here for the remainder of what will hopefully be a short life. There's a chance I could see them occasionally if I visited Proctus, but those opportunities would be few and far between. It's probably been five years since I last paid a visit.

There was foolish optimism that it could've been the catalyst to bring them together at last. They can deny it all they want, but their feelings are definitely mutual. It's obvious to everyone—Conin and Ezra are absolutely ridiculous. (Facts.)

One attainable, positive outcome emerged from my sudden (and ridiculous) outburst. Conin came out as well. It was not my intention to coerce him, but I could see it was eating him up, so I nudged him to say something because I knew if it were me in this situation, I'd like the truth to be out there. The number of times he gazed wistfully at Ezra was more than I could count. It was agonizing to witness after a while.

What happened after Conin's confession will remain a mystery. Ezra was dead silent afterward, keeping to himself on the couch. The evident panic in Conin's expression, however, painfully prompted him to flee into the bedroom. Ezra wasn't going to say anything to me, so I got the fuck out of there and hid inside my room. (I've been lying here since.)

Impulses to ram into the wall or repeatedly bang my head against the desk's surface are prolific. Why is this making me feel weird? Why did I say I'd miss them? Why did I say anything at all?

And why do I care so much?

I'm dying. Is this what dying feels like? I should have asked abu. (God, I'm a horrible, horrible, awful person.) Scratch that from the record. Please. It's official. I'm going to hell.

The panic raging ruthlessly, crawling through my skin and veins, might very well put me into cardiac arrest. The attempt to stand is worse. I pick myself up from the floor, my legs shaking vehemently under my weight to the point I almost drop to the floor again. I grab on to a shelf to steady my (systems-failing) body and wait for the sensation to subside.

This is a whole other level of worry I'm not used to feeling.

If something happens today, if the extraction goes wrong, I'll feel responsible because I had one job and can't fail them now. So, I dress in bland clothes and yeet myself down the steps to the bunker. Ezra greets me in the kitchen. He startles at my approach but it off with an attempt at a smile. I'd normally drink this image up, but the reminder comes that if I fail him, this could be the day we lose Ezra Gray forever.

Conin isn't here. He must be sleeping or preparing for the extraction.

"Are you okay?" questions Ezra as I pace the length of the kitchen.

"Sure. Yeah," I say.

A jumble of words spills out of Ezra's mouth. "This is driving me crazy. How am I supposed to leave not knowing what this . . . tether between us is?"

I come to a complete stop. And for some reason, his question angers me.

Because if you don't, you'll die.

I sure as hell don't have the answers.

"I don't know, Ezra. I can't leave. My place is here. And you need to go," I say, but each word is a knife to my own heart.

He flinches. "And if someone discovers you're a recidivist? What then?"

"It's never happened before. I'll be fine." It's a lie. The mercenaries are here, and they know Ezra and Conin are, too. By extension, aren't I in danger as well?

"Then we'll stay."

"You can't. We both know this."

"Aren't you curious what this means?"

This is probably the most I've heard him speak during his entire visit.

"Yes! Of course, I am! But this . . . this needs to happen. You need to go, and I need to do my job," I say.

Ezra has a retort tipped on his tongue when my phone rings. It's a burner number Ambrosia told me to look out for. Without a backward glance, I storm through the steel door, away from discovering our truth.

Chapter 37

Ezra

His striking, angered gaze lingers long after he vacates the bunker. It's vanished and, in his wake, my hope of discovering what this tether is. Atlas is not coming with us. If the Barclay Network discovers him and his operation . . . what then?

My thoughts are ruthless: our news channel debut, Atlas's and Conin's simultaneous coming out, the inescapable thrill of mercilessly kicking Callum, and the fact that neither I nor Atlas know why we're bound. It's like I've been catapulted into the air with no sure way down, eternally fearing when I'll crash to the earth. If I ever do. I'll be bits and pieces by then.

Conin commands the room when he materializes at the bedroom door. My heartbeat elevates, and drums like the wings of a hummingbird. This boy, no, this entire man's expression is ashen.

Had he overheard us? Or is the rapid beat of my chest because I've learned he's pansexual? That there's a sliver of hope he reciprocates what I've felt for so long? He's queer and I never knew this about him. To be fair, I never admitted my feelings, let alone my sexuality.

"I heard some of your conversation," Conin whispers.

"Oh," I say, deflating.

"You know." He swallows. I don't . . . know. Know what? "If it means anything, I hope you two find out what's happening. Someday."

Something uncanny is passing between Conin and me. My lips stick together as a lump in my throat forms, burning.

"But that's not what I want to talk about. Atlas made it very clear I should tell you and he's right, you should know. You should know why I came with you."

"Oh."

He bites his lower lip, arms embracing his broad chest. Conin groans from deep within and slouches. I stand aloof from him, but I can feel it. I can sense the weight of it. The urge to quip and lighten the mood is uncomfortably stifled.

"I have another confession I need to make."

I'm rocked back in the astral plane, feeling the impact as I slam full-force on the ground. Conin moves slightly closer, gentle in his approach. He dismantles my entire being, dissecting and prodding at what remains. He seems calm and collected on the surface, but there's more underneath that stoic façade.

"I've noticed how you and Atlas have been around each other the past few days. It makes me happy—"

"It's not like that at all!" I exclaim. Because it isn't, it *really* isn't. I like Atlas as a person, and a friend, but nothing more.

"Well . . . regardless. I'm just going to come out and say it. I . . . feel guilty for not admitting my feelings earlier. With everything that's transpired. I don't want any secrets between us."

"Conin?" I question.

Feelings?

"I love you, Ezra." And the world stands still. "Not in a friend way. More than that."

I'm still. Frozen. Unable to speak.

"I want to be with you, Ezra Gray. And if we die today, I want you to know that I love you."

Bereft of words, I gawk at Conin with my mouth clamped shut. The proper thing to say eludes me the longer we stand here through the silence I've created. Because if I'm truly straightforward with myself, I never thought this would happen. I never thought my best friend would see me as any more than a friend or brother. I grasp for the subtle indications—any evidence that might've given him away in the past. There, of course, were the sudden, brief slips of his mask, his willingness to follow me to our impending dooms, everything he's done for me over the years.

I was too stupid to realize I owned Conin's heart.

His face falls, eyes sad. I'm ruining this. I'm ruining this moment. This should be beautiful, and profound, leading to a confession of my own. I open my mouth. Hope glints in his azure blues. That's when Atlas's voice rings from above.

He comes barreling down the stairs, the metallic hiss of the door sounding a second later. "We need to leave! Now," he says.

Conin nods, turning for the bedroom to gather our possessions before I can get another word in. To be continued, I suppose, more than crestfallen.

We have everything we need within two abnormally large backpacks, courtesy of Atlas. All we had from before is stowed away, so we slip on the bags and follow Atlas to the bunker's exit. When we enter the MacPherson's home, a Black woman with blonde dreads and a white man with bright, gleaming red hair is there to greet us.

"Ambrosia. Matt. This is Conin and Ezra. Conin and Ezra, Ambrosia and Matt," Atlas says in a slew of speech.

"We'll make introductions later, but we don't have time for pleasantries. Let's get you to the van. It's on the outskirts of town," Ambrosia commands.

Matt nods grimly. When we make for the door, Atlas follows suit.

"I'm coming to say goodbye," he says and my heart collapses.

I smile because that's all I can do before we're ushered out of the home and into the backstreets of Eureka. We don't even get a chance to thank Atlas's parents. I follow the Angelics with a narrow tunnel vision as if we're in some thriller or action movie.

Our path takes us through the main street, the center of town. The nondescript white van the Angelics arrived in can be spotted next to a turnoff for a car shed. Our gait is poised and nonchalant, the perfect pace not to draw unnecessary attention. But I feel an uneasiness—dart my eyes in every direction, afraid the Barclay Network will rain down everything they've got at any given moment.

Time suspends, stretches. The pattering of boots sounds from the asphalt behind us. I crane my neck and watch two black-clad mercenaries and an all-too-familiar skull mask barrel in our direction.

Chapter 38

Conin

The mercenaries are upon us before we can react. There's nowhere to flee, nothing Ezra, Atlas, and I can do in time—

"Levi Finch," Atlas says breathlessly.

Callum's brother.

I get confirmation when a wave of heat and smoldering flames nearly burns us alive. If not for Ambrosia's timely counterattack, we would've been goners. The fire narrowly misses with the swipe of her armored hands. The flames disperse both ways to reveal Levi Finch's twisted grin. I notice the familiar features he shares with his brother. Same sandy hair, same psychopathic stare, same piercing green eyes with the underlying need to kill. He sports no scars of his own, but his wild expression is enough to send chills down my entire body.

Ambrosia and Matt are armored head to toe—where the armor materialized from, I can't say, but I recall the emblems attached to the center of their chests in the MacPhersons' which center the suit's breastplate. Next to Levi, with lightning crackling between her fingertips, is Mara Barclay, skull mask a haunting reminder of that night days ago. I didn't kill her. I'm not a murderer.

She releases the lightning with a thunderous bang. I step down on my ankle and pain shoots up, though I manage to pull Ezra to the ground. Atlas takes the rear. Matt uncaps a canteen looped on to his armor. Water spills out. As he rapidly raises his arms, I'm reminded of Tommy as Matt barricades us from Mara's attack with a wall of slopping liquid.

"MAFU!" Ambrosia screams.

A car door slams, and a large man in thick armor sprints in our direction, but he isn't quick enough. The white van is yards away and Levi's throwing fire like he's trying to avenge Callum's name.

"Give us the boy!" Levi bellows.

Ambrosia refuses to humor him and pushes back with a burst of her telekinetic powers. He stumbles to the asphalt, the dark clothing on his flesh scraping against the rough ground. Meanwhile, Mara relentlessly fires bolt after bolt at Matt. Ezra squirms underneath my weight, but I hold him down and use my arm to communicate he needs to stay where he is. Atlas is motionless beside us, fear in his eyes.

I remember the gun stowed away. I should have known better than to believe this would go according to plan. Such is our luck. I reach for it in my backpack, but fear grips me tight. What do I do?

It's foolish to believe we could have escaped unscathed if Ezra had transformed before our departure. Creating scenario after scenario won't change what's already happened, and realistically wouldn't have avoided this conflict. Horrifically, Levi bounds into the air and rains fire down at us. It is so quick that none of us can react in time.

Ezra emits a bloodcurdling cry. Flames lick up his arm. I smell scorched flesh—it's nauseating, like leather over fire. Ambrosia pulls Levi back to her and flings him farther than before. The act strains her, evident in the red of her eyes and the drooping of her shoulders. Ambrosia moves on to Mara so Matt is able to do what he can to aid us with water. We're splashed with it, drenched from head to toe, but it doesn't matter. All I fear for is Ezra, who continues to elicit small groans of pain.

In the distance comes a roar. I check on Ezra, then crane my neck up the road. Two black vans cruise down the street. As soon as they halt to a stop, soldiers in black file out with automatic guns.

Chapter 39

Ezra

The cauterized skin on my arm screams in agony. Underneath the scorching Utah sun, the pain is unbearably worse. Tears fight to pour out of my eyes while I resist the urge to press on the wound.

"Mafu! Call in for backup!" screams Ambrosia.

She swipes both arms in opposite, horizontal movements, telekinetically tossing several men aside. Conin reaches for me and hoists me from the ground. We're moving fast, considering. Pustules mark my crimson skin, capturing my attention to the point I almost forget where we are and what's happening around me. It swelters and cries, pleading for reprieve.

Thax never inflicted anything like this. Tears sting and encompass my vision.

"Atlas, get them out of here. We'll handle it," Ambrosia says as she redirects the trajectory of a blitz. Mafu, a large, yet slender, Polynesian man with buzzed hair, arrives, determination in his eyes. He extends an arm to his left. A long, thin plate of metal soars, then hovers before him. He crafts a makeshift shield and places it before the soldiers sprinting at us in droves.

"Now!"

Fire soars into the sky in a plume of waves, a brutal reminder of the pain in my forearm, which surges with every movement. My uncompromised hand is gripped tightly by Conin's as Atlas leads us up a hill and back into town. The heavy weight of our backpacks, Conin's injured ankle, and my burns impede our progress, though stopping is a matter of life or death.

Is returning to town the smart thing to do? Won't that put other's lives at risk? My life isn't worth it any more than the citizens of Eureka, but Conin's determination says otherwise, and Atlas leads us ahead with no clear trajectory. This is spiraling out of control.

I'm much more aware of the charred layer of skin as we sprint for our lives. There's a crackle of lightning in the distance. The night we fled Mara Barclay overtakes my vision in a brief flash. Terror courses in my veins, pumping blood to every corner and crevice of this tattered body, fueling me with adrenaline. My throat burns with deep, labored breaths. *Gotta keep going.* The subconscious will to survive from a masochist. The fucking irony.

Conin winces from the pain in his ankle. I try to communicate he can lean into me with a nudge, but he's determinedly pushing himself harder than ever. Some of Barclay's men have broken from the fray, pursuing us. Atlas, Conin, and I navigate the backyard of someone's home. We turn abruptly left and almost splat into a brick wall. We adjust our course and then proceed ahead as the harsh thuds of boots sounds from dangerously close by. The soldiers trail toward us, but Atlas redirects us down an alleyway.

Ahead is Main Street. That won't do us any favors. We're putting so many at risk, but it's too late—the soldiers behind have found us and continue with a vengeance. Our trio spills onto the road just in time for Levi Finch to surprise attack from above. He ascends into the air with blasts of flame, then rains down the raging inferno upon us. The three of us scatter and I lose contact with Conin. I can't see him, but Atlas is at the corner of my eye. He vanishes, then rematerializes on top of Levi's shoulders, wrapping both arms tight around the man's throat.

I cry, "Atlas!" just in the nick of time. A blaze builds in the whites of Levi's eyes. Atlas pops from existence as the mercenary hurdles himself into the air again.

This is one of Conin's favorite superhero movies come to life—a fucking nightmare. And I'm at the center of it all.

One moment Levi is suspended midair, the next he's being tugged down by Atlas in one fell swoop. Levi crashes through the glass of a storefront. Barclay's men file onto the road with barrels raised, while duplicate white vans charge in. Angelics spill outwards from the inside, adorned with the texturized, signature white suits.

Atlas pops and reappears before Conin and I, the lines of his face determined. He's solid, fierce, as if he was always meant to fight, meant to be one of them: the Angelics. Seeing him like this is jarring compared to the image he gave off in the bunker. His resolve makes it hard to believe he had no idea what he was doing after his grandfather's passing.

Screams emanate from the small market. Bruised and battered, Levi stands and peers out the jagged window with shards of glass sticking at odd angles along his skin. He brushes them off as inconsequential. Blood drools down his forearms, his palms. Atlas tugs Conin and me aside as Matt erects a water barrier between us and the vindictive mercenary. Eureka citizens hide behind shelves, attempting to escape through the mess of battle. All I feel is the scathing burn and the wrongfulness of innocents dying because we came here in search of safety.

My body shifts into the disguise from the motel.

Let's see if this works.

I'm being dragged once again. We dodge flying bullets and soldiers eager to get their gloved hands on us. Angelics with a wide range of abilities fend off the soldiers as if they're swatting flies. Mara and Levi, skilled and overpowered from obvious years of training, make our efforts difficult. Crackled lightning intersperses in the air followed by a loud, threatening detonation reverberating off Eureka's mountainous walls. Angelics overpower and apprehend Barclay soldiers while the rest interlock in battle.

"No!" screams a woman. Mara, unmasked, throws herself up the alleyway, tiny wires of electricity branching out of her fingers. She stumbles, then fires, and a burst of lightning barely grazes the tips of our hair. The smell of ozone permeates my nostrils. It chars a hole into a wall. We're running, running, running, and she's pursuing, but before Atlas thinks it better to teleport and stop her, Mara freezes. She's flung into Ambrosia's clutches, though she retaliates with a swift kick to the Angelic's ankle.

"Go! We'll find you when we've handled this," Ambrosia yells. Her last words are knocked out of her mouth when she clatters to the asphalt.

Mara's about to slice through the impenetrable-looking armor when she's enclosed in a body of water. I watch her drown, the horror on her face, preserved in the bubble—the realization she can't do anything if she wishes not to zap herself into oblivion. Tommy drowning Callum at Emery's party comes back to me.

Conin and Atlas don't stop. We're suddenly inside a car garage, a repair shop in various stages of work, abandoned and now isolated. I'm on the concrete floor, back pressed against a brick wall, while Atlas and Conin traverse the claustrophobic space to barricade the doors with whatever they can find.

Now that I'm not moving or caught in the adrenaline of our threatening predicament, the burn on my skin swelters ferociously. It's cold one minute, then brutally hot the next. I suck in my teeth. My lips press into a tight line. I inhale deeply and then exhale, drawing my breath out as if this exercise will help me. What occurs instead is that familiar, numbing sensation. It returns with a debilitating vengeance.

Conin abruptly shoves a tool cart in front of the back door we came in. The numbness disassociates my thoughts as they spread out into the cosmos. Lost in space, in my increasing worries, they wash over and pull me down until I suffocate.

Chapter 40

Conin

The distant pops of gunfire work their way to our ears. We're barricaded in this car shop with whatever could be mobilized—wrenches, crowbars, and worktables. No one speaks as we set up to treat Ezra's wound—a gaping second-degree burn that wraps and builds up the length of his forearm. I can barely eye it without feeling squeamish.

With the adrenaline from a moment ago fading little by little, I step onto my bad ankle. It wails in agony, screaming for me to relent, but finding a first aid kit for Ezra takes priority. Atlas absorbs my sorry state, most likely aware of my injury, and tells me to keep Ezra company while he seeks out treatment for the burns. I huff, then acquiesce and settle next to Ezra's frame. He sucks his teeth in. His breaths are deliberate but distressed. The longer he and I remain this way, the more my ankle throbs.

Ezra's burn comes first.

"Can I?" I ask, indicating his arm.

He concedes, then raises his forearm for me to assess. Atlas rummages through the car shop's office in the background. The gunfire tapers off but still sounds in occasional, staccato bursts. Ezra jumps at each one. His arm jolts, instinctively retracting from me, but I gently pull it back. The burns could've been worse. So much worse. When I've finished studying the extent of the injury, I slither my hands to his own and lace my fingers with his. He glances at me questioningly, but my heart's too much of a mess to say anything.

"Co?" he whispers.

"I'm sorry," I say, "for springing that on you earlier."

"It's—"

"But I needed to tell you in case something bad happened. And something bad has happened, so you deserve to know the truth."

He says nothing this time. Somehow, this makes it much harder to continue. I want to be a writer, yet finding the proper words to say in real time may be the hardest thing ever.

"I've loved you for so long," I confess again, letting the words ring true. Atlas was right. Admitting this to Ezra releases a burden that was weighing down my shoulders, but it does nothing to stop the racing thoughts.

More rustling from the office. A yelp of success.

Ezra shudders and inhales a bated breath.

"I love you too," he says softly.

Those four words spark wisps of euphoria that electrify my skin, raise the hairs on the nape of my neck, make my blood rush warm, and breathe life into me in a way I've never felt before. I bite back suppressed tears and feel a harsh sting as my eyelids brim.

"Y-you do?"

"Yes. For so long . . . too long," he laughs. It's forced and jumbled, but fuck, his mirth sounds paradisical.

I feel like I'm floating in midair. Ezra's hand keeps me grounded, tethering me to this earth. I forget about the tether that binds him to Atlas, about the past week and all the weeks before. I forget about the battle that ensues outside. Because Ezra loves me, and I love him.

"When this is over . . . when we get out of this, because we *will* get out of this, I'm going to kiss you so fucking hard, so you better not die," I promise.

An incentive to stay alive.

"Kiss me," Ezra breathes. "We might not live through this, so kiss me now. No regrets."

It's a dreadful statement, enough that I almost hang back. Want fuels the verdict instead.

"Drop the glamor, Ezra. I want to kiss *you*."

He looks affronted but then comprehends my meaning. He melts into himself, recognizable once again.

I draw his head in, pulling him close. Our lips touch. For the briefest of moments, all is right in the world. His lips taste of lingering tequila and every word left unspoken. They fit into mine perfectly, molding into the contour of my mouth. His eyes are warm and radiating. The kiss is fleeting, though the spark that was there was enough to ignite a fire.

We *need* to get out of this.

When I search for Ezra's eyes, he's staring at something behind me. Atlas is looking at us. He casts his eyes away once he's spotted and fumbles with the gathered supplies.

"S-sorry," Atlas stammers.

Ezra chuckles while Atlas picks up what he dropped.

"Here," he says and moves toward us. "I couldn't find any clean towel to compress the burn, but I did find some ointment, bandages, and a water bottle."

He starts uncapping the bottle, scrupulously pouring the liquid over the burn. Ezra hisses and shuts his eyes tight. I stroke the back of his head, raking fingers down the length of his hair. An ointment is applied next. Atlas dabs swabs of the lotion over every inch of the burn after washing his hands with the remaining water. A blue and a green iris peer at me. The pain behind them shatters my heart.

"I've been through worse," Ezra says.

I know he has. It doesn't make this any better.

"I wish you hadn't," I say back.

Atlas sighs, upset. I don't think Ezra's broached that topic with him yet.

I assist Atlas in wrapping the bandages around Ezra's forearm. Atlas breaks the fabric into two with the sharp edges of his canines and we tie the loose ends to finish it off.

"I'm sorry. There weren't any painkillers."

Ezra nods, then studies our handiwork. Once we've applied what we could, we wait. The gunfire has ceased, but it's foolish to believe we're in the clear. Seconds bleed into minutes. The three of us huddle together. Neither Ezra nor I have objected to Atlas molding into our clump—the press of his body is oddly a comfort. Interpret that as you will.

We wait and I begin to feel bravely optimistic.

Until something collides with the front door. The crowbar lodged between the handlebar remains steady. An unknown force smashes into the door again, which noticeably bends the bar, wedging it tight against the handle. Ezra freezes next to me. Atlas, on the other hand, slowly stands in a ready position.

"Whoever it is will get in. Find a weapon," commands Atlas. He moves for the plethora of tools that line the back wall.

"It could be the Angelics," I say.

"Or not."

The gun's in my pack. I could grab it—have this be over the moment they break in. Keeping it on my figure had been a ruse in the bunker and I got lucky with Mara, but who's to say that luck will persist? These are bad guys, though. They want Ezra. They want me and Atlas dead. If I killed them, I'd be saving the fate of other recidivists. Discovering Mara was alive was a relief. If I killed this time . . .

No, it's not something I want to think about. I will do what I must.

Fire blasts the door from its frame, sending the equipment careening through the repair shop. I grab a hand tool instinctively and bolt for the entrance as Levi barges in. His twisted expression could kill, but the flames hovering over his palms may do the trick. Maybe I should've grabbed the gun, after all. Levi doesn't deserve to live. The flames climb higher, encroaching on his arms. His smile reveals bloodied teeth.

"This will be fun."

The mercenary releases the fire and flies away in a blur when Atlas's hand materializes from nowhere, clinging to the fabric of Levi's collar. He rams into the plexiglass, buckling to his knees. Atlas streams ahead and knees the man on the nose. Crimson drains from Levi's nostrils. The mercenary makes a disquieting noise as Atlas rams the crowbar into his stomach.

"Ouch," he exhales.

Fire plumes from Levi's fingers. Atlas teleports away. The flames spread, blackening the area with their touch. I take cover behind a vehicle suspended by a lift and feel the heat scorch my clothes. They're no longer drenched but singed and battered. Boots click on the cement floor, drawing dangerously close. Fire erupts again. There's a faint clatter from the far end of the shop. Seconds later, Ezra is at my side with a morbid, frenzied look.

"Hand me the Glock," he whispers.

I hesitate. Ezra blinks, holding out an expectant hand. Behind us, Atlas distracts Levi, and it's only a matter of time before he finds us. This is the only way.

You're a coward.

I rummage through the contents of my bag and feel the cool, metallic sheen of the handgun. My hands shake violently as I pull the weapon from the depths and proffer it to Ezra. While Levi and Atlas parry in the background, Ezra attempts to pry the gun away from my grip. I can't let go.

"Conin," he says, "give it to me."

Ezra *knows*. Of course, he does.

"We're wasting time."

"Okay," I concede. He takes the Glock and rounds the vehicle. I follow, witnessing when Levi decks Atlas in the gut. He hunches over on the concrete, gasping for air. Flames lick the length of Levi's arms. Atlas's moves are stagnant as he backs into the garage door. The emergence of yellow and orange flame burns bright, then releases. Ezra cocks the barrel of the gun, firing at Levi. Atlas drops to the floor. His wail is painful.

The fire dissipates at the release of a bullet. Levi turns in the nick of time, his attention drawn to the loud noise emanating in our direction, and gets grazed in the cheek by Ezra's lone bullet. In reply, the mercenary loses balance and slumps against the garage door. He holds a hand to his bloodied face in blatant shock but has no time to react when Ezra fires again without hesitation.

The bullet misses. It shatters glass, remnants raining down on the injured mercenary. This buys Levi time. Atlas has moved to the far corner, hunched behind a worktable. My eyes flick from him to Levi, who's trained his gaze on Ezra and pursues the death blow. Levi's irises are murderous as blood trickles down his cheek and dribbles from his mouth, his sandy hair disheveled and his forehead scrunched up, features livid.

"Fucking bastard," he growls.

The Glock clicks, out of ammunition.

"This will be satisfying."

He slams a fist into Ezra's chest. The boy I love rams into a tool cart that clatters away and tilts to the floor with a swarm of tools that spill over the concrete. I raise the hand tool I gathered as Levi homes in on me. He crumples his hands into fists and readies himself for a punch, but I'm set. The hand tool swings at his ribs. Levi loses his purchase on the ground and falls on his ass, so I raise my weapon, getting ready to drive it in his face. Armor-clad people rushed in and tackle the mercenary before I can finish the job. I'm disarmed and held against the wall by an Angelic I'm not familiar with. Ambrosia appears, blurred, while I take large, gulping breaths.

"Stand down," she commands.

I'm not doing anything.

"Let him go!" someone cries.

Ezra fills my vision.

"It's okay, love. It's okay," he says.

Love.

Chapter 41

Ezra

I reel from that kiss and the promise of more. I'm on cloud nine, despite the situation we find ourselves in. It's also pain, but a comfortable pain—tolerable and wanted. I invite it in. Because I never thought this would happen. I've dreamed of it, conjured up scenarios where Conin and I would be together, living our best lives. Deep down, there was always that unequivocal denial.

And to let it happen today of all days. What is this life? Certainly, it's not mine. It's something good to quell the bad that exists. I just hadn't realized it was always there. Always Conin.

My dreams aren't dreams anymore. For the first time in a long time, living doesn't sound as painful. Living doesn't sound quite that bad.

In some morbid way, I'm grateful for this. Maybe I'm selfish for thinking so, but right here, right now I don't fucking care that our lives aren't the same, that we had to leave what we knew behind. Maybe I was meant to be found by the Barclay Network. Perhaps it was the driving force redirecting me to happiness. Or maybe I'm just fucking delirious.

Am I not allowed mercy?

I'm cooped up in the back with Conin's attentive arm slung over my shoulders while Atlas stares down Levi as if he'll wake at any moment. I saw how hard Conin hit him. It shouldn't be any time soon.

While the Angelics handle the fallen mercenary, Ambrosia pulls Atlas aside, whispering silently to him. Tears brim his brown eyes, obscured by his glasses. His forehead creases in three horizontal lines, something resembling dread. His mouth dips down, parted slightly at the lips. Atlas looks trapped in time. If I look away, I'm afraid he'll crumble or never move again. He's alive and it's only by the slight twitch of his fingers that I can tell. Fingernails rake up his palm and clench at his sides. That's when I realize I've been ignoring Matt. Conin nudges me, helping me stand.

"May I?" Matt inquires. I nod, then he observes the burn.

He beckons an Angelic over who also asks for consent—I'm not used to it—not by strangers or people who pretend to be family.

Conin was always the exception.

"It's a nasty burn," the Angelic says, matter-of-fact. She observes it a while longer before ungloving her hand. "I'm a healer. It will take some work and won't immediately go away, but I can subdue the pain and lessen some of the scarring."

Right. The scar. My exposed arms reveal the aftermath of Thax's brutal tirades with the burn as a nice touch.

"Sure," I say.

Conin tenses beside me, observing the ethereal glow emitting from the healer's hand. She runs it along the length of my forearm, deliberately. Slowly. It isn't painful, but it's not comfortable, either. It's air on an exposed wound, a soothing wind. Trickling water on parched, dirtied skin. I sigh a breath of relief when she finishes. The scar is still there, evident by the burn's streak, but it's duller now. The pain's gone. I smile weakly and mutter a "thank you." She grins, asking Conin if he has any injuries. They discuss his ankle, finally.

Atlas catches my attention. An onslaught of tears streaks his face. He says something, Ambrosia nods, and then Atlas is escorted out with an Angelic in tow. My heart pangs for him—I feel a sudden jolt in my mood: grief, loss, and fear, though I've lost no one.

Our tether ebbs and flows, coalesces and disperses, but lingers stronger than before. I wonder why he's upset and what the Barclay Network coming here will mean for him and continuing his grandfather's work. Is that even a possibility now?

"Alright, let's get moving. Angela must be sending in reinforcements as we speak. It won't be long before law enforcement gets involved, if they aren't on their way here already," says Ambrosia.

Some Angelics load Levi Finch onto a stretcher and follow Ambrosia out. Matt leads Conin and me to the white vans aligned on the main street. An Angelic converses with an official-looking woman near Eureka's tiny town hall. She nods, unperturbed that recidivists have overtaken her city. I know not everyone's prejudiced. Maybe she's one of the good guys. She could be grateful we apprehended the mercenaries. Or, perhaps, she's humoring us until law enforcement arrives to whisk the responsibility of the predicament away from her. Either way, it's not my problem. Not anymore.

There weren't any casualties. That comes as a relief. Some injuries, sure, but no lives were lost. In my periphery, Mara is loaded into the same van the Angelics took Levi's stretcher in, her wrists inside power-suppressing handcuffs.

Apprehension hits me full-force. Where the fuck is Callum?

"Conin!" His name comes out as a hiss.

"Yes?" he asks. He seems confused by the tone of my voice.

"You didn't see Callum anywhere, did you?"

Conin looks around as if Callum will take shape from out of nowhere. I suppose he could, having the ability to navigate through mirrors.

"I don't remember seeing him at all. Should we ask?"

I'm about to object because I detest confrontations, but—

"Excuse me. The man on the stretcher? His brother is—" Conin says before he's interrupted.

"Callum Finch. What about him?"

"Is he here? Did you capture him?"

The Angelic straightens. He detracts his mask with a simple press of a button, then peers around. Mara laughs. It's sinister and discomforting.

"That pathetic, incompetent loser will be out of commission for a while," she snarls before the doors of the van are shut, cutting off her voice.

The motel we fled to with Tommy was the last time we saw Callum. Callum had been rendered unconscious by Conin's brute force, but something must've gone down in the aftermath. Mara would have stumbled upon a comatose Callum Finch, vulnerably frail. Realistically, his injuries should've prevented him from pursuing us any further. It makes the most viable sense. But that fear, strong and curdling in my chest, hollows itself deep inside, rests against my bones until they ache.

I'm nudged on the arm. We're in a van, the Angelic we'd been speaking with only moments ago is gone, and we're idling alongside the curb.

"Are you okay?" asks Conin. His expression is neutral, but I catch him making indirect glances as if the police or more of Barclay's men will spill out and attack us at any given moment. The longer we wait here, the more we're put at risk. Why haven't we left yet?

"I zoned out there. Sorry," I say.

"We were told they'd investigate it, but I have a feeling nothing will come from it. They're clueing in to what Mara said, and given everything, I think it's the least of their priorities."

"Do you believe that?"

"I'm not sure," he says, thoughtful. "But I trust that we're safe now. The Angelics will protect us from here on out."

That's not how he felt before. His opinions were in flux. Seeing the Angelics in action probably changed his mind.

Safety was our end goal. Putting our trust in these people feels too far a stretch now that it's happening, contradictory to my earlier beliefs. I have to remind myself the Angelics are like me. They've undergone similar situations, some much worse than my own. This is only paranoia—the Angelics aren't against me and they sure as hell aren't the family I left behind. I trusted Atlas quickly. And maybe it is the strange, innominate binds that tie us, but if Atlas trusts the Angelics, I should, too.

Guilt, sharp and quick, sinks its teeth in. Leaving without Tommy feels wrong. There is nothing we can do, but that doesn't relieve the guilt's piercing hold. For a second I forget to breathe. It might be better if I forgot about him.

What's wrong with me?

The set of twin doors at the back of the van abruptly open. Atlas: golden-skinned, disheveled hair, and tired, wild brown eyes fill my tunnel vision. His cheeks are puffy from tears and a dark shade of maroon sets in. He bends at the hip, sidling by so he can sit on a seat opposite us. Staring at him, heart aflame with self-inflicted culpability, all I can feel is relief. It washes over and masks the guilt.

The tether pulses.

"You're coming?" Conin asks. I sense relief in his voice.

"It's not safe for me anymore," Atlas says brusquely.

An unspoken question blankets the air. What will become of his parents? Why won't they flee with us if their lives are potentially in danger, too?

It will remain unanswered, unmoored for now.

In a procession, the Angelics' vans file out of Eureka, then disperse at a crossroads. Sirens wail from a distance.

Chapter 42

Atlas

"We may have apprehended the mercenaries, but Eureka's now on the Barclay Network's radar," Ambrosia says, traces of her cordial grin, which she offered my parents, who stand beside me, fading. She was always fond of them.

But the way she smiles, following by the horrifying news, makes every part of me ill at ease.

"Even if they aren't aware of our operation . . . it's not safe for you here anymore. Eureka has attention on it that it didn't before," pa tells me while ma stands demurely by his side.

The aftermath of this battle has shaken her up. She clutches pa's hand, fingers trembling.

It's certainly been terrifying for me. Fighting's not all that it's cracked up to be in the movies. My entire body is on fire, each muscle, bone, and tendon screeching for abatement. There's nothing I can give. Preparing myself for next time is all I can control.

What's more, burdening me is the extreme trepidation, loss, and grief that races through every corner and inch and crevice that makes up my body. I *can't* leave my parents behind. This wasn't part of the plan.

The plan was for me to continue abu's legacy. He created this operation, and I was supposed to keep it alive for as long as it took for the Angelics to make a difference in this world where recidivists wouldn't be called recidivists, and we could live our lives openly and freely. A world where no Scarlet Letters existed and no one had to pin a sign onto your chest, labeling you for the world to judge. Now the operation is dying with me. My parents refuse to have it operational any longer.

"Mi corazón," says ma before pulling me in. I almost burst into tears. "It may not be the life you always desired, but it's the life you deserve. At least . . . at Proctus . . . you're freer than you have ever been."

That's not true. She, pa, and abu have given me the best life I could have here. Here is all I've ever known. But maybe . . . perhaps, there is some semblance of truth to her words. Though, without them, what kind of life will it be?

And, reminding myself, isn't this what I wanted? A life free of the bunker, away from responsibility, and abu's impossible shoes to fill.

"Can't you come with?" I ask, breaking away from the embrace. My vision strictly finds Ambrosia, whose faux smile has shifted downwards. "Can't they?"

"Of course they can," she answers.

"But we can't right now, hijo. We still have work to do," says pa.

"What work—"

"Abuelo left much work to be done if we decided to end the operation. That time has come . . . It's too much to explain in detail now, mijo, but we promise we will one day. When all is said and done, we'll meet you at Proctus. Deal?" ma says.

"Deal," I whisper and the dam in my eyes breaks.

"You did good. We love you," my parents tell me.

That was hours ago. We traverse now through the miles and miles of desert stretch in Utah. Ambrosia and Matt navigate up front while Mafu keeps me company at my side, though neither of us speaks. The sun hangs low in the sky. Across our row, Conin and Ezra doze off. I'm not sure how they can rest after everything, but good for them, I guess. They don't have to stew in their own self-deprecating thoughts.

Even when my parents were active in the church, I was never devoutly religious. I suppose that alluded to what my future held, discovering my queer and superpowered identities and how the world would treat me for them.

I find myself praying. For the first time in a very long time, I silence my mind and focus. I pray my parents will be safe and that I will get to see them again one day as they and Ambrosia promised.

Then grief bulldozes me over, more powerful than before. I grieve for abu's loss and his legacy. The operation ended today, but his legacy was strong, vibrant, and ceaseless. I hold on to that reassurance as we chart our course into a new life.

Chapter 43

Conin

The mask of night swallows an endless landscape hours later when I wake up. There's a weight on my shoulder—Ezra fast asleep, head resting between my chin and clavicle. I'm tired, tense, and sore, but his body relying on mine releases a flock of birds from my stomach. He's radiating even as he sleeps. His breath caressing my arm lights my heart aglow, igniting a frisson of chills.

Dubiously, I wonder if this is a dream. I'll wake up and things will return to how they were before the attack in Eureka. Ezra's confession, my confession, all of it a hoax. But it's the throbbing, ebbing pain reminding me this is real. I'm awake and his head really is resting against me. He's here. This is happening.

We're very alive.

A half hour later, Ambrosia stops to put gas in the vehicle. She and Matt press down on the emblems attached to their chests. The armor detracts, dematerializing before my very eyes, fading from existence until all that's left is the winged emblem stitched to the fabric of their shirts. Uniformly, they remove the emblems and hide them in the glove compartment. Ambrosia exits the vehicle to fill it up while Matt detours to the convenience store. Ezra stirs and lifts his head, blinking away the grogginess. I smile at him when he looks at me with bleary eyes.

"Hello sleepyhead," I coo.

I want this to be our new normal.

His smile is genuine but weak. It doesn't quite reach his eyes.

"Where are we?" he asks.

"Filling up on gas. You can go back to sleep."

He nuzzles into me and my heart implodes. This is too good to be true.

When we're back on the road, the rumbling noise from the van lulls me into a restless sleep.

It's very early once I regain consciousness. Every inch of my body aches, but the pain is another reminder I'm alive. The weight from before is no longer on my shoulders. Ezra's awake, grinning softly when he notices I'm up. Mafu's silence is loud next to Atlas. The metal-wielder studies the road ahead. Atlas, however, has his gaze cast down on the vehicle floor. Periodically, he'll blink as someone should, but his eyes are soulless—his face blank and steeled. A part of me hurts for him. The pain of leaving family behind is no easy task.

Matt's at the wheel while Ambrosia navigates with a touchscreen display mounted to the vehicle's dashboard. A green sign on the highway's ledge grows larger. As we pass it, I notice the infamous *Welcome to Las Vegas* printed on the metal.

It comes and goes, but at the pit of my stomach is an endless dread.

"Where are we going?" I ask.

The blinding, twinkling Vegas lights surround us, interspersed by rays of dappled sunlight. Buildings climb, and a crowd of vehicles appears. We idle alongside them as early morning traffic hinders us from reaching our destination, wherever that is. Ambrosia soaks me in, expression wry.

"The Excelsior. Esther's father owns it. We'll be safe there," she says.

The GPS mumbles something inaudible. Ambrosia redirects her attention to the screen and tells Matt to exit an off-ramp. We descend to the bustling streets of Las Vegas's strip as people begin their day. But all I can think about is the Excelsior—the many people there and our likelihood of being caught. Why aren't we heading directly to Proctus? Aren't we more exposed this way?

"Why are you taking us to the Excelsior?"

Mafu's disgruntled disposition sets me on edge. A defensive flare lodges itself in my chest, ready to fight if the predicament arises.

"Standard procedure. The Excelsior is technically a safe house. It runs like a resort, people are constantly coming and going, and if it stays this way, no one has any reason to expect the owner's housing powered individuals waiting to be transferred.

"We were supposed to meet Leeanne and her crew here for a transfer anyway, but it seems they've encountered a hindrance on their latest recruitment mission. So, in the meantime, we'll keep on the down low here," says Ambrosia.

"Is there a reason you can't take us to Proctus?" I ask. I have no intention of pushing any buttons, but I require answers. Mafu exhales a guttural sigh.

"Again. Standard procedure."

"Well," Matt says, trying to shatter the tension, "we can't go to Proctus. Our jurisdiction is Utah and Utah only. We're not properly equipped for a trip to California, so this is as far as we go."

"To Vegas?" I say it sarcastically.

"The situation called for it."

"And besides, Leeanne's crew are the only Angelics with Proctus's exact coordinates. They're a group of handpicked individuals with special skills and assets, so naturally, Esther trusts them with the location. Leeanne is the only one who can take you there. With an influx of mercenaries and bounty hunters crawling around the western states, we have no choice but to wait."

"Are you fucking kidding me? You're telling me that not one of you knows where the safe haven is?" My anger rises, and I feel Ezra's grip tighten in warning.

"Not the exact location, no," Ambrosia answers.

"It may seem flawed to you, but it's worked for us—we've avoided countless confrontations. If we don't have the exact location, our enemies won't have the means to find us," Matt says.

I say nothing, too pissed to utter a single word.

"We're here."

There's some logic to this protocol, though it's hard to believe no one's thought to branch out and discover the haven's location. Unless restrictions are heavily implemented, their process is flawed at best. Witnessing the Angelics in action firsthand wiped away the last bit of uncertainty I had. In the present, it's obvious I was premature in my assumption. I want to put faith in these people who've helped us escape death, but Ezra and I have been through so much.

Matt turns into a driveway with rows of palm trees on each side. Some tropical-themed resort is to our right, an arena ahead, and a large sphinx perches in front of the Excelsior. I remember coming here with Mom years back—our attempt at a vacation when the worst of my parents' marriage came crashing down. It was intended to be a distraction, but the trip only postponed the inevitable. We didn't know what would happen back then.

My heart pounds in my ears and blood rushes all over, muddling my senses. If I'm a mess, I can't imagine how Ezra feels. He clutches his joggers, nothing but the embodiment of anxiety. I squeeze his bicep, offering a smile. He can barely manage one of his own.

"Trust us, please," Mafu says.

The driveway veers to the left, stretching underneath the sphinx. This early in the day, the only activity is the line of cars and taxis ready to pick up guests checking out. Several valets tow bell carts sporting stacks of luggage to the awaiting vehicles. I spot the occasional security guard here and there. How many of these people are recidivists? Is it that easy to come and go or are these people merely a facade? Whatever the case, there are people, and lots of them. We have a missing person's report looming over our heads. It's a stretch saying they'd recognize us, but I can't rule out that scenario altogether.

Ezra's entire body is tense against mine. I move my hold from his bicep to entwine my fingers with his, hoping it'll bring him some reassurance. His shivers soften.

Atlas watches from across the row. He could be staring into space, but that's unlikely because his eyes trace in circular motions like they're tracking a movement. My thumb over Ezra's palm mimics the same motion. I swiftly divert my notice. Strange.

In front, Ambrosia shifts to take us in. She tugs her lips into a frown, subtly singling Ezra out.

"Mafu," she says, "armor down. You're coming with me to let them know we have arrived. Matt, stay here with the others."

Matt nods as Mafu presses down on the emblem. His suit detracts, leaving the signature Angelic wings attached to his civilian attire. He hands it off to Matt, who stashes it with the others.

"Ezra, I need you to shift. There's a slim chance you'll be recognized, but you never know who's watching," Ambrosia tells him. "Alright, Mafu. Let's go."

Ezra didn't tell the Angelics about his abilities, but I wouldn't be surprised if Atlas said something.

Occupying the space next to me is a larger, thicker man. Tatum stares back with hazel eyes and a sculpted frame plucked from an art gallery. This variant is indeed hand-some—all broad shoulders and bulging muscles—but it's not Ezra. This variant is what he wishes he looked like. He didn't need to say anything for me to figure it out. It breaks my heart that he'll never see himself in the same light I see him. Having confessed my feelings for him now, I hope he'll start to realize I love him. No facade will change that.

Ambrosia and Mafu disappear in the Excelsior. Moments later, they return with key cards in hand. The van shakes as they enter. Ambrosia presents six key cards, one for each of us, and disperses them. Ezra and I share the same number: 3.

"Matt and I will share a suite. Atlas, you're with Mafu. And Ezra, you and Conin will be together."

My face flushes. If anyone notices the beet red of my countenance, they say nothing of it. Ezra's flustered, his cheeks hotter than mine. My heart races at a speed I won't be able to slow, not as long as I stay next to him. It'll be our first time sharing a bed since he and I admitted our feelings for one another. The thought of it sends eclectic jolts of electricity through my entire nervous system.

"Alright. Let's move."

We're directed to the tower where we've been assigned penthouse suites on the upper floors. Ezra and I are on the very top, the room across from Mafu and Atlas. A grand suite greets us when we enter. Ahead is a glass wall, reflecting Las Vegas's skyline. I gawk at the luxuriousness of our suite, much like the bunker in Eureka. There's lots to soak in.

Ezra gravitates toward the bed. Exhaustion creeps at his eyelids where red, irritated lines have sheened over. How is it that he can still sleep? I had hoped we could discuss the idea of *us*, and where we stand. How do we define our relationship after such a monumental kiss?

"Ez—"

"Co', I know you want to talk about us. We will, but I'm tired. I'm . . . freaking out. I promise we'll talk later. I just need sleep right now."

"It's okay," I mutter. "I understand."

He returns to himself, molding into the boy I love, and dives onto the bed, groaning as he sinks into the mattress.

"This feels heavenly."

I watch as he passes out. Meanwhile, I'll die from self-immolation.

Chapter 44

Atlas

Forgetting is the hardest part.

And it's truly driving me insane.

But trying to forget these intense emotions about my parents and abu and failing my job is too much. Frankly, it's impossible. That's why I stalked to the minibar the moment my eyes spotted it when Mafu and I arrived at our suite. It's not like the Angelics promote casual drinking or ruining your liver, but they had the same idea I did (the right idea).

I need to dull the edges, make this bearable. After I down two shots, Mafu steps imposingly in front of the bar and swipes the glass from my hand. His stark eyebrows furrow and his smooth skin crinkles in disapproval. I miss those long locks because the buzzed hair on Mafu's scalp displays his exasperation entirely. He scoffs, stealing the bottle of vodka away too. I frown at him.

"Maybe you should slow down," he says.

"And maybe you shouldn't butt into my business," I say. "Give it back."

"No. If I'm going to share a damn room with you, you're not going to be piss drunk."

"Fuck off," I hiss, teleporting to catch Mafu off guard.

With the forward momentum, I snatch the bottle from his grasp and fall gracelessly onto the carpet. I get to my feet, feel an intense pounding in my head, and the world vibrates and sways until I gather some composure. (There were, like . . . twenty other bottles in the cabinetry . . . I could have taken one of those.)

"Goddammit, Atlas! You're not the only one here going through shit," he says, his voice rising.

"Oh please, you have no idea what I'm going through."

Mafu takes a step forward. He's lean, but large, and not the type of person to start something with. I take a step back. The bottle is brandished like a weapon in my hands, ready to strike if he tries anything funny. He could easily overpower me any day, both by his special abilities and strength. I almost flinch, but I have more self-respect than that.

"I had to leave my life behind, too, you know."

"I remember," I grunt.

"Then you should understand."

I'm too upset to let him win this fight.

"But your leaving Eureka was voluntary." If the blow hits him, he's too collected to let it show.

"You know it wasn't," he says, "Ofa left. Mom and Dad followed. They didn't give me a choice. And come on, man. Do you not think we didn't get shit for being Polynesian in an entirely white, rural town?"

"Ma, abu, and I aren't white . . ."

Mafu's expression softens. I hate when he shows this side of himself: the kind half, the one often hidden behind his gruff disposition.

"Atlas, you know that's not what I mean. What I'm trying to say is that it wasn't safe. You staying there wasn't either. I know it sucks to leave what you knew behind, but this will be better for you. For all of us."

He's right. Of course, he is. I'm not having it, though. Not today.

"At least you have a family to return to."

Mafu sighs, defeated. He shakes his head and veers toward the couch. "I thought you would be happy to see me. Abuelito meant something to me, too, you know."

Abu's absence still carves a cavity in my chest. I sometimes discover lingering traces of his presence. A ghostly hand on my shoulder, an imparting of wisdom whispered into my ear. In the later years, there was only so much he could do. It felt like he was constantly occupied with something, trying to complete as much work as possible because he knew his life was slowing to an end. Mafu helped me through many of the darker days, but then, as they always do, he left. And I remained behind.

I understand why he withdrew. His family stayed in Eureka for as long as they could.

"Take the bed," Mafu mumbles. "Just don't drink yourself silly."

No promises.

Chapter 45

Ezra

I awaken to unfamiliar settings swaddled in soft, white sheets, that permeate a pleasant scent. Warm light drifts through the window wall, the lights of Las Vegas beaconing even when the afternoon sun is in full effect. I blink away the grogginess in my eyes, pushing myself up. The pillows propped against the headboard are heaven on the ache crawling up my spine. I inhale, hold my breath, and exhale, reminding myself I'm alive.

The penthouse suite's bedroom is large and spacious, with richly cream-colored walls and a window that spreads the length of the left-hand side. Furniture is modest and features all the necessities: nightstands, a desk to my right, two upholstered lounge chairs with a spiraling white motif separated in the center by a coffee table. The art on the wall is basic even as it attempts at modernity and pretentiousness. It unsettles me. This whole room does, as the sun beats down and life ensues outside as if we weren't nearly beaten to within an inch of our lives.

Shudders crawl through my skin. I rub my forearms, then pause to study the faded burn. The scar blends in with the others—a perfect, tattered tapestry. It's difficult not to wince. My bare feet land on the dull, gray carpet with its rigidness and subtle abrasions, a total juxtaposition from the alluring cloud of the bed. Before returning, I force my legs to carry me out of the bedroom.

This morning was a doleful blur—I hadn't noticed much before passing out into a dreadful sleep. The window wall spreads further, expanding the entire penthouse. The parallel wall is closed off and safe, reassuring me we're not entirely exposed. There's a bathroom leading to an elevated tub, a minibar stocked with liquor, the kitchen, a billiards table, and Conin spread out on the sofa bed, which can't be comfortable.

He slumbers on the couch in the clothes he wore in Eureka. His arm hangs off the ledge, fingers brushed against the floor. He's coated in dirt and the occasional streak of crusted blood smeared in mottled browns. If we hadn't been led to a private entrance, I can only imagine the stares we'd be getting.

Conin snores, cuing a smile. My cheeks relish in the pain over how ridiculously happy he makes me. Then the guilt comes rushing back. Making him feel like he couldn't sleep at my side was not my intention. I should have expressed this before scouring for the bed. It was hopelessly optimistic to believe he'd join me without prompt. We parted with a sea of questions and answers between us.

Creeping over to join him, I gently rest his feet on my lap, turning on the television and lowering the volume. Some sitcom plays. I don't care about it, but it's a distraction. Time passes, and I'm both oblivious and very aware of its ebb and flow. Somewhere, my thoughts take hold of me. And the pain, that culpability, grips again.

I wish I could have done more in Eureka, but I was useless. Neither Atlas nor Conin were injured in our scrimmage with the Barclay Network, but it hurt knowing there wasn't much I could do to protect them when it boiled down to it. Even with an injured foot, Conin led me along as if he hadn't been wincing with each stride. He took me to safety and protected me despite his injuries. I did nothing but fire the gun, missing when it counted most.

Levi Finch takes a threatening shape, transforming my feelings of inadequacy into a mold of fear. He gauges my reaction after the flames had licked my arm, the malicious, hedonistic eyes of a killer. Finding out he's Callum's brother weakens my resolve. The connection was easy to make—their similar green eyes and dimpled chins, the shared last name. The realization that not only one recidivist would turn on their kind, but two, is appalling. What went so wrong in their lives that they felt the need to slave for a network hell-bent on killing people like them? And Mara Barclay of all people . . . daughter of the network's leader. It's despicable.

The thought of anyone stooping so low as to become a jingoist makes me sick.

Then there's a jarring knock on the suite's door. Conin, to my surprise, doesn't wake. He stirs slightly as I wait to see if it will pass. I feel an inkling of relief when I gently remove his feet off my lap and make way for the door. I'm hesitant to approach, but grateful for the peephole and the familiar face beyond the threshold.

"I took a nap and I'm still not entirely sober, but damn does my fucking head hurt, and I need some food," the boy says as he nurses his temples. A small chuckle parts my lips.

It's surprising, almost, the emotions he evokes out of me. I've opened myself to Atlas in ways I never thought possible. Whether it was due to our strange tether or his charismatic personality, my pragmatism is kaput. I like Atlas and the idea of that eviscerates me. It's not romantic or an attraction, but my willingness to be open with him far outweighs any hostility felt when we had first met.

"Would you like to come with me? Alcohol was a mistake," Atlas inquires.

"Sure," I say.

A new mold shifts underneath my clothing. There's some restraint, but the husk is comfortable overall. Atlas's face is stricken with horror when he gets a good look at me.

"What?" I ask.

"You—" Atlas gulps. "You shifted into Tommy."

"Fuck—" It had been instinctive, though why I chose Tommy probably stems from my immense guilt over his fate. Familiar faces are easy to manipulate, so I settled on an appearance that would take little energy. In doing so, I unwillingly traumatized the boy who's been kind to me since our arrival in Eureka.

"I can try for someone else," I say to rectify what I've done.

"No, it's okay. It caught me off guard, that's all," he whispers.

"I tend to shift into people I know well because it's easier. It takes a lot of concentration to craft a new facade, especially if I don't have a mirror to see what I've managed to do. Shape-shifting takes a lot of energy. Too much, sometimes . . ."

Atlas nods as if he understands.

"Teleportation is draining, too. I was afraid my body would give out on me during our encounter with the Barclay Network. I hadn't teleported that much in rapid succession like that before."

We're still perched underneath the suite's door. With it wide open, you can see the perfect view of a resting Conin. Atlas notices and silences himself, then motions for me to follow.

"So," he says, and I know exactly where this is leading. "I thought you two weren't a thing."

"I'm not sure what we are," I confess. "I didn't even know he liked me in that way."

Atlas smirks, his plump lips widening into a smug sense of victory. His eyes, however, don't display the same radiating light. Is he . . . upset? Is this about Conin and me or is it leaving his parents behind? I don't ask when we enter the elevator, keeping any thoughts and opinions from exiting my mouth. Better that way.

But I need to know. "You knew, didn't you?"

"I may have gotten him to confess a thing or two," Atlas says.

We start our descent when a sudden thickness lodges itself in my stomach. Bile rises in my esophagus—my larynx constricts. I try not to let my panic show, suppress it like Conin would—paint on a stoic facade with this faux face. Atlas is none the wiser.

The elevator halts. The steel doors push aside and reveal two of our Angelic comrades. Ambrosia has a slim purse to her mouth, with creased eyebrows. Matt's indifferent, but his expression isn't unfriendly. They slip in to occupy the space next to Atlas and me. The gates shut and we continue descending.

"Where are you two going?" questions Ambrosia, giving me a once-over.

Does this form unsettle her too? How well did she know Tommy, if she knew him at all?

"We were going to get something to eat," Atlas says.

"We'd rather you not. How about you return to your rooms, and we'll get you what you need. Whether or not you're recognized is irrelevant. It's safer to stay in your rooms until Leeanne can extract us."

"Sure," he replies, and that smile doesn't quite reach his eyes again.

He and I exit at the next stop. Ambrosia nods, satisfied, before she and Matt slide out of sight. Though my anxiety ebbs at first, a sudden, irrevocable spike catches me off guard. The walls on each side start to cave in. Atlas blurs while the ground below me sways. An image of Lukeman Gray raising a hand to strike me finds its way to the surface. Shards of ebony. Fragments littering the floor. I try to find Atlas, but he's nowhere to be seen, and the walls only grow tighter against me. I sense the first retch, my body instinctively fighting against it, because this sucks, this sucks, this fucking sucks. Crippling apprehension rattles my every limb until I wander aimlessly in search of a restroom. There's one nearby, thank god, just a turn down the adjacent hallway.

"Ezra?"

"Ezra?" he repeats. The voice is too far away.

I'm not sure what triggered my relapse. Maybe the past week's events have finally settled and my body decided to reject them the best way it knows how. I hate this body, this skin, these scars, this face, these eyes, my very fucking, cruel existence.

I'm so sorry, Tommy.

Barriers surround me, a stall climbing up. My throat thickens, fingers raking down the tissue. I don't want to see it. I don't. The fear in me pulsates, pushing harder, and I gag, vomiting into the porcelain what little contents remain in my stomach. It's not much. Saliva droops, pools on the rim of the toilet seat. I divert my eyes. Two gentle hands cup my shoulders. They surprise me at first, which rockets me closer to the toilet, but I acquiesce, lean into the touch, and relish it.

They're not Conin's.

Atlas's soft, gentle hands never leave my side. He mutters reassurances, loud enough for only me to hear. Atlas waits and never probes. He's patient until the wracking shakes subside, helping me to my feet while stroking soothing fingers down my spine. Even as they grace the knobs, warmth blooms with each caress from the hands of someone I met a week ago. A fluttering sensation in my stomach crawls upwards and quickens the beat of my heart.

What the hell?

He assists me back to my and Conin's suite, lets me know I've shifted into myself. These clothes feel normal against my body, something I can at least live with. Atlas helps me inside, where Conin is still fast asleep on the sofa bed. He must've slept very little on our ride to Vegas, though that's no surprise. What we went through in Eureka is not something so easily forgotten. Atlas lowers me onto a plush chair, then occupies the one opposite the coffee table. He seems amused by Conin's slumbering form. Brown irises find mine.

"Want to see if any *Star Wars* reruns are on while we wait?" Atlas says in his low baritone.

"Sure." My heart catches.

He and I discuss favorite movies from the saga, where I again disclose my unfettered love with the second film. Our conversation veers into the series, the independent films, the ones slated for release in the distant future. Atlas's knowledge, which far outweighs Conin's, and is almost on par with mine, comes as a pleasant surprise. We talk for a long while. My cheeks won't relax, stretching painfully wide.

We avoid the previous day's events, the millions of questions unasked, our thoughts, feelings, and emotions in favor of this shared interest. I hope one day we'll talk about what we keep silent about for now, but for the time being, I am perfectly content at wasting away in a fictional universe.

And there, still present in my stomach, is the unnerving sensation of butterflies taking flight.

Chapter 46

Conin

Ezra and Atlas are lounging in the chairs when I regain consciousness. A *Star Wars* movie plays on TV and they're chipping away at takeout—Chinese, I think when the scent wafts over to my nose. The two are engaged in an enthusiastic conversation, probably something regarding the fictional universe, but it oddly enough puts a smile on my face. Seeing Ezra enthused about a topic, talking with a friend, and branching away from his comfort zone is a breath of fresh air. I sit up and hug one of the pillows to my chest. Atlas briefly stops speaking when Ezra turns to me with a small grin.

"We didn't want to wake you, so there's takeout for you in the fridge," he says.

"You looked like you could use the sleep," Atlas mentions.

"Thanks," I say.

I feel far from rested.

I don't know how I will be after yesterday's events.

My feet carry me to the kitchen, where I find the Styrofoam box of Chinese food waiting amongst empty refrigerator shelves. I scoop the box's contents onto a plate and start microwaving it. Leaning my frame against the granite countertop, I watch Atlas pick up where he left off. Ezra's eyes are trained on the TV. He's actively listening, subtly nodding, and agreeing with other parts of Atlas's speech. Ezra rarely displays this side of himself.

I never meant for Ezra to do anything he wasn't comfortable with growing up. But I always challenged him, invited him to parties or events, and ensured he knew he was wanted. He'd at least attend my football games, usually accompanied by Mom. His presence there meant the world to me. Suddenly, there had been a pep in my step, an invigorating boost when I'd spotted him in the bleachers. Of course, Ezra would reject the other, countless social engagements I invited him to, but he had tried. I sincerely love him for it.

I may not understand this tether between him and Atlas, whether this makes them more than fast friends, but whatever the case, I accept it: without jealousy, without animosity, and without feeling as if Atlas will take Ezra from me.

Atlas treats him the way he deserves—in the way the guys on the football team should have. He's thoughtful and genuine, serious when he needs to be. He and Ezra already share so much in common. Atlas's eyes are alight with passion as he gestures widely with his hands in animated bursts. His tousled hair waves with each movement, his glasses askew, tipped at the nose, while his lips sharpen into focus.

Atlas is attractive as hell. That'll be two times now that I've confessed this to myself.

But before panic settles in, Ezra's face dampens, turning sour. His mouth tilts downwards, his fork suspended over the takeout box holding an unbitten piece of chicken. He sets the food on the coffee table, excuses himself, and proceeds to the bathroom. The door shuts loudly in his wake. Atlas roams to the kitchen, his gaze fixed on where Ezra departed.

"He doesn't seem to be taking everything in well," he whispers.

There's that pain again—that intense understanding only years of friendship will get you.

"Ezra's always kind of been this way."

"What is it?"

"He's never outright told me, but I think it stems from his anxiety. When it happens, I give him the space he needs," I say.

That might sound like I don't care, like I can't be bothered with his mental health issues. Truth is, I'm too scared to push Ezra away.

"Before you freak out," Atlas says, "Ambrosia told us to come back, but Ezra and I went out to get food . . . didn't make it past the third floor. He started to have one of these . . . spells and puked in the restroom. Do you think it's an eating disorder?"

"Maybe," I replied, cringing at the bluntness of his question. I have no clue what it is. We never talked about it. And the idea of that makes me feel horrible and scared and a plethora of other crappy emotions.

I plaster on a smile, remembering the food in the microwave. After several bites of the takeout, its contents grow dull and tasteless in my mouth. Each bite leaves bitter entrails.

Eventually, Ezra returns and sits on the couch as if nothing happened in the first place. Neither I nor Atlas acknowledge it. Instead, we return to our seats and watch the movie in silence.

Atlas strikes up a conversation again. Whatever he says breaks Ezra out of his spell. He guffaws and bursts into a stream of heavy laughter. Atlas grins, watching Ezra clutch his stomach and roll into the pillows on the chair.

"What'd you say?" I ask, leaning conspiratorially toward Atlas.

"It wasn't even that funny," he says, chuckling. "I was just saying Ezra's more expressive when he's sad and mopey than Hayden Christensen could ever be."

"But we like Hayden Christensen, right?"

"We *love* him."

The Nevada sun starts to set on the horizon. There hasn't been much for the three of us to do, so we've interlocked in conversations as movies play on in the background.

"God, I was so infatuated with him. It's so cringy to look back on." Atlas laughs.

"Oh no, what happened?"

"I waited until we were in a secluded part of the school to ask him out. And I did because I'm an idiot with no filter . . . I wasn't subtle about it. At all," he says and buries his face into his hands. "We live in some hick town in rural southern Utah, of course his reaction wasn't going to be good!"

Ezra's mirth is contagious. He hugs his legs against his torso, peering over his kneecaps.

"He looked away, rubbing the back of his head like he was some stereotypical anime schoolgirl, and I took that opportunity to teleport the fuck out of there."

We howl with laughter.

"That sounds like you," Ezra says.

It does . . . sound like him.

"So . . . what about you two?" Atlas questions. "I was talking to Conin several days ago and that crush of his was still unrequited. What happened?"

Ezra's red in a millisecond.

"Well," he mutters, "I've . . . loved him for a long time, too."

We haven't had a moment to discuss this yet: he and I, us two, alone. His words erupt my skin into a furious blush. I can hardly look him or Atlas in the eye, finding a focal point somewhere on the floor. The leg of the coffee table suddenly becomes very interesting.

"So, you were both oblivious? How cute!" Atlas coos in a mocking tone. "You know, I told him he should confess. I am the perfect matchmaker."

Ezra's expression is torn between many things, but cheer prevails, and he spews it like a geyser. "So, I've heard."

Our conversation halts abruptly after a knock at the suite's door. Atlas is the one to answer it. He peers through the peephole and opens the door to reveal Ambrosia, Mafu, and Matt stand on the other side. They walk in, situating themselves around the lounge area. Ezra sits up, all traces of relaxation gone. His posture is straight, and his shoulders are tense, drawn back against the slope of the couch. Ambrosia whispers something into Atlas's ear. His face incontrovertibly relaxes.

"Leeanne and her crew are on their way. They should arrive sometime tomorrow," Ambrosia informs us.

Atlas nods. Ezra's tight-lipped, staring off into space.

"I understand we haven't been completely transparent with you three. You deserve some explanations."

"We do," I say.

Mafu sits on a stool at the kitchen island—he's impassive, watching the sun drown under the cerulean sky. Matt has his arms hugged to his chest. He's concentrated, yet still manages to display a jovial front.

"Truth is, the Angelics are spread incredibly thin. Our numbers are dwindling. A lot of this has to do with an influx of mercenaries, bounty hunters, and recidivist trafficking networks. Laws and alliances are rapidly changing because of the attack on Buford Elementary. We're noticing increases in shifting allegiances with people we once relied heavily on, even in states that are known to protect recidivist rights.

"The fight's more brutal than ever before. Leeanne's crew . . . their latest recruit was a trap set by a local network. Several died. They just barely managed to escape. So, when they arrive, expect them to take extra precautionary measures. Luck's running thin. We must be more careful."

"So, why here? Why in plain sight?" I ask.

"It's a lot easier to run our operation this way," Matt answers. "The last thing people would suspect is for an Angelic operation to be running amid so much activity. It's the perfect cover-up."

"You mentioned earlier Esther owns the Excelsior? How's that?"

Ambrosia opens her mouth to answer, but Atlas interjects.

"Can I?"

She gestures for him to continue.

"The CEO of LAM Resorts is Esther's father. He bought the Excelsior back in, what, 2006?"

Matt confirms this.

"Erwin knew his daughter was an Angelic when she was very young—of course, the laws on mandatory testing and patient confidentiality were much stricter then. Erwin had to pay millions of dollars in hush money to keep Esther's abilities secret.

"But he bought the Excelsior and lets Esther use it for secret Angelic operations. Essentially, it's like our own underground railway. She's in charge of aiding runaway recidivists and getting them safely to Proctus. So many of the workers here are people like us—Angelics with abilities they've hidden their entire lives."

"Precisely," Ambrosia cuts in. "Now you know. Be prepared for when Leeanne arrives."

"Thank you," I say.

"You should get some rest," says Matt.

The trio takes their leave, abandoning the rest of us to think about what they said.

"I'm gonna shower," Ezra says after a while.

"I'll go," Atlas sighs. "I'll see you tomorrow."

Ezra disappears around the bend after Atlas says his goodbye. I stay suspended, ruminating over all this new information, feeling the world crumbling and crashing down on my shoulders. We're so small in the grand scheme of things that this feels too much to handle. Water starts in the bathroom. His voice is soft, and inaudible at first, but when he repeats my name, my heart skips a beat. It sounds like a prayer.

"Conin," he says. "Can you come in?"

Chapter 47

Ezra

Steam swirls and sticks in a sheen of dew over the glass. The hot water cascades the length of my back, loosening the tension off my shoulders, traveling down and unknotting the deeply rooted aches. Regardless of how divine it feels, my heart is on fire.

There's the hesitant pattering of footsteps on granite tiles. I turn my back to the shower door, ass exposed, eyes concentrated on the granite before me and the showerhead above. My heart patters, patters, patters an inharmonious beat. At any moment, it'll burst out of my chest, present itself in all its bloody glory for Conin to see.

"Ezra? Is everything . . . okay?"

"Yeah," I say quickly. "Um—"

I want, no, I *need* his proximity, his closeness, the intimacy of our naked bodies. Someone to ease the staggering loneliness and quiet the thoughts that roar and roar and roar and won't shut up. If this is selfish, then so be it.

"Can you . . . come in?"

The soft rustle of clothes falling to the floor reaches my ears despite the rush of water. The glass door opens and shuts quietly. I stare at the wall, nerves shot to hell. My scars, my body, everything that I'm not, up for display—up for judgment. My arms wrap tight around my abdomen, grazing the foundation of scars healed long ago. Conin's dick is hard as he presses his stomach into the small of my back. There's a noticeable difference in height between us; I'm several inches taller, but Conin rests his chin perfectly near the nape of my neck. He kisses me softly, kindly, lovingly.

"Is this, okay?" he asks.

It's more than okay. It's all I ever wanted, but my insecurities claw and rake forward, loud and destructive in their approach. I attempt to quell them, beg for them not to ruin the moment. It requires every ounce of energy I have, but I manage. They're suppressed at the sidelines for now. This is okay. Conin wouldn't do anything I didn't allow him to.

"Yes," I whisper.

The shower sprays over us as Conin trails kisses down my neck. Spine-chilling, but warmth blooms after each contact.

"Can I kiss you?"

"Yes."

He turns me around, my ass planted on the tile wall. Conin kisses me fervently on the lips. They're soft and knowing, his grin magnificent as he carefully explores. It sugarcoats my mouth, imparting a lingering sweet tang.

Spray runs in rivulets off his wet curls. Conin searches for my acknowledgment, then leans in to press our mouths together again. They glue against each other—fitting perfectly in their interlocked embrace. I graze his tongue, peruse his teeth with my own. He groans, a deep noise from his belly. I press a finger to the soft bulge of his stomach. My eyes open in want for the invitation. He opens his own as well and leans his head back.

"C-can I?" I stutter.

"You like that I'm fat?" he asks as if he doesn't believe me.

"I love it," I say.

"Okay. Yes."

We're back to discovering our mouths and the directions they take us. My hand cups his belly, where wanting fingers press and feel this vulnerable part of him only I have permission to uncover. My fingers search for the skin, the tufted happy trail, the hair on his chest, and the spots that freckle it. Conin drinks in my image, my body, the scars that run up and down, twirl, and slash, the lacerations forever etched into my canvas.

Conin inches closer. His thumb brushes over a scar that gashes through my navel. I recoil. He reels back, watches me for permission. He won't hurt me. He couldn't ever do that. I tilt my chin up as an offering. He kneels, then presses his mouth on the scar, which memory is difficult to recall. I'm grateful for this.

"Your scars are beautiful, Ezra," he says.

They're painful reminders.

"I love them because they're a part of you. I love everything about you, Ezra Gray."

"I—"

"It's okay," he says quietly. "You don't need to say anything. Just tell me if I need to stop."

He tests the waters, exploring while I discover what feels okay, what's more than sublime, what I never want to do again. In the whirlwind of pleasure, I am oblivious to the dizziness settling in, and the heat amplifying it. I tell Conin and he smiles, then we wash each other of the dirt, blood, and grime from yesterday. He's tender and I reciprocate his attentiveness. Conin's all smiles, barely able to hold his glee. Once we're toweled off, naked and bare, Conin laces his fingers with mine and leads me to the bed.

We are canvases—our hands, the paint. In flushed pink strokes, we trail and brush in technicolor. Our hearts beat like metronomes, a rhythm that far outpaces any possible tempo: Vivaldi's *The Four Seasons*, calm then abruptly chaotic the next. I hear the trill of vibrato. The echoes of strings. The beginnings of a symphony. Call me dramatic, but I know the lyrics to my song now. I know what needs to be said. It's there, tipped on my tongue, ready to be sung.

Does he know? Can he hear them already?

We resume our expeditions across the planes of our figures. The sunlight wanes in the sky. Golden hour is upon us. The city, the Vegas lights. As the day transitions into night, I feel everything in me relax, and a sense of safety takes shape. The world around us falls asleep. We're masked in the dark and seen only by the eyes that matter. My heart thrums excitedly. The subtle luminescence from afar glows. It surges, flashes, and casts kaleidoscopic colors onto the sea of white and the paleness of our skin.

Conin traces a thin scar. He plants a kiss on my lips, displaying love along the laceration. I freeze as a phantom pain jerks awake a ghost of the past. Lukeman Gray's brutal hands and his belligerent stare. The insults rolled off his tongue as each became more natural than the last. Years and years of practice were evident in their creativity. They were the precursors of what came after. Thax's cruel blade and its unrelenting nature—the planes he destroyed—the innocence snatched and the sacrifices it had cost.

"Ezra? Do I need to stop?"

I blink.

"I can stop," Conin whispers in the dark.

I see his dull outline, the bleak edges, and make eyes only for Conin.

"Where are you?" he asks because he would know.

He always does.

"I was lost there . . . for a moment," I answer truthfully.

"I'm sorry," he mutters. The apology is sincere, broken with guilt. "I went too far, with your—"

"I'm happy you did," I say. The truth, again. "I never loved that part of myself. It feels ugly. Wrong. You made me feel *good*."

The pain or hatred might never go away, but right now, this is okay.

"I will never forgive them for what they did," Conin says, "and if I hurt you in any way—"

"You're not them. You're you. You love me and I . . . I love you, too."

His irises are glassy. He blinks the tears away and digs his nose against my flat chest. Conin plants his cheek there and a solitary drop splatters my tattered skin. I caress my hand through his wet hair, trying to exude every bit of love I can. There's that smile again. Progress.

"Fuck. I love you—"

And for a moment . . . for the briefest moment, all is right in the world.

How did we get here, Conin? From childhood friends to . . . what does this make us? Boyfriends? Are me and Conin boyfriends?

"Come here." He listens.

I find his mouth. He meets me halfway. For our first time, it's better than I could have ever hoped for. It's later in the night when we finally succumb to sleep. His heart is quiet underneath all this muscled flesh. Our limbs tangle. I dream of a boy with wild hair. I dream of his effervescent smile, the swing set in the sweltering sun, sweating ice cream cones in hand, and a future of limitless possibilities. Conin Bresshet—I dream of you.

CHAPTER 48

Conin

Nausea pins me to the slick chair I find myself in when the world takes shape. I'm pulled from the recesses of a pitch-black dark—my head pounding so excruciatingly tight, it's like I've been drugged.

I blink away the bright flash of a floodlight that overstimulates my senses. The beam forces my eyes closed; all I see is red. They sting every time I attempt to open them. The tap of boots sounds from a concrete floor, approaching, an ominous noise that makes my heart race. I try to break free. It's a futile attempt. Rope binds my hands to the chair frame and my ankles to the legs. Naturally, panic sets in.

"They're coming to," says a gruff, unfamiliar voice.

"Fetch Leeanne," someone else says.

Minutes, maybe hours pass. Where was I before this?

What happened?

Oh my god.

Ezra and I—we were in the penthouse suite making love . . .

And now we're *here*. Wherever here is.

Thank god I'm clothed. The fabric brushes against my skin as I shift to get comfortable. My wrists chafe against the rope. If it's true that Leeanne's here, why are we tied akin to prisoners? Hostages.

Next to me are the stirrings of other individuals. Ezra, Atlas, and the three Angelics that transported us to the Excelsior are here beside me, waking from the same binds, from the same drug-induced coma. Ezra is in the seat over. He blinks life into those special eyes, just as confused and dazed as I was.

"Co," he stammers.

"I'm here," I whisper.

I can't reach for him. I crave his skin, I want it, I need it to alleviate the fear of what's to come next. This isn't right. The Angelics wouldn't do this to us.

"We'll be okay," I say. "It'll be okay." I'm not sure if I'm placating him or myself. If anything happens to Ezra—

"You're awake. Good," croaks an older woman, voice hoarse from years and years of cigarettes. "I apologize for the sedatives, but they were a necessary precaution."

The woman approaches further, but my only thoughts are for Ezra, whose eyes betray the fear that must be wracking him from the inside.

"Don't touch us!" I yell.

She promptly stops.

"I'm sorry," she says.

She has a deep, ethereal red flow of hair that falls elegantly from her head, cascading off her white-clad shoulders. Her skin is a golden tan from countless hours in the sun, with matching green irises that pierce into anyone who dares to stare at her straight on—an imposing presence I respect, given the predicament we find ourselves in again.

"I'm Leeanne," she introduces. "As I'm sure Ambrosia has told you, needing to be unconscious for the trip to Proctus was crucial for secrecy. We, of course, do not want our enemies to know of our proper coordinates."

"We're in Proctus?" I ask.

"Yes."

"Why the binds, then?"

"Recidivists' reactions can be unpredictable."

"I don't have powers—"

"Bresshet, cut it out," Mafu grunts.

I suppress the rise in anger by biting my lips. Leeanne shrugs and then appoints Angelics to untie us from our ropes. There's an urge to run, rooted deep inside me, but that's shoved onto the backburner. I take a deep breath and exhale at a snail's pace—no need to be premature with my anger.

"Ambrosia, Mafu, Matt . . . you're free to follow Darcy and Malek to the briefing. The rest of you will be questioned. Precautionary measures," informs Leeanne.

If I hear that phrase one more fucking time, I'm going to lose my shit.

PART 3

PROCTUS

Chapter 49

Conin

The admissions process into Proctus is lengthy. Their security is no joke, and while I appreciate it, the questions feel like unnecessary probing after a while. The Angelic sitting on the chair opposite the metal table starts with the basics, dragging the questions on in a monotonous drawl. My patience dissolves the longer we do this.

"Full name, please."

"Conin Conroy Bresshet," I say and peer into the camera, watching my reflection stare back. "Is this necessary?"

They cast their gaze away from the clipboard and frown.

"Yes," then proceeds with, "Where are you from?"

"Ogden, Utah."

"Were you in school?"

Were. No longer.

"Yes. Ogden High," I answer, clipped.

They move down the line of questions with the tip of their pen.

"What year?"

"Senior."

"How old are you?"

"Eighteen."

They jot something down.

"Do you possess transcendental abilities?"

No mention of recidivists. No mention of the Angelics.

"No."

They jot another slew of words.

"Does the person you arrive here with possess transcendental abilities?"

"Yes."

"What's their name?"

"Ezra Gray."

"Relation?"

Relationship? What are we? We confessed our feelings for one another, said, "I love you," and even made love . . . so what does that make us? Partners? *Boyfriends?*

"He's my significant other," I settle on.

They quickly write that down, then move to the next question without hesitation. A blanket's been lifted, or a weight I hadn't realized was there, but it's suddenly easier to breathe. My stomach isn't churning like it was before. With such a prejudiced world, why wouldn't it be easier to be ourselves here?

Question after question after question. They become so mundane, so invasive, I have half the mind to flip the clipboard from the Angelic's hand and storm out of the room. I don't because they'd view me as hostile, and I'd rather not jeopardize our shot here, or Ezra's safety. I'm expecting another pointless question next when the Angelic mixes things up.

"How did you come in possession of the Glock-19 stashed in your backpack?"

The gun.

My things.

I don't have them.

Leeanne's crew must've stripped me of them when they discovered what my backpack contained. I can't imagine they'd want someone walking around with an unregistered handgun, would they?

"I stole it from a mercenary pursuing Ezra and me," I reply, brief, deliberate.

The Angelic finally looks up.

"Which mercenary?"

Were they not told?

"Mara Barclay, of the Barclay Network."

The Angelic blinks, then rapidly puts ink to paper.

"What happened?"

"She was apprehended by the Angelics in Eureka."

"Is this where you came into possession of the gun?"

Don't lie. Don't give them a reason not to trust me.

"No."

"Can you tell me what happened?"

"Is it pertinent information?" I ask sarcastically. "I'm sorry, I don't see how any of this is necessary."

"The more we know about you, the better," they say, yet elaborate no further. So, I reluctantly retell the story, from the encounter in the motel to the events on the highway. They write studiously in their notes, as if trying not to leave out a single detail.

"Alright, we're finished here. I'll pass you along to Katherine for orientation and room assignment. She'll give you back your stuff, but the gun will be held at Headquarters."

"Thank you," I lie and wait to be escorted out.

———◆○◆———

I'm led to a meeting room in the vast warehouse where the Angelics are keeping us. Neither Ezra nor Atlas have been seen since our interaction with Leeanne, which deeply unsettles me. The room's vacant when we arrive, and I'm told to sit down anywhere in the rows of fold-up metal chairs. These chairs remind me of the many times Mom and I were late to church, subject to sitting in the overfill for latecomers at the back of the hall.

I choose a seat at the back of the room, an eye on the only entrance and a solid wall behind me. I'm dressed in clothes I wasn't wearing in the suite. If memory serves me well, I wasn't clothed before succumbing to sleep—limbs twisted with Ezra's, his head propped underneath my chin. Next, we were in this warehouse, and I was clothed in a shirt and sweatpants kept in my backpack.

Ezra appears across the threshold, gaze transfixed on me. My worries dissolve at the sight of him. Atlas trails behind, seeming a little worse for wear.

"Are you okay?" I whisper to Ezra.

"I'm fine. You?"

"Yeah." I close the space for a kiss.

He wasn't expecting the move, so he and I get an awkward peck on the edge of the lips. His smile's coy, while I brush it off with some playful laughter. Atlas is dormant next to us, staring at the carpeted floor. I feel a sense of loss for him.

A lady enters. Her eyes pan from the front of the room to where our trio sits, as if she were expecting us to sit closer. I have no plans to satisfy any request to move, not while this wall is at my back. "Ah, I see you've all survived our extensive questioning," she says to brighten the room.

None of us laugh. Atlas looks as if he's seen a ghost. Ezra and I hold hands, myself watching her in reproachful disapproval. She grins awkwardly and moves for a chair, grabbing its back, then shuffles over to sit close. She clasps her aged hands above her kneecaps.

"I'm Katherine," she sighs, "but let's cut the pleasantries. You three have been through a lot. I'd rather not have you sit through another hour or two of orientation you'll be dreading the entire time. So, how about this? We get you some food, I'm sure you're starving. Then we'll take you to your assigned rooms so you can get settled. Here—"

Katherine groans and walks to the front, where she grabs three large packets. She returns and hands us each one. They're intimidating, binder-thick. Katherine nods gravely.

"You read these at your leisure. No rush, but these packets are an entire rundown on Proctus and its comings and goings. Do make sure you read them at some point, however. They are important.

"Alright. Let's get you fed and then show you where you'll be living during your time here in Proctus."

She tells us to wait here while she returns with food. It's another ten or fifteen minutes before Katherine arrives again with another Angelic in tow. They carry trays of food for each of us and hand them off, waiting in front of the room while we eat.

The food on our plates is fresh, which is surprising. Fresh-grown vegetables, cheese, and a nicely put-together sandwich. I'm finished in minutes. Ezra, on the other hand, eats half of what's on the tray, but I'm glad to see he's consumed something of substance.

"Finished?" Katherine asks.

"Yes, thank you," I say.

"Thanks," Atlas mumbles.

Ezra nods.

"Shall we show you to your places?"

She introduces the other Angelic: Bobby, who sports a long pixie cut in a vibrant purple, with faux gold glasses to match. They smile and wave, a gesture that eases some rooted tension since waking in the warehouse. When Ambrosia said we needed to cooperate, I didn't have sedatives and bonds in some warehouse in mind.

Bobby's assigned to Atlas. Me and Ezra, however, are with Katherine. We say strained goodbyes with Atlas before parting our separate ways. Ezra appears crestfallen, then tries to mask his expression with a more upbeat, positive one. I don't buy it for a second.

Katherine shuffles into a room housing our backpacks. She acts ignorant about the Glock's disappearance, but I decide it best not to pry any further. I suppose the gun isn't needed anymore, anyway.

The warehouse is near the location of the place we'll be staying, so we don't have much walking to do. We're on the main street at the heart of the town, passing through old brick buildings with a nostalgic feeling I love. It's homely, to a certain degree. Katherine rummages for the keys in her pocket and unlocks the door to a set of stairs leading up. We climb after her, the steps groaning beneath our feet, but the noise is comforting, in a way.

"You have the entire apartment to yourselves. It's a one-bedroom, newly renovated and furnished. Esther is ensuring we make every occupiable space feel new and homey."

A random surge of excitement blooms in my chest.

"Welcome home," Katherine says and unlocks the door.

Chapter 50

Atlas

Separating from Ezra and Conin incites an epiphany. When they walked away, my heart and body felt the magnetic pulse increase, begging to close the space between us. It's strange being apart from them now that they've remained a staple in my everyday life over the past week. And the worst part of this all?

I'm attracted to them both. No matter how hard I deny it, it's the irrefutable truth. I think I understand now, partially, what pa meant in the motel, proffering my big heart like it's no big deal. Because of that, I'm drowning in the demise of my emotional promiscuity.

Can you call this jealousy? Maybe. I've had my fair share of jealous plights, but nothing to this extreme. Conin and Ezra love each other. They're childhood best friends, so on top of their infatuation are years of history that I don't share. I'm scrambling for ways to cast the idea of them out of mind, but that frustration returns.

(God! When did I stoop this low? Pining after people I can't have?)

Watching Ezra and Conin kiss was even worse. I tried to act like it hadn't bothered me, playing the part of a flustered boy who was caught accidentally watching an intimate moment between two lovers. *Two* lovers. Would the idea of another partner be too much for them to fathom? The thought had certainly crossed my mind on numerous occasions. I've never been in one (a polyamorous relationship), but that's me, and I know it. It's just . . . particularly in Utah, a part of oneself that's deeply frowned upon. (I'm looking at you, Joseph Smith.)

There's a connection between us three and it's more than just the tether that keeps me bonded to Ezra. Imposing might ruin the friendship I think we've created over their time at the bunker. A week ago, I had no idea who these two were. Now, it's like . . . they've always been a part of my life. It's hard to imagine one where their friendships aren't valued. It would be nothing short of a miracle if Conin and Ezra felt the same.

Bobby taps me gently on the shoulder. I'm so engrossed that by the time we reach our destination, I can't remember why we're here. We're in front of a trailer home surrounded by a community of more trailer homes.

"I've been assigned here?"

Bobby's sheepish as they try to mask their discomfort.

"It's not glamorous," they say (truly the understatement of the century), "but this is where we pair, um . . . *lone wolves* with others so they're not on their own. See it as a buddy system—a means to have someone always watching your back."

Lone-*fucking*-wolves?

"You can just say people who don't have a family," I deadpan.

With them. A family with them, to clarify. Bobby turns paper-white.

"Um . . . yeah, I suppose you're right. You've been assigned a unit with several others. Let me introduce you to them," they mumble.

They knock on the trailer door. I count a minute before someone answers. Mafu's lean, yet broad, frame, looms on the other side.

"You've got to be kidding me," I groan.

My anger at him rekindles. With how high his eyebrows rise, he doesn't seem happy to see me, either.

"Hi, Atlas," Mafu says, as if our conversation from the other day hadn't played out at all.

"You have a family. Why are you here?"

Bobby's head whips in my direction with an incredulous glare, their mouth agape in mortification. They're probably trying to signal me to shut the hell up and right the fuck now.

"I had a . . . falling out," he says.

Bobby looks as if they wish they were anywhere but here.

Me too, Bobby. Me too.

Chapter 51

Ezra

Proctus has some getting used to. It feels like the real world but better, and far more inclusive. Smiling faces herald us wherever we go, and I can't help but sense a fakeness to them. Rich coming from me, the actual faux. The entirety of this place is a front. If I searched hard enough, I'd find weaknesses in the cracks, the crevices that threaten to expose them for what it truly is: a masquerade to distract these people from the outside world's threats.

Maybe I'm just paranoid.

On the next day, we're collected from our apartment and shown around what was once the town of Dunsmuir. Proctus is in northern California near Mount Shasta. Dunsmuir fell victim to one of California's many wildfires years ago. The entire town was evacuated, the outskirts burnt to the ground, but what remains is purely thanks to the Angelics' leader, Esther Brown.

She restored what could be salvaged, paying the local government millions of dollars in hush money, so no one would pry or give up their locale. Essentially, she bought the entire town. California is one of the more accepting states—Scarlet Letters aren't mandatory, but that doesn't completely abolish abuse or prejudice. Many have sought refuge in Proctus to get away from the constant vitriol, but there are just as many people from all over the country who have come to wipe away their past for clean slates.

Conin, Atlas, and I are amongst those people. And Conin, like others, is here because of family and loved ones they couldn't part with.

A rotund woman with a bob of red hair arrives to retrieve us. She was so unbearably congenial, that ripping both ears off so I wouldn't have to listen to her acute, upbeat falsetto any longer didn't sound half bad. Put a wrench through both my eyes while you're at it.

We follow the steps down to the street below our apartment building. Dunsmuir Avenue this early in the morning is devoid of human life, though I hear the echoes of voices from farther ahead and see the hint of canopies. The woman introduces herself as Sandra, then promptly leads us toward Town Hall, which happens to be on the same street as my and Conin's new apartment. Sequestered between an old pizza shop and the town's community center, the Town Hall is an unremarkable two-story brick and stucco building with a stone staircase leading to a set of glass doors. Sandra smiles at us, then gestures to follow her inside.

"Alright," she says while we trail after her into a small meeting room, "first we'll assign you occupations and then I'll have Matt show you around Proctus. He says that he was one of the Angelics to extract you from Eureka. Terrible what happened there."

Conin slaps me on the shoulder.

"You're frowning. Stop it," he whispers to me. Sandra doesn't take notice. I arrange my face into something hopefully impassive.

My fingers grip an imaginary bottle, an amber glass of tequila, and its phantom memory. The numbness creeps forward—the want solidified. Conin nudges me again gently and I reel myself back to reality, focusing on Sandra and the file she's just procured from somewhere. The hems of my long sleeve ride up, exposing scarred flesh, and I'm swift to lower them to the wrist.

Sandra opens the manila folder and leafs through its contents before settling on a select few pages.

"Ah, here it is."

Sandra taps a page. She drives her finger down the column, murmuring to herself.

"Mr. Gray," she says kindly, offering me a look. "How does horticulture sound?"

"Horticulture?" I question, vaguely familiar with the term, "What does that entail?"

"You would be cultivating our crops here at the fields. Tending to the fruits and vegetables, gathering them, proffering them to our sellers at the Shop. Would that be alright? We could use all the hands we can get."

"What are the other options?"

Sandra blinks, grins, and returns to the page. She lists off the occupations available, but they all sound as mundane as the last. I finally settle on horticulture and let bygones be bygones. Truthfully, I don't have the energy to argue, nor is it my right to. The Angelics have already done us a major service by bringing us here, despite my dilemma of facing a false sense of security. In an abrupt change of pace, Sandra turns her attention to Conin. Her mouth twitches, but she locks the smile into place. I'm partial to kicking her teeth in.

"Now, we don't allow significant others to hold the same position, so we'll have to assign a different job unless horticulture sounds interesting to you, in which case it's up to you both to discuss who will take what. But do any of the occupations I listed before strike any interest?"

Conin is silent for an uncomfortable length of time. I count the seconds in my head while he peruses the list Sandra passed over with obvious disinterest. He looks back, adjusts his position on the chair.

"I want a guard position," he says bluntly.

Sandra blinks with that persistent fake grin of hers.

"Come again?"

"I want a guard position," he repeats. "I want to do my part to protect Proctus."

My heart somersaults, soaring to the skies. I would do so many things to him right now if fucking *Sandra* wasn't in the room with us.

"Ah, well . . . I'm afraid it's too dangerous for someone without special abilities to take up a guard position. The liabilities . . . the repercussions. I'm sure you understand." She swallows.

"I've seen guards armed with guns man the walls! Are they recidivists with defensive powers? Not everyone possesses offensive abilities, you know—"

"We prefer not to use the term recidivist here. Angelic will do."

"My bad, I'm sorry. Who are the Angelics with the firearms, then?"

Guns are not something I believe in, but if it's one thing the past week has proven time and time again is that we need methods to protect ourselves, no matter how rooted in controversy or the dangers they've presented. Conin's seriously going to fight for this. It's only right that I let him, though the idea of his potential endangerment terrifies me from head to toe.

"They are indeed Angelics without offensive abilities. It is rather unorthodox for a normal individual to hold a guard position. It's simply for their safety," Sandra says, congenially.

"Bullshit," Conin says and there's fury in his azure blue eyes—fury I haven't seen in a while. Sandra's aghast. She sputters a few words, though nothing concrete, then purses her lips. Nothing can be said to placate a heated Conin. Good luck, bitch. I've tried.

"So, people are ostracized here, too? Love to see how things haven't changed. I'm not justifying the blatant xenophobia around the world, but I had believed Proctus would be different. I believed everyone here would be a unified front, not rooted in ableist ideologies. There are people here who have lost so much, who have sacrificed everything to ensure their loved ones' safety. People like me—without any powers of their own. I'm just as capable as those without the ability to attack. Give me the means to protect myself and I'll be just as effective as anyone else on the line. You have my word."

I could kiss him.

Get the hell out, Sandra.

She swallows again before standing.

"Stay here," she mutters. "I'll speak with the council. It's not up to me to decide, but I will ensure they consider your proposal."

Proposal. I almost scoffed.

She's out of the room in a blur before I press tight into Conin and kiss the ever-loving fuck out of his mouth. He groans, then sighs, but leans forward, my entire body aware of his presence. We part and he must see the wild hunger in my face as a mischievous glow sprouts over his own. I've been deprived of Conin romantically my entire life, the least we can do is kiss as if the world's going to end. In my defense, it very well might.

"Christ," he says under his breath.

"You and me. Tonight," I whisper.

Conin bites his bottom lip. His Adam's apple bobs.

"What the hell's gotten into you?" he asks.

"You," I say. "I don't think you understand what it means to be me. I don't like people, Conin. And I don't just mean that I hate people—"

"I know what demisexuality is, Ezra," Conin chuckles.

I'm not sure why I'm choosing here out of all places to discuss this with him—to lay my feelings bare on the table. We discussed it briefly after our first time having sex, but we were so caught up in the heat of the moment that there wasn't much I could say. Something's gotten into me, something good. A boost of confidence, maybe? Hopefully, Sandra will stay away for a little while longer.

"I know you do. What I'm saying is . . . there's been no one, not until you . . . and then, it's always been you." I don't know how to articulate this. I'm not as eloquent as Conin is. "Everything you've done since the night at the party . . . until now with not backing down on what you want, wanting to protect the people here . . . I love you so fucking much. Shit, you really make this impossible."

His stoic facade crumbles for a moment—a brief moment—before Sandra inserts herself into the room, Matt in tow. I hate this woman. Fuck you too, Matt.

She hands me the paperwork I'll need to begin my occupation, with the proper job description and the pay detailed toward the top. The Angelics have a currency exchange system in place here. Admittedly, this comes as a surprise. Sandra focuses on Conin and plants a faux smile onto her mouth, a smile that doesn't quite reach the rest of her face.

"I've expressed your interest to the council, and they told me they'll consider it. I'll inform you when a formal decision has been made, so in the meantime, just hang tight."

"Thank you," Conin says. His cheer is fake at best.

We exchange awkward goodbyes and then Matt leads us down the street, where we pass a small art museum masked as a storefront, a hardware shop, a hair salon, and a bar with a flamingo as its mascot. On the corner of the road at a three-way intersection is a pavilion claiming Dunsmuir to have the best water in the world. Matt veers us to the left down Cedar Street where the old police station watches our descent. I wonder if any of these businesses or buildings are still in use or if they've become homes for Angelics and their families.

"The police station has been converted to the guards' headquarters. Hopefully, we'll have you join us there soon, Conin," Matt says with a sheepish grin.

Conin lights up at this, chin held high.

Once we reach Sacramento Avenue, I peer to the right and notice a few other faceless buildings. Matt instead directs us left, where the town starts to show signs of people and activity. A small train yard aligns perpendicular to the row of buildings across the road—trees graze the landscape on climbing knolls, some burnt and withered away, others thriving underneath the scorching California sun.

We follow the trail of electricity poles and the crescendoing hubbub of a cluster of canopies, the ones I noticed earlier. Matt points at a coffee shop dubbed "The Wheel-house" that he says is still in business and acts as both a bar and a place to grab imported coffee. When we've joined the throng of Angelics, Matt introduces us to the Shop, a place where we can buy food, imported goods, and whatever else vendors offer that we may need. Conin appears genuinely interested, but all I feel is an overwhelming influx of conflicted emotions. I keep tight-lipped, proceeding with the tour as if I'm not suffocating on the spot. As if integrating back into a somewhat normal society isn't the most jarring experience I've ever gone through. And I only left the world I knew behind eight days ago.

We're shown the high school, which serves as a house of education for all grades and ages. The gardens are nearby and they're genuinely impressive. Trellises of tomatoes and a plethora of fruits and vegetables in garden beds stretch on and on. A tiny, miniscule part of myself wants to believe that working in horticulture won't be so bad.

Finally, we're led up a winding road that passes a cafe converted into food storage, what was once a boutique, another bar, and a tattoo shop. There's a hotel that houses Angelics, a theater across the street Matt says is still in working order, and a library just up the road a bit. Conin asks if we can go inside to have a look around.

"Well, I suppose this is where we can conclude your tour. You're free to roam now if you like. In case you need me, I'll be at Headquarters." Matt waves, leaving us to explore an unfamiliar town.

Conin looks like a kid on Christmas, grateful he still has book access. His palpable excitement rubs off on me. He and I enter the scant space, brimming with an array of all sorts of titles and spines.

"I love it," he says, then instantly absconds to peruse the collection.

After a while, there's a shuffle of someone entering the library. I turn to see Atlas MacPherson in the flesh. There's that tug, the tether acknowledging the arrival of the person I'm bound to. I have the sudden desire to draw myself close, to wrap my arms around him, to claim him and call him mine. I blink and he's hovering above me with a wide, jovial grin.

"Fancy finding you here," he says, and my heart skips a beat, leaping out of my chest.

What the hell? When did that happen?

Conin joins us and we pick a table at the far end of the library. There's tension in Atlas's shoulders, the way he constructs himself, and the mechanical twirl of both his thumbs. Up and down, up and down, up and down.

"So, which occupations were you assigned?"

"I challenged the council for a guard position," Conin says. Atlas's eyes widen.

"No way. How did that go?"

"Well . . . not great. Sandra said she'd pass the proposal along to the council and would get back to me on their decision."

"Damn," Atlas sighs. "That was really cool of you."

Conin's smile is breathtaking. He truly does seem pleased with himself. Ecstatic is one of the words I'd use to describe this feeling inside me.

"Horticulture. I'll be working in the gardens."

"Shut up!" he exclaims, pounding his fist.

The librarian hushes him.

"What?" I ask.

"I've been assigned horticulture, too!"

Conin's upturned lips falter for a brief second before he corrects them. I decided, instead, to redirect the conversation elsewhere—his sudden change in mood is stifling.

"Would you like to come see our apartment?" I ask.

And so, we show him around. He's particularly vocal about his jealousy and complains all about the trailer home he shares with Mafu and some other guys. But I'm no longer listening, no longer paying attention to his words. My eyes are transfixed on Conin. His expression is unreadable, his emotions tucked underneath all the barriers he's erected to protect himself. I'm not sure what I find, but whatever it is . . . it doesn't sit well with me.

Chapter 52

Conin

Ezra has his feet lounged over my lap when a knock comes at the door.

"I got it. Relax," I say.

There's some awkward navigating and untangling, which feels oddly reminiscent of being in a relationship with him—almost like I have no idea how to act when we've been friends our entire lives. I love him, though, so these baby steps and the awkward fumbling are entirely worth it.

Sandra's returned, but this time with a grim expression. My hope crumbles, any chance for a position with the guard subdued.

"Well, the council has collectively come up with a decision," she says, disgruntled.

"And?" I question, matching her energy.

"The Council has granted you clearance to become a guard, but with conditions. You'll need to speak with them on Wednesday morning. Ambrosia will then meet with you to go over the ropes. Make sure to be at the police station at 8 a.m.," Sandra tells me.

She's made it abundantly clear that she doesn't approve.

"They were impressed . . . with what you had to say. Make a good impression, okay?"

She departs with a smirk, bidding us farewell before climbing down the stairs. No matter. Elation overcomes me when I shut the door. Ezra's tall, lean form stands near the coffee table, his face fixed into a broad smile.

"You heard?"

"Yeah," he says.

I'm more satisfied I won my case than anything else. This goal wasn't long sought out, but it feels right. And seeing Ezra, hair out and loose, with a beaming smile that matches how I feel inside, I could kiss him until our lips grow sore. He crosses the distance between us with four long strides, grabs the nape of my neck, and presses his mouth firmly on mine. We kiss and stumble, finding our footing on the laminate wood floor.

Ezra bumps the coffee table, emitting a tiny chuckle with a breathy "Ow" before I playfully push him onto the couch. His long limbs spread out, bangs over his forehead, his cloak of hair draping over the couch's arm. He stares up, one blue eye, the other green—filled with twinkling stars—I almost lose myself in them, in the distant galaxies they create.

"You okay?" he asks.

No. But right now, with him? I think I will be. Eventually.

It's better with him.

It somehow always is.

I lean down and kiss him.

An indeterminate amount of time later, our clothes pile in heaps on the floor.

⋅•◦•⋅

Ezra's chest is firm, our naked bodies flush against each other. He strokes my hair and breathes warmly on my ear. We stay like this for a while, silent, the only noise our breathing lungs. His beating heart is in unison with mine, a reminder he's alive. We're both alive despite everything we've been through. Despite all odds.

But something's been gnawing at me since we made love for the second time. I don't want to ruin this moment he and I created, so it's better to stow it away for some other time. As always, Ezra senses a thought troubling me. Like how I can sense when something's off with him, he seems to have honed that ability, too.

"Where are you?" he asks.

"Did you mean it? When you said you were okay with me kissing your scars?" I question, cutting right to the chase. The quiet before he answers lingers for a beat too long. I screwed this up, didn't I?

But a small part of me, a tiny part of me, feels as if he's lying for my sake.

"Of course I did. I do. It's you."

"Sure, but—you're not just saying that, right? It's okay if it's not, Ez. I'll stop."

Ezra ponders what I've said for a little while longer.

"I'll tell you if it ever becomes too much," he whispers.

"Okay," I say, taking whatever solace I can from his words.

"And what about you? What about me, uh, touching your stomach?"

"I don't think about it that often. Yeah, I don't have a six-pack anymore, so I guess sometimes it feels bad . . . like I didn't care enough to maintain it—that I was too lazy."

Ezra looks a bit sad, but most of what flashes across his face is guilt.

"I'll stop," he says.

"You like that I'm chubby?"

"Yes, Co, I like that you're chubby. I *love* it. I think it's cute, sexy—"

His affirmations feel good. Genuinely good.

"And?" I joke.

"Do you have any of those fancy words you know that are synonymous with sexy?"

"Provocative? Voluptuous? Titillating?" I say seductively.

He gasps, "Don't you ever fucking say that word again. I hate it!"

"What? Titillating?"

"Ew!" he screeches. "Gross! Get off me!"

He shoves me off with faux disgust and bursts away to our bedroom, his bare ass disappearing behind the door. I chase after him and try for the handle, but it won't budge. Ezra's locked it, leaving me ass-naked in our living room. I pound on the door, bursting out in an uncontrollable fit of laughter.

"Let me in! I'm naked!"

"Your clothes are next to the couch, you fiend!" he yells.

Good point.

I pound on the door again.

"Let me in!"

"As long as you promise me that you'll never say that word again!"

In my mind, my fingers are crossed.

"I promise!"

"Fine."

He cracks the door open to reveal his strikingly gorgeous self, all loose hair and piercing eyes.

"Can you and I lie down again for a bit?"

"Sure," he concedes.

Together, we lie on the bed and find a comfortable position where skin touches skin.

"I love you," I say.

"I love you, too," he says.

"Promise me you'll tell me if I do anything that makes you uncomfortable. If I trigger you?"

"Of course. Can you promise me that, too?"

"I promise," I say.

It's a Wednesday in mid-October and the sun is peeking over pine-infested knolls. Main Street is alive with early goers beginning their days and the scent of freshly baked bread wafts, then lingers in my nose. I walk in the middle of the road, devoid of any car or vehicle, taking in the sites and the historic brick buildings. The Angelics have a nice setup. Perhaps I was rather harsh and overprotective these past days, but one can never be too careful, considering what we'd gone through to get here.

I pass the pavilion, finding a red brick-and-mortar building with rows of windows and white framing. Matt and Ambrosia wait out front with a man I've yet to meet. He's all broad, toothy smiles as I approach, suddenly putting me back on the defensive. Regardless, I switch the apprehension to a mask resembling something cheerful as if I'm grateful for the chance to be offered a position that shouldn't have been withheld from me on the basis of prejudice in the first place.

Has anyone without special abilities fought for the chance to be a part of the Angelic Guard? I can't be the only one.

"Conin, meet Brett Rosenbaum. He's head councilman of Proctus," says Ambrosia in place of a greeting.

"Conin Bresshet, so nice to meet you," Brett says, all white teeth as he extends a hand for me to shake.

I reach out, hoping he doesn't see my timidness. If he does, Brett says nothing at all.

"Nice to meet you."

"Do you mind if I tag along while Ambrosia and Matt here give you a tour?" he asks.

Why?

I thought we were going to talk.

"Sure," I say. "I don't mind at all."

"Wonderful. Shall we?"

The four of us enter what was once Dunsmuir's police station, now converted into headquarters for the Angelic Guard. We're greeted by a receptionist behind plexiglass and a hallway with checkered linoleum flooring. Ahead is a four-way intersection with a hallway cutting through that leads to rows of other rooms and temporary holding cells, but we proceed forward, where a staircase leads to the basement.

They store their armor, weapons, and whatever else is needed to protect the walls in the basement. Proctus's walls are indeed impressive. They span the entirety of the safe haven's borders, consisting of metal and steel structuring.

The walls aren't a dead giveaway, as opposed to my earlier belief. A protective magical barrier encompasses Proctus like a half-globe. It was conjured by Benji, one of the Angelic's own, years ago. It masks Proctus under its spell, projecting fields of barren wasteland and crumpled buildings behind a barbed wire fence that tells any curious onlookers not to trespass. I've heard of close encounters in the past, but the Angelics have generally been able to handle the problems.

There are locker rooms where they house their armor and personalized weaponry. We proceed to the armory, with industrial shelves stacked with guns, ammunition, and other medieval weapons. I'm not sure why they have them, nor do I ask, but no one explains, as if the sight of them is normal.

Some presumably more dangerous, high-tech weapons are locked up behind cages. Several safes are off to the side, one stacked over the other. Ambrosia tells me that only Angelics with special clearance can access these weapons. I nod because this is normal. This is what I signed up for. There's no reason to give them an excuse to strip me of this position before I've even had the chance to start.

"Alright, well that concludes your tour!" Matt says enthusiastically. "We'll give you the rest of the day off but come here again tomorrow so we can go over your shifts and begin your training."

"You'll be training with me," Ambrosia says.

"Okay." She's reclusive and closed off. It'll be interesting training with her.

"Conin," Brett whispers, "can you and I chat for a second?"

He pulls me aside to a vacant room down the way. He shuts the door behind him and folds his arms, a smile still spread wide across his face.

"Was that too overwhelming?"

"No, sir, I'm excited to get started."

Brett considers me a moment.

"Those were some inspiring words you said to Sandra the other day. And I think you're right. I think we should allow anyone here to join the guard if it's what they truly want, with or without powers."

I nod.

"No one's put up a fight like you have. Keep up that fire, okay? Welcome to the Angelic Guard," Brett says, that smile not faltering for a second.

"Thank you," I mutter.

Minutes later, when I'm out of the headquarters, I find my feet carrying me beyond our new apartment. Thoughts start to cycle in me: everything from those blissful moments with Ezra to the fake charm all these Angelics try to exude. Someone calls my name.

"Conin, hey!" Atlas greets.

He jogs to catch up, all grins and gorgeous brown eyes. His smile is contagious. Woe is me.

"Hey, how are you?"

"Ah, well . . . not sure I'm digging the trailer home arrangement with the other family-less guys, but I suppose it's better than nothing. Just got off my first shift at the gardens and got to see Ezra there. I think he's back at your place. What are you doing here?" Atlas says so quickly, it's a struggle to keep up with his train of thought.

"Uh, not sure," I confess.

"I was about to head to the library. Wanna come with?"

Do I? I think I do. Why do I want to, so badly?

"Sure," I say.

He leads the way and my heart trips over itself.

Chapter 53

Ezra

The first few days on the job are strenuous work. I underestimated the effort put into gardening and how out of shape I was. It's somewhat enjoyable, like I'm making a change with work integral to feeding the citizens of Proctus. Like I've finally done something useful in all this—for once pulling my weight, instead of cowering behind others.

Atlas and I take lessons together, though we'll be partnered up after our training, once we have a handle on the fields' operations. Neither of us has any prior horticultural knowledge, which must be irksome for the Angelic conducting our training lessons. After each eight-hour day, Atlas vents his clear frustration with their teaching methods.

"I'm not a quitter," he said when I asked why he didn't just seek out another occupation, which I didn't want. Not at all. "Besides, you make the job worth it." He winked. I melted on the spot into gelatinous goo.

And how my heart *soared*.

The time came for us to receive hands-on training, so naturally, Atlas and I were paired as newcomers under the supervision of a seasoned Angelic. Ofa was Mafu's older sister. She arrived at Proctus years before Mafu did, according to Atlas, who was once good friends with them both. The details of their falling out are foggy from there, leaving lots to the imagination.

We learned to garden, harvest, and manage the crops. When Ofa left us to our devices, Atlas would strike up a conversation with a friendly cadence, an ease that could fool anyone into thinking we'd been friends for a long, long time. I *reveled* in it. Our conversations sent my heart tripping over ghostly obstacles I couldn't best.

We would talk and talk and talk about everything. It stemmed from *Star Wars* and branched into every aspect of life, discovering our mutual love for *Sleep Token* and music in general, to our hopes and dreams and aspirations—a future so bleak and unobtainable, nothing but a dream. I urged him to inquire about a teaching position, somewhere he could start simply by teaching younger students.

However, with his tutoring experience, there was confidence he could do so much more. He beamed when I told him, casting careful glances my way that became sloppier as the day wore on. He was not discreet. Maybe a part of him wanted me to see. Every time I caught his eye, I'd trip over again, covering the upward tug of my mouth like I was wiping perspiration off my top lip. That damn grin was glued to my face for the remainder of the day.

We cast secret glances, smirked through the foliage and tomato vines. He'd brush up against me and my body would ignite, flame and embers spreading everywhere. I was afraid they'd be visible for the world to see. Atlas made me forget. He made me forget the bad and the ugly, the evil and the dangers of the world outside Proctus—the life I had left behind. He shared stories of his childhood and adventures with Ambrosia, Mafu, and Matt when they were younger. Atlas would trail his abuelo everywhere. He told me how his family came to settle in Eureka, falling in love with the small-town life, the abandoned ghost towns that littered the area and land around them, and how his abuelo would take him to every one until they had explored each bend and crevice.

The day his abuelo died, Atlas could no longer feel his presence. It was painful that he was constantly reminded of his abuelo's passing—when Angelics who knew him or were helped by Augurys's operation approached Atlas to thank him or offer condolences. Their tokens of gratitude were another mnemonic that he had failed to continue the legacy.

Tears welled in his brown eyes. I clung to him and let him grip my shirt. We sat in secret amongst the evergreens enshrouding the high school. He understood the tether with his abuelo to be a familial bond, but the one between us was unexpected, unfamiliar. He thought to ask Ambrosia and said he would, but getting my hopes up wouldn't do any favors, so I masked the brewing worries with careful nonchalance. Atlas saw right through that facade. I was getting lazy with my poker face.

Repaying in kind, I told him of the time Conin and I first met at the park beneath the sweltering sun with ice cream cones, the stories about my violin, how it was my most prized possession, and recounting the drastic moment Lukeman Gray shattered it into bits and pieces. I told him about Thax, the strained relationship with my mom, her detached submissiveness, but of her instincts to patch me up—about Conin, Conin, Conin.

Doubt trickles in, pitting in my stomach, craving my attention. Conin and I are happy. We're *finally* together, so why does that pit feel like a never-ending hole? It craves more, but I can't give it more, because I don't know what *it* wants. Conin's filling it, but not completely, and that terrifies me.

What the hell is happening?

"When did you fall in love with him?" Atlas questions me one day. We're sequestered between a bed of potatoes and a line of evergreen trees. His expression is indiscernible and he's just as stoic as Conin is. A good chunk of the garden is in the high school's track field. Students run around its perimeter on the asphalt. I can't help but feel they're watching us, judging, waiting for the inevitable.

"A long time ago, I think. I, uh, didn't realize then I was demisexual, but I knew without a doubt Conin was the one. I never thought he'd reciprocate those feelings."

"I think he's always loved you too," Atlas says with a knowing grin. "From what I observed."

He chuckles, magnetizing me with his infectious mirth. We cultivate the potatoes, placing them roughly into a wicker basket at our side.

"So, when do I get to hear you play the violin?" he asks.

"Never," I say.

He's crestfallen or it's a ruse, but I'm rushing to tell him that I promise I will, I'm a bit rusty, I was only joking because I'm a sarcastic little—

"You were being sarcastic," Atlas says.

"Yeah."

"Well, stop it. I'm serious. I want to hear you play."

Soon, I promise. He nods, content and satisfied, and returns to his work.

I picked up the violin again a mere few days ago. Conin said he discovered through the grapevine that two Angelics in the community were offering lessons. Instruments were limited, but there were several slots still open. I hopped onto the opportunity immediately.

Sometimes you don't realize how much you miss something until you lose it. The thrill of the violin underneath my chin, its long, curved frame reaching my extended arm, and the scintillating sensation of the strings brushing against my cuticles. I missed it all, from the upkeep to its sweet trill. The notes resonated far after I released the bow.

The ebony instrument was back in my possession, I was attending lessons again, and life felt okay. Somewhere along the way, lyrics popped into my head again—the same song I'd been testing the waters with before shit hit the fan. Turns out, a relationship isn't the cure-all for life's obstacles. The words were difficult to come by still but committing them to a blank page felt more attainable than ever.

A week later, Conin left on a shift with the Angelic Guard. He kicked off training and returned each day with palpable enthusiasm. I'd smile, kiss him full on the lips, and snuggle with him on the couch or in our bed, where we'd drift peacefully to sleep. Pride welled in my heart, geared my mouth upwards into an unabashed smile that couldn't easily be negated. Conin would beam back, rake his fingers down my hair, and tell me with familiar persistence that he should tie it into a bun again before he became rusty. I let him every time.

"I'm so proud of you," I'd say. He'd kiss me until my lips grew numb.

Now, he is away for guard training, and I am home alone, left with a brain full of thoughts and a stringed instrument waiting to be played. I pick it up. The strings are familiar, the weight of the bow a comfortable reassurance. I raise it to the tip of the frog, then swipe down with an elegant thrust. My index finger wobbles, emitting a smooth vibrato, which hums deep into my hands, traveling upwards. The sound settles in my ears and brain. It is alive, alive, alive. I am alive. Familiarity washes over me, taking me to wherever it pleases. And finally, unprecedentedly, a knock sounds on the door.

The knock tells me to freeze, so I do. The violin is set down.

With pent-up anxiety, I amble toward the front door, willing for the knocks to recede and for whoever is behind the entrance to go away. Instead, more come. I sigh, grip the handle, and pull it open.

Atlas MacPherson stands over the threshold.

The first thing he says to me is, "I heard you."

My face heats, but it also feels like all the blood's been drained out of me.

"You sounded amazing," he says next. "Can I come in?"

"S-sure," I reply.

Atlas slips in and takes in the interior of our apartment, which he's seen plenty of times before. He sidles up to the violin placed on the glass coffee table. I watch to see if he'll pick it up. He doesn't.

"I thought you were some neighbor coming to tell me to keep it down," I say.

"If I were your neighbor," Atlas smiles, "I'd tell you to play all the fucking time."

"Oh."

"I went to the library to meet Conin for book club, but he never showed. I thought I'd come to check if everything was alright."

My heart deflates. Embarrassingly, I had hoped he had come to see me.

"He had to pick up a shift," I say.

"Oh, well. Fancy seeing you here."

It picks back up, performing somersaults upon somersaults. A quick beat of silence. Then, "Play me something," Atlas demands.

"I—" don't want to.

"Please! I won't judge. I promise. I just want to hear your prowess."

For fuck's sake.

"Fine."

With the violin back in my clutches, the rest cups my chin, and then the bow finds my fingers. I hold the horsehair near the frog for longer than necessary. Atlas watches with patience, eyes lit with childlike enthusiasm. He awaits the performance of a lifetime, and I fear I'll subvert his expectations. Burn them to the fucking ground. It's not a big deal. I take steady breaths. He waits, smiling, patient, attentive. I stroke the bow down and the beginning notes of John Williams' "Across the Stars" resonate through the tiny apartment. Atlas's smile could brighten the world.

The prelude swells into the dramatic chorus. I cast a brief, wary glance at Atlas, whose eyes are wide with wonder, mouth agape. Jolts of pleasure shoot up my spine, striking my heart in its epicenter. The surge to play more powerfully, to show Atlas everything I have overcomes me. I use our tether to hold on to him, making it impossible for him to let go. Every ounce of energy is put into the vibrato when the outro arrives, echoing far after I've concluded the piece. He stares in awe. My heart pounds frivolously against my chest, threatening to break through blood and bone, muscle and sinew. The butterflies are out of control.

"*Wow*," he mutters. He's breathless. I have that effect on him. *Me.*

"So?" I question and look at him without looking at him.

Wow could mean anything.

"You memorized it?" he chokes on his words.

"Yeah."

"Of course you did."

Atlas stands. There's a slight tremor in his knees.

"Was that for me?" he asks, but I can barely hear him.

"Yes," I say.

And it's the truth.

The press of his lips is soft against mine.

Fireworks erupt from our bated breaths.

He grips the bridge of the violin and pulls it from my grasp. There's no space between us, but he parts his mouth, searches deep into my eyes. It's agonizing. My lips open in expectation. I don't object, I only stare, only wait for him to kiss me again. And he does. It's wonderful, otherworldly, perfect.

A wave of panic crashes over me.

Atlas breaks away quickly. Horror laces his expression and the wide curvature of his eyes. My heart's descent causes whiplash as it drops deep into the earth.

"Oh my god," he whispers.

"Atlas—"

"Oh my god," he says again, "what the hell have I done?"

"I kissed you back," I say, uselessly.

"What the hell have I done?" he repeats as if he could take back what he just did. What I reciprocated.

"Conin—" and the words are lost.

Conin.

I—did I cheat on him? Have I betrayed him? Would he understand? Would this be okay for him? Would he allow it? Does he feel the same?

"Ezra, I'm so sorry."

"I–it's okay."

"No, it's not. I don't want to ruin what you and Conin have."

"It's okay," I say. But I don't know if it is. I don't know if I believe it. All I know is that I love Conin, but there's obviously chemistry between Atlas and me.

"This isn't how I wanted you to find out. I shouldn't have done that to you."

I kissed back.

"Find out what?"

"That I like you. And that I like Conin."

"Oh." *Oh. OH.* "Have you two—"

"No," Atlas quickly interjects.

"So, you're—"

"Yes."

"Oh."

"I'm sorry, Ezra."

"It's alright," I say because maybe it is. "I think I am, too."

"You are?"

"Yeah. I believe so."

"Well, shit," he says, breathless.

"Shit," I say.

One second, two, three.

"What now?" he asks.

"This," I answer.

I pull him close. Our bodies flush hot near each other. The kiss I give him is a promise: soft, subtle, warm.

Maybe this is okay.

Maybe we will be alright.

Chapter 54

Conin

"**F**ancy seeing you here," Atlas says.

He says this every time we meet. I find the starts of a giggle lodging in my throat and the eruption of tingling nerves along my skin every time—without fail. A magnetic force gravitates me toward Atlas, almost like a tether binds him and me together like it does him and Ezra.

There's his undeniable charm everyone loves him for, and when I say everyone, I quite literally mean *everyone*. He knows every Angelic already, although that could be because of his abuelo's operation. Regardless, a bevy of beaming, enthusiastic people are always surrounding him. A thimble of jealousy lodges itself in my stomach to the point where I can feel an irksome itch in my bones, a sprouting annoyance I have no means of stopping.

But when Atlas is with Ezra, that clawing plight dissipates. It feels right that they're in each other's orbit. I'm far less ill at ease when I know they're working together or when I come home from Headquarters and they're sitting on the couch in an animated conversation. Ezra lights up the room when Atlas is in it and perhaps I should feel jealous, but I don't.

My heart is full and it's not only because of Ezra. It's because of Atlas, too. If Ezra knew, would he understand? Would he feel the same way?

Atlas plops this week's book club pick on the table. He sighs and leans back in the chair, getting comfortable since we've become regulars.

"I didn't like it," he says, exasperated.

"Boo," I say and take a sip of my coffee. "Why not?"

"I just don't know how I feel about a cisgender man writing the experiences of an intersex character, no matter if it is fictional. Though, at the same time, I acknowledge we need more stories about intersex people, as they're often the most repressed in the queer community. God, I'm conflicted."

"Wow, okay," I mutter. "I didn't think that deeply about it."

"I still don't understand why you keep reading these books with me when I'm nothing but overcritical," Atlas laughs. I giggle alongside him, then thumb through the book's pages.

"I don't know. It's fun. I like to hear your never-ending rants."

"They are never-ending," he concedes. "You're never able to get a say."

"And I'm perfectly fine with that."

"Any other thoughts on the book?" I question. He'd normally be lost in a full-on tirade by now.

"Nah. I think I was mostly disappointed. How about you?"

He's not invested, not how he usually is. At this point in our conversation, Atlas would be fully engaged in his analytical ways, but he's not. He's distant.

"I approached it from a more technical aspect, which—"

Atlas rolls his eyes.

"Which you told me not to do, but you know me. I'm a writer."

"Yes, that you are," he says. "And that's fine. The author does have some beautiful prose in there."

"Yeah, he does!"

Atlas leans in, resting his elbows on the table, and clasps his hands together. "Anything that stood out to you in particular?"

"No, but it's like you said. His prose is great. I tried studying to see what techniques I could implement in my own writing."

"How's that going, by the way?"

"I've finished the first several chapters, but I think I'll go back and touch up on the outline before continuing any further."

"Nice! I hope that goes well."

"Thanks. I do, too."

Atlas's pupils dilate and his lips curve upwards. A pleasant burgundy flushes his cheeks, his eyes crinkling behind his spectacles. His entire person gravitates toward me. I reciprocate his cordial smile after discreetly catching my breath.

"I'm glad we're still doing this," he whispers.

"Me too," I say.

"And I'm glad I ran into you that day."

"Me too."

After my conversation with Brett, and running into Atlas near the library, I followed along without question. There were two copies of a book he'd waited to read for a while. He'd asked if I'd be willing to read along with him. My mouth agreed before my brain realized what I'd done. The next time we visited, Atlas proposed a book club. I just wanted to spend more time with him.

The way he's speaking, and the way he looks at me, makes me wonder if I'm missing any cues here. I sift through everything he's said to me, attempting to find the hints underlying each word. He stares at me longer, his grin fading. "I should go," Atlas says, standing.

"What?" I stumble. "Is everything okay?"

"Yeah," he says, though his reply is not convincing. "Sorry, I remembered Mafu invited me to a game night tonight."

I sometimes forget he and Mafu were childhood friends, given how cold he acts toward others. That, and they haven't been on the best of terms lately.

"Sure," I say. "Have fun. See you Tuesday?"

"Yeah," he mumbles, offers a weak grin, and hurries out of the library.

◈

Ezra's fingers brush through my curls. He's acting as the big spoon because of the several inches he has over me, but I can't complain. It's soothing, wrapped in someone's arms for once, protected and safe.

The sun's gone down and moonlight drifts through the blinds, casting us in its milky glow. Ezra tells me about his day and the projects the horticultural supervisors have given them to accomplish. He drones on and on about plants and vegetables, the music he's learning in his lessons, and how Ofa is constantly hovering over his shoulder. He doesn't mention Atlas once. I haven't confronted Ezra about him yet. That would lead me to confess feelings that aren't ready to see the light of day, but the absence of Atlas in this conversation doesn't help my suspicions.

The avoidance almost confirms them.

"Are you okay?" Ezra asks when my silence has dragged on for too long.

"Yeah," I say. Sleep threatens to pull me under, its arms cradling my tired consciousness.

Time. I need more time to figure out what I'm going to say and when.

"If there's something on your mind, you can tell me. You don't need to be afraid to open up to me and talk about your emotions," he says.

"I know, Ez. I'm just tired."

"I don't want you to be the only one carrying this relationship. I want to do my part, too. Be there for you when you need it."

"Thank you, love."

The sheets rustle, followed by the tender placement of his lips on my cheek. Minutes later, he's dead to the world. I consider what he told me, but he and I are at an impasse. He must have his suspicions, too.

I'm not ready to tell him, but I have to figure out something before we crash and burn.

Ambrosia pulls me aside in the locker room, the second the Angelic emblem clasps to my chest. The wings are weightless, which continues to surprise me. On my second day with the guard, Matt told me that their armor suits consist of nanotechnology, courtesy of Esther's father and his endless stream of cash.

Ambrosia snaps her finger in irritation.

"You've been distracted lately. Is everything . . . fine?"

"Yeah. Sorry."

She peers at me skeptically, but it's back to business with her.

"Leeanne informed me of a supply mission her crew can't make with our private distributor. She tasked the Eureka group to fulfill it—"

"The Eureka group?"

"Everyone in Eureka that day who helped fight off the Barclay's mercenaries. I told her how you handled yourself with Levi. Leeanne was impressed," Ambrosia says.

Normally, I might've preened over the praise. "Listen. I want you to come on the run. This could be a good training exercise—get you a feel of what we're tasked with sometimes."

"Sure," I say.

But on the inside? I'm rattled to my core.

Going out on a supply run potentially means leaving Proctus's borders and leaving Ezra and Atlas—

So, Atlas has crept in there now.

No wonder I've been distracted.

Ambrosia leads me to the armory. My HK-47 hangs suspended on the wall at the far corner, locked until I type in the specific code assigned to me. Her gaze is nothing but cold disapproval. Ambrosia vouched for me to join the guard, but maybe she's starting to regret her decision.

The HK slides from its clasps and into my gloved hands. I stand there for a moment, maybe a moment too long, to cover the tremors.

Ambrosia looms behind me.

"Is this going to be a problem, Conin?" she asks.

"Is what going to be a problem?" I say, dubiously.

"I've noticed your hesitancy with a gun in target practice. Is having one on your person going to be an issue?"

Of course she noticed.

"No."

"Are you sure? I can't have you freezing up out there."

"I promise it won't be."

"You'll tell me if it does become a problem?"

"Yes."

She assesses me again.

"Good, let's go."

Dread comes rushing back in waves.

Chapter 55

Conin

The van bounces along the winding boreen. The road worsens the farther we go, instilling trepidation in my chest that can't be placated. The farther the distance from Ezra, the more that fear grips me. Distancing from Atlas is certainly not helping, either.

"I thought you said you didn't know Proctus's location," I say, exuding some of Ezra's signature sarcasm.

"It wasn't a lie," Matt admits sheepishly. "There's miles and miles of dead trees and forest. Without a GPS or signal, it's easy to get lost."

"Besides, Ambrosia's the only one here with the coordinates," Mafu says. He chuckles.

I turn to her, peeved. She doesn't seem perturbed at all. "Why aren't you a part of Leeanne's elite, then?"

Ambrosia ponders this question for a minute.

"Because I didn't want to be. I wanted to be where Matt was," she replies.

I wondered. Matt's face flushes.

"And I grew up with these guys. We know each other well, and work great together as a team."

"Wait, okay. How do you know the coordinates and no one else does?"

"Esther's my aunt," she deadpans.

Shocker. I stare at her dubiously, but no one denies it. Instead, the van hits an uncomfortable patch of road. The mountainous area is dead, void of civilians and cars. What turns out to be an additional half-hour stretches to feel longer, but we arrive at last, and at a warehouse no less. Next door is a rusted, abandoned gas station and an old cottage down the way. A pair of trucks are parked underneath the roof housing the gas pumps. Ambrosia is the first to exit the van.

I grip my HK harder.

"Voices low. Weapons and powers at the ready. We should be in the clear, but you can never be too careful. Mafu, check the perimeter."

Mafu stalks off while Ambrosia motions for me to follow her and Matt, a suitcase in her grasp. She raps a specific set of knocks on the warehouse door. It opens a second later to reveal someone wearing a black balaclava. Their eyes pierce through the cover's slit, training on me before looking away and asking Ambrosia for the password. She recites something I can't quite hear, but we enter the warehouse shortly thereafter.

Inside is dark. In the center is a floodlight illuminating a stack of cargo and four other men. The leader, dressed apart from the rest, watches us impassively.

"Just you," says Balaclava, pointing at Ambrosia.

She nods and steps forward, but Matt's hand holds her back.

"Wait—"

"It's fine," she says.

He lets her go and watches with worry as she crosses the dark expanse to the man in the middle. Matt's canteen is slung around his belt while I clutch on to the HK for dear life.

"You take a corner. I'll take another," Matt whispers.

We part ways. Outside, another vehicle approaches.

"What's that?" asks the man.

"More Angelics. Don't worry, they're here to help pick up the supplies," Ambrosia says.

They're here in case this run goes awry.

Something tells me it might.

"Now, let's talk money," the man says.

I recede into the corner where the darkness envelops me. The sound of boots clatters beyond the warehouse's thin walls, muffling all traces of voices and obscuring the discussion ahead. Even surrounded by nothing but shadows, I feel more exposed now than ever.

My chest hurts, my throat closes in, and my mind shuts off.

Matt is hardly visible from so far away.

"Esther discussed payment with you, I assume?" Ambrosia questions.

"She did," the man drawls. Top hat, pedo-stache, glasses tinted black. "Fifteen million."

Fifteen-fucking-million? Is she insane?

Ambrosia hesitates with the suitcase, then lowers it back to her side.

"We agreed on twelve million."

"*Fifteen* million," Pedo-stache hisses. "For all the trouble we go through to help you."

"Fine," she says. "Twelve million is all I have on me right now. We'll wire you the rest."

"We need full payment *now*. Esther knows how I feel about indirect transfers."

Ambrosia's quiet, too quiet, resulting in an eerie silence as everyone holds their breath, waiting to see how this will unfold.

"I'll radio her. She can have it sent to you in seconds."

"You and I both know there's no signal here."

Then why the hell did we come out here?

The HK rattles in my grasp. I'm grateful for the suit's gloves because my hands would be sweating up a storm by now.

"We have a problem here. How do you reckon we solve it?" Pedo-stache says.

Ambrosia disservices him by not answering. Pedo-stache takes a deliberate step forward.

"I wouldn't do that if I were you," she warns.

He raises his handgun.

"Was that a threat?"

"No—"

"Fucking recidivists!"

Ambrosia swipes her hands in sweeping, opposite directions. The crate of equipment in the middle remains mostly unscathed, but Pedo-stache and his men aren't as lucky. They careen through the air, landing brutally on the cement. That's when it starts raining hellfire from beyond the warehouse walls. Bullets clang on metal, some creating sizable dents in the structure. I fell to my knees, letting the strap of the machine gun loose, which was weighing me down. The drum of my heart is louder than the chaos that breaks out.

Our supply mission crumbles before my very eyes.

Matt's on his feet, moving with grace as elegant as the water he masters. The water soars out of his canteen, hitting the nearest man to start getting to his feet. He molds the liquid into a bubble, the same as he did that day in Eureka. Mara flashes in my vision, her body crumbling to the ground, her venomous stare, the lightning crackling in between her fingers. All of a sudden, I'm frozen. The HK hangs uselessly, draped over my torso. I blink. Lost.

"Conin, get the hell out of here!" Ambrosia bellows.

Her voice pulls me from my waking nightmare and I'm hauling myself up, machine gun in position. She tosses another of Pedo-stache's men to the roof, followed by a booming crash. The man drops to the concrete, his bones squelching from the weight of the impact. Blood pools at his head. Meanwhile, Matt releases the water, and the person he's trapped falls, seemingly dead.

I have the instinctive urge to vomit—my feet glued to the concrete, my mind racing a million miles a second, and I can't formulate a thought long enough to move into action. A group of Pedo-stache's backups files into the warehouse with guns raised. I'm a deer in headlights, a perfect offering, but my hands instinctively react like they did on the interstate, and I'm suddenly firing several rounds. Someone drops. The others are not yet aware I'm here.

"Ambrosia! Matt! Get outside!" Mafu screams.

The two Angelics dodge and weave while the men release a hailstorm. Ambrosia uses an enormous amount of strength, pushing them aside. Stray bullets gut the interior, tiny pinpricks of light illuminating their mark. I narrowly dodge the blast of hail. Ambrosia urgently motions at me. My body reacts and I'm at her side, racing out of the warehouse into the pines.

"Get back!"

We stumble to the forest floor.

Something aches in my abdomen. There's a wetness inside my suit. It blossoms fiercely, spreading throughout my midsection. I turn on my back, reaching for the breached chink of armor, but I can't reach, and instead watch Mafu mold the warehouse to his will—it crumbles into metallic heaps over Pedo-stache's crew. My peripheries are starting to blacken. My vision blurs. My senses numb.

"Conin!"

I close my eyes and there isn't a world to return to.

Chapter 56

Ezra

There's a tight knock at the door. Atlas and I are slow to respond, neither of us wanting to break from our comfortable positions on the couch. When it knocks again, this time more quickly and urgently, I get a gut instinct something isn't right. Atlas shuffles away to stand up and I trail behind him for the door. Matt greets us from the other side, though he no longer wears his signature, cordial countenance.

"Good, you're here. We need you two at the infirmary, stat," he says. He doesn't even question why Atlas is here. Matt's level of distress triggers the anxiety already pitting in my stomach.

"What's happened?" Atlas asks because I apparently can't get my mouth to open.

"It's Conin," Matt mumbles and I've shoved past him, sprinting down the steps as fast as my bare feet can carry me. I hear Atlas call my name, but I don't pause, I don't freeze in submission. My feet slam against the pavement, each step drawing a fresh scrape. He teleports in front of me, extending his arms out to get me to slow down. I won't. I jump into the road and let these feet and legs and body lead the way. Because this can't be happening. This *isn't* happening. I'll arrive at the infirmary and it'll be nothing but a misunderstanding. Conin will be *fine*.

"Ezra, stop!" Atlas cries.

I take the turn near HQ leading to Sacremento Avenue, letting the momentum of the decline leverage me forward. In several instances, I almost trip, but remain upright, continuing as if there wasn't a hiccup. I veer a harsh right—Atlas is at the front entrance, waiting alongside Ambrosia, who has her arms folded tightly against her chest. She's out of her Angelic garb, her dreads a mess, her eyes wide with ladened fear.

"Ezra—" she tries.

I push through the threshold and storm right in, Atlas on my heels. The infirmary is a chaotic mess of orderlies working tirelessly. Injured Angelics either wait at the makeshift lobby or are being tended to farther in. I tear my eyes around, searching, hoping, wishing I'll find Conin and find out there was nothing to worry about in the first place. Atlas wraps his fingers around my biceps, but I flinch and launch away from him. He seems like he's about to cry. Ambrosia's careful gait makes me defensive the closer she gets.

"Where is he?" I yell. "What happened to him!"

She hesitates, sucking her lips in, biting them until a bead of blood wells. She's struggling to maintain eye contact with me. Atlas stands by my side, awaiting the same devastating news.

"He . . . he came with us on our supply run—"

The more she talks, the more her words muddle together. I try to understand what she says, but nothing that comes out of her mouth makes sense. She tells me and Atlas everything from beginning to end. I hold my crumbling pieces together, try to remain intact the longer I absorb this news that cannot be real.

"He's in critical condition. The healers are operating on him now."

"Oh my god," Atlas whispers.

The sight of Ambrosia makes me sick. Fury builds and collects until I'm a meteorite of rage crashing, crashing, crashing. I ram into her with all my weight. She clatters to the floor, drawing the attention of everyone near us. Some Angelics rush to her aid while others move closer, standing nearby in case they need to intervene. I want to kick her in like I did Callum that night—I want to so badly when Matt picks the perfect moment to enter, watching with wide eyes at the scene unfurling before him. He spots Ambrosia and rushes over. She sits up and instead of acknowledging Matt, she looks at me.

"I'm so sorry," she says.

I don't fucking care.

"I WILL NEVER FORGIVE YOU!" I bellow. "YOU DID THIS. YOU DID! IT'S ALL YOUR FUCKING FAULT!"

She vouched for him to become an Angelic guard. She convinced him to go on that fucking supply run. She . . . brought us here, somewhere that was supposed to be safe. This never should've happened. Conin shouldn't even fucking be here. "He's in shock. We're working on him now," someone says.

I don't feel anger anymore.

The earth caves in.

Chapter 57

Ezra

T he words sound wrong in my ears. I don't know what to make of them. I don't know what they mean. We're supposed to be safe. Proctus is supposed to be a safe place—a haven where we can't be touched by the outside world, where the Barclay mercenaries can't find us.

They lied.

The Angelics fucking *lied*.

I don't fucking care Conin's one of the Angelic guards.

I don't care that this was his job.

He was injured,

he's in a coma,

I need to see him,

I need to fucking see him,

I need to see him right the fuck now.

Atlas is blurred at the edges. My mind tries to process him, my vision, the boy ahead. A ringing crescendo sounds like the aftermath of a gunshot to my ears. It builds, it builds, it builds while I suffocate, search for air, but it's been sucked out of this room. It's been sucked out of me. I claw for it as I spiral. Down, down, down.

This is my fault

This is my fault

This is my fault

Atlas speaks to me, but the noise goes in one end and out the other. Useless. Utterly fucking useless.

He raises attentive hands, places gentle palms on my shoulders, and then his fingers pierce in. I snap. My hand flicks him away and I'm stumbling off the couch, kicking my legs to get away, get away, get away as a scream tears through my lungs, scalds my throat, rips it apart at the seams. Each sinewy thread snaps and breaks and opens me up. Atlas isn't there anymore. All I see is Lukeman Gray . . .

Lukeman Gray thrashing.

Lukeman Gray threatening.

Lukeman Gray, red-faced, broken bottle in hand, bellowing his heart's content while spittle rains down on my face.

I see Thax.

Thax—Thomas with a switchblade.

Thomas with a malicious grin.

Thomas in a belligerent rage.

Thomas carving out chunks of skin, watching the blood well, then fall and stream down tattered skin, creating a constellation of scars.

I'm eleven years old again.

I'm an untouched canvas.

"What's wrong?" someone asks.

"Is he okay?"

"Mr. Gray, it's alright—"

It's not!

Atlas is near. His presence hits like a shockwave, our tether pulsating in fear, horror, and rage. Mourning. I see all my inflictions and imagine the worst, imagine them on Conin, bloody and battered—bruises and lacerations beyond comprehension—beyond saving.

"I need to see him," I croak. "Please—"

"You can't, love," says Atlas, his voice so, so far away. "He's in critical condition, Ezra. They need to operate on him quickly."

None of his words make sense.

I need to see his injuries.

I need to see how bad they are.

If Conin's repairable.

If Conin can come back to me.

I need . . .

I need . . .

I need to get *away*.

My feet carry me far, far away from there. I sprint and break into a full-on run. Atlas cries for me, but his voice diminishes as I vanish into the night, to the inner depths of Proctus. I run and run and run.

And I don't look back.

Chapter 58

Atlas

Panic courses through me. My feet are glued to the floor like quicksand sucking me in the longer I remain dormant. When I blink, Ambrosia zooms into focus at the end of the hall where Ezra left her, staring intensely at the floor, as if the ground leads to all life's answers. Our shared immobility prompts me to wake the hell up and get moving before Ezra does something rash.

"Bring him back to us!" I yell.

She blinks, looking up in confusion. But one glance at me and I *know* she understands.

"Find Ezra," she replies, nodding.

My feet carry me out of the infirmary and into the night. Proctus is *alive* with people going about their business, socializing, meeting for a drink, or mingling among the cluster of canopies at the Shop. I dart my gaze around Sacremento Avenue, my eyes stumbling upon the first group of Angelics near me. Sprinting their direction, a few are startled out of their animated conversation.

"Atlas?" says one of them.

A distant lamp illuminates the speaker—it takes me a bit to realize who it is in the granularity of the dark. It's Percy—Ezra and I work with him in the fields.

"Are you . . . okay?" he asks.

"Have you seen Ezra? He darted out of the infirmary only minutes ago," I say, but the panic makes the question incomprehensible.

"Yeah," Percy mumbles, "we saw him run up that way."

He indicates the road that leads to Main Street. I think I know where Ezra's headed. I frantically nod, rushing a "thank you" before teleporting to the top. There's no trace of him at the three-way intersection, so I vanish again and rematerialize in the living room of their apartment. At first glance, Ezra isn't here, but the door to their bedroom has been left ajar. I amble carefully in that direction, hoping he'll be behind those walls. My fist wraps firmly around the handle. The door creaks open. He sits on the bed, elbows on his knees, chin carried by the palms of his hands.

"Ezra?" I whisper.

He doesn't move, doesn't look at me, stays suspended where he sits, completely oblivious to the world around him.

"Ezra," I repeat. "Sweetheart?"

Ezra gradually lifts his head. His hair is frantic and unkempt, bangs spilling over his eyes, so I can't see his reaction, or what lies underneath.

"Are you okay?" Stupid question. "What can I do for you?"

"I'm fine," he mutters hoarsely.

He sounds far from fine . . .

"Ezra—"

"I'm going to sleep," he says and falls underneath the sheets, burying himself deep inside.

I watch warily from my post near the door. My gait is gentle and quiet over to the opposite side of the bed. For a second, maybe two, I withdraw and step back before hopping in with him. Would Ezra want me here when he's grieving and torturing himself over Conin? What would Conin think if he knew?

Ezra needs me. If he tries anything, I must be there to stop it. My heart beats frantically, but my body decides for me, turning to face him. A subtle rise and fall of his chest are a telltale sign he's alive, so I match my breaths with him and keep pace. We fall in a shared, eurythmic cadence as the night wears on.

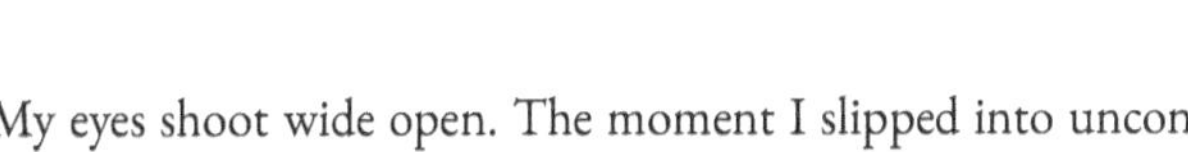

My eyes shoot wide open. The moment I slipped into unconsciousness is unclear, but the panic is back, and it's blaring louder than before. I toss quickly to my side. Ezra is no longer there—a mound under the sheets. The covers have caved in—the imprint of his body the only trace. I jump to my feet in a blur. Light-headedness crashes into me, forcing me to hold an arm out to steady my balance. When the worst of it subsides, I bolt out of the bedroom, searching for him in the expanse of the living room and kitchen.

"Ezra?" I say, panicked.

No reply. Instead, noise from the bathroom reaches my ears. Then, suddenly, a crash echoes from inside. I stumble for the door.

"Ezra!" I cry.

The handle won't budge after several jerks. I keep shaking for it to relent, but it remains locked.

"Ezra! Open the door, please!"

I press against the door, leaning all my weight into it, when I remember I can teleport inside.

My brain doesn't want to process what it sees. The sickly, egregious sight of spilling crimson over the side of the tub, the tiled flooring, intermingled with vomit that missed the basin of the toilet. Ezra is in the center of it all. He's slumped against the wall, arm draped over the lip of the tub and eyes staring blankly ahead as if he no longer has the sight to see.

There's blood. So much fucking blood, it's all I can see.

Ezra's drowning in it.

After the initial shock has worn off, I rush to him and kneel down. A knife is planted in his outstretched palm, which lies lazily at his side. A plethora of lacerations climbs up the length of each arm, exuding blood. It sloshes down the forearms, pouring onto the floor. Everywhere. It drapes down everywhere.

Something morbid climbs up my throat and escapes through my mouth. It echoes in the bathroom, ringing deep in my ears, vibrating fiercely, and tearing away at my organs. I scream. I scream his name, I scream for help, and I continue even as my throat cries for mercy in response.

"HELP! HELP US!"

I wedge my arms underneath his armpits and try to lift Ezra from the floor, but he's too slick with blood, and now it's coated all over me. He's too tall for me to carry and I don't have enough strength to get him to the infirmary. I could teleport there, cry for help until someone comes running, but Ezra's bleeding out. There's no time.

I call out for help again. And again. I try to staunch the blood with towels and whatever else is nearby, but it's useless. What was once white is now stained in a deep crimson.

"You'll b-be okay, love. It'll be o-okay," I stutter.

I scream until my voice grows hoarse.

Chapter 59

Atlas

I fixate on my stained shirt, mottled with blood that's soured a dark brown. My hands and forearms are caked with it, crusting and breaking off into tiny motes that flake the linoleum flooring. Healers come and go. I'm sure they asked me how I was doing at some point, but everything's numb and cold, a world void of their warmth and light.

Ezra's being tended to the same as Conin. While Ezra has a higher chance of a full recovery, Conin's situation remains bleak. Healers surround him at regular intervals. They have some of the best tending to him. Regardless, Conin is on constant oxygen with blood transfusions pumping back the excess blood he lost. The bullet grazed so deep that Mafu had a difficult time pulling out the various fragments.

When I make another round, Ambrosia impedes me from pacing any further. Her cold fingers grip my biceps tightly, keeping me at arm's length. She searches my line of sight and tries to gather my attention.

"Let's get you cleaned up," she whispers.

I don't protest.

Ambrosia slips her fingers around mine, tugging me gently to a restroom at the far end of the hall. We sidle in, the door is shut gently behind me, and I start to feel the raw stirring of coarse hands scrubbing away the crusted-on blood. By the end, I'm freed of the crimson stains at the cost of my stinging, abraded arms. The sink drains the brackish water and leaves residual streaks of red. I look in the restroom's mirror, glasses askew, lips mangled from where I've been chewing them.

"Stay here. I'm going to find you a change of clothes," Ambrosia says.

The reflection gazes drearily back at me, suspended in time.

I could've prevented him from hurting himself. I should've never fallen asleep.

Ambrosia returns before any stupid decisions are made. She knocks softly.

"Eureka101, it's me."

She gives me privacy to change. I shuck out of my pants and underwear, strip my torso of the blemished T-shirt, and let it fall to the ground with the rest of the tainted clothing. I study the indents on my ribs, the lean muscle on my chest, the bruised patch on my shoulder from cradling Ezra in my arms after stumbling over the sleek tile.

The clothes fit loosely over my frame. I crack open the door to let her know I'm finished. Ambrosia inserts herself, then sits me down on the toilet seat. She leans against the wall, arms folded, staring down at me like I'm some kid in need of a scolding—or, I don't know. (She kind of always has a scrutinizing expression on—a no-bullshit attitude.)

"You might've just saved his life," she tells me. The checkered tiles below my feet zoom into focus.

"I could've stopped him," I mumble.

"Could you? You told me what happened, and all it sounds like to me is an unfortunate series of events. At the end of the day, Ezra made his decision. You made yours by calling for help."

Ambrosia may be stern and standoffish, but she always knows what to say, without fail.

"I've missed you," I say.

She kneels and wraps me in her warm embrace. She smells oddly of mint, permeating from her thick locs. I breathe her in, nestling my nose into her skin.

"I missed you, too."

There's a subtle set of knocks. Ambrosia mimes an apology and goes to answer the intruder. The silence builds and as it looms, tension mounts. She cracks the door open to a sliver, then shuts it momentarily to look at me.

"It's Mafu," she says.

"*No.*"

She frowns. "Come on, Atlas. You two should talk."

There's nothing I want to talk about, not when everything's in shambles, but it was bound to happen sooner rather than later, so I might as well get the confrontation over with (much to my chagrin). I gesture for her to let him in.

"I'll be right outside," she says.

Then it's just me and Mafu in this tiny restroom, alone. The silence is brutally uncomfortable. My eyes don't leave his feet, instead staying suspended, neither panning down nor moving up to look at him in the eyes. He reclines against the porcelain sink. His gaze burns into my head, leaving singed skin, hair, and my waning, dying composure.

"I'm so sorry about Conin and Ezra. I hope they recover," he murmurs.

So, he knows.

My heart on a goddamn silver platter.

Another stretch of empty words left unsaid.

"Are you really going to stay mad at me forever?"

I contemplate what Mafu said with my lips sealed. He squirms, his foot tapping relentlessly on the tile.

"Fine, I'll go," he says.

"Wait," I blurt out.

I—

"—I'm not mad at you."

He doesn't push any further—he waits idly by. I still can't look him in the eye, which usually isn't a problem for me, but now it's unfathomable, shirking myself of this protection. I have no more vulnerability to give.

"Things were changing too quickly. I wanted familiarity before it was stripped from me. I wanted things as they were and not the responsibilities I knew I was going to have when abu passed away. You and the others made it bearable. When you left, it felt . . . I guess it felt sort of like a betrayal," I say, the words tumbling out one after the other.

"I wanted to stay," he says, "but I felt the need to follow them after all the sacrifices my parents made. And, well . . . the operation was yours and abuelito's. It felt wrong intruding."

He and I are at an impasse, momentarily, while we collect our thoughts. The tension has faded and there's only familiarity in the space between us, a lifetime bursting with our shared experiences.

"I'm sorry I hurt you."

I sigh.

"It's okay. I'm sorry I was an ass about it."

Mafu chuckles.

"All is forgiven, dude."

"But why the trailer homes? Why not stay with your family if that's why you left?"

Mafu groans, repositioning himself.

"You had to ruin the moment, didn't you?"

"I'm infamous for that . . ."

His smirk is playful, and he relaxes his eyebrows.

"Well . . . we disagreed one night—about what, I can't remember. I accused them of being cowards, screaming at them that we should've never left home. We haven't exactly been on the best of terms since," he tells me.

"Oh. Sorry."

"We'll get there eventually."

He helps me to my feet, and he and I exit the restroom together (which totally looks like we were caught in the act). Ambrosia greets us with a solemn nod, letting us know there aren't any updates on Ezra's and Conin's conditions. My heart won't slow, no matter how hard I will it to. My thumbs excessively circle in tireless intervals.

Our estranged trio sits in the lobby, waiting for scraps of good news to reach our ears.

"Atlas, is that you?" sounds a voice from above where I'm hunched over. The voice is, at first, unrecognizable, until I peer up to match the sound with a face. Several years have passed, but I'd know her anywhere.

"Delilah," I say, standing to greet her. "How are you?"

"I'm good . . . safe, because of you and your grandpa. I'm sorry about his passing. Augurys was one of a kind," she says.

"That he was. Thank you, though. I'm happy to see you doing so well."

As much as I'm delighted to see an Angelic abu and I successfully housed to safety, these interactions grow too cumbersome. My energy depletes and the strength in my legs gives way. Mafu leverages me to the bench, where I attempt to hide my embarrassment. Delilah grins fondly at me. There isn't a hint of judgment on her face.

"Your friends are going to make it out of this, okay? I'll do everything in my power to ensure they do," she says confidently.

Abu was adamant about getting her to Proctus in one piece, whatever it took, however high the risk, because of her healing abilities. Being around Delilah and the Angelics, symbols of his legacy, makes these shoes feel impossible to fill. I'm hanging on by a loose thread—emotions over the precipice of no control.

"Thank you," I whisper.

Delilah places a tentative hand on my shoulder before disappearing around the bend. Ambrosia, Mafu, and I sit like we're in solitary confinement, waiting until the ceiling inevitably falls on us, silencing my voice along with those I'm afraid to lose.

You offer your heart on a silver platter, pa had told me.

I didn't realize it'd been plucked from my chest.

Chapter 60

Atlas

Neither one of them wakes up.

That's the worst part.

Their hearts keep beating, their chests instinctively taking in air, but their souls remain in stasis and their fates are left undecided.

Staying in the infirmary did no one any favors, so I force myself out by sheer will and spite. Ambrosia trails behind, pursued closely by Matt, while my feet carry me to unexpected places. I know they're following me. They're not being discreet about it. There isn't a bone in my body that gives a damn enough to complain or command them to leave. (So, I don't. I let them follow.)

And suddenly, we're in Conin and Ezra's apartment. The polished floor is the same, as is the sunken coffee table, the dark gray futon, and the empty shelves. It's all the same as it was. Instead, this time, Ambrosia and Matt are in this bubble—this frozen, untouchable remnant of Conin's and Ezra's lives.

"Stop looking at it," Ambrosia says.

The floor, the toilet, and the lip of the bathtub are stained with Ezra's blood. The stains have congealed over in speckled patches. He's falling again, the crash rattles the floor and vibrates up my spine. The knife that was resting in his palm when I found him lies complacent near the toilet.

I emit an unrecognizable noise.

It feels like falling, but it's actually my feet carrying me forward. Every towel within the nearby vicinity ends up piled on the floor. I wet them all and start furiously scrubbing at the blood. Flakes unglue themselves, but there's still so much, and it spreads along the walls and ceiling until it completely enshrouds my vision.

Crimson, crimson, crimson.

A pair of hands drag me away from the scene and rest me on something soft, like a cloud. Those same hands shape into a firm body and crawl next to me. Another figure sidles up at my other side. He has red hair and dotted freckles, with a dim smile appropriate for the situation. Matt reaches forward and slips away my glasses, discarding them gently on the nightstand. He blurs, briefly, before returning to me.

"It's going to be okay," he whispers. "I love you, Atlas."

I love you, too.

Ambrosia embraces me. My shoulder blades pressed against her chest. Her chin rests against my neck, brushing hot air against my skin. My eyelids well with the accumulated pain from the past day, and they're threatening to break the dam, but I don't want to shut down now because I can't shut down now.

Then Matt places a tender kiss on my forehead, and it's over for me. The water rams through and spills everywhere. Tears flood the sheets, drip onto my hands, splashing Matt while he strokes my hair. Ambrosia clutches tighter, reassuring me she's still there.

I wish ma and pa were here. I wish abu was still alive. In some fucked-up way, this feels like losing him all over again, but worse when Ezra's and Conin's lives are on the verge of no return. Abu's voice breezes in. It's hard to discern what he says, but it's unmistakably his voice. He's speaking in Spanish, akin to a song, like distant echoes rising. The longer I attempt to decipher what he's saying, the more I realize it doesn't matter. It's a melody. Abu is singing.

He croons the lullaby he sang to me as a kid, the one he taught ma, who would take his place on busy nights. I can't tell whether his voice is a figment of my imagination or a call from beyond in the spirit realm, but it's a wave of reprieve.

"You hear that?" Ambrosia asks. "Abuelito's singing."

"I can hear it, too," Matt agrees. Even through the tears, it's clear he's soothed by it.

"You can hear him?"

"Of course. He never really left, Atlas."

No, I guess he didn't. I couldn't feel him anymore when he passed, but there were still traces of his spirit in little fits and bursts—just as stubborn as he was in life. Abu had a powerful, indelible presence, one that couldn't easily be wiped from existence. He's still here and still watching over me, rooting for the Angelic cause.

I liberate myself with a deep breath. If I search around, Ezra's tether is still there and pulsating with teeming life. It's duller than before, but it remains, and I won't let go. The tether beats with Ezra's heart. It beats with mine. What tortures me is that I can't say the same about Conin. I can't feel him, his life force, his beating heart. It's truly agonizing not having that confirmation.

Matt and Ambrosia never let go. They stay, molding their bodies with mine until we're one big, amorphous blob. The tears taper away. An emotion resembling calm trickles through me, and my eyelids suddenly feel heavy.

I dream of drowning in my own tears.

⸻◆⸻

Matt's arm is draped around my chest. His knee bumps into mine, and I can't help but let a chuckle escape. He snores softly, like he always does, that same one I'd listen to like a lifeline on the nights we'd spend together. (My, my, the unrequited crush I had on this boy. It's too bad he ended up straight, and I had to respect he and Ambrosia were exclusively a thing.)

"Matt," I whisper. He rolls away with a grunt and clings to an imaginary blanket. We fell asleep without climbing into the sheets, so he must be cold. I slip away, noticing Ambrosia's absence and the lingering creases like the ones announcing Ezra's departure the night I found him slumped over the tub.

Panic slams into me. I grab the fuzzy blanket placed at the foot of the bed and draw it over Matt, then proceed out of Conin and Ezra's room in search of Ambrosia. I realize I was premature with my worries when I find her standing in the kitchen, preparing food at the stove.

"Good morning," she says. "I let you guys sleep in. Matt wouldn't admit it, but the stress was getting to him. This is the most he's slept all week."

Lured in as if by some magnetic pull, my gaze falls to the bathroom where every speck of blood has been wiped clean. No evidence remains that Ezra harmed himself. The room is bereft of any knife and stripped of the towels I mottled with Ezra's blood.

Ambrosia's silent, the only noise coming from the food she tosses around in the pan. She feigns ignorance as she casts tiny looks my way.

"What?" she questions.

"Thank you," I mumble in reply. "You didn't have to."

She lets out a grunt of breath through her nose and silences the stovetop. She ambles over to me. I brace for her touch and wince when it never comes. Ambrosia remains at arm's length, her posture rigid as she studies me up and down. Her stoic mask breaks into melancholy.

"Can I hug you?"

"Yes. Please."

Her arms wrap around mine, and we're chest to chest, so close that I can feel her pulsing heart. It's fast, scurrying like a mouse. She's trembling. She shudders, and the noise that escapes her mouth sounds like a suppressed choke.

My best friend doesn't cry. She's strong, unlike me. She's a force to be reckoned with, a leader when people need her, but she's undeniably crying. There's a breaking point for everyone, and Ambrosia has crossed the threshold.

Her sobs are torturing and frail, a result of a lifetime of unfair treatment and living. Her nails dig in, then let go, as she cycles through grasping my shirt. It flashes me back to the day we were waiting for the results that would later diagnose her with autism.

"I knew it," she said.

"You know nothing's wrong with you, right?"

She smiled weakly and tugged at a blue dread.

"I know. It's a relief . . . having an answer for what this is."

Her fingers raked in, then receded. I knew all about wanting answers.

"Can I tell you something about me?" I asked.

She nodded and laced her fingers through mine. I gripped hers tightly and held it against my chest, right where she could feel my heart.

"I'm queer," I said.

"I fucking knew it!" She guffawed.

My mouth was torn between scolding her and smiling giddily. Of course, she wouldn't care.

"And you know what?" she said.

"What?"

"There's nothing wrong with you, either."

Ambrosia clenches the fabric. She cycles through a few more tics before resting her chin in the crook of my neck.

"Sorry," she sighs.

"For what?"

"You're hurting, and I sprung this on you."

"Shut up. It's fine. What's troubling you?"

"This," she replies immediately. "I shouldn't have made him come. It wasn't fair. I knew better, and I knew the risks of bringing someone without special abilities. And now he's . . ."

Dying, though neither of us says it.

"It's not your fault. You know that, right?" I say.

"You weren't there," she replies.

"Sure, but I know Conin wanted to be a guard. You were taking a chance on him, and not one of you could've known it was a trap. These are . . . unpredictable, scary times we live in. There's only so much we can do."

She laughs weakly.

"Well, look at that. Augurys did impart some wisdom on you."

I remove myself from the embrace and slap her on the arm.

"Shut up! I was trying to help," I scoff.

She grins. For a moment, it seems off, when I haven't seen a smile on her in so long. I capture this moment in my head, this brief still in the movie that's our lives, and commit it to memory. Happiness is so few and far between, it's nice to see it pop up amongst the gloom.

"It did help," she says. "Thank you."

We stand there in silence, neither of us ready to move, waiting for life to resume.

"Do you think Ezra will forgive me?" Ambrosia questions unexpectedly.

"I don't know," I answer, because it's true. There's a lot about Ezra that remains a mystery. It's sort of . . . disheartening to think about. "I think . . . he's angry with himself. He feels responsible for Conin, for dragging him into this. He lost it in all the chaos and took it out on you.

"I think when he . . . harmed himself, he woke up. He couldn't justify pinning the blame on you anymore."

Ambrosia's stare is calculating, brows furrowed in question. She opens her mouth and then quickly clamps it, starting to chew her lips. I allow her to go through her process, but my patience is wearing thin.

"You appear to know him well," she whispers.

(About that . . .)

"You love him, don't you?"

(Ah, that's a loaded question.) Maybe not love. Maybe more so that I'm falling for him.

"Yeah," I say, because it's true in some sense. "And Conin."

Her brows rise further to the sky. She ceases the assault on her lips, going slack-jawed. "Do they know this?"

"Ezra does, but I haven't figured out how to tell Conin yet."

She waits for more. I'm preparing for her judgment, telling me this isn't a good idea and that I'll have to back out while I can, or for her to never say anything to me again.

"We kissed."

"Did he kiss back?"

"Yeah."

Ambrosia reclaims her position and hugs me. "When Ezra wakes up, you figure this out, okay?"

Not if. *When.*

"Okay," I say, exhausted.

"What'd I miss?" Matt asks with a beautifully chaotic bedhead. Ambrosia groans.

Chapter 61

Atlas

Ofa saunters over to where I'm harvesting the last of the corn. November is underway, the air not so prickly but dampening as the sun relents. Overhead, an eagle cries. Its call rings in my ears, drowning out Ofa's attempt to grab my attention. She waves a hand over my line of vision. Her hair is tied up and sits on a mound atop her head, while her lips, uncannily identical to Mafu's, grin in understanding.

"I thought I told you not to come in today."

"I needed the distraction," I reply.

"Go home," she says.

"And be melancholic there? No way. They won't allow me to be in the infirmary unless there's a critical update, so I'm here. Get over it," I rebuke.

"Jeez, okay. Lots of pent-up anger—"

"Ofa—"

"Understandably so! I get it. If being here helps, then stay."

She turns to leave me alone but halts mid-stride. Her look is apprehensive.

"Have you considered goin' to therapy?" she asks.

"Please—"

"Can you hear me out for fuck's sake?" Ofa clips, shutting me up.

(Consider my lips thoroughly sealed.)

"We have several therapists here. Utilize them, please? You've been through a lot, and it hit you all at once. Therapy might be what you need to let it out. I attended when I arrived here alone, and ensured Mafu did when he came along."

"Mafu went to therapy?" It doesn't seem like him.

"He's still going. Don't tell him I told you," she says, and I agree with a curt nod. "Just . . . consider it, please?"

"Sure," I concede. "I'm sorry for . . . taking this out on you."

"Don't sweat it. Now get to work."

Matt brushes past Ofa on her way out, muttering a slew of apologies, and darts straight for me. There's urgency in his eyes. My nightmare has come true. One of them is dead.

"Don't—"

My knees give out and buckle under my weight. Matt dives, catching me mid-fall. He helps me back up and locks his arms in place to keep me afloat. His instincts are always on point.

"You okay?"

"What happened?" I ask, instead.

"He's awake, Atlas. Ezra's awake."

━━━◆○◆━━━

The strength in my legs returns with a vengeance. The fields fade away, replacing the surroundings with white walls and the intense smell of rubbing alcohol. I rush to the orderly behind the counter, startling them half to death. They instinctively clutch the cross draped around their neck and whisper something.

"Ezra Gray. Where is he?"

"And you are?" they ask after smoothing the wrinkles near the cross.

I glare blankly at them.

"A-Atlas MacPherson."

"What's your relation to Mr. Gray?"

We kissed (and nothing more). We held out on the conversation until we figured out how to tell Conin, but it never came to pass. The realization sends me scrambling for a response, and I can't just answer that we're . . . friends. A best friend is pushing it.

"Does it matter? Let me see him, now!"

"I'm afraid I can't—"

"Delilah!" I scream. "Delilah!"

"Mr. MacPherson—"

"Where's Delilah?"

I push my way down the hall when Matt comes striding in, panting within an inch of his life. He spots me from the entrance and calls out my name, but I won't let him hinder me. Healers poke their heads out of rooms to see who's responsible for the fuss. It's me. I'm the hailstorm barging through, searching in every goddamned room for Ezra.

They're keeping him from me (that must be it). The fury, the tornado bursting from my stomach, comes to a screeching halt when Delilah enters the hallway, holding Ezra upright. His hair is untied, falling in loose strands down the sides of his shoulders. He's unkempt and pale, but those blue and green eyes are brimming with so much life. His mouth is parted in bewilderment—probably in surprise that I'm capable of creating a fuss when I want to.

"Ezra," I breathe and run to him.

"Atlas?"

"He's still weak. You need to be gentle," Delilah says.

My feet slow down before I collide with Ezra, and it's like the world drowns around us because I kiss him in that hallway without paying mind to anyone watching. Delilah steps away because I have Ezra, he's in my arms, and I can keep him upright. Ezra's surprised by the sudden kiss, as I'm sure everyone else must be. Before, it was known that he and Conin were together, inseparable, as some would say. Rumors will fly now. Their perception has (definitely) been skewed by my inability to be discreet.

"Can we talk?"

"Yeah," he says, "but I need to see Conin first."

⸺◈⸺

Conin lies in a hospital bed, bundled in the sheets, an oxygen mask clasped over his face, and an IV drip pumping chemicals in his veins. Ezra leans over beside me and watches, stony-faced, while I keep him upright. The EKG beeps periodically like it has the choice to decide Conin's fate. My gaze trains on the device, for fear it will flatline the second I look away.

"I'm going to therapy," Ezra murmurs. His voice is raspy. He sounds like he's gargling water. "I want to get better."

Ofa's advice returns, and Ezra saying this must be another sign that I should get help, too.

"That's a great idea," I say.

Ezra scoffs, his smirk pained.

"It was Delilah's idea. But she's right, I need to. It's time."

There's so much I want to ask him. Are all his scars from self-harm? Are his sick spells because of anxiety or eating disorders? Are his eyes the color they are because of heterochromia or a result of his shape-shifting abilities? (Okay, admittedly, I've wanted to know this since the moment we met.) But I can't ask these questions. If he wants me to know, he'll tell me—I trust him.

My fingers brush against the bandages wrapped around his arm. Ezra startles and withdraws, but this unbalances him, and I wrap my arms around his waist before he topples over.

"I'm sorry!"

"It's okay," he pants. "I need to work on that, too. Touching is . . . a sensitive spot, I guess."

"We'll work on it together. Okay?"

"Yeah. Thanks."

Ezra nestles at my side—a plume of warmth bursts from his touch. It sends shivers down my spine, but they're happy and wanted. We watch Conin for what feels like hours, waiting for the inevitable moment he awakens from his coma.

"He'll wake up," I say. "He has to."

"I know."

"We should tell him . . . when he does. About us."

"I know."

Even behind the glass, the beeps are loud and clear. Conin's heart is still beating. Underneath all that flesh, he's fighting to stay alive, he's fighting to come back. I don't need a tether to know this.

"I love you, Atlas."

"And I love you, Ezra."

Chapter 62

Conin

The world is pieced together in shards and remnants. At first a void, now a stream of memories and images. My senses are the first to return: the scent of a clean and sterile hospital room, my touch next, and the static noise of existence. My eyes flutter open, slow and exhausted, revealing a white sensory overload. The ceiling is cracked with dunes and abrasions, a vast, pale sea that forces me to close my eyes again, waiting for the harsh stings to subside.

I remember the supply run, the men with guns, the wetness sourced from my abdomen, and the collapse of a warehouse. And then it hits me like a body colliding with the pavement. I was *shot*. The residual memory blooms a phantom pain near my obliques—though I'm not sure whether the pain is real or I'm imagining it.

For a second time, I open my eyes and gaze at the ceiling. I'm in less of a daze, so I risk my capabilities further by panning my line of sight down, confirming what I was starting to suspect. I'm in a hospital bed. And to my bewilderment, next to me is Atlas. He's dozing on a chair. His head rests against the wall, his mouth slightly agape, arms in a tight embrace against his chest. What is he doing here? And where is—

Ezra!

I don't want to wake Atlas, but finding Ezra is now a top priority. The pain that spreads from my side is too much for me to get up and go looking for him.

"Atlas," I say, voice hoarse. I try to cough away the buildup of phlegm and let my saliva placate the intense inflammation in my throat.

"Atlas!" I say louder.

His snore wakes him up from his slumber. He blinks groggily and turns his attention to me. He's not wearing glasses, which slightly catches me off guard. I can see his beautiful brown eyes so much clearer. Atlas grins, sits up, then leans forward.

"I'm happy to see you awake," he whispers. "We were very worried."

Atlas was worried? About me?

"Where's Ezra?" I ask, cutting to the chase.

I can't be distracted.

Atlas's expression immediately turns grim. He reaches for his glasses on the bedside table, putting them on while he bites his lip with worry. There's a crease in his forehead and his nose scrunches up. It would be adorable if my heart wasn't pounding with incessant worry.

"Where's Ezra?" I repeat.

"Do you remember what happened on the supply run?" he questions me instead.

I do, up until the collapse of the warehouse. The rest is a blurry haze.

"Yes."

"Well, you were shot. The armor absorbed most of the blow, which it was designed to do, but these men had bullets that could penetrate the integrity of the suit. A bullet lodged itself in the side of your abdomen. Mafu did what he could to pull out the remnants."

"I don't care about the specifics! Where's Ezra? What happened?"

"He didn't react well when he discovered you were in critical condition," Atlas mumbles.

My heart stammers.

"He . . . harmed himself. I found him in the bathroom with—"

I squeeze my eyelids shut—heart racing, head spinning, my arms tingling and going numb. Atlas stutters, trying his best to ease me. He even goes as far as placing his hand on my forearm. I hate that it sparks something deep within me.

"Where the hell is he? I need to see him," I say, sitting up.

It hurts like hell, but I don't care. Atlas protests and I ignore him in favor of attempting to slide off the bed and go in search of Ezra.

"You can't! You need to rest. You're still healing, Conin," Atlas says.

"Does it look like I care? I need to see Ezra. How long has it been?"

"You've been comatose for a week, Conin. Ezra was only a few days, but he's been seeing a therapist. I think he's there now."

"Here?"

By the way Atlas fumbles for an answer, I know that Ezra is in the same building. I stand, Atlas running to my aid, but I shove him back—a weak push, yet enough to tell him I mean business.

"I'll tell them you're awake! Just please lie down," he implores.

"No," I say with finality.

But before I reach the door, I stop. I unplug the IV drip from my skin and let it fall to the ground. With a large breath, I take Atlas in and stare. He fidgets under my gaze, unsure of how to conduct himself.

"I need to know. Is there something happening between you and Ezra? Something more than that tether?"

"You know about the—? Of course you do. We should've told you sooner. I'm sorry," he says, his eyes downcast.

A deep pressure has been lifted from my chest because it all makes sense now. When I haven't said anything in a moment, Atlas peers up again. His eyebrows furrow in a question.

"I'm happy for you two."

"Conin—"

"But Ezra's also mine, if he still wants me—"

"Of course he does!" he exclaims.

"I'm happy there's someone to love him just as much as I do," I say.

"Conin, Ezra's polyamorous! I am, too."

I swallow whatever else I had planned to say.

"When did he find that out?"

"He just met the right people," Atlas says with confidence.

Oh. Shouldn't I feel betrayed? Realistically, I should be livid Ezra hadn't told me sooner, that he and Atlas came together behind my back, but I'm not. I'm surprisingly calm. This is Atlas we're talking about—a genuine soul who cares deeply for my best friend. I couldn't ask for anyone better worthy of my boyfriend. Suddenly, I want to kiss Atlas so badly.

"If you reciprocate these feelings," I mutter, "can you and I be something, too?"

His eyes bug out of his head. He can barely contain his grin, which ignites one of my own.

"I want that. I like you, Conin. A lot. And I like Ezra. I didn't mean to get between you two, but I'm happy . . . so happy you feel the same."

My gut instinct is to be shocked, but the more I reflect on Atlas's words, the more I realize I'm truly not surprised.

"We need to talk about this later, but right now I need to find Ezra."

"Fine," Atlas acquiesces. "Let me help you."

He assists with the door and leverages himself against it to help me out. Seconds later, we're about to head down the hall when Ezra turns a corner and comes face to face with me and Atlas. Collectively, we freeze. And before I can so much as utter a word, Ezra's countenance contorts with anger.

Chapter 63

Ezra

"Lie down on the goddamn bed, Conin," I demand.

His eyes linger on the bandages that wrap tightly over fresh scars.

But he concedes, struggling to raise his feet onto the mattress. Atlas already has a handle on things, shifting Conin's feet onto the bed. My boyfriend is scarlet in the face, diverting his eyes and picking a focal point somewhere outside the window. It's evident in the way they move: Atlas's pupils dilated, zipping from me and back to what he was doing. His scrunched nose, the early onset of wrinkles creasing his forehead. Conin, silent as a mouse, finding the outside much more interesting than the boys in front of him.

Trees and their branches flitter in the breeze. An Angelic or two cross the road with baskets, and I vaguely remember them from the fields. I realize I'm distracting myself from the conversation that needs to happen, much like the two before me. Atlas takes the seat I left him in and I join him on the chair beside it. After an excruciating beat of silence, Atlas stands and moves for the door.

"I should let someone know Conin's awake," he says.

But before he can escape, Conin stops him with the sound of his raspy voice. It tears me apart, knowing the pain he went through—the mental casualties now tainting him. And knowing, deep down in my core, I was the catalyst that started them all.

"I want to talk first," he rasps.

Atlas freezes under the doorframe with a white-knuckled grip. He's slow in facing Conin, while simultaneously masking the panic in his face. He's terrible at hiding his emotions, unlike a certain two people.

"This concerns all of us," Conin continues, his eyes finally pried away from the window. "I want to talk about where we go from here."

He knows. There's a screaming, palpable tension in the room. It blankets us, siphoning the space of its air. I wait for something to happen, anything to happen to get me away from here, but as minutes creep on, it's clear nothing will come from my hopeless cynicism. He chose to discuss our relationship over everything else after regaining consciousness, so there's no way we're backing out of this.

And suddenly, succinctly, shifting into another alias and moving off the grid doesn't sound so bad.

Atlas is the first to break.

He shuts the door and leans back. His eyes close—when he reopens them, piercing, glassy-brown irises take their place. Atlas glares at the ceiling, waiting for it to unfold all of the universe's mysteries.

"You know," I manage to say.

"Of course I do," Conin whispers.

"We kissed."

Atlas stifles a whine.

Conin shifts to look at me with a blank stare.

"I thought I'd be angry, but I'm not. I'm not even jealous . . . not anymore. I'd be a hypocrite, saying that I was . . . because Atlas quickly grew on me, too. It wouldn't be fair to make you guys believe that all this miscommunication is your fault when I've been culpable for keeping secrets as well."

"I wanted to tell you," I explain, "but I was worried that if I did, I'd lose you after I'd spent my entire life wanting you. Atlas made me realize it wasn't fair to keep you in the dark. I mean, you and I danced around this for fourteen years of our fucking lives."

Conin releases an amused chuckle.

"It's clear he makes us both happy. We make each other happy. So . . . why not see where this can go?"

"Hello! I'm right here, you know," Atlas laughs.

"Right," Conin says. He switches from me to him. "I like you, Atlas. Like, a lot. You're sweet, funny, and mad intelligent. I could drone on and on about books with you all day and listen to your little tirades. It would make me extremely freakin' happy if I could share Ezra with you."

Goddammit. This boy is brilliant.

"I really freakin' like you too, Conin," Atlas mumbles. "You guys helped me through the hardest part of my life. So . . . thank you for that."

I smile at him, trying to communicate where words would otherwise fail that he deserves the world.

"So, um . . . where *do* we go from here?"

They're driving me nuts.

"Oh my god, just kiss already!" I say because it can't be helped. The excitement that this is happening at last is entirely too much to bear. But we can weather anything, Conin, Atlas, and me.

Atlas beams, a striking contrast after the gloom of before. He looks from Conin to me and back to Conin, a question furrowed in his brow. The infirmary ceases to exist as Atlas carefully ambles forward. He leans in on the mattress, freezing as his fingers ruffle the sheets. Conin propels upward, his mouth parted with expectation. Atlas lingers there a moment and then shatters the space between them.

Atlas presses his lips to Conin's. My boyfriend kisses him back.

It's fleeting.

But it happened.

And I feel as if my chest could burst.

Atlas retreats with a grin that could brighten the sun. Conin's pleased gaze remains transfixed on him.

"I'll go find an orderly now," he says.

He pecks Conin on the mouth again before he leaves, siphoning his last breath in the aftermath. The silence that follows Atlas's departure speaks volumes. We're left grasping for straws in his wake.

"I'm going to see a therapist," I finally manage to say. "After . . . you know . . . I want to get better. I don't want to feel this way anymore."

"You don't need to tell me yet, Ezra. Not if you aren't ready."

"I want to," and I find that it's the truth.

"Do you think you can handle this? How are you feeling?" I ask.

"I'm fine," he says.

I find that hard to believe, but I don't tell him. Tears slip down my cheeks and hang loose on the cornice of my jaw before I can suppress them. My chin trembles and I can't do anything about it.

"Fuck," I sob.

There's a creak on the bed. Conin's strong, muscled arm wraps around my neck and pulls me tight against his chest. Sobs wrack my body. The numbness returns.

"I'm so, so sick of this. I'm sick of craving alcohol every time the depression comes back. I'm sick of . . . feeling sick all the time—feeling useless—feeling like a fucking nobody."

"You were never a nobody," Conin placates. His breath is warm on my ear. "You were always someone to me."

I'm hysterical—inconsolable. He lets me cry for as long as I need—for what probably ends up being hours.

"I wish you could see how amazing you are," Conin says after most of my energy's been depleted. I take in shuddering breaths. He strokes my back with the arm he slung over my shoulders, a comforting graze that settles my nerves.

"Can I tell you something?" he says.

"Sure."

"When we were kids and I first saw your eyes—I was truly, wholeheartedly captivated. I thought it made you some kind of superhero because I never knew someone could have two different colored eyes. And, you know, then it turns out you actually have superpowers, which makes you a million times cooler in my eyes. My point is . . . I was always in awe of you.

"I feel like shit that I didn't see how much you were suffering. And the little I did know . . . I did nothing about it. I'm so sorry, Ezra."

I nurse his hand in mine while the appreciation I feel for him multiplies.

"You couldn't have done anything then," I choke out.

I grip his hand to reassure him that it wasn't his fault, that he and I are fine.

"But you did what you could when it came down to it."

Conin squeezes back.

"Where are you?" he asks.

"I don't know. I've been lost for a long time," I admit.

"You want to tell me about it?"

I recall what Ms. Bernard said a month ago, something that was along the lines of putting trust in others. I've always trusted Conin and I always will, but I think I understand now what she was trying to tell me. She was trying to get me to open up to her then, but I wouldn't with anyone. But I think the time's come to say something.

And so I do.

Chapter 64

Conin

I've always envisioned Ezra in a field of green, white roses dotting the landscape in a perpetual horizon. He'd stand there, still as a painting, watching the sun dip below the stretch of land. His hair billowing in a wind I could not feel. Once the sun fell, he'd turn to me with a smile etched on his face and his blue and green eyes piercing into my soul. But this time when he turns, the night doesn't fill to the brim with stars. The sky is a soulless black and Ezra's irises have darkened with it. Around us, the roses change from white to a bloodened crimson. The flowers exude a blushing scarlet that spills until it drowns the land in its horror. Ezra slumps into the blood, cuts and lacerations racing across his skin.

I wasn't there to witness his relapse, but I can imagine it in my head as clear as day.

It's why I can write stories so well; the way I envision images scares even me.

"I don't know why I did it . . . why I kept doing it. When Thax tired of doing it himself, I'd take the blade and continue his work," Ezra mutters, so low I have to strain to hear.

"I think I understand," I say. "You did what felt normal to you . . . what took away the pain Lukeman and Thax caused. I'm so sorry, Ez."

He nods but doesn't tell me it's okay. Because it's not. None of this is.

"In that moment, when I found out what happened to you, I felt . . . I knew, that all of this was my fault," he says.

I refuse to let him believe this. He didn't choose to be discovered, for Thax to turn him in, and for the Barclay mercenaries to pursue him relentlessly. And it was I who decided to go along with him. I chose *him*. Ezra. I would do it again in a heartbeat.

"You'd be home with your mom writing your books, preparing for college . . . maybe even you and Melissa could have been . . . a thing. And I took that all away from you."

I cringe at the mention of Melissa, feeling guilty for not having thought of her since the start of all this. The same can be said for Tommy, who we abandoned all those weeks ago . . . who may not even be alive now. Worst of all, I feel guilt that Ezra believes he stripped me of my entire life. If I'm being truthful, a life without him would be pointless.

"Ez, I want to make this clear," I say firmly.

His sad gaze finds mine. We stare at each other before I find the proper words to speak.

"First of all, Melissa and I were only ever friends. She knew how badly I was crushing on you. And second, you didn't take away anything from me. This world's cruel . . . it stripped us of everything—you above all. Yes, it's not fair, but that's not because of you. I would've followed you no matter what. I made that decision. *Me.* It was mine alone. And I decided that I couldn't live in a world without you. That I didn't want to live in a world without you. You are everything to me."

He blinks away the tears that fall no matter how hard he tries. I curve my finger around his chin and press up so he can look at me. He averts his eyes, but I keep my finger placed there for as long as it takes. With my other thumb, I wipe away the stream that's slid down his cheek.

"I love you," I say, "and that's not going to change."

"I love you too," he whispers.

I pull him in. He stands awkwardly at the side of the bed, but he stays there as I rake fingers down his hair.

"You and Atlas have helped me so much in seeing my worth, so I want to fight. I want to protect you now, Conin. And . . . before I can do that, I need to get better. Cutting myself then was a relapse and I know things may get worse before they get better, but I'm going to do my best. With the drinking and my . . . eating disorder, too."

"Thank you for telling me."

"Atlas helped me through one of my episodes that one time. I think that's when it clicked."

Anyone who treats Ezra like a king is someone I want in my life. I just didn't know it'd be such a turn-on for me.

"And you will get better. I believe in you."

"Thanks," he says.

I pull out of our embrace, kissing him gently on the forehead. His smile is weak, but he chuckles, which makes the entire gesture worth it. He keeps his lips sealed, pursed together, and watches me for what seems a very long time. It's not uncomfortable and I reciprocate his looks, drinking him in, admiring one of the boys I have deep, deep feelings for. The boy that I love.

"Admittedly, I should seek out therapy, too," I confess after a while.

"You think so?" Ezra asks.

"Yeah," I say. I take a deep breath and hold it. Ezra's been so honest with me, I feel I should respond in kind. It's only fair, to lay bare my emotions. "I . . . I've bottled all these feelings for so long, I don't know what to do with them. I . . . don't know how to let them go."

Ezra sits on the forgotten chair and scoots it close to the bed. He takes my hand with both of his, waiting for me to say what's been boiling inside me for far too long.

"Growing up . . . I always felt the need to suppress what I was feeling. It didn't help that my parents were constantly fighting—getting at each other's throats. When my . . . when my *dad* would leave days at a time, I'd take those isolated periods to comfort Mom and do my best to make her proud—at school, with extracurriculars, with friends, and helping out around the church. Which, you know, is why I never told her about wanting to change schools, for wanting to follow you wherever you decided to go or travel to in the future . . . because I *knew* wherever you applied for, you'd get in. You're insanely talented and I wanted to prove to myself I was worthy of that."

"Conin—"

"It's true, Ez."

He leans into me. My heart flutters.

"But eventually, when they divorced, my mom and I put a lot more time and effort into church—attending every meeting and providing our due diligence in whatever act of service they assigned us to. Some women in the Relief Society started to passive-aggressively prod her over the divorce. Even the bishop expressed he wasn't a fan of what they'd done and not-so-subtly told her she should've tried better, she should've forgiven my dad, and she should've prayed to God more so they could repair whatever had broken in their relationship.

"The thing is, my dad was a terrible person. And I know you know this. I can't say he was as bad as Lukeman, but he was still extremely intolerable. He cheated on Mom. He stole some of her money so he could spend it on nice things for whatever woman he was hooking up with at the moment. And the LDS church said we should forgive him? After he made mine and my mom's life a living hell? Fuck no! So, we left. I comforted Mom.

I continued to suppress my feelings so she wouldn't know how badly I was struggling inside.

"Eventually it became the easiest thing in the world—to lie, to forget, to bury my emotions so deep down that they could never see the light of day. All the guys on the football team started looking at me differently—all our friends did as well since, you know, so many of them were in our ward. I never told Mom, but . . . I started to go back to Tuesday youth activities again to convince everyone I hadn't left, that I still believed in their fucked-up religion . . . Through it all, Dan and Melissa helped me out the most. They understood when no one else would. Melissa's fine, but Dan . . . I'm sorry. What he said about you was screwed up."

I pause, take a deep breath. Ezra's listening attentively. He hasn't interrupted to ruin my flow. I grin at him gratefully.

"While all of this was happening, my feelings for you were wild. And we both know how the church feels about queer people. The only people I told before you were Mom and Melissa. Melissa was finally the person to make me realize why the church was so screwed up. I'd tell her about you. She made me understand that the way your family was treated, the way you were treated . . . it wasn't okay. That was only a part of my decision," I tell him.

"Why didn't you say anything to me?" Ezra questions and he appears genuinely hurt.

There goes that guilt again. Relentless.

"Because you were going through so much. I didn't want to burden you with any of my troubles. It didn't seem fair, especially with . . . how brutal Lukeman and Thax were. And then—then I discovered about your special abilities and the Barclay Network, and coming clean just didn't feel right anymore. It wasn't the right time. Now that we're here at Proctus, I feel safe enough to tell you. I feel you deserve to hear it from me now," I answer.

"Thank you for telling me," he says.

A tear streaks down his face. He kisses the back of my hand and leans his chin on it, gazing at me with those brilliant eyes of his.

"And thank you, for everything," Ezra whispers so only I can hear. "We're going to get better, you and I."

"We are," I say.

Ezra's being brave. I admire the hell out of him for coming this far. He's been through so much and the world was never kind, but he overcame the worst of his adversities. I never thought I'd see the day he would put this much trust in other people. I've seen his faith in the Angelics grow. I believe that means something. It has to.

We're going to be okay. I know we are.

"You miss your mom," Ezra states.

"I do. So much," I choke.

"I miss her, too. But I know she's alright. She has to be. She's a very strong woman."

And for the first time in a very, very long time, I cry.

PART 4

9 MONTHS LATER

Chapter 65

Conin

The nightmares aren't as prolific anymore. I wake up peacefully rather than drenched in an excess of sweat, panting for dear life. The space next to me is empty of a body once there. I reach out to feel his lingering traces, the scent that reminds me so much of him. Ezra's lying on his stomach at the far end of the bed, drool dripping from his mouth. He's in nothing but his underwear, healed scars exposed, and hair spread out everywhere. I sit up, moving in search of my missing underwear discarded in the mess that litters the floor.

What can I say? Three men live in this tiny one-bedroom apartment together.

I find Atlas in the kitchen. He's put on a T-shirt that drapes over his boxers while he constructs a peanut butter and jelly sandwich.

"Hey you," he says. I love it when he says that.

"Hi," I say.

My arms slither their way around his midsection, and I plant a kiss on his neck. Atlas isn't overtly muscular, but I love the feel of his flat stomach against my palms. I trail them underneath the shirt, the hair on our skin grazing each other's. He shudders from my touch.

"Babe, I'm trying to make a sandwich. Please don't make me horny," he sighs.

"Sorry. What time is it?"

"Six a.m."

"Shit. I have to be on shift in two hours."

"Don't go," he complains.

"You know I need to," I say.

He cranes his head back and rests it against mine. This tiny act of affection has become normal, comfortable even. It seems easy now, after everything. It took us a damn long time to get here, but we're here now.

"That was amazing . . . what we did earlier," he whispers.

"It was," I mumble into his ear.

He turns on me and pushes me against the island counter.

We kiss ferociously, hungrily, with a desire that shouldn't be there this early in the morning. His hands find my ass and squeeze it hard.

"Mmph, thick," he breathes into my lips.

Atlas tastes like peanut butter and jelly. We're locked in for another five or so minutes before we break apart. Something is happy between his legs.

"Jesus Christ. How?" I guffaw.

"I have the endurance," he jokes.

I playfully shove him. He snorts and I dive for his sandwich to take a bite. He grabs it away from me with an enormous frown. Atlas scarfs the sandwich down whole.

"Fiend," I say.

"My sandwich," he pouts.

"Yeah, yeah," I say, "I'm going to shave."

I escape to the bathroom. Inside, I gently massage the shaving cream on my face, noticing the acne dotting the mound of flesh on my chest. The groan I emit is long and harsh, made even worse the longer I fixate on my belly, which is fatter than it was several months ago.

"You look great, babe," Atlas tells me from the bathroom door. He sidles in and plants a loud, wet smooch on my cheek, excess shaving cream splattering his lips. He wipes his face clean, returning to the kitchen. My mouth cracks from the pure joy he elicits.

Atlas and Ezra love my belly. I'm aware of their support if I decide I eventually want to be rid of it, but at times, it feels like I'm allowing myself to be me. At others, the self-consciousness gnaws at me like a leech. I think, perhaps, if it wasn't a societal expectation to be fit and skinny, I'd be perfectly content with how I look.

"A bigger belly means more to love," Ezra had said once. I stared at myself that night. *Yeah*, I had admitted. Bigger bellies were pretty damn attractive.

The scar on the right of my stomach, the residual aftermath from the bullet wound, is even more painful to face. I blink and Mara's there, smiling maliciously with her skull mask cracked over her lips. I blink again and she's gone—a memory of the distant past.

I know I've killed. It wasn't Mara, but those men at the warehouse. It was in self-defense. I know this, but she still haunts me.

The razor slides down the grain on my cheek. Atlas rematerializes and watches the painstaking process. His grin is sweet and tender.

"You're not discreet, you know."

"Guilty as charged," he says. "You're just adorable."

"Quiet, you." Another stroke to the cheek.

When he doesn't reply with a quip, I turn my neck to see his gaze transfixed at the corner where the bathtub meets the wall.

"Stop it," I say.

"I'm sorry. I can't help it."

Scarlet blooms in my peripheries. I wasn't there, but I didn't need to be.

"Come here," I say softly.

"But your face is covered with shaving cream."

That didn't stop him before.

"Fine, hold up."

I finish and wipe my jaw clean. Atlas stares out into space, most likely reliving the horrific images he had to witness almost a year ago. I lace my fingers with him, rubbing his back with my free hand.

"Want to watch something?"

He sighs audibly.

"*Star Wars*?"

"Ezra will kill us if we watch *Attack of the Clones* without him," I deadpan.

"So *Revenge* it is," Atlas snickers.

The two of us, half-naked, take to the futon together. I retrieve a blanket and plop it over our legs. We snuggle into one another.

"So," Atlas says, "when did you know?"

"Know what?"

"Come on, Co. When did you know you liked me?"

"Buy me dinner first," I scoff.

"I'm serious. I want to know!"

"It's embarrassing, but . . . I thought you were attractive from the beginning. And then, well, you were very persistent in hanging out with me, so here we are."

"I got you beat. I loved you since the moment I laid my eyes on you," he says and giggles.

"Oh, whatever!" I say and twist his nipple.

Atlas yips. Thinking the same exact thing, he and I dart our gaze to the open bedroom door, shushing ourselves with tiny giggles. Ezra's conked out under the sheets, seemingly unperturbed by the sudden disruption. Atlas and I laugh.

"Love, huh?" I ask, remembering his subtle mention of the word.

"Well, yeah . . . I . . . love you. And Ezra, of course," he says coyly.

"Of course. We're a packaged deal, he and I."

"I know." Atlas grins.

"And I love you too," I confess.

We're no longer watching the movie. As the film plays on in the background, Atlas grinds on top of me. Electric jolts spark from the friction, coursing through my veins, up my spine, into my erection. He trails kisses to the waistline of my briefs, ducking underneath the blanket and working his magic. While I breathe in euphoria, the touch of a third-party member bristles the goosebumps that have erupted all over. Ezra pushes my chin with his index finger, luring me in for a kiss.

"You didn't wake me up," he murmurs.

Atlas hits a particular spot that makes me squirm. I hold my breath and wait for the sensation to subside.

"You looked like you needed the sleep," I shudder.

"I did, but round two without me? No fair."

"I didn't—" Intense shivers wrack every inch of my body. I gasp, unable to help it. "I didn't know this was going to happen."

Atlas's head pops from the cover, all boastful grins and crinkly eyes.

"He said he loved me."

"It's about time you told each other!" Ezra exclaims, slapping me on the deltoid.

"I know, I've been waiting forever," says Atlas.

"Sorry. I've just . . . I've been afraid," I say.

He climbs up my torso and lays his head in the crook of my neck. Ezra sits on the carpet. He squeezes an affirming hand on my forearm, taking the leftover space on my shoulder.

"I understand," Atlas says. "I worry about us sometimes, too."

"Why?" asks Ezra.

"I . . . there are times I feel like I'm intruding. I'll listen to one of your conversations, then realize that I don't share the same history. There's this guilt I feel for allowing myself to be swept away from the high of a new relationship. I didn't actually pause to consider or reflect on the entire lives you shared before you met me."

So, the time for this conversation has arrived. I had an inkling we'd need to discuss this eventually. I brush the back of my hand over Atlas's cheek, feel him breathe in an uncertain breath.

"Ezra and I may have an extensive history, Atlas, but the second you believe you're not an integral part in this relationship is the second this, as amazing as it's been, falls apart," I say, driving in every syllable to emphasize the truth to my words.

"I'm sure I can speak for both Ezra and myself when I say that we were also swept away with the excitement of everything. But . . . I think that's okay. We're young. We're discovering. We love each other. You came into our lives and you just didn't want to let go. And I don't want you to."

"Neither do I," Ezra says. "You mean so much to me."

The cogs in Atlas's head turn. It's a while before he says anything, but Ezra and I don't pry.

"I've never felt like this before," he says eventually.

"Do you want to tell us how you feel?" Ezra questions.

Atlas sighs.

"I thought it was some silly crush. These two cute guys show up in a town I've lived in all my life and I was going to send them on their way and that would be that. I didn't expect everything to happen the way that it did. I . . . didn't expect to eventually want what you two have. I definitely didn't think I'd fall for you both."

He's spiraling—it's in the edge of his voice, signaling emotions that run deep; because that's who Atlas is. He's a well filled to the very brim. I haven't seen him like this in a long time. This must've been bothering him for quite a while.

"Oh, love, you care about this a lot, don't you?" I say.

"Yes. I'm scared to lose it," he murmurs. A tear splashes my chest. Another, then another.

"You're not going to lose us," I say. "We're in this for the long haul."

Ezra squeezes me. He and I . . . we're on the same page.

"Ezra and I—" I search for the words in me. "We've loved each other for a long time and it's increased now that we have you. Someone else to love. Someone else we can share it with."

"We love you just the same," Ezra assures.

"If anything, we're complete now."

"Thank you," Atlas says in barely over a whisper.

The sun brightens and the outside buzzes with the promise of a new day. We touch, we feel, we keep close to one another—hearts beating, lungs breathing air. And we're alive. So alive.

Chapter 66

Atlas

Sandra finds me bent over at the knees, pruning a vine of tomatoes with Ezra. I pinch the suckers with my nails and pull them clean off. Ezra nudges me. I stand at full height and find her holding a clipboard, exuding a fake sense of kindness. (I could see right through you from the beginning, bitch.)

"Can I have a word with you, Mr. MacPherson?" she says.

She's never been informal with any of us since the moment we arrived.

"Sure," I say, not knowing what to expect.

I feel Ezra's gaze sear into me the farther Sandra and I go. Students run alongside the tracks, and elementary-aged kids play at the swing set. Ofa waves as she passes by the stalks of corn. Sandra taps her pen on the clipboard, which only makes the suspense worse. (God, I hate this woman!)

"How are things here?" she asks. "I see you and Mr. Gray are still working together nicely."

She one hundred percent knows about us. Her disapproval rolls off her in waves, but I ignore the snipe and decide to play friendly.

"Things are fine here," I answer.

I will not give her the satisfaction of small talk. (Absolutely not.)

"Good, good." Sandra returns to inspecting her clipboard and the mysteries its pages must hold.

"Well, I came by to extend an offer. The school board here was impressed with your interview. They're willing to offer the opportunity for you to teach middle grade math if you're still interested."

"Yes!" I blurt out. She startles and almost drops her pen (and I'm not about to apologize for it). "Absolutely. I would love to." She fixes her face, then smiles fakely once again.

"Splendid. I'll communicate your answer to the board."

Sandra's about to walk away and leave me to my devices when she stops in her tracks. She lifts a finger, hesitates briefly, but twists around to face me.

"Oh, and congratulations. I'm sure the news about your parents was wonderful to hear," she says, then finally leaves.

I return to Ezra, who's finished pruning the last of the tomatoes. He dusts off the light coat of dirt that's stained his pants. I watch the particles rain into the grass. He shucks off his gloves and sidles alongside me, smiling as he notices the bright grin that sits on my face.

"You're happy after an interaction with *her*?" he says, chuckling.

"Of course not. It's what she said that I'm happy about," I answer.

"I'm intrigued. Proceed."

"I got the job."

"You got the job?"

"I got the job!"

Ezra rushes forward, scooping me up for a kiss. My feet hover above the ground for a split second and in that second, I wonder how it feels to fly, to fight against the binds of gravity. I feel like I'm soaring in the skies with him—a power all of its own. (Sometimes I wish I was born with that ability instead.)

"I'm so happy for you," he tells me once the excitement has settled into an enjoyable buzz.

"Thank you. I can't wait to tell ma and pa," I say.

"They'll be so proud."

Ma and pa have finally settled down after completing the work that needed to be done since abu's passing. Essentially, they needed to erase all traces of the bunker and contact the powered individuals abu had connections with, which is about the extent of my knowledge regarding the situation. I'll be happy to hear from them when they arrive at Proctus to live here for good. It's been nine months, so the excitement is tangible.

Ezra's forearms are chiseled from the hard labor working in the fields. I find myself entranced for the umpteenth time at the musical notes and elongated lines that wrap and spiral up his arms—the evergreen trees and colorful, sporadic swirls that have been elegantly tattooed all over, admiring Claude's handiwork. Ezra pulls away, looking me straight in the eyes. His one blue and one green iris are home. The way his hair frames his face perfectly steals a breath queued on my lips.

We have a good thing going on here. I never want it to end.

Chapter 67

Conin

The space is not a welcoming one; white painted cement walls were an attempt to brighten the room, but only worked in making it more unsettling. The floor's gray, the metal table centered in the middle is gray, and I sit there with my leg jumping in place, waiting for the next set of arrivals to question. Leeanne and her crew have brought more and more people in since the rise of trafficking networks and the fall of recidivist protection laws.

Recidivists vs. Buford Elementary sparked an uproar all over the country. The court case created an unnerving surge of pandemonium. We may be isolated from the rest of the world, but that fear is still very present in our hearts.

And, of course, I'm one of the several selected to question these frightened refugees ever since I was critically injured at the warehouse nine months ago.

The news of my injuries infuriated many of the people here without special abilities. I placated them by saying it was my choice that I went. It was a sacrifice I needed to make to ensure Proctus's prosperity.

Now I'm no longer allowed outside these walls.

A knock sounds at the door—dull, almost muted, but I've picked up on its noise over time. Matt walks in with fresh faces. They're a couple, perhaps somewhere in their late thirties. I hope the questioning will go by quickly, but two identical children trail after them. My heart plummets. It devastates me to see children affected by our world's cruelty. I blink away the well of tears, focusing on the cordial smile I've practiced. The mother offers one back, but the father's tense, stiff shoulders make me pause. Meanwhile, Matt goes in search of additional seating.

"Hi, welcome," I say. Remembering to stand, I outstretch my hand for them to shake.

"Hello, dear. My goodness, you're young," the mother says grimly, then pops up as she stretches over the table to take my hand. The father follows reluctantly. The children stay glued to their sides.

"Well, we all have a part to play," I reply.

She nods gravely. Matt returns with two smaller chairs for the kids, departing with a half smile. The family situates themselves on the seats, but the male twin looms behind his father with a skeptical glare. I clear my throat.

"So," I say, "my name's Conin. I'm going to be conducting a survey I'll need each of you to answer so we can get to know you well while you're at Proctus."

"The same shit the government pulls?" the father grunts.

"*Adam*," hisses the mother.

He smooths his features, though he stays rigid. I'll have to be careful around him.

"We want to make sure we can accommodate everyone. The more we know, the better we can fill your needs. And, of course, we won't have you wearing those nasty Scarlet 'R's' around here. The Angelics want to see their people grow and thrive. They named it Proctus because it's a derivative of the word 'proctor.'"

I study the kids' dubious expressions.

"A proctor is someone who watches students during a test or examination to make sure they're doing what they're supposed to. Now, you four are not here to be tested or examined, but we like to carry that same principle in how we conduct ourselves. Instead, our goal is to promote growth and not discipline, though we do expect everyone to follow our rules for safety purposes. Don't worry, it's not too overbearing. We really just want to ensure happy, full lives. Lives that were stripped from you in a world that doesn't understand people like us. So, we called our little safe haven Proctus. It felt fitting," I recite. None of it sounds natural, but I hope the point gets across.

"I like that," the mother says.

Adam's loosened, as if I knocked one of his walls down.

"Wonderful. Shall we start?" I ask.

"Hold on, dear," the mother interrupts. "I don't mean to intrude . . . you said people like *us*? Matt said you were normal . . . like myself and Adam."

I cringe at the word *normal*. The term implies anyone with special abilities is not like everyone else and, therefore, outcasts.

"We're a family here, whether or not you possess powers."

"Of course. My apologies, Conin. We're tired from the trip."

Sedatives. Waking in a cold, dark warehouse. Leeanne better not have subjected this family to the same shit as when we first arrived at Proctus.

I don't ask.

"I understand."

"And goodness me! I forgot to introduce ourselves," she says, looking pointedly at Adam. I won't mention I was about to ask them to state their full names, but this works too.

"I'm Beth Pershing. This is my husband, Adam, and our two children, Reece and Rebecca. They possess special abilities. Came as a shock to Adam and me when they grew into their powers!"

The Pershing children are so young. Atlas's abilities manifested when he was eight and Ezra didn't even realize he had any until the age of eleven. I study Reece and his twin counterpart, Rebecca, perched on her mother's lap.

"I have super speed!" Reece exclaims suddenly.

The parents startle. Beth's about to scold Reece when I feel the sudden, instinctive urge to intervene. "Super speed, huh?"

The boy grins and before I know it, he's poking me on the shoulder from behind—there one second, gone in the blink of an eye, reminding me too much of Atlas.

"Oh wow," I gasp, "you are *very* fast."

Reece giggles—I'm glad I got through to him. It must feel liberating to use powers in the open without the need to hide. I gauge the parents' reactions; Beth is all teeth and praise. Adam has the beginnings of a grin creeping over his mouth.

"Me next! Me next!" Rebecca squeals and jumps off Beth's lap.

She totters over to me, places out an expectant hand, confused at first when I don't immediately react.

"Turn to me," she commands.

"Yes, ma'am," I say.

Once I've shuffled enough in my seat, fully facing the little girl, she closes the space between us and presses a gentle hand on my sternum. The warmth of a summer day blooms somewhere deep within me, expanding, growing, and filling me whole. Butterflies take flight and tickle every inch of skin. At the forefront of these thoughts is a familiar face. Someone who reminds me of home. Rebecca reveals a toothy smile.

"I can make people feel things," she says.

An empath.

"You're happy about something," she adds.

Beth clarifies. "She can often tap into an emotion that's already there and amplify it."

"I *am* happy," I admit.

The resurgence of tears, happy tears, wells sharp and quick. That familiar face. The feel of home.

"Why?" asks Rebecca.

"My mom finally gets to come home."

Ambrosia waits for me at the end of the hall. Her lips are pursed as usual, her arms folded tight against her civilian attire, and her dreads fall to her shoulders, sporting a deep shade of purple. She appears tired—so tired I can see the bags under her eyelids.

"I see you changed things up," I say jovially.

She peeks at the amaranthine dreads in disinterest, then redirects her insipid gaze to me.

New vocabulary. Nice.

"I'm so glad you went back to blonde. The red was hideous," Ambrosia deadpans. A second later, she loses her composure, falling into boisterous laughter.

"You're hilarious," I say.

She gestures for me to follow as she lets out the last of her incessant giggles. We enter an alcove that separates in two opposite directions. Ambrosia steers me to the left, closing the office door after I enter the room.

Her aunt, the leader of the Angelics, appointed Ambrosia co-captain of the Angelic Guard. Feels oddly reminiscent of my days on the football team. Some would claim nepotism, others would fault her after the incident at the warehouse, but I think she's deserving of such a regarded position. She sits down on the leather chair and lounges her feet atop the desk, considering me.

"You okay?"

"Any news?" I ask instead.

Ambrosia frowns, but she doesn't pry any further. I'm always appreciative of how she never butts in more than she should.

"It took us a while, but I think we finally waited out most of your mom's unwanted attention. It's safe to bring her to Proctus now."

"When?" I shoot, excitement coursing through my veins.

"Soon. You and Ezra are officially declared dead, and everyone's returned to their lives. The police no longer care for a mother in mourning, so their eyes are directed elsewhere now. We just need to find a team that can extract her."

How morbid.

"My mom thinks Ezra and I are dead?"

"No. She's aware you're alive. We've been in touch."

The relief that floods inside me is paramount. Mom gets to come here, live with me and Ezra, and although I'm grateful Atlas's parents finally concluded it was about time to see their son again, I have no idea how our living situations will work once they all arrive. The MacPhersons have each other, but Mom has only me. She can't live alone in unfamiliar surroundings. Atlas could continue to stay with us, but what if Mom doesn't like him? What if she doesn't come to love him the way she loves Ezra?

Of course she'd love Atlas.

"Earth to Bresshet?"

Ambrosia uses my last name to get under my skin. It pulls me out of my reverie quite efficiently.

"Sorry. Thinking," I quip.

"Yeah, I can see the smoke coming out of those cogs of yours," she says.

Haha.

"Thank you for taking the time to do this for me. She means a lot to me and Ezra."

"I know she does," Ambrosia mutters. Her entire face scrunches in concentration and she mercilessly chews her bottom lip as she does when something is bothering her. I know this because she had that same look every day after I was discharged from the infirmary—every instance she saw me.

"What?" I say.

"How's Ezra?"

"He's fine."

"That's good."

"Would you like to come to his performance Friday night?"

She's reluctant, twisting her thumbs in awkward motions, permeating that awkwardness all over. She shakes her head quickly.

"I probably shouldn't. He wouldn't want me there."

"Ezra's moved on, Ambrosia. He won't mind."

"Really? Because the last time we talked, he said he'd never forgive me. It's been nine months."

A flare of heat, anger, and annoyance sparks simultaneously throughout my body.

"You know what? I don't care. I want you to come."

She glares. Drawing a bead of blood from where she ripped the skin off her bottom lip, she twirls her fingers for good measure and stares out the office's window.

"Why?"

"Because how you were treated wasn't fair. It was because of me . . . because I chose to be part of the Angelic Guard. Ezra will come through eventually."

She thinks.

"Please come," I whisper.

"Okay," she says.

The silence that follows speaks volumes.

Chapter 68

Ezra

Performances always scared the living hell out of me. There's a scintillating thrill to them, an intense, frenetic energy—the obligatory attendance from friends and family, but their wholesome willingness to cheer you on and congratulate a performance well done. The Grays never showed up for any of mine, but Conin and Ms. Bresshet took it upon themselves to never miss a single concert. I'd see Conin in the crowd with his mother at his side and my heart would swell twice the size. My frantic pulse would keep me on edge, but their presence never failed to amplify how well I performed.

But I always wanted to perform perfectly, especially when a certain boy was in attendance.

It was the watchful eyes of others that sent my anxiety racing—their possible judgments and their expectant stares for an inevitable mishap. A small portion of me waited for cruel words to strike. A vile glare, a contorted, hostile expression worthy of Lukeman Gray's consideration. But they never came. It was reassuring after a while, knowing the awe I evoked out of others. Many would congratulate me. My confidence grew, but Lukeman Gray's words would tear me apart when I returned home. Thax's blade would search for a new stretch of skin left unscathed.

And now it's been almost a year since I last performed in front of an audience. Those daunting reminders rush at me in droves, but I attempt to stifle them with the coping mechanisms Quincy taught me. I thank myself for every moment I took a step back today to reflect and meditate. I think of the good that's happened and remind myself of the good that's in my life: this violin performance, my song, Proctus, and our safety. Me, Atlas, Conin. I bunch up the unwanted thoughts and picture them as printed polaroids on an empty desk, scattering them to the floor to be forgotten. I inhale, hold that breath, then exhale until my heartbeat slows, the tunnel vision soothes to a steady plane, and I no longer feel the sting of anxious tremors.

I feel okay. It might be momentary, but for the time being, I'm okay. I've come a long way from the man I was before therapy, before arriving at Proctus, before leaving the life I knew behind with the Grays. Realistically, there's still so much that needs to be worked on. I occasionally relapse and cut myself when the depression hits the hardest. When before I'd choose my forearms, I moved on to my legs, to the familiar planes of my stomach and chest. The self-harm has lessened the more I've tattooed my body. Claude is the best.

There have been instances where Conin and Atlas have grown frustrated, we'd get into an argument, and something or another would trigger a memory of Lukeman Gray or Thax's cold brothership. In those instances, I had to remind myself that neither of my partners were my estranged brother and father. And that I am *not* my anxiety. I'm *not*.

Conin's PTSD has been on and off; the night he shot Mara—despite her being alive, from what we know—and abandoning his mother at home without a proper goodbye continuously haunts him. He misses her immensely. Ms. Bresshet is being monitored by an Angelic until Callum Finch is found. Callum was reported missing days after the Eureka incident, but the news didn't reach our ears until weeks later. Ambrosia and Matt returned to Utah for a few days to relay what happened with Esther, but now they've returned to Proctus indefinitely. Their reasonings were unknown, but I know Conin and Atlas are happy to have them here.

Therapy's been great for all of us. It's no linear path, but it has helped me further understand how the past year has affected us in more ways than one. It's certainly helped our . . . throuple (*god, I hate that term*) grow closer. There are nights when Atlas and I need to placate Conin from a nightmare that jolted him into a screaming fit. We'd cuddle from then on out, Conin squished in the center, the three of us a tangle of limbs and bodies and warmth. Atlas continues to struggle with guilt from abandoning his grandfather's work. And, you know . . . I have my issues. We're works in progress.

Someone breaks me out of my reverie with a five-minute warning. Gracie's at my side while she resins her bow. Several others talk animatedly behind me; a gaggle of kids younger than I am converse over how nervous they are to participate in their first performance. The familiarity of the setting crinkles the corners of my eyes. Gracie smiles back cordially, then returns to her pre-performance ritual. These people, the Angelics around me, resemble friends, in some regard—people I look forward to seeing in practices or around the haven.

The Angelics are family, in some semblance or another.

The younger instrumentalists are called to the stage. When they file out, Gracie and I peek out the side of the door to take in the packed audience gathered here tonight. We're sequestered in an open space between Pops, and a converted art gallery. Edison bulbs string overhead in a zigzag pattern that illuminates the setting in an orange glow. Both brick walls are a painted tapestry of flowers, fields, mountains, and trees. An old bicycle wheel is mounted onto the art gallery's wall—an abstract installment I still can't understand.

The various age groups play their pieces until it's time for Gracie and I to take the stage.

"Break a leg," she says, and mimes a snap with the bridge of her viola.

I take the rear, immediately spotting Conin and Atlas in the second row with Ambrosia at their side. My stomach flips uncomfortably. I suppose this means I'll have to reconcile with her afterward—I've prolonged the inevitable for far too long now. Her presence is most definitely Conin's doing.

Atlas's eyes brighten at my approach, his glasses glistening under the glow of the Edisons. Conins's more reserved, but I can see the subtle enthusiasm in his expression while he laces his fingers into Atlas's. Ambrosia nods with an upward tug to her lips while I shuffle behind Gracie. An emphatic murmuring rises in the crowd—I feel the strong itch to get my fingers on the strings of my violin. We set our sheet music on the stands, pause momentarily, and then harmonize the opening notes together.

I get lost in the melody, in the sound of our instruments clashing eurythmically together, in Gracie's solo when I've finished mine. I cast surreptitious glances toward my boyfriends: the awed, childlike wonder of Atlas's countenance and Conin's peaceful, relaxed expression. Somersaults and butterflies, warm afternoons and nights intertwined. This piece reminds me of them, of how lucky I am to have them in my life, to have them as my own. The last faint echoes of the vibrato smooth out into oblivion and the raucous applause of the audience swells. Gracie and I bow—we're joined moments later by the rest of the crew. When it's all but me left on the stage, Maggie, my instructor, makes an appearance.

"Now, don't leave quite yet, folks. We have one last, final surprise for you tonight. Give it up for Ezra Gray, who after months of endless writing and editing, has a special song for two very special someones in the crowd here."

My traitorous legs almost lead me away from the microphone. I hold the mouthpiece close, gaze pressed on the boys who mean the world to me—the only two I can see in this endless wave of people.

"Conin and Atlas, this is for you."

Chapter 69

Conin

I think my heart skyrockets out of my chest. That's just how excited I am when Ezra takes the stage again, looking antsy at his feet—a white-knuckled grip on the microphone, lips brushing against the mouthpiece. In the seconds of silence that lead up to Ezra's encore moment, I turn to gauge Atlas's reaction, wanting him to experience that same eagerness. His eyes bug from their sockets. Ambrosia's lips are tight as she watches Ezra from the seat over Atlas.

"Did you know about this?" I whisper.

"No, not at all."

The only times I'd see Ezra crawl out of his shell were the days he had scheduled orchestra performances or when he'd attend my football games with Mom. In the fifteen years I've known him, he never once mentioned singing—never once expressed interest in lyricism or branching out from the violin. Is this what he meant when he said he wanted to compose music? I thought that entailed movie scores or his own fame-bound symphonies.

But this is Ezra—he's chock-full of surprises. The fear of leaving his comfort zone held him back most of his life, but watching him on stage tells me one thing. He's ready to break free. The sight of him sends adrenaline pumping—my excitement pulses with Ezra's static breath. He swallows and looks up. His face is red juxtaposed to the pale of his skin, but he overlooks the crowd. His one blue and one green eye spot me and Atlas in the throng of the audience. I gift him a reassuring nod. He grins, ever so slightly.

His voice is silk, raspy in a way I never imagined possible. His baritone is heavenly to the ears. When the chorus crescendos, he procures a falsetto that ignites every organ in my body. I'm transfixed and I know that the crowd is, too. Ezra sings with an unbelievable prowess that's both equally poignant and raw. The lyrics are gut-wrenching, vocalizing every single one of his emotions—his story of the life that he lived. A tear caresses my cheek. There are so, so many people around me, but I'm unabashed in my emotions because the only three people at this moment that matter are Ezra, Atlas, and me. The world falls away and the spotlight lands on us—the rest, a dark backdrop.

His final note lingers, resonating far after he's ended his song.

The audience erupts into rapturous applause. The sound is deafening from our spot amongst the crowd. Ezra mutters a small thank-you, then points at Gracie on the piano. Atlas has tears spilling down his cheeks. He claps and hollers louder than anyone here. Even Ambrosia has emotion tainting her tight composure, applauding with the rest.

Suddenly, Atlas rushes to the stage before Ezra can escape the outpouring of attention. He takes him by the arm, helps him off, and kisses Ezra with dramatic gusto. Atlas certainly has a flair for dramatics. Hoots and hollers are voiced from the obstreperous audience. I'll take that as my cue to join my people. Cheers burst from the crowd when I press my lips to Ezra's. He's flushed, but the smile adorning his face is undeniable. Ezra is *happy*.

"It needs some work, but . . ." He pauses, equal parts flustered and embarrassed. "Was it okay?"

"It was brilliant!" Atlas exclaims.

The look Ezra turns to me is hopeful. I lace my fingers with his, searching beyond his eyes to convey with all that I have just how brilliant I truly think he is.

"I'm so proud of you."

His beaming smile is electric.

"That was really good," says Ambrosia, who's joined us from the sidelines.

Ezra startles. Ambrosia already seems dismayed, ready to back out of the situation.

"Thanks," he mutters.

Behind us, the applause dies down and Angelics start to pour out of the venue. A few congratulate Ezra before leaving, but in our tiny, clumped group, an uncomfortable silence ensues. Ambrosia initiates another stilted conversation with him that I try to eavesdrop on, but Atlas pulls me aside. We place ourselves under a tapestry of colorful mountains that span a nonexistent horizon. He interlocks his fingers with mine and we watch as Ezra's reluctant discussion with Ambrosia becomes more animated.

"You okay?" Atlas asks.

I'm not particularly worried about them. I know they'll work it out—Ezra is aware how close Ambrosia and I have become over the months since the warehouse incident.

"You know what?" I say. "I'm happy."

"Me too," he says.

He rests his head against my shoulder, which I can't imagine is comfortable, as he's about an inch or two taller than me, but he and I lean against the bricked wall of Pop's while the conversation increases to a buoyant cadence.

"You excited to see your mom?" he whispers to me.

Atlas knows that I am, though I think he's just trying to get my mind off the two in front of us.

"I think she'll like it here. I can't wait for you to meet her."

"Do you think she'll like me?"

"She has to. I mean, she likes Ezra . . ."

Atlas hits me playfully on the arm but giggles nonetheless.

"I'm sorry you had to leave her for so long."

"I'm sorry, too . . . for how everything abruptly ended for you. If Ezra and I hadn't shown up, you'd still be there with your parents—"

"Stop," Atlas says firmly. "It was never completely safe there, not even when abu was alive. Besides, it was my job. Aiding people with special abilities was a decision we made collectively as a family. I wouldn't have had it any other way."

"I'm excited for them to come here—come home," he whispers.

Because Proctus *is* home. If you had asked me when we first arrived if I ever thought that possible, I'd have said no. But it's true. I can't wait to live our entire lives together here.

"Me too," I say.

"I can't wait to tell them about my teaching position!"

"They'll be so proud."

I scoop him up, kissing him passionately on his beautiful lips.

"I'm proud."

"Hey, you two," Ezra warns, "there's people here."

Ambrosia chuckles. Ezra shuffles our way to join in on the fun.

"Did you know she cosplayed as Aayla Secura? *Queen.*"

I knew he'd gain a significant amount of respect for her after learning about her cosplaying days. She looks pleased but keeps a respectable distance from us. I nod and mouth a thank-you.

"Well, I need to help take everything down. Meet you guys at WellWorks after?"

"Of course, love," I say. Atlas squeezes his shoulder.

Ezra disappears into Pop's, leaving the three of us alone in the venue once teeming with enthusiastic Angelics. We saunter to Sacramento Avenue, the night alive with palpable vigor. Many crowd into WellWorks for late-night drinks and food, so we follow along, basking in the hype and liveliness.

It's a testament to how far we've come, a promise of a long, fulfilling life with people who've undergone so many of the same experiences. My heart soars and I'm happy. Happier than I've ever been.

Chapter 70

Ezra

His head pokes around from the tips of the growing tomato vines. I see the bleached highlights of his otherwise dark hair and the glint of glasses as he rounds the corner of the trellis. Excitement courses through my veins like it does every morning he and I do this. I rush over with a basket in hand, body expectant and tingling with elation. Atlas's face scrunches up in concern while he studies a particular vine that wraps messily on a spool. When at last I approach, he sighs, deep and guttural. He folds his arms but smiles when he notices my arrival.

"Hey, you," Atlas says warmly.

"Hi." I grin. "What's wrong?"

He studies the tomatoes, feeling the frayed leaves.

"It's this vine," he mutters, tracing fingers along its twirling figure. "I'm not sure what happened, but it wasn't like this a few days ago."

"There's too much extra foliage. No one pruned the poor thing," I say, angrily ripping away a few excess leaves.

"We've been so busy with the corn, I think we overlooked it."

"Who was in charge of the tomatoes last?" I ask.

"Kyler," replies Atlas.

I grunt with exasperation. "We'll have to tell Ofa. I think he's still mad."

"No shit."

Atlas instructs me to reach for the roller hook at the top of the trellis. I retrieve it from its clasp, then we tug the vine from its square-foot-spaced roots in the soil. Atlas saunters off with the spool and tomato vine to dispose of them. I start to pick the ripened tomatoes in the wake of his absence, but five minutes pass and he hasn't returned. Two distinct fingers poke into my sides—they tickle, and I release a sudden burst of laughter. Arms wrap around me, pulling my waist to his. Atlas digs, then nestles, his nose into the crook of my neck. He tugs, I lose balance, and then we're toppling on top of each other to the grass bed below. He lands on my stomach, but his arms catch the brunt of the fall. His deep brown irises gaze into my blue and green, and his lips press hungrily into mine.

I don't know how long we lie there kissing as Angelics busy themselves with the early crop. No one can see what we do. Tomato vines and wooden trellises encompass the area he and I lie in. We bask in the privacy as long as we can.

"Get back to work, you two," says an inconspicuous Ofa from somewhere nearby.

Caught red-handed.

We return to picking the tomatoes as if we weren't kissing in an R-rated fashion. Once the basket is brimmed to the top, Atlas and I head in the direction of the Shop. He nudges me in the divots of my hips, because of course I'm the one tasked to carry the basket. A few tomatoes topple to the grass, but I flee, so he'll be the one to pick them up. Instead, Atlas careens my way, hands positioned for attack. At least he didn't cheat by teleporting.

Gunshots echo across the valley. I hear the way they ricochet off the buildings of Proctus, the way they travel to where we stand. That's when we hear the screaming and the explosion of the front gates. They come crumbling to the ground in a heap of smoldering flame.

CHAPTER 71

Conin

Matt finds me at the end of the hall after my shift. He smiles big and bright like he usually does—I can see what Ambrosia loves about him so much. He's a great, cheerful guy. The two pair so well together.

"I'm sorry I couldn't make it to Ezra's performance."

"It's alright. I'm sure Ambrosia told you all about it," I say.

"That she did," he chuckles.

Matt follows me down the hall to the exit, past Barbara behind the front desk. The sun beats down on us immediately. It's a hot day in August, but kids run along the road in hordes—Angelics chat and mingle, go about their jobs like they genuinely love the work that they do. It feels nice to be an active part of a community like this.

"I was going to stop by the Shop for some supplies," I tell Matt as I veer in that direction.

"I'll come with," he says. "I need to pick up some tomatoes for dinner tonight anyways."

"You better praise them. Ezra and Atlas have been working so hard."

We feed off each other's laughter while we make for it down the road, spilling onto Sacramento. In the near distance, the cluster of pop-up canopies await in what was once the parking lot of the Dunsmuir train station. Matt nudges me and points off to something in the far distance when the heat of the sun increases a hundredfold. He and I stop in our tracks, collectively peering up at the sky. I shade my eyes with my hand, noticing that something is amiss. The glisten of Proctus's protective barrier is gone. I can no longer spot its hexagonal pattern.

"What's happening?" I ask.

"I—" He fails miserably at a warm smile.

Rachel, a member of the Angelic Guard, materializes from around a bend. She acknowledges me with a curt nod, but beelines it to Matt and starts conversing with him in hushed tones. I overhear something about Benji, that he's gone missing or something. I'm not sure. But my attention is pulled from them and to a fracas that's erupted down the street near the gate.

"There's only one reason the dome would disappear," I catch Matt saying.

"... he must be dead—"

In a chain of events too swift for us to comprehend, Proctus's gate comes crashing down. We freeze in tandem. Nondescript, pitch-black vehicles are waiting on the other side. At least a hundred men stand beside them, carrying machine guns, dotting the road that stretches through the wastelands ahead. I hold my breath. A dead, eerie silence drapes over us like a crushing, weighted blanket. I hear an eagle's cry from far away. And that's when the gunfire begins.

I move, but my body protests and I'm falling to the asphalt, where I scrape my forearms. I try to get up, try to get moving, to get the hell out of here, and watch as bullets tear through Rachel's chest. She slumps to the ground. Matt barely has time to cry out when an outlier shoots clear through his forehead. Blood drains from the entry wound. The life leave his eyes, his mouth open in a perpetual state of horror. He falls to the road next to Rachel, his skull cracking from impact.

I can't scream.

But I need to move or else I'll face a fate as terrible as theirs.

At the front of the fray is Levi Finch and Mara Barclay, followed by a platoon of men. I thought they . . . I thought they had been apprehended? Mara sends bolts of lightning ricocheting off walls, targeting stray Angelics as they attempt to get away. Meanwhile, Levi sets nearby trees and buildings on fire, watching as they burn with sadistic glee. They're yards away and I'm a dead man if I stay here any longer. Finally mustering enough strength to run, I bolt back up the road Matt and I came down only minutes earlier. I need to find my boys. I *need* to.

A bullet makes impact with my skin.

Chapter 72

Ezra

We're sprinting into the heart of town. Ash rains down. Smoke coalesces and rockets to the sky in great plumes. Everywhere, people scream, darting past us. My chest is on fire. I search for Conin amidst sudden chaos, keep Atlas nearby by holding his hand. Angelics cry to reach the tunnels, which are Proctus's last resort in the event of an attack like this one. I won't go. Not yet. Not until I find the other half of my whole.

"There you are."

He bloodies Atlas before he can teleport away.

"You little shit," says Callum Finch.

Before I can react, the mercenary knocks me to the ground.

The prominent, puckered scar on his cheek mocks me. I see him in the mirror at Emery's party. I see him in my constant nightmares, his gun raised, and his decrepit grin. His hands come down to the base of my throat. In a flurry, Atlas teleports and comes at Callum from behind. He wraps his long, slender arms around Callum's neck, gripping the skin with ruthless force. Blood slips from Atlas's fingernails where he rips at skin. The mercenary wails while I attempt to get to my feet. Callum throws Atlas off, but not before Atlas disarms him—the gun clatters into the grass. I watch while the two dive to retrieve it.

I rise to my feet and sprint toward Callum to dissuade him from reaching the weapon—a scream tears at my throat. I feel the burn, the inhalation of pungent smoke, the moment Atlas takes hold of the gun and sets to aim. He fires, but the bullet misses Callum by mere inches. The crack of gunfire relays in repetitive bursts—Atlas is being fired at. With a grim, panicked expression, he teleports but doesn't reappear. I dart my head every which way. He never comes back.

"You fucker," the mercenary roars.

I'm whipped in the head. The weight of my body crashes into the earth. My vision is compromised, and blurry, but there's no mistaking Callum's snarl. He seizes my wrists and starts to drag me away, Barclay's men surrounding him in support. I blink, dazed by my downfall. My mind screams for Conin and Atlas. Black clouds cover the sky above.

I gasp for my last dregs of air.

Chapter 73

Conin

The stray bullet knicks my tricep. I fall on all fours, my botched palms drawing blood against the road's surface, crimson draining in rivulets from the bullet's graze. Before I find Atlas and Ezra, I need to obtain both my Angelic suit and the HK from the armory inside Headquarters. So, I get moving, careening up the hill as flames encroach on the wildlife and buildings behind me.

Angelics scream and cry for help, many of them sprinting in the direction of the tunnels. I wonder if that's where my boys have headed since they were together working on the fields. That's where I'll go once I have the armor and gun in my possession. I round the corner and beeline for the entrance. I need to be hasty since it's only a matter of time before Barclay's soldiers find their way here—before the flame climbs, claiming the land around us.

When I enter HQ, a stream of Angelic guards adorned in their armor sprint out and make their way toward the action. I'm backed against the wall, panting and watching as smoke starts spilling over the streets. It's thick and dark and blocks any view of the street beyond. Barbara clambers from the desk and spots me hunched, back pressed against the bricks.

"What are you doing?" she exclaims. "They're coming!"

"I'll follow after you!"

She hurries through the exit, but the second she reaches the outside, the smoke swallows her whole. I hear the *brat-brat-brat* of a gun. Crimson stains splatter over the glass door. The horrifying image is enough to send me sprinting toward the stairs that lead to the locker room. I make it about halfway before I trip over myself and go barreling down head-first over the remaining steps. My body's on fire and I ache from head to toe.

Nothing's broken, at least not from what I can feel, so I sit up, brush my hands against the metal railing, and pull my body to stand despite everything in me resisting.

I'm slower moving toward the locker room. I keep my hand against the wall, letting it scrape against the concrete, but it's enough to keep me upright. The room approaches and I slip in, but halt when I see two figures hovering near my locker. Their faces are coated in sweat and grime. I recognize them both and it's enough to send jolts of hope all through my aching body.

Ambrosia's purple dreads are a little worse for wear, while Atlas's glasses are shattered in one lens, his hair disheveled, poking up at odd ends. Ezra isn't with them, but they have to know where he is. They *have* to.

"Here," she clips, tossing me my emblem. I attach it to the fabric of my beaten shirt, pressing down hard. The armor wraps around my frame and tugs against my stomach. I place two fingers on the neckpiece, feeling the confines of a helmet appear from thin air. The ventilation kicks in and it becomes significantly easier to breathe. The others follow suit.

Ambrosia turns to me, eyes wild.

"Where's Matt?" she breathes.

I can't do this now.

"I was with him . . . he—"

"No," she says. Her visor shakes, glints from the fluorescents above reflecting off it. "No, no, no."

The pain in her voice shatters my heart.

"I'm so sorry," I croak.

An intense pounding crescendoes down the stairs. I twist to look behind me and see the crude outline of a figure in the darkness—through the smoke that starts to drift in. Ambrosia releases a bloodcurdling cry and the figure rises into the air, smacking into the ceiling, before falling onto the cement in a piercing crunch. Whoever that was could've been one of us. Vomit rises in my esophagus, threatening to splatter the visor of this helmet.

"Ambrosia—"

"These suits have night vision, Co. They were a soldier," Atlas says.

"I can't feel him," she stutters.

I have no idea what she means, but the longer we sit here, the higher the chances are we'll be caught.

"I can't feel him!" she screams.

"We need to move," I say and push past the two for the armory. "Help her up."

The armory's already looted, but my HK remains clasped to the wall. I punch in the code, feeling the weight tug down on my shaking arms. The strap falls onto my shoulders. Once I'm situated, I search for a weapon to give Atlas. Ambrosia's abilities are a weapon of their own, so I don't worry about her, though I'm not optimistic she'll be useful at the moment. And for good reason, too. When the two inch into the room together, I extend a SIG Sauer to Atlas in hopes he'll take it. He eyes it warily but doesn't protest as he hesitantly grabs it.

"We need to find Ezra. Where is he?"

"I don't know, but he's alive."

"What happened?" I ask, growing impatient. "Weren't you with him?"

"I—I was with him! Callum intervened and took Ezra. I've never seen Callum before, but that scar . . . Ezra's not dead yet. I can still feel him." Atlas quivers.

I don't need to see his face to know he's crying, but he's much more composed than Ambrosia, who leans against the threshold, clutching her emblem.

"Do we have one for him? When we do find him?" I say, indicating the one on my chest.

"Yes," he says.

"Let's go find him. Maybe he escaped."

The distant cracks of bullets being fired ring close. More and more smoke collects in the basement—a window must be open somewhere.

"Go on without me," Ambrosia sobs.

"We're not leaving you here to die," I say firmly while everything inside me falls apart.

I'm reining in every last drop of energy and adrenaline I have to remain composed, but I feel myself bursting at the seams. Not having Ezra here with us is making me lose my mind, but if I fall apart before we can do anything about it, I just may never get to see him again. And that's not going to happen.

"Please," she says.

"No," I say. If this makes me the bad guy, then so be it. "We have Angelics out there counting on us. And forgive me if I don't want my friend to die."

Ambrosia leans against the outline of the exit, then slowly straightens to her full height. Her visor is directed toward the floor. Seconds later, it finds Atlas, and then me. She nods. A sliver of hope wedges itself inside me. We're going to do this. Ezra will be fine.

"Let's move."

I lead the way while Atlas takes the rear. Boots bang against the linoleum over us and I prepare the HK for inevitable confrontation. The first black-clad soldier takes a step down. I fire, releasing a stream of ammunition into the helmet. A cherry-red stream sprouts from the exit wound and cakes the cement behind the fallen soldier. More arrive—I'm about to send another flurry of bullets their way when I get shoved to the side. Ambrosia's dreads spill out the back end of her helmet, her gloves gripped tightly into fists. The second soldier takes the place of the first—they have barely any time to react. Ambrosia releases her fingers, splaying them out wide, and fills the hallway with her screams while she furiously sends the lineup flying down the hall.

Atlas teleports to the end, where Barbara's blood stains the entrance's glass. I climb the last step, watching him put a bullet through the head of every Barclay soldier. Each shot rings in my head—each shot reminds me of Mara's fallen body, of the man whose life I ended at the warehouse—Matt's fractured skull. The soldier whose crimson life force scatters the wall below me—another testament that I'm a murderer.

I can't see Atlas's expression behind the visor, but each bullet to the brain is another puncture to the heart, another reason to fear for him. If he's okay. If he'll be able to live with himself.

"Atlas—"

"No time to stall. There'll be more soon," he says.

Ambrosia swipes the bodies to the side and clears a direct path to the door. Atlas is the first to exit. A whirl of pungent smoke in hues of gray and black wafts through the space. The thick clouds obstruct our vision. Even the suit's visor has a difficult time picking up anything through the intense layers. I follow Ambrosia out, stepping over Barbara's cadaver, slicked with blooming blood from multiple entries to the skull and chest. That urge to vomit resurfaces and I try my best to swallow it down.

We file onto Main Street, the occasional clearance in the air allowing us to see ahead by several feet at a time. I keep my eye trained on Atlas, ensuring he stays within my view. I can't lose him either. I won't. It's my peripheries that notice a shift in the landscape—a life form that wasn't there before. Infrared outlines an approaching radio signature. It moves slowly, negligently, without a care in the world—without fear that a town burns around them. Unless they're injured, this can't be good.

From out of the thickened haze, a figure dressed in the bare minimum in sheer black swaggers in our direction. Flame tattoos wrap around the length of his forearms like a spindle—fire hovers above his palms. Levi glares triumphantly through the heavy smog, cradling death within his hands.

"Whom do I have the pleasure of burning?" he bellows maniacally.

He's deranged. Frenzied. And he's enjoying every goddamned second.

Atlas dissipates in the smoke and rematerializes behind Levi, draping an armored hand around the mercenary's neck, the other hand holding a gun to his temple.

"Atlas!" I wail.

"Where's Ezra Gray?" he seethes.

Levi's mouth betrays him and a delightful laugh escapes. Atlas digs the SIG Sauer deeper into the mercenary's skull.

"Oh, it's you two," Levi says. His laugh grows uncontrollably, but his entire frame stays unnaturally still as Atlas keeps the gun trained on him. "Angela has him. If I'm correct, they'll be siphoning him of his abilities any moment now."

I lose all feeling in my legs.

"No!"

Instinctively, Atlas presses the trigger. Even in the pandemonium that captures the valley, I can hear the audible click of the gun—the indication it's still in safety mode. Levi grins and shoves Atlas off, consuming his suit with flames. Atlas disappears. Ambrosia raises clenched fists. I let gunfire loose, spraying the area around Levi. He vanishes in a flare. I lose sight of him as the smoke covers his every trace, raining hellfire around the vicinity. Ambrosia keeps back and I hope that Atlas has the instincts to do the same. A light flares behind a fresh cluster of clouds.

The equivalent of a meteor barrels right at me. I lunge away from the blast's radius and right into Ambrosia's figure. She stumbles and loses her footing. I land on the asphalt with a loud thud. The smoke clears, revealing a brief flash of Atlas falling on top of Levi. The two come clambering to the ground. Fire erupts from the mercenary's palms and Atlas has to once again teleport to safety. Ambrosia is quick to her feet, swiping her hand aggressively to the right. Whether her attack did the trick or not, we're not sure. Levi cackles, vanishing into the smoke. Behind me, I hear the thump of heavy boots, watching Atlas rejoin me and Ambrosia.

"Motherfucker!" Atlas roars.

Infrared is hardly doing its job. Where Levi vanished off to is a mystery. I peer around, HK trained and ready to fire. Seconds bleed into minutes. Time passes excruciatingly slowly. I take a large gulp of ventilated air when Ambrosia is once more swept off her feet.

She slams to the ground on her ass. Levi mercilessly sends waves and waves of flames all over her suit. I twist, releasing more heavy gunfire. The mercenary deflects what he can with an erected wall of fire and flees the brief exchange. Ambrosia moves to her knees and flicks her wrist, managing to lift Levi in the air before he can escape. He drowns in the very smoke he's guilty of conjuring.

I gun the trigger. A large detonation implodes and Levi's figure careens through the sky. He's swallowed by flame and smog. Atlas unclicks the safety on the SIG Sauer, waiting for the mercenary to resurface. Levi charges, freeing sporadic fire darts that hail past us. Some find their target in my armor, singeing the seemingly indestructible material. Ambrosia twists her frame and pulls Levi into her telekinetic embrace. She lifts him high, high, high, mimes grabbing him with two strong fists, taking hold of both ends of his body. She pulls.

Atlas teleports and reappears at Levi's bottom end. He grabs the mercenary's feet, and in one cruel, sweeping motion, Levi Finch splits in two.

Chapter 74

Ezra

A ngela Barclay stands before me in the flesh—the head of the Barclay trafficking network—the bane of my fucking existence.

Callum won't shut up about his success. He'd been watching the Angelics for months through the mirrors, gathering intel, searching for Proctus's weak points. He was in Eureka during those final moments when Mara and Levi attacked us during our extraction. Callum knew to bide his time, hide out in the reflections of Eureka's storefronts, in the mirror of the Angelics' vehicles. It was there he took several captive after causing a collision; Callum interrogated them with the help of Angela, which was where they discovered Levi and Mara's location and where to find the elusive Angelic safe haven.

"I killed Benji, too," Callum boasts.

The urge to rip his throat out prevails amongst the myriad of emotions circling inside me. If my hands weren't bound, I'd claw and tear at every one of these bastards for what they've done. Benji was the kid responsible for Proctus's protective magical barrier. He made it possible to live our lives in peace, and this is what he got in return.

"Your friend Tommy led us to Eureka, which led us here. How does it feel to know the Angelics perished by my hand?"

I do what I do best: I keep silent and bide my time.

"You made a stupid decision running from me that night," he says.

Tommy and innocent Angelics are dead because of me. I should have surrendered when I had the chance.

Angela laughs despite the ensuing chaos around us. It's depraved and cold. I shudder in the hands that clasp me down. Her gait is relaxed as she eases toward me. She glares down in disdain, eyes alight with victory.

"And you, Ezra Gray, are my consolation prize. A bonus for all our hard work. I still plan to siphon your powers, of course," she says malignantly.

"Why?" I say, knowing my words are futile.

"For my personal use."

Angela absorbs the scene unfurling ahead.

"Your capture set into fruition our plan to eradicate the Angelics. Senator Cornwallis will pay us handsomely for our achievements made here today," Angela says. "And I will possess your power by the end of it."

"Now, Thomas. It's time."

Thax materializes through the throng of men.

For a moment, I wonder if I've imagined him—a mirage, but not of paradise. A harbinger of what's to come. When he stalks up to punch me square in the nose, I know he's not a conjuration of my imagination. Blood spews from my nostrils. I taste iron on my tongue and splutter, expelling the phlegm from my mouth.

"Now, now Thomas. Don't damage the merchandise," Angela says buoyantly.

"Fuck you," he spits, but it's not at Barclay. His spit lands on my forehead and grazes my bruised cheek.

"Thax—" I gasp.

"Go to hell!" Thax screams. It's loud, and deafening, even amongst the gunfire that echoes around Proctus. Hate fuels his irises. I'm not sure I ever had a brother to begin with, but the man above me is unrecognizable.

"Bring him to Miss Zagan. If you wish to prove your loyalty to us, Thomas, you will be the one to deliver Ezra to his demise." There's a playful mirth in Angela Barclay's voice. The sound of it sickens me. "You can make it painful, but leave him alive." Her smirk is conniving.

"Come here, Ezra," Thax says, but it's not his voice.

It's Conin's.

"It'll be okay," he says, this time in Atlas's.

Which is impossible.

Thax doesn't know who Atlas is. He never met him.

Unless . . .

Unless the two boys I love most in this world are dead.

Chapter 75

Conin

"I can't . . . feel . . . my legs," Levi groans.

Copious amounts of blood pool from his severed torso. His intestines spill over the road, flabby tubes and excrement mingled in with a deep crimson. The sight is sickening. I don't think he's aware that we hover over him, watching as the life drains from his eyes.

"Put him out of his misery. Please," I say.

Atlas unmasks and retches on the asphalt. Vomit mixes in with the blood and guts that drift away from Levi's body. He wipes his mouth and coughs excessively after inhaling too much smoke. He stands to his full height, sliding a finger over the trigger. I don't want to have my boyfriend bear this burden, especially not after severing the man in half. Ambrosia is capable enough, but a layer of green sickness has overcome her face. She tilts, evidence of how much energy this fight has drained out of her. Through her mask, I can tell she doesn't have what it takes to finish him off.

"Stop," I say, lowering the gun in Atlas's hand. "Let me."

"Conin . . . you shouldn't—"

"*Let me,*" I repeat.

"Please . . . help . . . I . . . I can't feel . . . my legs," Levi gasps.

His spine is shattered in two. Bone fragments litter the viscera, the rest of the spine protruding at a misshapen angle. His tailbone juts out while muscles pulse with exuding blood. I look away from the ripped tendons and ligaments to the handgun in Atlas's possession. I steal it from his grip, aiming the barrel at Levi's head. A milky sheen now coats his irises. I don't think he can see anymore. He stares blankly at the smoke-coated sky while cherry droplets spill out of his lips and onto an exposed area of his neck.

"Help . . . me," he gurgles.

The bullet relieves the end of his suffering.

Mara. The man in the warehouse. The soldier on the stairs. Now Levi.

Ezra's in danger.

I wait for the moment to pass and for my mind to settle, as much as possible, given the active destruction of Proctus.

But *Mom*. What will we do now? Where will we go? How will I see her again?

"We need to move," Ambrosia says with defeat.

Soldiers sporting oxygen masks similar to ours march our way with guns poised at the ready. At the front of the pack, familiar, skull mask and all, is Mara Barclay. She spots us, intermittent crackles of lightning dispersing between the pads of her fingers. The flow of electricity bursts forth and misses us by inches. I grab Atlas's hand, he takes Ambrosia's, and we sprint from the scene and into the scorching inferno.

We don't see her again. The last I hear of Mara is her piercing cries for Levi to wake up.

"YOU BASTARDS!" she wails. "I WILL FUCKING KILL YOU!"

We bolt past St. John's Catholic Church where the trees and buildings await the fire's wrath. The flames reach and lunge, but we keep moving.

"Ezra! What about Ezra?" Atlas cries.

He releases his grip, stalling in the middle of the road.

"We can't leave him behind. Let me teleport and save him!" he pleads.

He has a bloody nose. It drips, small flecks dotting the screen of his visor. He's in no condition to teleport. Neither Ambrosia nor I respond to him. Instead, I close the distance, grip his wrist tightly, and tug him away.

"Help me, please?" I say.

Ambrosia claims his other wrist. We pull him along together while he protests and attempts to wriggle away. His firm figure disappears and I'm left clutching at air. Atlas pops back into existence several feet from us. His legs buckle from underneath him. He falls to his knees, hand masking the visor where more blood has spilled.

"Can you still feel him? His presence?" I ask.

It takes an entirely painful minute for him to reply, but he eventually says, "Yes."

"Then he's still alive. And maybe he'll escape. We don't know if Levi was telling the truth or not."

"Besides," says Ambrosia, "you won't come out alive if you teleport to her. They'll kill you on sight."

"You'll hurt yourself," I add.

"Callum snatched him, Conin! I didn't do anything about it . . . I couldn't. How will he escape now?"

"Ezra is a survivor. We'll find him, but going back there is a death wish. We're useless to him dead," I say.

Every instinct screams at me to be the hero, to run into the fray and save Ezra from a deadly fate. I didn't come this far to lose him like this. But if I go, I know I won't make it out alive. Attempting to save him would be a suicide mission. I can't do that to Atlas, but I'm missing a part of my heart—a hole only Ezra can fill.

"He'll make it back to us. He has to," Atlas says with more determination than before.

"That's right."

"We've got to keep going. It's only a matter of time before Mara pursues us with a vengeance," Ambrosia says, tearing us away from this moment. "We need to find the other Angelics. Once we regroup, we can discuss next steps."

The fire spreads, licking with its long entrails, and beckoning whatever's in its path to burn along with it. The flames are unnatural, burning far brighter than I've ever seen possible. They're wrapped in an ethereal sheen while simultaneously pulsating and cursing in an innominate chorus of crackled voices. We charge through the areas left unscathed, charting our course to the tunnels.

Chapter 76

Ezra

I'm selfish and desperate. That's what I remember in these final moments.

"You won't feel a thing," Miss Zagan coos. She's kind, unlike the others. How did a gentle, cordial soul like her wind up with the most conniving, infamous trafficking network in the States? "This will be swift."

I was never a good person.

"Relax for me, please."

Smoke slithers through my nostrils. I feel a deep want to succumb to its hazy sensation. Around me, Angela Barclay and her men wear oxygen masks. High-tech. State-of-the-art. The masks will protect them from the effects of smoke. Not me. I don't get a happy ending.

I was selfish and desperate. Of course, I don't deserve a happy ending.

"Find where the others fled to! We have enough in our possession—kill the rest."

"Don't listen to them, dear. Pay attention to me. We're almost done," Miss Zagan says.

Conin and Atlas are not dead. They're not, no matter how much Thax tries to manipulate me. They'll have a happy ending, but I won't. I don't deserve one.

"How do you feel, Ezra?" Miss Zagan asks.

"Tired," I say.

I am so, so tired. Let me sleep. Let me forget. It'll be better if I forget.

I can't see the sun anymore. There's too much smoke. Perhaps it's better that way. Everything's so fucking bright, even when the pitch-black tendrils enshroud the sky.

"You can rest, dear. If you're tired, rest," Miss Zagan whispers. Sweet. Cool. Not calloused with malicious intent.

I was selfish. Desperate.

Sleep. Sleep will help.

"How do you feel now?" Miss Zagan asks.

"I . . ." My body is numb. Everything's so bright. So fucking bright. "I can't feel anything."

"Don't worry, dear. That's normal. You'll be okay," Miss Zagan says.

I believe her.

"We're almost done, Ezra. You're doing so good," Miss Zagan coos.

Finally. Something I've done right. I always mess shit up. But she said I'm doing good. We're almost done. Then I can sleep. I'm so tired.

I was a terrible excuse for a son. I was a terrible excuse for a brother. Thax wanted what I had, what I couldn't give up, even if I tried. Thax wanted to take out all his pent-up anger on me: negligence from parents, our untreated mental health issues, our displacement in the world. Neither of us belonged, but I received the blunt end of it. Always me. His pain became mine. I bore the burden of our pain. *Me.*

I held Conin back. He had a scholarship. A team. A writing career to look forward to. I stripped it from him. I stripped those dreams and aspirations and squashed them. My burdens became his. He felt the need to chase after me. He felt the need to protect me. But here we are. What was the point of his sacrifices if I'm dead anyway? At least he has Atlas. At least he has someone who won't disappoint him.

Imagine if I lived longer. Imagine all the hurt Atlas would go through because of me. This is for the best. Of course, it is.

Just know I loved you both.

I love you.

"Ezra, are you still with me?"

I can no longer speak.

"Oh, dear. It's okay. Rest now. You're allowed to rest."

Thank you.

Chapter 77

Conin

Deer Haven Drive is long and winding. The farther we run into the forest, the more the asphalt cracks, and large chunks of road jut out. Weeds and wildlife reclaim the land. The trees grow taller, towering far above us and obstructing any view of Proctus. We sprint even as every inch of our bodies protests in sheer agony. We sprint because our lives depend on it—Ezra's life depends on it.

The thought we've left him behind stabs me repeatedly in the chest. What if instead of running toward him, we're running *away*?

Each breath I take in is more difficult than the last. My esophagus is raw with inflammation, my body protesting against every stride taken. Adrenaline has me moving with a vendetta, but it's a slap to the face realizing how out of shape I've become, now that I've no longer had the responsibility for football drills and workouts—I've been confined to HQ, so I haven't actively been working like the others. When the road ends, Ambrosia leads me and Atlas through the thicket, along a winding boreen. Once the uneven path gives way, we rely solely on Ambrosia's memory. It feels like an eternity, but she pulls through.

Behind shrubbery and a dense entanglement of branches is a wall of stone. The stone climbs, creating an overhang, and about twenty more feet above is a cliff. She pulls a tarp away. It's tufted with fake grass and bushes, rocks and miscellaneous twigs. Underneath is a metal hatch. There's a lockbox to the side where she punches in a code. The lock clicks open. Ambrosia tugs at the flap, letting Atlas in first. I allow her to follow him, then proceed after. I drag the tarp back, repositioning it as best as I can before shutting the hatch. LED lights mounted on the wall flash to life. We descend into the cold. After climbing down the last several rungs, I steady myself on the solid foundation underneath and look ahead. A concrete hallway stretches into the mountain. Overhead lights snap on.

Ambrosia hurries toward an additional steeled-off entrance. They're an extremely thick and durable set of doors which shelter off the rest of the labrynthine tunnels. She types in another code and the sliding doors glide effortlessly into their slots. Ambrosia stands back. Behind the steel is an image that shakes me to my core.

The surviving Angelics dot the wide expanse of space in clumps. I soak in the injured, which from a faraway glance, seem to far outnumber the uninjured. I search frantically for Ezra, but I can't see him. At least, not at first. Atlas detracts his armor, jumping on the balls of his feet. After a press of the emblem on my chest, I sidle in next to him and draw him close.

"I don't see him," he mutters.

Atlas rushes through the cots and crates, toward each Angelic, calling for Ezra, a plea in his voice. When he inquires for Ezra's whereabouts, people either shake their heads or suggest checking somewhere else. I catch up to him once he's moved on to the stragglers in the back. Atlas approaches someone with their head slouched over and elbows rested on their knees. She perks up, unshed tears welling in her eyelids. Ashen and soot-stained, the woman is a little worse for wear.

"Penelope . . . right?" he asks.

"Y-yes?"

"Is this everyone? Is there anyone further in the tunnels?"

She sniffles. "No one that I know of . . . apart from the remaining council members," Penelope chokes out.

"I'm sorry to bother you, but . . ." Atlas kneels on a leg. "We're looking for someone. His name's Ezra Gray. He has really long brown hair that's probably tied up in a bun, with one blue and one green eye—"

Penelope smiles weakly. The tension once abundant on her face has eased, if only a little.

"The one who sang at the concert? Your boyfriend?" she says, looking from Atlas to me.

"Yes!" There's a glimmer of hope. I grasp on before it can fade away.

"I haven't seen him. Not yet. But that doesn't mean he isn't here. I'll keep an eye out for him, okay? I'm sorry." She sounds sincere. I deflate because Ezra would have surely approached us if every remaining Angelic was indeed in this room. But I refuse to believe he's dead until I see him with my own eyes.

"Thank you," Atlas whispers, and stands.

When he turns and takes me in, his facade shatters. Tears spill over his cheeks. He presses a hand to his chest and lets out a strangled sob. I move in to embrace him.

"This is agony," he cries. "I can still feel him . . . but not knowing where he is . . . or what he's going through . . . is killing me."

"He'll come back to us," I say, because I *can't* handle the alternative.

What if he did escape? Is he trying to get here?

The Barclay Network didn't travel all the way here for the sake of one person, but Angela won't give him up. Faux are rare, and she wants his power.

"If they . . . if they succeeded in stripping Ezra of his abilities . . ."

"It would kill him," Atlas says.

Ambrosia makes eye contact with me after materializing from an adjacent hallway. The look she gives me sends my heart racing. Is this what Ezra's anxiety feels like? It's bullshit. My palms are clammy, I sweat along my hairline, the small of my back, and feel the world around me muddle into nothingness. I can't take it anymore. Ambrosia plods over, dropping her voice an octave so only Atlas and I can hear.

"The council is discussing our plan to get out of here. From what I understand, Esther's mobilizing what forces she has left to come rescue us. We're stretched thin as it is, so who knows when that will be."

"Have they any idea how the Barclay Network knew where to find Proctus?" I ask.

"Benji was murdered, and by Callum, no less. It's safe to say he watched over us for months. We thought he was incapacitated—"

A child sobs somewhere nearby. The sound of their distress chips away a little more of my remaining composure. Ambrosia stares blankly into space. Her cheeks are wet and there's a small quiver in her bottom lip.

"Are you okay?"

It's such a horrible, stupid question that I instantly regret saying it. I wish I could take it back. She blinks, squints, and comes to. Teardrops begin to slide down again, staining the concrete below.

"I will be," she answers, then, "but right now, it hurts. It hurts so fucking bad."

I glance at Atlas. We break away and I go in to embrace Ambrosia. I wait, gauging if this is okay with her, and she nods. Her arms remain limp at her sides.

"I'm so sorry. I wish I could've saved him. Matt was . . . he was an amazing guy," I say.

She doesn't speak. Not at first. Her tears fall—I try to absorb her shivers, hold her still, make it right. But there isn't anything that can make this right.

"They're going to have to pay . . . for what they did to him," she mumbles.

I don't entertain her thoughts, but I agree. The Barclay Network will pay.

"Earlier," I say, treading carefully, "you said you couldn't . . . feel him."

We detach. Her gaze is fixated somewhere on the floor.

"Atlas and Ezra probably told you . . . Powered individuals can, more often than not, feel the presence of someone like themselves . . . someone who also possesses abilities. When . . . when you bond with another, like Matt and I did, it amplifies. You feel them . . . all the time. It's intoxicating, at moments."

"Ezra said he couldn't feel others, not until Atlas. Do you know why?"

"Some people just can't. There's no apt explanation for any of it," Ambrosia says. Atlas joins us now that our discussion has veered elsewhere. He gives her unarmored shoulder a gentle squeeze.

"His presence was so strong in Eureka. I've felt others' before, but nothing like his. It was like Ambrosia said. Now that I think back on it, it always felt like an innate bond. I still feel it. It's not as strong, but it's there. Ezra's alive," he says.

He leans in for a kiss, his lips slick with sweat and perspiration. They linger until he pulls away gently to study me. Tears freckle his soft flesh and I run a finger over them, cupping his cheek. I wipe one away with my dirtied thumb.

"I love you. So much," Atlas tells me. "I admire your resilience, Co, but it's okay."

"I can't. I *can't.*"

If I break, there will be no coming back. Instead, I press my lips to his forehead. They're salty and taste a smidge of ash, but Atlas is here. He's alive, in the flesh—in front of me.

Six rapid *pops* tear behind the steel entrance. Angelics swivel their heads to see what's happening. Others gasp or scream, while that lone child wails and wails. Another muffled bang follows and then complete, utter silence. Ambrosia armors up. Two Angelics geared with their suits follow her carefully to the doors. She types in the code. I raise the HK, training it where the door splits through the center, each side returning to its designated spot. I hold my breath.

A skull-masked mercenary stands on the other side, hands raised in the air for surrender. Soldiers surround Mara, their guns and bodies in heaps on the floor. Blood cascades from the freshly deceased. It's a harrowing sight.

"Hold it," someone says.

Mara's figure starts to warp and bump, shrink and grow taller. Out emerges Ezra Gray, alive and well.

Chapter 78

Conin

I fall to my knees.

"Stand down!" Ambrosia yells.

It's alright, Ezra's here, all is okay.

I can't feel my legs; my knees tingle and a numbness inside spreads. Atlas, however, doesn't waste a second. He darts for Ezra and jumps in his arms. They stumble sideways, but they're sobbing, kissing, hugging. I see one of the men I love most in this world, a man I tried desperately to find and return unharmed, but the Mara he was before replaces all the relief I felt. What if . . . what if this isn't Ezra? What if this is Mara wearing Ezra's face? Angela didn't desire the power for herself. She wished her daughter to possess it, instead.

Suddenly, I'm on my feet. I burst through the surrounding Angelics to get to Atlas.

"Get away from him!" I bellow.

Ezra . . . no, Mara finds me, her irises glassy, though the same blue and green Ezra's have always been. But I don't buy it—not for a second. Not after everything. If Ezra's dead and this son of a bitch killed him, I'm going to make them suffer until they beg for the sweet release of death. I have my HK trained at the imposter's skull.

"Conin, what the fuck are you doing!" Atlas screams.

The imposter whimpers. The audacity sends an infuriating jolt up my spine. I can't help but grip the gun tighter, move the barrel closer to Mara's forehead. Ezra . . . I mean, the *imposter* stumbles to the concrete and backs to the wall. They're crying. Tears fall in rivulets down their sunken, exhausted cheeks.

I think I . . . I think I made a big fucking mistake.

"Conin? What are you doing?" they say.

I'm brutally shoved away. Atlas hovers over me, face contorted with fury. My gun smacks on the ground and pain jolts up my tailbone. He teleports, takes the weapon from my reluctant hands, sends it clattering into the abyss. He then rematerializes in front of me and slaps my face with enough force for me to regain some sense.

"What the fuck is wrong with you?" he hisses.

"I . . . I thought . . ."

"Mara Barclay is dead," Ambrosia exclaims.

The bold declaration is enough to drive us from our heated altercation. I don't even bother to turn and look. My eyes stay locked on Ezra—the *real* Ezra. I'm wrought with extreme guilt. I've betrayed him. I . . . I don't know what to do. Hopelessness burns through me. The glistening tears on Ezra's face accuse me of being traitorous. What have I done?

"Ezra . . . I thought—"

"You saved our lives, Ezra," Ambrosia interrupts. "Thank you."

He doesn't answer. His mouth is glued shut, eyelids wide, staring at me with unbelievable horror.

"Are you okay, love?" Atlas questions, but he's not asking me. He kneels over Ezra, tending to him, surveying his skin for any bruises or scratches.

An imposter wouldn't have killed Mara. An imposter wouldn't have gunned down their own people. I sit on the floor, festering in the pain I rightfully deserve, quiet because otherwise I'd be a blubbering mess. Ezra's attention has shifted to Atlas. He whispers something and then asks to stand. Atlas assists him up. Once Ezra's on his feet, it's grueling, every step that he takes in my direction.

I've failed you.

He bends over and falls to his knees. And instead of hitting me like the punishment I know I deserve, he kisses me. His lips are gentle, warm, and kind. The guilt is still so obviously there and I know I will always feel it deep, deep down, but perhaps the joint meeting of our mouths can make the burden more tolerable.

A promise.

"You aren't them," Ezra whispers and I know who he speaks of. I'm not *them*—Ezra's father and brother—the mother he adored, but who always batted an eye.

"You thought I was someone else," he says—a statement rather than a question. "You thought they took my powers."

I nod.

"And you were protecting Atlas." There's a pause. "It's okay, Conin."

He leans in further. We hug as Atlas's presence lingers above us. We're huddled longer than we perhaps should be, but letting go of him now is not something I think I can do. The thought of his dead corpse was so visceral. If our bodies detach, I'm afraid I'll lose him forever.

Meanwhile, the Angelic council members reconvene. Ambrosia joins them alongside the Angelic Guard that came to her aid moments ago. They converse, huddled in the open space near the set of steel doors. Atlas and I are alone with Ezra, or as alone as we can be.

We trudge over to a free space alongside the wall. Ezra wears jeans, an ill-fitted T-shirt frayed at the hem, and holes that dot the fabric. His face and hands are caked with dirt. I look at the healed burns that stretch up his forearm—and at the tattoos that now paint over them. Nothing fresh. He doesn't appear to have been caught in any of the fires roaring outside. A wave of relief washes over me.

"Are you . . . alright?" I ask.

I can't imagine how it must feel to have gunned down six people.

"I'm not sure," Ezra concedes. "I think I'm dehydrated."

Atlas promises he'll return with water. He leaves in search of some. Ezra, in the meantime, rests his head against the crook of my neck. He sighs into me. His breath is hot against my skin. It means he's alive. Ezra is alive.

"I didn't think I'd see you two again," he whispers.

"You found us. That's what matters," I say.

Atlas doesn't return, but Ambrosia does. Several council members flank her from behind. Brett Rosenbaum isn't amongst them. It's safe to assume he perished in the attack. They look stern, unsure. Our predicament is a dangerous one I'm sure is weighing down heavily on everyone. I worry they're not positive how to handle the situation.

"Ezra," Ambrosia says kindly. "How'd you escape? What did you see out there?"

I'm suddenly defensive when I have no right to be, but Ezra's been through a lot. Maybe he doesn't want to talk about it. He doesn't object because this really can't be avoided. He blows out a gust of air.

"Mafu saved me right as Angela attempted to siphon my power. He manipulated the metal of the vehicle, crushing them."

"His prowess is unmatched," chimes in a councilman.

"He mentioned hearing gunfire, then screaming. He came rushing into town and found me before it was too late. So many of Angela's soldiers are dead, but I'm not sure what came of her. Mafu's currently leading a resistance against those who remain with a group of Angelic stragglers. They're putting up a good fight," he says.

"They have their suits?" asks a councilwoman. Ezra nods. "That fire is going to continue spreading. If we can take control of the fight, we'll see what our water-users can do about the flames."

Ambrosia's stone facade, once an impenetrable force, falters for the briefest of moments. Matt was a water-user. And a damn good one, too.

"When should we expect Esther's reinforcements? And what of Leeanne's crew? Where are they?" a guard says.

"Esther's scrounging up who she can from Washington, Nevada, and Arizona. We're stretched extremely thin. We've lost so much of our forces from the government retaliating and the local cartels, that managing enough reinforcements might be a longshot. It may not be enough," someone says.

"We've radioed Leeanne. No word."

"There's one more thing," Ezra interrupts. The group's attention returns to him. "Angela mentioned an agreement with Senator Cornwallis. I think it's safe to assume he promised the Barclay Network reinforcements. We need to act quickly in case they retaliate."

"Would they intervene?" questions Atlas. I hadn't realized he had returned.

"I'm not sure," Ambrosia says. "I don't believe Cornwallis would get directly involved if it could be avoided. I think he'd rather watch as we wipe each other out."

"A fair assumption," says the councilwoman.

For now, we're on our own.

Cornwallis must've always known of our location—meaning, because of his greed, we no longer have protection. It appears he was willing to look the other way for the Barclay Network.

"If we rendezvous with the others, we can wipe out what's left of Angela's men," Atlas says.

"I agree," Ambrosia says, folding her arms. She turns to the room.

Other utterances of agreement echo in the bunker.

"Mafu and the others may not have much time. We must act quickly."

"I'll take every abled body I can," Ambrosia instructs. "We'll use the other passage out. Employ the element of surprise."

In total, we rank ten Angelics strong. Better than nothing at all. We clad ourselves in the signature Angelic white, emblems gleaming on our chests. We turn down a passageway that stretches far into a bleak darkness. Lights flicker on the farther we go—our boots clack against the cement of the tunnel. We're met by another ladder that climbs up to an inky blackness. LEDs buzz on and we ascend upwards.

Once we reach the top, a hazy sunlight drapes over us. It's hot, but the inferno tearing the landscape down burns hotter. Smoke superimposes the environment. Tendrils rise into the air. Bursts of orange and yellow consume the evergreens and wildlife. Ahead is the unknown, but ahead is where we must go.

Chapter 79

Ezra

We're running in blind. Radio signatures aren't picking up, so we have no idea where the remaining Angelics are cooped or the locations of Barclay's men. There's so much left burning that the tar-black smoke far outreaches the white. We stumble through the dense foliage that sits complacent, content to be set ablaze by the spreading fire. I saw Levi Finch's severed corpse on my way to the tunnels. If he's dead, all that risks this landscape from further scorching is what's already burning. It's some solace, but not enough. This is California, after all.

We're headed directly for Dunsmuir station. Tracks materialize under our feet, showing the way forward. The fire reaches its destructive hands. The Angelic armor is flame retardant, but can only suppress so much. With enough pressure, I'm positive it could border on dangerous. The fire licks and beckons. The Angelics persist until the river can be seen below and our feet hit gravel. That's where we find the brunt end of the battle.

The Shop is smoldering. Clumped behind a small warehouse is a cluster of the Angelic stragglers that saved me from Angela's clutches. Several without offensive abilities fire aimlessly with their guns. Barclay's men have taken refuge at the station. Portions of the building have succumbed to the destruction, to the growing flame.

Bullets rain relentlessly against our remaining Angelic comrades, holed up with little leeway. We sprint and don't stop, but one of our own is hit by a stray bullet through the arm. Because of the thickness of the armor, it lodges itself deep in muscle and tissue, evidently not the same bullet that ground its way into Conin's body many months ago. Blood spills on the tracks. Ambrosia lifts herself into the air, twists, and grounds in a three-point landing. With a strong motion of her arms, she renders Angela's soldiers like rag dolls flailing in the air. Ammunition litters the tracks. More soldiers pursue through the thick smoke. Ambrosia boosts up once more before joining us behind the warehouse.

"How's the wound?" someone asks. Who, I'm not sure. I stare down at the injured Angelic, unaware of their name and their story.

"Where's Mafu?!" Atlas yells.

"Here," he says. "I'm so . . . drained."

"You've done a lot," Ambrosia says, "but we need you to do one more thing."

"They're advancing!"

I watch in horror as Conin aims his automatic, sending bullets after our enemies. Ever since that night, ever since Mara, he's been different. Yet he kept stubborn about defending Proctus's walls, about keeping a gun on him at all times. Mara hadn't died then, not until I'd finished her, but I know it's traumatized him. I wonder if I'll end up the same. I ended the lives of Mara and those soldiers without hesitation. And . . . I think I'd do it again.

"Can you retrieve the bullet from their arm?"

"I can try."

"FUCK! I'm out of ammunition!" Conin exclaims.

"Here." An Angelic trades him. That same Angelic twists on their heels and extends their hands in the direction of a water tower yards away. In a burst, the tower implodes. Water hovers midair while the legs collapse to the ground. The Angelic hurtles the liquified bulbous form toward the advancing men. Several drown in the water's depth, hovering in the sky. The Angelic releases it and those trapped within smack onto the rails. I can hear the crunch of bones from where we stand, hidden behind our cover. Water-users: a dime a dozen, but damn useful.

"This is going to hurt like a bitch," Mafu mutters.

"Just . . . do it."

Mafu lifts a quivering hand and places it over the entry wound. He scrunches up his features before the trapped bullet falls into his palm. He grips it with trembling fingers, releasing it to the ground. Blood spews and pools in the gravel.

"Cauterize the wound. Quickly now," Mafu informs, slumping against the wall of the warehouse. And to my surprise, here comes another Angelic—Bobby I think her name is. Her fingers heat, growing red on the pads. With a searing touch, she places them firmly on the Angelic's skin. They wince but don't complain. I hear them draw in a hiss.

"They've taken cover. For now," says Conin.

"Let's strategize," Ambrosia suggests.

I gaze at the fire, somberly watching it eradicate and eat and leave nothing but charred remains. I think of that night and the car. I think of the flames that engulfed Conin's vehicle, Levi's attacks in Eureka, the ghostly touch of the burn that stretched up my arm. It was a reminder that I was alive. I'm still alive and I don't plan on leaving this earth. Not today and not for a long time.

The Angelic that can manipulate water directs what little is left to the spreading flames. The trees are lit in a fiery, scalding light. Soon, it'll find its way here.

"I'm afraid Mafu can't do much in his condition. Neither can Taylor."

"I can teleport behind their ranks, take out who I can," Atlas says.

"It's risky, but we may not have a choice."

"No," Conin argues. "That's dangerous. You could be killed."

Atlas grins sadly and places an armor-clad hand over the glass of Conin's mask. Conin is terrified. I can see it in his stance, in the way the gun in his grip shakes, the way he takes a shuddering breath.

"Right now, it might just be our only option. I've done it before. I'll be fine," Atlas reassures. It brings absolutely no fucking reassurance whatsoever.

"You're injured," Conin argues.

"I'm fine," Atlas shoots back.

"I can test the range of my telekinesis. Perhaps I can reach some of the men closer to the warehouse," Ambrosia says.

"I'm afraid I don't have much water to work with," pipes up the water-wielder.

"Atlas can create a diversion. In their distraction, we'll make an advance. We have some ammunition left and we could use Gavin's ice and Ambrosia's telekinesis."

I nod and prepare myself. It's time I finally carry my weight.

Chapter 80

Ezra

Angela's soldiers will have to run out of bullets eventually. This isn't some episode of *The Walking Dead*.

Yells from far away carry to where we take cover.

"They're here! Leeanne's group is here!"

Collectively, we breathe a sigh of relief.

Together, we combine our powers and strength to push ahead. Atlas vanishes, then reappears seconds later to tackle a soldier onto the tracks. I stay glued to Conin's side with a handgun that has a single round left. I need to use it wisely and I need to trust in those around me to keep me safe. We're few and limited, but together we're a force to be reckoned with. And with Leeanne's return, the Angelics might just have a shot at winning this battle.

I'm terrified.

But I'm not alone.

I never was.

Leeanne phases through a slew of gunfire aimed in her direction. She sprints toward a woman clad in the Barclay attire and passes through their body uninterrupted before coming into possession of the weapon the soldier was holding. She tries her luck several more times, handing each firearm to a member of her squad before moving on to the next unfortunate soul to cross her path.

Atlas scuffles with a man who grabs hold of his frame to boot him off. The weapon scatters in the process, but the man isn't finished with Atlas, who struggles to his feet. He's kicked repeatedly on the visor, over and over. Atlas's head lifts, then thuds against the gravel, while the Barclay soldier aims to shatter glass. Conin and I aren't quick enough.

We pick up our pace, a bloodcurdling cry slips from Conin, and I cock the barrel, set to aim.

Yet it's Gavin who beats us to him. The soldier's boots freeze in place, icy shards climbing until they reach the padded shins. The man's head comes next. It's encompassed in a bulb of pure ice, which snaps apart from the rest of the body. Both figure and head crash into a dead heap. Gavin assists Atlas to a standing position, but Atlas is wobbly on his feet. We reach him a second later. I keep him upright while Conin thanks Gavin, who then returns to battle. We're in the eye of the storm with little to protect ourselves.

I sling an arm around Atlas's shoulder, and in my peripheries, the flash of a familiar face makes the entirety of my being freeze. Thax is on the outskirts of the ensuing pandemonium, a deer in headlights. I can't help but look at him, feel my will and composure freeze. We can't see each other's eyes, but I know without a doubt we're looking at each other.

"Ezra, who is that?" Atlas says.

My mouth won't function.

"That's his brother," Conin whispers.

I failed to mention Thax was here, but I gather nothing from Conin's expression, which is stony-faced and slack behind the visor. I will myself to get moving before we're killed where we stand, but I grind to another halt as Ambrosia careens in front of us to telekinetically toss Thax into the heart of the train station. He breaks through walls and plaster, glass and embers. I don't take any time to consider what I do next. I bolt for the raging inferno and the building it consumes. Not a single thought flickers in my head despite one single word: *closure*. Whatever that might be. Whoever lies in the rubble: brother or foe.

This is the end. Maybe we can salvage something before it comes crumbling down over our heads.

"Thomas!" I shout.

My partners shriek my name.

There's no stopping me.

The flames climb and lick the infrastructure of this tiny station. I fall into place right in front of the hole Thomas's body created when he went crashing through. I enter and the building groans in greeting. Sparks rain from overhead—the roof starts to cave in. And I yell his name.

"Ezra!" Thomas shouts back.

"Where are you?"

His voice is hoarse, labored. It physically pains me to hear.

"O-over h-here!"

It's faint, but he's ahead. I push through the smoke, the billowing clouds of tarred obsidian, the pervasive fumes that work to inch into my suit. Thomas writhes on the ground. On top of him are wooden beams. He's coated in drywall and plaster. The sound of my name crescendos, but I ignore their pleas, focusing on the man who made my life a living hell.

I'm no savior. I'm doing this for me.

"Help," he strains. "Please."

I hook both arms underneath a beam, squat, and then attempt to lift its heavy mass. It hardly budges. Thomas shudders beneath it and elicits an elongated groan. I crouch again, attempting to create enough space for him to escape. When the beam lifts ever so slightly, Thomas catches on, pushing with all the strength he can muster. Conin and Atlas are growing louder. I think I can hear their impending footsteps above the chaos.

Thomas pushes and pushes, I pull and pull, and the beam gives way enough for him to slip through. He crawls from the space, panting and gathering the air forced from him. He's on his hands and knees, gasping for breath, but the fire invades his nostrils. He hacks and splutters. I gaze down at him in what probably resembles pity. Now confronted with Thomas, I have no idea what to say . . . what to do. Instead, I stand there as the train station holds on for dear life.

"Don't think this changes anything," Thomas says. I wonder if I heard him correctly or if my mind's machinations are leaning into the familiar.

I'm gravely disappointed.

"Thomas—"

"I hate you."

"Let's get out of here!"

"I said I hate you!" he bellows.

"Yeah?"

I'm not surprised. I'm not surprised in the fucking slightest.

My partners are somewhere behind me.

"Ezra!" they call. "Ezra!"

I laugh. I can't stop it. I'm hysterical, eyes only for Thomas, who cranes his neck to take me in. He's nothing but loathing and detestation. His face is contorted with seething cruelty. All it does is make me laugh.

"Fuck you," he coughs.

"I should've let you die," I hiss.

He's done nothing but make me hate myself. He's done nothing but hurt and scar and make me wish I was dead so I wouldn't have to face this painful existence. For a moment there . . . for a small, minuscule moment, I thought the rift between us could be repairable. When I search his face, I find the scorning, hateful likeness of Lukeman Gray. I see a family in shambles, beyond salvation.

A life that could've been, but will never be.

And the world that drove us apart.

That hurt us both and left us for dead.

He and I are both products of what our failing society created.

Amalgamations, less than human.

Brothers with no semblance of family.

With no parents to love them.

Thax bulls into me, driving me to the littered ground. His hand locates the emblem centered on the suit's chest plates that detract the entirety of it from my body. He presses down. The only protection I have dissipates. I'm vulnerable to the elements. Thax takes deadly, squeezing fingers to my neck and crushes. He presses on skin and muscles—tighter and tighter. As I gasp for air, I inhale an abundance of fumes and ash.

"*You're a disgrace*," Lukeman says through Thax's mouth.

"*I wish I never had you as a son*," comes the impoverished likeness of Rochelle Gray.

"*We never loved you*," my boyfriends say. Thax's lips close. I don't care how he came to know their voices, I just want him to *stop*.

"Let him go!" yells Conin, automatic weapon slated to kill.

I barely make him out in the blurred corners of my vision.

Thax's grip loosens. His frame trembles.

"Let him go or I will kill you!"

The world fades to black, but I feel his hands detract.

"Leave or I shoot," Conin says. "Get the hell out of here!"

The thundering of boots tapers off.

I heave and cough, hack up copious amounts of blood.

There's a sensation of being lifted in the air, armor rebuilding into place, a visor sheathing my head. Atlas fights off a soldier and wins, but barely.

Everything darkens.

"I'm sorry," I choke out.

Unconsciousness claims me.

Chapter 81

Callum

Callum had let the boy slip away for the last time. He wasn't going to make those same mistakes again. They were in his sights and he had the havoc of the battle around him to his advantage. With Angela Barclay missing, Callum could get away with anything he wanted. Ezra Gray would finally die. He had been waiting for this moment since he lost his chance to apprehend the boy at the party.

Amid the chaos, he watched the burning structure Thax had escaped from. Callum didn't care where his friend had run off to. In fact, after today, he wasn't expecting to be alive any longer. But if he was to die, he was going to take the life of the boy who had made his life a living hell—a joke amongst the Barclay Network's inner circle.

From the thicket, he spied. Callum saw Conin, the boy's lover, carry him out of the collapsing station. He was disgusted. Their obsession with each other was insipid to Callum, the true driving force to why he failed every time he got so close to capturing Ezra. Another Angelic was with them, a man he could not recognize. No matter. He'd handle this quickly enough. It would make no difference who was there to back Conin up.

Callum stepped out of the thicket. He navigated the battlefield, avoiding the Angelics, and watched as Barclay soldiers were downed ruthlessly. He cowered behind train cars and piles of debris, narrowly missing an encounter with an Angelic he shot twice through the visor. The recidivist dropped to the tracks. When at last Callum surpassed a long procession of carts, he rounded the end and found himself yards away from Conin, his Angelic comrade, and the boy in his arms.

He raised the gun. And fired.

When Callum blinked, the godforsaken bullet had missed its target. He didn't have time to fire again before he was being tripped up by a swift force to the ankle. He knew then who the third person in their party was. Atlas teleported and lunged for Callum's weapon, but Callum wasn't going to let him have it. Callum spun and threw himself at his attacker, lashing out and attacking the man's visor. The force shot jolts of pain up his knuckles and wrist. Before Atlas could strike again, a woman gained on Callum's right. If he was going to go down, he wasn't going to do so quietly. He released a final bullet from the gun's chamber, and where it landed, Callum would never know.

The woman used every ounce of her strength to lift Callum high, high into the air. *Ah*, he thought. He also knew who this was. Ambrosia released her hands, the same very hands that had killed his brother, and watched as Callum fell. His ankle was the first to crack. Then came both kneecaps. He knew the moment his body made impact with the gravel, he was paralyzed from the waist down.

"You'll pay for the lives you took," Ambrosia said, kneeling beside him. "Imagine how differently this could have gone if we hadn't turned against each other."

Callum didn't give a shit what she said. He just wanted to know if his bullet had found its mark . . . if the boy was dead. The terrible truth was, he would never know. Ambrosia attached a thick material to his chest. Callum could already feel his airflow grow tight. He knew what was happening and what was worse . . . he'd never get the closure he so desperately needed. The woman pressed hard against the material and white armor coursed across his paralyzed body, molding over his broken legs as they bent and snapped.

Callum's world closed in around him. A familiar visor overtook his vision—the ventilation system whirred on and started to flow clean, filtered air into his lungs. But it wasn't enough. He could no longer breathe. Callum peered down and could see Ambrosia's fingers tightening into dangerous fists. He was . . . suffocating. His chest was being crushed. His eyes were overcome with coppery blood. He could feel himself drown while it pooled to the brim in his mouth.

The last of the world he saw was smoke and ember, blood and red, and the woman who would take his miserable life away from him forever.

Oh, the sweet relief of death.

Chapter 82

Atlas

When Callum's dead, I feel the worst has passed.

Everywhere I look, Barclay soldiers are being detained by Leeanne's crew—the remaining Angelics after we lost so many. They free the detainees from the black vans; men, women, and children pour out, screaming and crying and watching in horror as the world around them burns. I see a bleak future, but a future where the Angelics persist no matter how much we lost today.

No sign of Angela, though it is only a matter of time before she perishes with the rest, if she hasn't already.

God, I hope she suffers.

Conin carries Ezra's unconscious body in his arms and watches the landscape for signs of help. Callum is crushed into a bloody pulp by our feet—mangled flesh macerated underneath the weight of armor that betrayed its wearer. Ambrosia stands, looking off into the horizon. She shakes her head and groans. After breaking from her transfixed state, she limps our way and assesses Ezra.

"What happened? Is he—"

"No," Conin blurts out. "He's still with us, but just barely. Thax . . . Ezra's brother . . . he detracted his armor, choked him. He inhaled too much smoke."

Ambrosia doesn't ask about Ezra's brother or why he was here, but it is closure I hope to get one day. Instead, she nods and starts ambling toward the clump of Angelics that's formed near the destroyed gate.

"I'll find a healer," she calls back.

Conin is dormant where he stands, Ezra limp in his arms. I round to face him, carefully glance at Ezra, who's raspy breathing indicates he is struggling to stay alive, and then look through Conin's visor. Tears fall helplessly off his cheeks. They break my heart.

"Do you need to rest, love?" I say gently.

We were shot at. We could've died. Fire blazes around us. Ezra grapples for dear life. We need a fucking break. A rest to last for eternity.

"I—he needs help. Let's move," he strains to say through the tears.

"Okay," I say. "Come here."

I lead the way. We traverse through gravel, onto the road, through the abandoned parking lot, toward Proctus's gates. My fear increases the closer we get, scared shitless over what will happen now. We can't stay here. Everyone will know where the Angelics were hiding, and with most of the town burned to utter devastation, the land uninhabitable, the only way is to resettle somewhere far from here.

Thoughts of ma and pa hit me like a sucker punch, brought to the forefront of my mind over the uncertainty of our future. What will happen to them? Will I be able to see them again? I look around as we approach the cluster of Angelics grouped near the gate and I know that many of these people are thinking the same exact thing—have the same exact worries. It makes me feel no less tormented over the idea. It's too much suffering for me to feel that any scrap of good can come from this. In some terrible, deplorable way I don't believe it possible we can return to the way things once were.

"Do you think he'll forgive me?" Conin says unmistakably under his breath.

Ambrosia is in active conversation with one of Leeanne's team. At our steady approach, they glance our direction.

"I do," I say without doubt. "He'll come back to us, Conin."

Ezra will.

If today has proven anything, it's that he will. He's strong. He's a fighter. We'll make it through this together.

Nine blissful months with these two. I want nine more, and all the years to pile on afterward. I want a future with these two, whatever future we can make from the ashes. Wherever Conin and Ezra go, I'll follow. I'd follow them to the edge of the world. And perhaps I already have. I cling to our tether, holding it close.

The area here has been doused with water. The remaining Angelic Guard move in and squander what they can from the wreckage. Meanwhile, Leeanne's crew herd in the survivors. I hear something about them moving to the tunnels to rescue those alive. I hear nothing about where we'll go and what will happen now that we have no place to call home. Because that's what Proctus has become: a home against all odds.

A part of me grieves leaving Proctus behind. In some small way, abu's work was an extension of the good the Angelics did and still do. Our goal was to aid people like us to the finish line and send them to a safe haven where they could live hopefully happy, fulfilling lives. With Proctus decimated, it feels as if all ties have been cut from abu. I have nothing but his memory now. But keeping his legacy alive is what fuels me amongst all this loss and defeat. It's what I'll hold on to as we continue forward.

When we settle and when Ezra is okay, I know what I'll do. Leeanne and I are going to have a very, very long conversation. But I'm ready. I tell myself this as Ambrosia introduces us to the healer. I tell myself this when we hop into the van and the work to keep Ezra alive begins.

The MacPherson legacy will continue.

Chapter 83

Conin

I would've killed Thax. I could have, but I didn't. There's been enough bloodshed today to last a lifetime.

Ezra weighs nothing in my arms. His eyes flutter—his agape mouth struggles to siphon air from the suit's ventilation system. If he perishes because of smoke inhalation, I'll never forgive myself. I could've run faster, held him back, kept him close before he dove into the battlements of a blazing building. That was preventable. Now, I'll have to live with the repercussions of Ezra's fate.

The healer ushers us into an Angelic vehicle as Leeanne shouts commands to her crew. I hear the Angelic say something about doing what she can to help, but every word uttered afterwards flies over my head into oblivion. Atlas perches beside me as we lower Ezra onto a cot. The healer presses down on his suit's emblem. When the entirety of the armor vanishes, I watch Ezra's face, painted with ash and soot, grapple with the fight for air. Several more Angelics file in, Mafu, Ofa, and Gavin recognizable amongst them. They take the empty seats on each side of the van, watching Ezra's deep struggle in the center with ashen expressions.

"Will he be okay?" Mafu asks, thinking about what must be on everyone's mind—what's plaguing me and Atlas to our very cores.

"I'm not sure yet," the healer says.

Her hands emit a golden light. It radiates a pleasant warmth that overtakes the vehicle. I try not to let hope overcome me, but I cling on to it with the last dregs of my strength, and watch the bitter rise and fall of Ezra's chest. Atlas grips my hand and doesn't let go. His glasses are shattered, and coagulated blood smears his upper lip, but he's alive and he's here. I squeeze to remind him that I'm alive too, and that I'm not going anywhere.

My fears claw their way up. They scream and slash, cut and try to outlast my waning strength, but I won't let them. If the past year has taught me anything, it's the undeniable knowledge that I can't control everything—I simply can't, no matter how hard I wish that not to be the unequivocal truth. I was always so afraid of what I didn't know, of what the future held, of it spiraling from my grasp into a path I couldn't move away from. If there's one thing I know for sure, one fragment of consolation I can hold on to, it's that regardless of the outcome, the goal is worth fighting for.

Ezra is worth fighting for. He was worth leaving my life behind and entering into one shrouded with uncertainty. He gave me his truth and I discovered mine. We met Atlas and lived an amazing nine months together. The more I reflect, the more I know that I need him alive. I need a future with him, whatever future we can dig out of the rubble, with Atlas by our side.

The van roars to life. It powers ahead, through the remnants of a forgotten land, and leaves behind a haven once teeming with life—a life survivors created to endure. Where we'll go now, I'm afraid none of us know. I suppose, the more I think about it, the more I realize we'll be alright. The Angelics have each other. Together, we'll tackle the world—face whatever obstacles come our way.

An image of Mom takes precedence for a moment. I wonder if I'll be able to return home one day, if I'll ever be able to see her again. That fear of what I don't know resurfaces, but I fight back, and I hold it at bay. What I can control is promising myself that I'll do whatever it takes to make our reunion a possibility. The idea of Atlas meeting her excites me and I cling to that feeling. I also cling to the idea that Ezra will see her again, too.

Atlas and I hold hands for an eternity. We watch Ezra, the healer's hands traveling up and down the length of his body. His breaths are labored, though he still breathes, and together Atlas and I hope.

I guess when it really boils down to it, hope is all we have.

Epilogue

Ezra

The sun is low as it sets over the Californian mountains. I hear an eagle cry—its call echoes, reaching us in this tiny park. The air is warm. Light filters through the foliage of the towering evergreen trees, drifting between the exposed gaps of the gazebo. Atlas kicks his feet back and forth as he lies on his stomach. He simultaneously reads while grading his students' math work. Conin jots ideas down in a notebook—his college essay, which I have high hopes he'll ace.

I've stopped playing the strings of my violin. Instead, I lie on my back and gaze at the ceiling. I raise my hand, catching the light, feeling its warmth, watching dust motes dance. They look like ash—their taste sooty on my tongue. I wish that every day could be like this one. What we have now is good, so good.

A grape hits my cheek and bounces away. I squint, rub the skin, and turn to see Atlas giggling without remorse. Conin chuckles but notes several more ideas on the lined paper. I grab the grape and chuck it at him. Atlas curls into a ball of laughter. I smile because I simply cannot help it.

"Hey! I wasn't the instigator!" Conin protests.

"Yes, but you aren't supposed to take his side!"

He grins and shakes it off. I groan and roll to Atlas. He strokes my hair with careful fingers. We lie here a long time in comfortable solitude, the sounds of Conin's pen and the flipping of paper carrying to us. I don't care. All I care about is that I'm here with them.

"What are you thinking about?" Atlas asks, quietly.

Conin has a subtle smile on his face as he flips another page. He'll get those scholarships, I know it. He'll be the best goddamn quarterback any university has ever seen.

"Just . . . how grateful I am."

Hues of yellow and orange stretch above, and the sun leaves and dives below the mountains. Conin's glued to my hip, our worries fading in the dark. Atlas's head rests on my shoulder, a silent thrum escaping his mouth.

Conin's eyes find me. An understanding passes between us. I don't need to say anything more. He nods because he knows, too. He knows what I'm thinking. And frankly, he always has. He always will.

I'm grateful he brought us here. I'm grateful he ushered me out that door. He came along with me, and he didn't look back, not after losing the life he made for himself, not after missing his mom, not after all the danger he and I went through together. Before, I would have given up. He didn't. Not once. Atlas is in our lives because of his bravery. We have a life worth living.

And even though it's our inseparable trio now, at one point, it was just Conin and me. I wouldn't trade our relationship with Atlas for anything, but I also cannot deny the history I have with Conin.

There was a time during my and Conin's middle school years when Lukeman Gray abused me for the first time over some petty argument. Thax had learned new tricks with his freshly serrated blade—cruel strokes to the arms. His relationship with Lukeman was as unhealthy as mine, and he always took his spite out on his younger brother. In my loneliness and hurt, I sought the refuge of Conin, who was unfamiliar with the troubles happening at home. But . . . I had no home with the people who claimed to be my parents. Home was where Conin was. And to Conin, I went.

"Ezra, dear. What's wrong?" his mom had answered. The door parted and there he was. He lies on the couch and looks at me. Tears are falling before I can do anything to suppress them.

"Oh, dear. Come in, love," she says.

Conin takes my hand and leads the way to his room. He shuts the door, joining me on the bed. Without hesitation, he tells me to lie beside him. Reluctant, I do. He wraps a tentative arm around my shoulders and pulls me in tight. We've never done this before, but it feels nice. There's an awkward tension at first, though even that disappears.

"Want to tell me about it?" Conin asks.

"Not right now," I say, but I will. I'll open up and Conin will listen. He will say that he plans to protect me and that nothing bad will ever happen to me. I can come and escape into his corner of the world whenever I need to.

I didn't realize it then, but that was the night I fell in love with Conin. Soon, we were under the blankets, on that tiny bed, us two, and the warmth of our bodies.

"You're safe here," he said.

I believed him.

There's the steadfast song of birds.

Forms made of skin and metal press against my own. They don't leave, they stay. Firm. Diligent. Familiar. It's dark now. It's too dark, almost as if I've lost the ability to see.

I was always fond of the dark. No one could see me. No one could judge. Lukeman Gray went to sleep. Thax escaped reality in the only way he knew how. And I would run to be alone, but alone with Conin. He would always make it better. Atlas makes it better, too. They put me back together, piece by piece. I carry myself the rest of the way there.

The taste of ash finds me.

I'm falling, falling, falling.

Conin's hands are on me, Atlas's too, and they're traveling over every corner and crevice, searching for the warm, sticky wetness pooled over the concave that is my stomach. I look down and I'm bleeding, bleeding, bleeding.

How unusual.

The world quiets. I hear soft voices, but I don't fret.

It's better now, I think.

Better when the sun goes down.

To be continued . . .

Acknowledgements

If you had asked me two years ago if I thought it possible I would be writing the acknowledgments of my debut novel, I would have most likely responded with an astounded "hell no!" But here we are. I did it, and frankly, I wouldn't have been able to do it alone. There are many thanks in order.

First and foremost, I want to thank my beautiful and loving partner, Riley, for being my rock in the worst of times. The past two years have not been easy, both mentally or physically, and if it were not for him, this book may not have ever been finished.

Mother, I get my love of books and writing from you. You are the most intelligent and steadfast woman I know. You made me believe it was possible I could write a book and publish it. Well, here we are. I'm happy to say that I've followed you in your footsteps.

Mardi and Briggs, you are two of my closest friends and were amongst the first to beta read my book. Your reactions and feedback were invaluable, and I will forever be grateful for the support you gave me and the tough nights you helped me through.

Tessa, you are probably sick of me at this point, though too nice to say it, but I can't write this without acknowledging your immense help and guidance. You answered every question I had and helped me through the worst of the anxieties and stressors that come from being a self-published author. Thank you from the bottom of my heart.

Sam, my first-ever editor, thank you for tackling my project. Your edits and suggestions put me at ease and furthered my excitement in releasing this book.

Bugghetti, your cover art for this book is nothing short of perfection. It encapsulates the tone and vibes flawlessly, and I simply could not have it any other way.

To my professor and the students of the Writing for Young Adults course I took one fateful Spring, I wanted to thank you for the support and the feedback you gave. While this book is now New Adult, your words made me truly believe I had a shot of publishing it.

And to my Kickstarter supporters, your unwavering support made the publication of this book possible. Thank you!

This is only the beginning.

About the Author

Hunter Hyde resides in the state of Utah where he attends the Creative Writing program at Weber State University. Hunter lives with his cat and partner of seven years in the mountains where it's cold and secluded, but oh-so-pretty. If he isn't reading, gaming, or studying Japanese, you can almost always find him daydreaming about a potential story. BETTER WHEN THE SUN GOES DOWN is Hunter's first book.